Critical Acclaim for the
Horror Anthology

PHOBIAS: STORIES OF YOUR DEEPEST FEARS

Edited by Wendy Webb, Richard Gilliam, Edward E. Kramer, and Martin Greenberg
Introduction by Robert Bloch

"The last two [stories] ventured so skillfully into familiar masculine psychological terrain . . . that they aroused shuddering emotions I didn't know I had."
—Clarence Petersen, *Chicago Tribune*

"Spine-tingling reading . . . The authors prove that a phobia doesn't have to be rational to be real."
—Larry Lawrence, *Reporter News* (Abilene, TX)

"[A] gripping anthology of original stories about people tangled in terror . . ."
—*Publishers Weekly*

AVAILABLE FROM POCKET BOOKS

Horror Anthologies Published by POCKET BOOKS

The Horror Writers Association Presents:
  DEATHPORT, edited by Ramsey Campbell
  FREAK SHOW, edited by F. Paul Wilson
  GHOSTS, edited by Peter Straub
  UNDER THE FANG, edited by Robert R. McCammon
HOT BLOOD, edited by Jeff Gelb and Lonn Friend
HOTTER BLOOD, edited by Jeff Gelb and Michael Garrett
HOTTEST BLOOD, edited by Jeff Gelb and Michael Garrett
The Hot Blood Series: DEADLY AFTER DARK, edited by
  Jeff Gelb and Michael Garrett
The Hot Blood Series: SEEDS OF FEAR, edited by Jeff Gelb and
  Michael Garrett
PHOBIAS, edited by Martin Greenberg, Richard Gilliam,
  Edward Kramer and Wendy Webb
MORE PHOBIAS, edited by Wendy Webb, Richard Gilliam,
  Edward E. Kramer and Martin H. Greenberg
SHOCK ROCK, edited by Jeff Gelb
SHOCK ROCK II, edited by Jeff Gelb

MORE PHOBIAS

Stories of Unparalleled Paranoia!

Edited by Wendy Webb, Richard Gilliam, Edward E. Kramer and Martin Greenberg

POCKET BOOKS

New York   London   Toronto   Sydney   Tokyo   Singapore

This book is a work of fiction. Names, characters, places and incidents are products of the author's imagination or are used fictitiously. Any resemblance to actual events or locales or persons, living or dead, is entirely coincidental.

An *Original* Publication of POCKET BOOKS

POCKET BOOKS, a division of Simon & Schuster Inc.
1230 Avenue of the Americas, New York, NY 10020

Copyright © 1995 by Martin Greenberg, Richard Gilliam, Wendy Webb and Edward E. Kramer

ISBN: 0-671-89547-8

First Pocket Books printing July 1995

10 9 8 7 6 5 4 3 2 1

POCKET and colophon are registered trademarks of Simon & Schuster Inc.

Cover photo by Nicholas Blair

Printed in the U.S.A.

Copyright Notices

Contents

Contents

Contents

MORE PHOBIAS

NONE ARE SO BLIND

Robert Bloch

CATS WILL KILL YOU," SAID THE BLIND MAN. "BEWARE."

Jess scowled at him, which was a waste of time, since his expression couldn't be seen. But actually he was scowling at himself for being such a fool. The hundred dollars had been wasted; he might just as well read the astrology column in the paper.

Actually, the person to blame was Liz, for steering him here, and he made a mental note to call it to her attention. With a scowl like the one he'd just wasted.

Jess put aside his mental notepad and leaned forward. Might as well try to get something for his money out of this. "You're telling me to beware of cats?"

"That is correct."

"Beware, you say. What exactly is that supposed to mean?"

"Be wary, I suppose. Be careful, cautious, alert."

"Around cats?"

"Exactly."

Jess checked his nod; that wouldn't be of much use with a blind man either. "Perhaps you can be more exact than that."

"I can only tell you what my inner voice tells me. Who you are, what you are, what you will be."

1

"We're not talking about inner voices. We're talking about why you think cats might kill me."

The bearded elderly man across the table smiled at Jess. "Being blind since birth, I don't visualize in terms of objects or words. The emanations received from you, the vibrations, the way they extend from your past and project into your future, prompt what I can only call an inner voice. A voice which warns me that you are presently in danger from cats."

"Presently?"

The psychic shrugged. "I can't determine if the risk will come within the hour, the day, or tomorrow. But I get a strong feeling that the problem is immediate and must be dealt with immediately."

"It would help if I knew how I'm supposed to be killed."

"It would indeed," the blind man said. "Unfortunately I can only sense that the threat is violent. And near."

"Cats will kill me, but you don't know how or when," Jess said. "Give me a break!"

"You will have to look to yourself for a break," the psychic said. "By heeding my warning."

Jess glanced at his watch, wondering as he did so how the blind tell time.

The bearded psychic stood up. "Hour's over," he said.

Jess blinked. The old man was right, but how did he know? Was he wearing a braille watch? Maybe he *was* psychic, after all. Or did that inner voice of his also furnish time signals? *At the sound of the chime, it will be exactly six p.m.*

No, Jess couldn't buy that routine about an inner voice. Which meant he wouldn't buy another hour of time in order to ask questions about himself and Liz, which had been the real reason he'd come here in the first place. That, and curiosity, of course.

So how had they gotten into the other stuff, about his own situation, and then this nonsense about cats? No matter, it was six o'clock, time to go.

"If you'll pardon the expression," the blind man said, "I'll see you to the door."

And he did.

Jess departed the modest little walk-up apartment with an

exchange of courtesies, farewells, and a final warning ringing in his ears.

Beware.

Liz was the one who'd best beware, Jess told himself. Why did she send him to this clown, this charlatan who couldn't read a word if its letters were ten feet tall, but who claimed he could read the future? What could he possibly know about the future of Jess D. Fallright, M.D.?

Granted, he'd scored a few hits. Identifying him as a physician before he gave his name was one. But Liz could have called to fill him in on who he was and what to say. No, rule that out: she wouldn't have told the guy to try putting a scare into him about cats.

Not that it had worked, of course. Jess wasn't afraid of cats, no aleurophobia for him. Or any other phobia, for that matter. Except, perhaps, when it came to alcohol. But this wasn't fear, just common sense based on experience. When you're ten years old and you see your own father literally dead in the gutter after a drunken binge, it tends to send a message. And not from an inner voice either.

Come to think of it, the clown had scored on that too, telling him one of his parents had been an alcoholic and met a violent death. That's something Liz couldn't have told him because she didn't know, nobody knew, it wasn't the sort of top secret a top-fee cardiologist wants spread around about his antecedents.

The blind man had told him about his practice. He said Jess had chosen his specialty before enrolling in medical school. And he knew why; the field could be highly profitable, the more bypasses the bigger the fee, and even pre-op and post-op care could be highly profitable. Particularly if you're smart enough to get licensed in a state where you can send patients to a radiology center that you just happen to own under another corporate name. The same goes for other lab work as well, and Jess had it all figured out in advance.

But how was it that the blind man knew? Normally, someone who wants to make a fast buck as a psychic isn't going to hint around at stuff that might reflect on the motives of his clients. But there'd been no hesitation in speaking of such matters, and he'd told the truth. Or was it his inner voice that spoke?

3

And could it have been telling the truth about cats as well?

But if the man was truly psychic, why was he living so modestly? *If you're so smart, why aren't you rich?* Jess wasn't rich either, not yet, but by God he was going to get there because he *was* smart. *Go for the gold. Eyes on the prize.*

That blind idiot couldn't even imagine gold as a color, his eyes wouldn't recognize a prize, and he wouldn't know a cat if one bit him. He had his other senses to go by, of course, but you can't touch tomorrow, and no inner ear can hear the sound of next year. No sense trying to figure out inner voices either; just a waste of time.

And Jess Fallbright, M.D., a medical corporation, knew that time is money. You didn't spend it foolishly, which is why he was hurrying now, hurrying across the darkening parking lot to his car and—

Jesus H. Christ, what was that?

It happened so quickly that Jess couldn't sort out the sequence until later. Something had suddenly slammed against his right leg just above the ankle, knocking him off balance so that he started to fall. His flailing arm struck the side window of a parked car, and his curled fingers found a purchase on the door handle. Firming his grip, he managed to check his movement before his head struck the glass, or went through it. As he twisted around and regained his balance he caught a glimpse of a shadow close to the ground, scampering off into the twilight. The shadow was small and gray, but as the old saying had it, all cats are gray in the dark. And this was just a kitten.

A goddamn kitten. A goddamn lousy kitten, running between his legs from out of nowhere, tripping and knocking him against that window glass. If he hadn't saved himself from falling, he could have cut his throat. The carotid empties fast. . . .

Cats will kill you.

How had the old man known?

Jess stood there for a moment until his breathing slowed. Nobody else in the lot seemed to have noticed the incident, and if they had, it wouldn't matter. This was quitting time; everybody was too busy rushing to get out of here, and if he'd actually fallen with a spear of glass sticking in his throat, they'd probably ignore him. Nobody wants to get involved, not if you're late for dinner and the game starts at seven.

Taking deep breaths, willing the slowing of pulse rate, Jess completed his walk to the car. His eyes scanned the asphalt beneath and before his feet. If the kitten came back this time, he'd see it, just as the blind man did. But he didn't see it, he *heard* it. His inner voice. Except that there are no such things or any organs capable of producing them. At least not on any of the anatomy charts Jess had studied in medical school.

Maybe it'd only been a lucky guess. Or an unlucky one. Either way, it hadn't done him any harm. And it was foolish to blame a helpless stray kitten for something that might have happened, but didn't. Jess thought it through while starting his car and backing it out to move toward the exit lane. Then, as he approached, he saw a blur of movement ahead.

Gunning the motor, he swerved, his headlights picking up a streak where the blur had been—if it had been there at all.

In the end it didn't really matter. What mattered was the loss of common sense. One moment he absolved an innocent kitten of blame, and the next he was trying to run it down. So much for the superiority of the human being with his powers of intellect, reason, and precognition.

It didn't add up. Reason alone would tell him there's no such thing as precognition. As for the power of intellect, Jess realized that for the life of him, now he couldn't even remember the psychic's name.

But then you don't always remember the names of the people in your dreams, and this whole thing had been a dream, a bad one, the kind you do your best to forget, with a little help from your friends; particularly a friend like Liz.

Because she was a friend, Liz didn't reproach him for being slightly late for dinner or ask where he'd been, and he didn't feel up to telling her right now. Because she was a friend, the dinner she served him was very nice indeed—the steak well-done, just as he preferred it, the potato baked and studded with chives, the Caesar salad truly imperial, the coffee strong, the cognac slightly chilled.

Because she was a friend, Liz had unbraided her hair to cascade across her bare back and shoulders, wore the earrings and bracelet he'd bought her. Because she was his friend—and wanted to be more than just a significant other whose apartment he visited on free evenings.

The way Jess felt tonight after the relief of an hour's relaxation—plus the second cognac—she might have a very good chance of realizing her ambition. And why not? After all, he was pushing forty (all right, forty-two, but who's counting?) and it was time to settle down. No more risks with receptionists or patients' wives waiting for widowhood. Liz was just right; older than most of the receptionists, younger than most of the widows. The beauty and sophistication that attracted him sexually could also serve him socially. A woman who knows how to use her charm can be a great asset as hostess to higher-ups in the hierarchy of the medical world. He and Liz would make a great team in public, just as they'd be in private, if only she'd see his throat man and get something done about her snoring.

Well, all in good time. Jess wasn't ready for the snoring problem yet. He'd avoided mentioning his visit to the psychic, because that could be a problem too. He knew Liz had bugged him about going to the old man so that he'd ask about his future—*their* future, actually. If Liz found out he hadn't even mentioned it, there'd be trouble; she wouldn't like playing second fiddle to the cats, and he wasn't anxious for her to learn about it now. What he was becoming anxious about, as she excused herself and went into the bedroom, was how soon she'd stick her head out again and suggest he join her.

That would be the perfect ending to a perfect meal; the dessert, the just desert for someone who'd gone through what he'd gone through with that blind clown this afternoon and that miserable runt-of-the-litter kitten that had almost robbed him of quality time, aka the rest of his life.

Not that he hated cats, but he didn't really like them either. They were too quiet, too stealthy. That kitten, popping up out of nowhere, was a good example.

All of which was foolish, he knew that, but it had been foolish to try running down the kitten too. The point was, he couldn't help the way he felt about things. Things that can kill you. *Beware.*

He could see why there were so many superstitions

concerning cats all through history, all over the world. Cats sucking the breath out of sleeping infants, black cats bringing bad luck when they crossed your path. Cats possessed by evil spirits; all those old legends about the witch and her cat.

The witch and her cat stood in the bedroom doorway.

"Surprise!" Liz said.

Standing in shadow, hair tumbling over the dark robe, she *did* look more witchlike than bewitching. And the creature perched on her shoulder lent a final touch.

"Where did that come from?" Jess said.

"Isn't it precious?" Liz's eyes were almost as green as the cat's. "He's a purebred; I've got the papers."

"What's it doing here?"

"Can't you see, darling?" Liz's voice was a purr. "He *lives* here."

"Since when?"

"I picked him up from the vet's yesterday morning. He's had all his shots, so there's nothing to worry about."

Jess rose, and she continued quickly, "Please don't be difficult. You know I've wanted a pet for company, and they won't allow dogs here. I talked it over with the vet and he recommended a Siamese—"

"I need a Siamese cat like I need Siamese twins," Jess said. He took a step forward, and the cat's stare became a glare.

"But darling, he won't be in our way, I promise! I'm already training him to sleep at the foot of the bed—"

"Get rid of it!"

The cat hissed.

Startled by the sudden sound, Jess raised his right hand. His gesture was involuntary; the cat's deliberate.

With a snarl, it launched its leap from Liz's shoulder. Before Jess could shield his face, the claws raked his cheek. The cat landed on the sofa and bunched itself, fangs bared.

"Poor kitty!" Liz murmured.

"Poor *kitty?* The damn thing tore a chunk out of my face—"

"It's only a scratch," Liz said. She was stroking the cat and didn't even bother to look up. "Poor little thing, you didn't mean any harm."

"Oh no?" Jess felt the tricklet of blood on his cheek, then

ran his finger upward to its source. "You see where he clawed me? Another half inch higher and I'd have lost an eye."

"Keep your voice down," Liz said. "The neighbors—"

"They're your worry," he told her. "Not mine."

She still didn't look up, though the cat did, and there was no mistaking the flicker of hatred in its slitted eyes. The creature knew what it had done, and given the opportunity, would do again. But there wasn't going to be any opportunity. *Beware.*

Jess took a deep breath. "Either that cat goes or I go."

Now Liz did look up, but there was no hatred in her eyes, only a hint of amusement. "Don't be such a big baby," she said. "Don't you see he was just frightened because you're a stranger? Besides, he probably doesn't like that cologne you're wearing. Neither do I."

"I guess you didn't hear me," he said. "I'm leaving."

"Jess! Don't act like an idiot—"

She turned to rise, but it was the cat who soared from the sofa to reach him first. Or almost reach him. Only the quick slam of the front door saved Jess from further harm.

And God only knows what else, Jess told himself as he drove off. Not that Liz really was a witch; that idea had just been the momentary product of cooled cognac and an overheated imagination. But the cat was real, and so were its claws.

Jess checked his cheek with the aid of the rearview mirror. Just a scratch, as Liz had said, but it was close to his eye, as he'd informed her. Too damned close. And even the scratch should be cleaned out; people wouldn't be so anxious to have pets if they knew how dangerous their infections could be. *Beware.*

Right now he didn't know whether to be grateful to the psychic for his warning or angry because of the trouble he'd caused. It was a question to think about, something to sort out, but not here at nine o'clock in the midst of midtown traffic.

Where was everyone going at this time of night? It wasn't until Jess inched his way through the tangle jamming into the parking area next to the Civic Auditorium that he knew the answer. It was spelled out on the marquee in blazing letters: JULY 10–13 NATIONAL CAT SHOW.

Apparently not everyone was afraid of cats. Well, best of luck and to hell with them. All he wanted right now was to get away from cats and cat lovers alike. No hard felines.

Jess headed west, avoiding the expressway to take the Abingdon Road route, which was the easiest exit from town. Once he got past suburbia and into the boonies he could relax, get a little fresh air to clear his lungs, clear his thoughts.

Gradually the traffic lessened, then the streetlights, then the roadway signs. Out here you could actually see the stars.

Jess pulled over to park on the right shoulder and did a little stargazing. That was a form of psychic activity too, wasn't it? Along with numerology and palmistry and reading the signs of the future in animal or human entrails. He still had no idea where the blind man got his powers, but today's events proved they existed, and for this Jess was grateful. Maybe he should also be grateful for the way things had led to the sudden and unexpected breakup with Liz.

Women don't need to practice witchcraft in order to be dangerous. And Liz had proven that she could be dangerous, if only to his self-esteem. But self-esteem was important in his profession; he didn't need a wife who would put him down, or what's worse, do things without consulting him. Beauty and charm weren't really such desirable qualities in a doctor's wife either, because they tended to divert attention from the doctor himself. And a woman who wasted so much time on cooking wasn't a necessity as long as there were so many good restaurants, where you didn't have to buy jewelry for the chef either. Besides, he'd paid forty dollars for that cologne.

So gratitude was definitely in order as he started the car again, turned on the deserted road, and headed back in the direction of the distant lights. It was only when he picked up the phone to call the exchange that he realized he hadn't done so since this afternoon. There'd been no emergencies when he left the office, and just two patients in the hospital, both post-op and ready for discharge. And if anything unexpected had come up, he'd have gotten word on the beeper. As it was, there was nothing from the exchange, and he was thankful for that.

Still, he'd forgotten to call sooner, and that was the psychic's fault. Maybe his warning had been helpful, but it was also harmful, the way it distracted him, disturbed him.

Disturbed. Another of those politically correct words used to gloss over harsh realities. Nobody's crazy nowadays, just disturbed. And nobody's afraid; what used to be called fear now finds scientific salvation as mere phobia. Did that bearded old clown do that to him, did he instill this fear of cats to such a degree he'd caused a prominent cardiologist to forget calling his own office?

Jess wondered how many people would still respect him if they knew how strongly he felt about cats. Calling it a phobia might be acceptable to some, but it didn't solve the problem. Which was, bottom line, that he never wanted to see another cat again for the rest of his life.

His life almost ended a moment later, when the car hit the back of the trailer.

How it happened, he never knew. A glance through the windshield showed the crossroad ahead perfectly clear; it couldn't have been more than a second or two later that the trailer came backing out of the side at his left.

The trailer was white, box-shaped, and windowless. Its color and shape didn't matter, but its lack of windows did; Jess slammed brakes but the car plowed into the solid midsection of the box and it toppled. If there'd been windows to hit, flying glass might have been disastrous.

As it was, Jess realized no harm had come to him, and no damage to the car, unless the impact did something to the bumper. The trailer lay on its side like some wounded animal, but animals don't have wheels to spin or sides that splinter. At least not as though they were being pried open from within.

Jess was out of the car, hurrying toward the wreckage, when the animal emerged. Not something white or wheeled or wounded, but a real animal. It was a frightening furry fury, its fangs and claws immense.

A tail lashed the night. Black stripes rippled across tawny fur, red mouth opened in a roar. The tiger crouched, coiling to spring.

None Are So Blind

Jess turned, racing along the side of the car as the roar resounded in his ears. He didn't look back, didn't do anything except tug the handle, yank the door open, hurl himself forward, then turn and slam the door just as the huge face rose snarling on the far side of the window.

Frantic, Jess turned the key in the ignition, his foot stamping the gas pedal. The engine flooded and died. And now a massive orange-and-white paw was rising outside the window, curved claws rasping over the glass.

Jess slid across the seat, trying to get out from under the wheel, trying to shield himself with both arms, trying not to think of what was going to happen, what was happening now as the tiger's paw drew back, readying to slam forward with full force, to smash the glass, to break the door open and claim its prey—

It never happened. At the moment of impact there was merely a thump, as though something had bumped against the side of the car.

Jess lowered his arms, opened his eyes. The view from the window on the driver's side was clear; the tiger had disappeared.

But the view through the windshield was another matter. He glanced up quickly at the sound of voices outside, then squinted through bobbing flashlight beams.

Three men were standing in front of the car. Their jeans, sport shirts, and baseball caps were similar; the only noticeble difference was that two members of the trio carried ifles and the third, slightly shorter man on the left, was randishing a dart gun.

It was he who rounded the hood to glance down, then wisted his head and called to his companions, "Over here!"

Then he moved up to rap on the side window, peering at ess through the glass. "It's okay. Open up."

Jess tried, but the door swung outward only partway efore encountering an obstacle. Jess stared down at the iger lying motionless against the side of the car. The short nan pointed at the shaft of the dart protruding from behind he ruff of the animal's neck. "Out like a light," he said, ride in his voice and grin. Then he sobered. "That was a lose one. You all right, mister?"

Jess nodded, then slid back across the seat to exit from the passenger side. Within the next few minutes it was determined that he was all right, the car was all right, and the Siberian tiger—all six hundred pounds of him—was all right too. But one of the rifle bearers, a man identified as Slim, was definitely not all right; the other two were chewing him out for improperly securing the trailer hitch to the van now parked on the side road.

As near as Jess could sort it out from all of the profanity, the three men were employees of the local zoo, to which they were transporting their captive from its former quarters in St. Louis. Hours behind schedule and weary after a long, nerve-wracking drive, they'd pulled off on the side road to sneak in a bit of rest before arriving at the zoo and spending all night unloading the tiger in its new quarters. Somehow, during their trip, the defective fastening had sprung loose, and after parking on the upward slope, the trailer broke free from the van to roll back down onto the highway where the collision occurred. As for the rest, the short man summarized it with a shrug.

"Lucky the first dart did the job. That trailer's special-built and we thought we had him secured, but nobody figured on something like this happening to it. See how he busted right through the side? Let me tell you, that baby's got power. Biggest goddamn cat I've ever seen."

Cat. Jess felt a chill not borne on the breeze. It intensified at the sound of the siren's wail.

The next half hour was a busy one, what with the highway patrol, the sheriff's deputies, the fielding of questions and the rendering of statements. More time than that might have been wasted, but it was established early on that they were dealing with Jess Fallbright, M.D., prominent local physician and personal friend of Sheriff Stanley Ottinger himself. Jess also volunteered that he was very tired and very busy—he'd been on his way to look in on two hospitalized patients when the accident occurred. And yes, it was an accident, but he didn't intend to file charges because there'd been no damages to his person or vehicle. He'd be happy to cooperate in whatever way they wished, tomorrow or whenever. But right now he was anxious to look in on his patients and get some rest because he had surgery in the morning.

Jess surprised himself at how well he handled it all,

handled it so well that nobody knew the only thing he really kept thinking about was the cat, the big cat that tried to kill him. *Six hundred pounds, out of nowhere. The size of those fangs, those paws and claws.*

But size isn't everything. Just stumbling over that tiny kitten could have resulted in a broken back, a broken neck, or smashing into the window and getting his throat cut with a shard of glass.

Jess relived the moment as he moved into city traffic. As he drove past the street where Liz's apartment was located, he thought about the way the Siamese tried to attack him. He must remember to look at that scratch; it was nothing to worry about, but out of nothing comes something. Suddenly, unexpectedly, and potentially deadly. *Beware.*

Once again he passed by the Civic Auditorium, and seeing the lettering on the marquee really shook him. Hundreds of cats in there right now, maybe thousands. Somewhere, he remembered reading that the cat population of the entire country numbered more than fifty million. The creatures were everywhere, everywhere you looked, everywhere the blind man didn't look, because he could see without looking, without eyes, see that cats will kill you.

You don't need to be a cardiologist to know when your heart is pounding. Jess drove on until he saw a bar on a corner. Turning into the cross street, he pulled over and parked at the curb. As he did so he thought he detected a flicker of movement beyond the side window, evoking a fearsome memory of the tiger's orange face.

But there was nothing looming up outside the window, nothing but the night. Nothing to be afraid of, and he wasn't afraid, not anymore. He'd faced three cats and escaped unharmed. The damage, if any, was psychological, and a drink would take care of that. Just one, because tomorrow would be a busy day. Call his lawyer, find out if he might have grounds for some kind of suit against the zoo people for putting him at risk. Couldn't sue for physical injury, but what about trauma?

And then there was the little matter of finding out more about the blind man. What was the legal status of fortune-tellers in this area? After all, when you get right down to it, that's what psychics were, fortune-tellers. He'd been out of his mind going to one in the first place, just because Liz recommended him and he'd been curious to hear about his chances of getting that appointment on the county health advisory council. All of which he'd forgotten, it didn't even come up after that clown had started in with his *cats will kill you* routine. There must be some way to sue him, at least to put the blind man out of business. Because he was a fake, a fraud, a scaremonger; tonight had proved it. Three cats in a row had proved he was all three.

And it had proved one thing more, the most important thing. Which is that Jess wasn't afraid of cats. They'd had their chance and nothing happened. Three chances. Three strikes and you're out. He'd drink to that, as soon as he got out of the car.

He did so, idly wondering if a report of the tiger's escape and recapture might be on the late news.

It was, but he didn't hear it, because the youth with the 9mm semiautomatic came up from behind him, grabbed the car keys, and blew off the top of his head.

The late news did report that, along with the capture and arrest of the murder suspect as he attempted to drive Jess's car away. Police told reporters that the young man's name was Joseph Katz.

NO END IN SIGHT

Carrie Richerson

PLODDING DOWN A DUSTY ROAD, BEHIND A BEDRAGGLED COL-
umn of soldiers. Tired, so tired. Eyes burning, tongue
furred, choking on the stink of mud and blood. Around me a
wasteland: shattered trees, burned stumps, pits full of greasy
water reflecting a sky that glows red and orange with
artillery fire. No sound. I can't hear the boom of the guns,
the groans of the wounded soldiers ahead of me, or even my
own breathing.

I notice that I am wearing only a housecoat and bedroom
slippers, but before I can wonder about this, I see that the
last soldier in the line is my son Jason. I call out his name;
for a moment he seems about to stop, then he limps forward
faster. There is something wrong with his curly blond hair, it
looks dark and matted, but I cannot see it clearly. I increase
my pace, running now, the robe flapping open, and I realize
with embarrassment that I am naked beneath. But that
doesn't matter, because I have finally caught up with Jason. I
put a hand on his arm, forcing him to turn around.

It *is* Jason—I recognize the dimple in his chin, the slightly
jug ears, the broad Future Farmer of America shoulders. I
birthed this boy, washed behind those ears, bandaged his
cuts. His body is as familiar to me as my own. But his
always-merry eyes are dull, blank—like the blank hole in

15

the center of his forehead. He is dead, has been dead for some time.

I step back, horrified, covering my mouth to keep from screaming. Then the rest of the battalion begins to turn in our direction. They are all dead, rotted, strips of putrid flesh flapping in the wind that has begun to howl around my ears. They raise skeletal hands and step toward me.

I look back at Jason. And now it is not Jason's face, but my own I confront. Naked, cracked bone; worms crawling from the eyeholes; the jaw opens and teeth spill like maggots from the rotten bone.

He turns to face me, and I see . . .

He turns to face me . . .

He turns . . .

Waking is like crashing through a plate-glass window; I am not sure if the dream or reality is worse. My heart thunders, I have pissed myself; surely my scream has awakened the entire hospital. But no, it seems that I am too weak to produce a good bloodcurdling scream. I have only whispered my terror to the darkened room.

Nausea rolls over me like a wave at the memory of the dream. I bite it back, with an effort of will that floods my thin carcass with stinking sweat. If I start to vomit, I will not be able to stop until the nurse gives me a shot. Then I will sleep, and dream again. . . .

The seconds tick off; my overstrained heart decides not to burst. Not yet. I will not die just yet. Cold, wet, filthy, I grin in bitter triumph. Still a little too tough for the big dark to swallow whole.

I didn't always fear death. In fact, in my sixty-five years I have never feared anything in this life. Born and raised in Bucksnort, Texas, way up in the Panhandle near the Canadian River. A lifetime of ranching on that vast plain, freezing and burning as the seasons turn and turn about, will teach anyone that fear is a luxury you just can't afford. I learned to survive, to cope, to do whatever necessary: butcher my own hogs, birth my own babies, shoot snakes and rabid coyotes, set bones and sew up ugly wounds. There was never time for squeamishness over critters that creep and crawl, or bodily fluids, or honest dirt, or small places, or the night.

No End in Sight

Even burying two husbands seemed like a natural part of life. Men wore themselves out on the land or had tractors fall on them or got et by the pigs—their widows planted them and got back to ranching. It took Jason's death, twenty-five years ago at Trin Lao, to make death real to me. To make it something to hate and despise—and fear.

And now I am dying. And now there is something more to fear even than dying and being placed in the cold ground and rotting. Now, for whatever reason, be it virus or plague or miracle visited upon us by a vicious cosmos, some of the dead are not content to stay that way. In their quest for justice against those who caused their premature deaths, they return and flaunt their decomposing flesh before the entire world. It's *indecent.* I cannot, I *will not,* allow it to happen to me.

I found the tumor by accident. I examine my breasts every month, like Dr. Myers showed me, but this lump was way back under my armpit, almost to my back. It felt so small at first I thought it was just a bruise, but it didn't go away after two weeks, and by the time I got in to see the doctor about it, it had doubled in size.

Dr. Myers ordered some tests. Just a precaution, she said. She should have known better than to try to put one over on an old cowhand like me. I could see the worry in her eyes, like a spooky heifer, for all the reassurance in her words.

It was cancer, of course. One of the new, aggressive strains, caused by pollution or pesticides or food additives or whatnot. I can remember when cancer was a word you whispered, as though it was a curse that might fall on you or your family just from pronouncing it. But now encapsulated tumors like mine are easily cured, thanks to the wonders of medicines like vincristine and Taxol, and Juprex, the true "magic bullet."

Like its predecessors, Juprex has a humble origin: the ash juniper, commonly misnamed "cedar," of my native state. Who would have thought that a trash tree like cedar, that ranchers hate because it grows like a weed and crowds out everything else, would prove to be a lifesaver? *My* lifesaver.

Dr. Myers referred me to an oncologist in Amarillo, one of the best in Texas, she said. Despite his youth, Allan

Forbes won me over quickly. Perhaps it was that he reminded me of Jason—tall and gangly, soft-spoken, patient, knowledgeable without a trace of arrogance. He didn't make the mistake so many of the young make, of assuming age had made me stupid or hard of hearing. And he didn't treat me like something that would break if he breathed on me. I liked him.

"Juprex works by strangling the tumor. We inject it into the tumor's center and it destroys the small vessels that are supplying blood for the abnormal growth. Eats it out from inside, you might say." He smiles shyly, proud to do his part in the triumph of science over the evil empire of malignancy.

"Like weevils in the wheat?" I ask.

He grins. "Exactly!" This boy should have been a farmer. But at the moment I am grateful that he chose a different career.

By the morning of my treatment my tumor was as large as a baseball, a hard, painful lump just behind my arm. I'd slept badly in the strange hospital bed, but I would only be in it for one more night while my response was monitored. Dr. Forbes had explained that the tumor would start to shrink within days and be totally absorbed within a month.

Two syringes on a tray. One containing Juprex, to be loaded into a mechanical arm that would guide the needle to the precise center of the tumor and deliver a calculated dose. The other containing a mild sedative to relax me through the tedious, sometimes painful process.

I don't know what went wrong. Something distracted Dr. Forbes, perhaps his own running commentary done to reassure me. In the process he forgot the first rule of medicine: Do no harm. Then he forgot the second rule: Check it, and check it again, and check it a third time. Only when he went to pick up the second syringe and saw that it was *not* the one containing Juprex did he realize that he had injected the wrong medicine into my vein. By then it had been circulating in my bloodstream for several minutes, and the damage was done.

At first, before I understood the implications of what he had done, I tried to reassure Dr. Forbes. He looked so shocked, so lost, even as he worked frantically to find treatments for the poison he had let loose inside me. For Juprex is a poison. It has to be, to do what it does so well. And what it was supposed to do to my tumor cells it was now doing throughout my body.

That night an exhausted Dr. Forbes outlined the path of destruction that Juprex was carving through my kidneys, liver, lungs, and heart. No antidote, no detoxifying agent. I had maybe ten days, two weeks tops, to live.

Allan Forbes, almost in tears, begged me to forgive him. "Call my lawyer," I said, and turned my face to the wall.

My hospital room is crowded: my lawyer, Herbert Grunberg, who disapproves of this attempt to negotiate; Allan Forbes; the hospital's and Forbes's insurance lawyers. I can't remember their names, even though Herbert introduced them to me just moments ago. The hospital's lawyer looks like a possum, and Forbes's insurance company's lawyer looks like a weasel, and both of them look like henhouse raiders and eggsuckers.

Herbert is arguing with the possum about the size of the hospital's settlement offer. It has been four days since "the accident," two days since I filed a massive lawsuit against the hospital and Dr. Forbes. I will not live to see the case pursued in court; that will be for my daughters and their husbands. But I want to accomplish as much as possible in the time remaining.

I ignore the raised voices and stare out the window. Since when have hospital windows become nonopenable? Since air-conditioning became universal, I guess. I remember being in this same hospital in 1943, to have my appendix removed. There was no air-conditioning then, and the summer heat in the Panhandle can reach over one hundred degrees every afternoon. Somehow there was more healing in that stifling ward, with few comforts and no privacy and the windows wide open day and night, than this TV-supplied, bathroom-attached, air-conditioned private room.

There isn't much view out the window anyway—just the flat, graveled roof and vent stacks of another wing of the hospital. And pigeons. They strut and peck outside the window in glittering, iridescent droves. So full of life. How I envy those sky rats.

"Gentlemen." I strain to made my weak voice heard over their wrangling. "I am willing to settle my claim without going to court—no, Herbert, let me speak—but I want something more than what the hospital and the insurance company are offering."

"More money?" eggsucker number one asks. "I assure you, Mrs. Coulter, our offer is generous and fair."

"Fair, Reigert? The woman's *dying!* There isn't a jury in the country that wouldn't find gross negligence here. Punitive damages could bankrupt this hospital!" Trust a skinflint like Herbert to kick the opposition while it's down. I'm glad he's on *my* side.

"Yes, and then your client would get nothing. Let her accept our settlement offer, and her children will be well taken care of for the rest of their lives."

"Are y'all going to listen to me or not?" They subside again. Forbes wears the look of a deer caught in a car's headlights, and there are dark stains under the arms of his white coat.

"I don't want to die. And it's in your best interests to make sure I don't."

They look blank. Young people these days. How dare they act as if the world were still the sane, ordered one it was a year ago.

"Don't any of you read the papers?" I ask. Still blank. I shake my head in disgust. "Y'all don't think I'm going to *stay* dead, do you?"

Herbert blinks thoughtfully. The weasel breathes, "Oh, sweet Mary." Forbes turns even paler; I can smell his fear from across the room.

Eggsucker number one doesn't buy it. "But this was an accident!"

"Malpractice. Wrongful death. So, Dr. Forbes, if you don't want my corpse showing up on your doorstep or in your waiting room to remind you of your failure and advertise it to the world, you'd better find a way to keep me alive. And you only have a few days."

Dying is hard work. I am so tired, and it is tempting to want to give in, let go, give myself up to the dissolution I can feel sapping me from within. I'm on dialysis now and receiving transfusions of whole blood and platelets round-the-clock; my liver is a bowling ball pressing upward into my lungs, which are filling with fluid from congestive heart failure.

Allan Forbes has come to report his progress, or rather his lack of it. His eyes are bloodshot and his hair has seen more of his fingers than a comb in the three days since the conference in my room.

"You need a shower," I say, wrinkling my nose against his smell.

"Don't joke. There isn't time." He looks as though he would like to hit me, and the shock of that realization shames him. He sags into the chair by my bed and drops his head into his hands.

"I'm not joking. You stink. How can you think straight when you smell like that?"

"It doesn't matter. There's nothing to think about."

"Sit up straight and tell me what you've found out."

He shakes himself like a puppy and drags himself upright. "There are no existing agents known to stop or reverse Juprex's effect on blood vessels. There's a class of drugs that inhibits its action in the test tube, but they only keep it from binding. Too late for that to help." He pauses, and his eyes threaten to close. I reach out and shake him awake.

"I swear I know more about this drug than its inventor now. If this were a research problem, I could theorize an avenue or two to explore, but it would take months, *years,* to even find out if I was on the right track, much less develop a usable drug. I'm at a dead end."

"Don't say 'dead.'" He looks even more miserable, if that's possible. "What other options are there?"

"None, I'm telling you! We can't find organ donors to match every one of your organs—and even if we could, we couldn't find them in time—and even if we could find them in time, you'd be too weak to survive all that surgery—and even if I could find transplant surgeons willing to operate, the damage isn't just confined to major organs, it's all over your body. Your whole circulatory system is turning into a sieve!"

"I'm not going to make a pretty corpse, Allan. And you're going to have to look at me for a long time. Every night at dinner, probably. I'll be with you on your rounds—how will your patients feel about that? In your bedroom at night, watching you sleep. Do you think you'll be able to sleep, Dr. Forbes?"

"Stop!" He covers his face with both hands. "Don't you think I'd undo this if I could? I'm a *doctor,* for God's sake—I'm supposed to cure people, not kill them. Don't you know that I would give *anything* to go back and change what happened? I'd even change places with you, if I could. Please don't do this to me!"

I want to pity him, but fear closes my heart. "You act as if I had a choice in the matter, Allan. Thanks to you, I won't have any choices, ever again."

He uncovers his face and opens his eyes. He is crying now, openly. *"Please* don't do this! I have a wife, a daughter. She's just two years old—she won't understand. . . ."

It is as impossible to hate him like this as it would be to hate and torture my own son. I sigh, and feel a little more of my life ebb away.

"Go home, Allan. Wash, shave, eat. Get some sleep. Maybe you'll think of something new."

He wipes his face with the dirty sleeve of his white coat, and leaves.

I count the ceiling tiles and wonder how long I can stave off sleep.

I dream that Jason comes back from death and visits me in the hospital. In the dream I *know* that I am dreaming, but I am also afraid that I am mistaken, that the dream is real, that Jason is one of the many returnees.

I watch him as he talks to me—the flat, boiled-egg look of his eyes; the hole in the center of his forehead, within a crater of impact-crazed bone; the way he never smiles. This is not my son, I think—but I know it is. I am so terrified of him that I cannot hear what he is saying. His mouth moves, but like my earlier dream, I am trapped in an eerie silence. He might be telling me secrets of the universe, secrets that one can only learn by dying, but I am so paralyzed by my fear that I cannot go to him, cannot take my own son in my arms and soothe his hurt. A mother should never be afraid of her own son.

No End in Sight

I wake to reality again, if that was a dream. This time I am too weak to scream, too weak to hold back the tears of frustration and self-pity. Life has *never* made me cry, but death, I have discovered, is a long series of humiliations.

When I open my eyes I know that I am dreaming after all, because it seems Jason is still sitting on the stool at the foot of the bed. Only this figure is covered completely in a long coat with the hood pulled low over its face. Then I see that Herbert is with it, and I know who this is.

"Herbert, please leave us alone."

Grunberg takes my hand in his two and searches my face for a long moment, but he doesn't speak. I have known him long enough to understand that he is a man who does not express his emotions easily; perhaps our similarity is why I have trusted him so much over the years. He places my hand gently on the blanket and leaves. I feel that I have seen him for the last time, and I am ashamed that I have not thanked him for all that he has done for me.

The returnee and I regard each other.

"I asked you here because I'm—I'm—" I cannot make myself say the words.

"You are becoming like me." Its voice is soft and dispassionate. I can't tell if there is any irony in it.

"Yes." Admitting it is so hard. I take as deep a breath as my tortured lungs allow. "May I see you?"

It stands and pushes back the hood, opens the coat. My stomach knots in distress, but there is really little to see. The returnee is female, and only a certain pallor, a waxiness of complexion and the dullness of the eyes betray her status. Rationally speaking, there is nothing to fear here, but my fear is not rational. Not at all. A whimper rises in my throat and I turn my head away.

The figure sits again. "What do you want from me?"

"I want not to die."

"I cannot help you with that."

"Then I want not to come back. I can't stand the thought of that. It's *unnatural.*"

She considers the problem, then offers, "Make peace with the one who has caused your death. Forgive."

"How can I forgive this!" For a moment I rage with something of my old strength—but the effort exhausts me and I fall back against my pillow. My bones are dissolving. "Is that what you did—forgive your killer?"

She stands and wraps the coat around herself. "No. I didn't," she says softly.

"How can I forgive?" I whisper.

There is no answer, and when I look up, the figure is gone. Maybe she was never there. Maybe I dreamed her after all. Maybe I am already dead, dreaming that I am dying.

I fight for every breath. My lungs leak fluid in, my arteries leak fluid out, my brain hemorrhages thoughts. But I refuse to let go; at this point, I am not sure that I could. They will have to pry my life out of my cold, dead fingers.

Allan Forbes sticks his head in the door. "What if I can arrange it that you don't die?"

I know from the look on his face that it isn't time to celebrate yet.

It is better than dying, I suppose. And one day the test-tube types may invent a way to repair this body, and I can be defrosted. In the meantime the hospital and insurance companies are committed, through Herbert's ironclad contracts, to paying for perpetual care for my cryogenically preserved body. The hospital even leaned on a judge, one of their directors, to allow the freezing procedure to take place before the legal moment of death.

But it will be a close thing. I am sinking fast, even as technicians scurry about inserting tubes and readying solutions. With almost the last of my strength I have said good-bye to my daughters, their husbands, my grandchildren. My daughters were strong, they didn't cry; I raised those girls right.

Allan Forbes is by my side, watching my heart monitor. And Jason—I imagine I see Jason standing against the wall. Maybe he has come to see me off. Maybe he has come to take me with him.

"Dr. Forbes," I whisper.

"Hold on," he says. "Only a few minutes more."

"Hold my hand. Please."

I can't see it, but I feel him take my hand in his. I know how cold my flesh is by how warm his feels.

"Allan—don't let this—shake your confidence. You're a—good doctor. Your mama must be—proud of you." His hand tightens on mine; a freight train is sitting on my chest. "I forgive you." I don't know if I am talking to Allan or to Jason, but I mean it for both of them. "I forgive you."

Here comes the dark.

THE MOVING COFFIN

Ed Gorman

1

ON THAT RAINY TUESDAY MORNING, HALF AN HOUR AFTER A car splashed me with mud, fifteen minutes after my left foot sank into a watery hole, my parole officer said, "Three times."

"Three times?"

"That you snuck off last week."

I started to defend myself but all that came out was a sneeze.

"It's really miserable out there, isn't it?" he said.

I'd always assumed that parole officers would be dour old gentlemen who wanted nothing more than to unnerve and exasperate their charges every time they got a chance.

Mr. DeConcini was not that way at all. His thirty extra pounds and bright blue eyes gave him a jolly effect, for one thing, and the yellow ties he favored continued the sense of quiet merriment. His personality was pretty much like that too. Here we sat in an office filled with murderers, rapists, perverts, and armed-robbery types, and Mr. DeConcini managed to be relentlessly friendly, like a campaigning politician on speed.

The Moving Coffin

"You know what I told him, Bob?"

"Told my boss?"

"Right. I said, if Bob disappeared for a few hours last week, he had a darn good reason. That's exactly what I told him."

"Well, I really appreciate that, Mr. DeConcini."

"Ralph."

"I really appreciate that, Ralph."

I sneezed again.

"Kleenex?"

"Thank you."

"So where did you go?"

"You really have to know?"

"I really have to know, Bob. I really do. I have a boss too, you know."

"I went to church."

At first he didn't react. Just sat there looking at me. Then he sat up very straight in his seat and said, "You wouldn't play with my feelings, would you, Bob?"

"No, Ralph, I wouldn't play with your feelings."

"I've been after you for months to get next to the Lord, and now you mean you've gone and done it?"

"Gone and done it, Ralph. Gone and done it."

He looked as if he were about to cry. Ralph had always liked me because I wasn't like, as he'd explained on my first visit, "the rest." By that he meant that I had a college degree in business and that before I became prisoner number 4832, I'd been an executive in a research company.

He looked at me and gave me one of those crinkly smiles people in TV commercials are always giving each other. His bright blue eyes watered a bit too.

"Good Lord, Bob, this is the moment a parole officer like myself lives for."

"It is?"

"Of course. A parolee who's denouncing his old ways and affirming his new ways by going to church three times in the middle of the day? This is going to be our lead story in next month's newsletter. We got one of those desktop publishing deals, so we can get it out monthly now. A parolee who's had the calling from God. It's just great."

27

You really believe that story I just gave you? I wanted to say. But not being crazy, at least not in that way, I decided to keep quiet.

"Mr. Carlson will be happy to hear about this."

"I hope so. I don't want to lose my job, Ralph."

"He'll be relieved too. He thinks you're a real good worker. Says you look nice in the clothes too. And that counts in an upscale store like that. You know, that's probably the most expensive store in the city."

"I've checked. It is."

"And you're their top salesman already—after only four months. I'm going to mention that in the newsletter story too."

"Good."

He leaned close, as if he were going to confide in me one of the universe's most important secrets.

"See all those people over there?"

"The parolees?" I said, scanning the line of sad and shabby and sometimes frightening men who sat angry and beaten and resentful in their bright plastic chairs.

He nodded.

"Yeah, I see them, Ralph."

"Hopeless," he said. "They're hopeless."

Then he sat up straight, his desk an oasis of orderliness in a vast gray room of cluttered desks and even more cluttered lives.

"If I was a betting man, Bob, I'd bet you were the only one who'll go completely straight the rest of his life."

"I appreciate you saying that."

"The recidivism rate is terrible. But you . . ."

The merry smile again.

"You always make my day, Bob. I feel that there's a little hope left in the world when you're around. I always tell my wife about you. I always say that on the days when Bob comes in, I feel like I'm actually accomplishing something."

"That's nice of you, Ralph."

I checked my watch. "Well, I guess I'd better be getting back. I wanted to use my lunch hour so I wouldn't take any more hours away from the job."

"You're thinking like executive material already, Bob. Already."

We stood up and shook hands in a solemn and sort of corny way and then I turned to go and Ralph said, "No, sir, if there's one man I don't have to worry about, it's Bob."

I nodded and turned toward the door and started walking quickly. I had one more appointment to keep before getting back to work. I had to pick up some burglary tools.

2

"You know how to use these things?"

"That's about all I did when I was in the joint. Lift weights and practice with burglary tools."

The tools were in a leatherette shaving kit that sat on the seat between us in the front seat of the taxi. The rain made the interior smell of cigarette smoke and dampness and perfume and aftershave and a few other odors I didn't especially want to identify.

Delia had picked me up after work.

She gave me a careful, appraising look. She was scruffy and cute in a lost-kitten way. Delia was a bottle blonde with quick, intelligent brown eyes and a smile that a dentist needed to do some work on.

She heeled the horn with her hand and spat a few naughty words and then said, "I hate bus drivers."

Delia drove her taxi with great psychotic glee. She seemed to be under the impression that the founding fathers of our little midwestern city had given her exclusive right-of-way on all streets and avenues twenty-four hours a day.

As she continued driving me back to work she said, "I followed him, the way you wanted me to."

"I appreciate it. I'd get a car but—"

"Terms of your parole. Tell me about it. Last time Kip was out, he had the same thing." She tamped a cigarette from her pack of Camel filters. I gave her a light from the Ronson lighter my wife Sara had given me for our fifth anniversary. I didn't smoke anymore but I always carried the lighter as a reminder of her.

Kip was her husband, whom I'd met in prison. When I'd told him what I planned to do, he said, "My wife'll help you, kid, long as you keep your hands to yourself. She's true-blue."

She was too. I'd seen any number of guys come on to her, and she'd always raised her hand as if she were about to send them the Finger, then suddenly she'd point to the wedding ring on her left hand.

She also knew a hell of a lot about burglary and burglary tools.

"All right, you got the tools down pat, but how about security devices?" she said.

"Kip told me a lot about them."

"He's my man, Bob, and I'd never say anything bad about him, but Kip doesn't know squat about security devices. Once you figure out where you want to break in, you let me know. I'll scope it out for you."

"I appreciate that."

"My pleasure."

We rode the rest of the way in silence. Or I was silent, at any rate. Delia frequently took umbrage at the way drivers chose to drive and pedestrians chose to walk. There was a war going on, and Delia was determined to win it.

As I looked out the window at the pedestrians hurrying to escape the rain, I thought of when I spent most of my time down here, in the loop area. The girls I'd taken to movies; the friends I'd hung out in record shops with; the small park where I sat and dreamed of a fine shiny adulthood that would see me with all the girls and all the friends and all the records a man could ever want. Well, that wasn't to be. For one thing, shopping malls squatted on three different edges of the city like invading armies and abducted all the retail business from downtown—and for another, women don't especially like to hear that you've spent your last few years rooming with guys named Lefty, the Skull, and Killer.

"So you'll be around at eight tonight?"

"Uh-huh. That's when he leaves the office?"

"Last three nights, he has."

"Hardworking man," I said.

"You sure you want to do this, Bob? Thing like this goes wrong a lot of the time, and then you end up back in—"

"I'm sure I want to do it, Delia. Real sure. Nothing else's

worked out for me. She told me something once, about MacDonald; and this shrink business may be just what I'm looking for."

Delia shook her head. "You ask me, it's the shrinks who're crazy."

"Could be."

"Last time Kip was out, they always made him go see this shrink and I always had to go with him, like I was his mom or something. The shrink was crazier than both of us put together. For one thing, he kept givin' me sexy eyes, you know what I mean? He even suggested that maybe I should come back alone sometime and see him."

"Sounds like a nice guy."

"Like I said, you ask me, shrinks're the ones who're nuts."

She pulled up to the curb of my ancient brick apartment house. Back in the thirties, when it was new, the upwardly mobile of their time had probably stood in line to get in here. Now the people who mowed the lawns and scrubbed the toilets of the upwardly mobile lived here.

"Maybe you can take a nap before I pick you up. Probably do you good."

"I don't think I could nap now. Too edgy."

She took my hand and gave it a squeeze. "You're one of the good ones, Bob. I just hope everything goes good for you tonight."

"Thanks, Delia."

3

I was wrong about not being able to take a nap. I went inside and took off the Stanley Blacker sport coat and slacks combination I'd worn today, and then went into the tiny bedroom and lay on the soft bed for ten minutes watching the lightning tear holes in the sky. Sometimes when the lightning struck, it lit up the framed photograph on my nightstand, giving Sara the same glow she'd had in life. I tried not to think about her, or how much I'd loved her, or how pointless her death had been. For seven years now I'd been trying to avenge her, but without any success at all. I had spent three work afternoons the last couple of weeks—the time off that so displeased my boss—trying to put together a few different plans. But none of them worked.

I slept.

In the dream, I was back in prison, as I was most nights when I dreamt, but this time my cellmate was Ralph DeConcini, my parole officer, and he kept claiming that he couldn't get our TV set turned off. It was set on a religious channel and the minister was down on his knees, sobbing. He needed more money quick or his ministry would die. Then Ralph himself started crying and said, "The poor bastard."

Thunder awoke me, the thunder of some murderous prehistoric era, rolling down the time lines like the voice of some angry god we no longer believe in. The angry god rattled a lot of windows that night.

When I swung my legs off the bed and put my face in my hands, I had to smile. God, imagine if I did get caught breaking into the shrink's office tonight, and if I were sent back to prison, and if my cellmate were Ralph DeConcini.

Talk about cruel and unusual punishment.

"There are two types, basically," Delia said a couple of hours later, explaining to me the kind of security devices I'd likely find on a small office in a duplex like the shrink's. "The most modern kind is called a digital keypad system, which only people who know a lot about computers can defeat—you know, hackers, creeps like that."

"And the other kind?"

We were nearing a suburban area of small, elegant shops and big, elegant aspirations. Perrier probably flowed from the taps. The night shone like a black diamond, the rain-washed streets throwing back the glow of traffic lights and neon signs. There was a curious beauty in this sort of bleakness. Wind whipped the still naked April trees and made the human heart—at least this human heart—pine for the warmth and glow of a fireplace and the solace of a good book. Or a nice lady, even better.

"Well, there are three other kinds, actually, but the first two aren't used much anymore. And anyway, if you run into them, you'll probably set off the alarm, first thing you do."

"Great."

"He probably uses something with an infrared motion detector."

"What's that?"

"It's very good at triggering alarms too, but there's a simple way to defeat it if you know what you're doing."

She then went on to explain that on the back door, cleverly hidden, would be a detector that noted any activity and would then pass this information along the alarm system. This all sounded pretty discouraging, but then, being good old Delia, she explained how I could trick the detector. . . .

Vertical wood siding gave the duplex a rustic look. It sat isolated and imperious on the shelf of a pine hill. Delia drove past, went halfway around the block, and then took the slanting gravel alley up to the duplex, cutting her headlights as she did so.

Delia was not only cute, she knew what she was doing.

"The one on the left," she said.

"You sure you want to wait for me? There's no sense in you getting involved."

"Hey, I help out all of my old man's friends. It's just my nature."

I smiled at her. "I appreciate it."

"Just remember what I told you about that beam. That could screw up everything. If there's any trouble out here, I'll honk—once if there's trouble, twice if it's all clear."

"I'll remember. And thanks again, Delia."

"Good luck, Bob."

I nodded, picked up the bag of tools and opened the door, wind and rain sprinkling across my face.

Then I went to try my luck again at the somewhat difficult art of burglary. Difficult for me, anyway.

The last time I'd tried something like this, I'd ended up in prison for four and a half years.

4

The detector setup was just as Delia had described it. Took me a few minutes to do what Delia had instructed me to do, but then I was inside, beyond the door my tools had helped open with little trouble, and standing in a darkness that smelled of slightly burned coffee and sweet furniture polish. In the pale light from outside, the waiting room could best be described as trendy-on-a-budget, a lot of dark, angular furnishings that looked awfully fragile. To the right of the receptionist's desks were three four-drawer filing cabinets, on top of which rested a half-dozen framed family portraits.

I started with the filing cabinets.

I learned where the good Dr. Wyman bought his paper towels wholesale; the fact that he was thirty days in arrears on his account at Bonanza Office Supply; and that he paid $65 a month to his late-night answering service.

Not exactly what I was looking for.

A few moments later I stood inside his personal domain, which was filled with just as much cheap flashy furniture and just as many framed family photos as the waiting room. There was a modern glass desk and spindly chair. And the inevitable Freudian couch, complete with an ashtray on one arm and a box of Kleenex—but from the arrangement of the leather armchairs, I suspected that this was where most of his business was done.

For a long minute I just stood there, imagining all the people who had been in here, all their woes and griefs—the faithless husband; the wife who felt her life was too confining; the teenager already far gone into drugs; the successful young man trying to make sense of the fact that he was dying of AIDS.

Not exactly a job I'd want.

I set to work, occasionally glancing up the hill to where Delia's cab sat, a dark figure against a darker night. By now the rain was little more than a mist.

The good doctor hid his patients' records in two filing cabinets tucked far back into a walk-in closet. I had to wind my way through a couple of raincoats and trod on a pair of rubbers that felt squishy as I passed over them.

Each cabinet was locked, but not very earnestly.

The good old burglary tools came in very handy.

I put the tiny flashlight into the corner of my mouth like a cigar and proceeded to riffle through the patient files.

I tried not to notice the personal information of anybody whose name didn't concern me. I figured I owed those folks at least that much discretion. There was only one name that concerned me.

Delia honked.

I closed the cabinet drawer I'd been looking through. I clicked off my flashlight.

I hadn't realized it till now but I was coated with chill sweat. I wasn't a natural-born thief. Burglary took both a physical and a mental toll on me.

I didn't know what else to do but stand there, breath coming in short hot gasps, fingers trembling slightly. Prison images filled my mind. Was I headed back there? At the thought, my stomach felt tight, sick.

I don't know how much time passed—enough anyway for me to go through a jury trial and a sentence hearing and to be assigned both a cellblock and a cell.

I even heard the prison loudspeaker barking for "Lights out!" on a steamy August night when you lay drowning in your own sweat.

A horn. Once. Twice. Delia.

All clear.

I went back to work.

I found the correct section—the M's—but I didn't find his name. A terrible thought: maybe he knew this shrink socially. Maybe they played golf together and he simply stopped in to see him sometimes and wasn't a patient at all.

I went through the next filing cabinet on the unlikely hope that somewhere else I'd find another M section.

I didn't find another M section.

There was no other M section.

I went back to the first filing cabinet, took several deep breaths, and forced myself to calm down.

He had to have a file in here somewhere. Had to.

I rolled the top drawer out on its oily wheels and started riffling through the tops of various file folders.

At last I came to one marked: NEW CLIENTS.

I took this one out, stuck the flashlight into the corner of my mouth and started looking through the material.

Whoever did the filing was a wee bit behind. Some of the "new" clients had visitation sheets that stretched back seven and occasionally eight months.

That's where I found him.

He'd been coming here seven months.

Tempting as it was, I didn't read the eight or nine sheets of scrawled notes that the good doctor had made about him.

There wasn't time.

I took the notes and went out to the front office and flipped on the Xerox machine.

The damned thing made a lot of noise in an empty office duplex like this one. Crisp electric fire outlined the lid of the copying machine. I hurried. My stomach was starting to act up again, probably in anticipation of prison food.

I made the copies, returned the originals to the file, closed up the cabinet, walked back over the squishy rubbers on the closet floor, and then went back to the front door and began to make my way out.

I crouched down so as not to set off the invisible beam. Less than a minute later I dropped myself into Delia's front seat and let her put a cigarette in my mouth.

It tasted a whole lot better than the flashlight had.

5

"I think it's great how much you loved her."

"Yeah. I suppose it is."

"Even after everything she did and all."

"That part I try not to think about."

"But we all do crazy things. That doesn't mean she was bad."

"That's how I look at it, Delia. That she just made a mistake was all. Just one little mistake."

She was taking me home after we'd had a few cups of coffee, during which she explained that she'd honked when a teenage couple had pulled up the driveway, looking for a place to make out. Everything had gone well.

"You still think about her a lot, huh?"

"Yeah, I do, Delia."

"You get ready to meet a nice lady, you call me."

"Oh?"

She laughed. "Don't worry, Bob. Not me. I'm true-blue. It ain't easy all the time, with Kip in the joint and everything, but I do all right. I was thinkin' about my cousin."

"Your cousin?"

"Betsy. Wait till you see her in a bikini."

"Nice, huh?"

"Nice? Boy would I love to have *her* chest."

"Maybe when this's all over," I said.

"Probably better you wait for a while anyway. She's tryin' to break it off with this Angie guy, he's this biker, and the last guy she tried to date, Angie smashed out all the windows in the guy's car."

"Guy ever call her again?"

"You kiddin'? But she didn't care anyway. She found out the guy was married, can you believe it, she sneaks around and gets Angie all riled up, and then the bastard is married."

You didn't need country western radio stations when Delia was around.

"Yeah," I said, "I think I'll wait a little while on Betsy."

"I can tell you're a little worried about Angie, and I don't blame you, but he'll be back in detox another two, three months, the way I figure, so you 'n' Betsy will have clear sailin'."

"That's good to know."

My apartment house took shape inside deep, windblown shadows.

Tonight when she pulled the cab over, I gave her a little kiss on the cheek and said, "I really appreciate all the help, Delia."

She nodded to the papers I had rolled up and stuck inside my blue windbreaker.

"I just hope you have somethin' in there you can use."

"So do I."

* * *

To caf or not to caf. That was the question.

Given all the pages I wanted to read through tonight, real caf coffee was probably what I needed to be alert. There were a lot of pages and I was tired from a long day's work at the store and I didn't want to miss some subtle message buried in the middle of the material I'd stolen from Dr. Wyman.

On the other hand, if I wrapped up early, I might find myself caffeine jitters staring at a long, hard night of bad memories and those little flare-ups of useless anger that makes dawn seem even more distant.

So I stood dumb, in all senses of that word, a jar of instant decaf in my left hand, a jar of instant caf in the other, weighing them as if they were jars of gold, and finally I decided to live a life of danger, and I filled the teakettle with water and set the kettle on the hot plate, which was about the only modern convenience in my wan little sleeping room, and then I spooned two heaping teaspoonsful of manly caf into a slightly cracked coffee cup.

And then finally I sat down and started reading about the life and times of one David George MacDonald.

During that long malaise of prison life, I became a serious reader, and some of the serious reading I did included André Malraux, whose *Man's Fate* contained a brief interview with a seventy-five-year-old priest. What have you learned in your fifty years of hearing confessions? Malraux wanted to know. And the old priest replied, "That there's no such thing as an adult."

I knew what he was talking about as I read through the file on David George MacDonald.

Here you had the rich, handsome, forty-year-old son of a wealthy investment banker. We were talking Yale. We were talking a five-year tenure at Mellon Bank. We were talking a six-year span at one of his father's investment companies. And yet . . . David had been inexplicably drawn to the dark side of American business. Contractors who skimped on promises and whose housing developments became rat traps after only a few years. Refinancing deals for home owners that were little better than the juice loans you could get from the mob. Used car wholesaling where turning back the odometer was mandatory. Expensive furs that were certainly stolen. And on and on.

You could see in Dr. Wyman's notes that MacDonald tried to pass himself off as a simple, honest businessman, but I knew his real background . . . and in the notes it became obvious that Dr. Wyman had at least begun to *suspect* his real background.

Here were his women, and they were myriad; here were his marriages, three in all, trouble with the law for beating all three of them; and here were the hookers he could never quite lose his taste for, the midnight cruise and the hasty hot reality of sex in a car seat with a woman who would please you any way you asked; and in passing once—just once— was a mention of my wife and how mad she'd made him because she'd tricked him into getting her pregnant.

At this point I set the material down, put my head against the back of the chair, closed my eyes.

I'd known she was pregnant, the autopsy had revealed that, but all along I'd assumed it was our child.

But now I knew better.

Their child.

One he hadn't even wanted.

It had died trapped inside her dead womb.

Really fucking peachy.

I spent the next fifteen minutes doing my self-pity aerobics—you probably do them yourself, at least sometimes. Has anybody ever been this betrayed before in all human history? Has such a bad hand ever been dealt to such an all-around wonderful human being as *moi* before? Has anybody ever deserved to feel such unashamed sorrow for his poor pitiful self before?

Fortunately, I got pretty sick of it all after a while and went down the hall to pee.

Sara hadn't been an ideal wife, but I hadn't been an ideal husband either. How about that cute little Nancy I'd spent one spring bopping in places as various as my office closet, the maintenance room in the basement, and the backseat of her ancient Buick war-wagon? Or the college-senior waitress I'd met at Pizza Hut? Or the Chanel saleswoman I'd had several nooners with at a motel out on Forester Road?

No such thing as an adult.

It wasn't virtue I was trying to defend here—it was justice.

Sara and I hadn't been all that morally superior to David MacDonald—but we hadn't murdered anybody.

David had murdered Sara.

And had gotten away with it, the police investigation dropped.

But faithless husband that I was, I wanted the killer of my faithless wife brought to trial.

My last best hope was that I'd find something useful in Dr. Wyman's notes. Nothing else had worked.

I had some more caf.

I even opened the window so the 43-degree wind would drive out any lurking sleepiness.

I started reading again.

Just before five and the first sharp cry of birds, I saw what I'd been looking for ever since I'd been released from prison. David George MacDonald had himself two very notable psychological anxieties. . . .

I saw the way I was going to nail his gold-plated ass to the wall.

6

Next day on my lunch hour, Delia drove me over to the library, where I checked out six books, three of which applied to one subject, three to another.

"You're going to be busy tonight," she said.

"Yeah. I will be."

"You closin' in on MacDonald?"

"I hope so."

"I hope so too."

The afternoon went slowly.

A customer named Burgess came in, a customer I ordinarily enjoyed talking to, but today everything he said irritated me. I knew why. I didn't want to be here. I wanted to be home with my library books.

Burgess bought a blue blazer and a pair of gray slacks. He

needed some additional clothes now that he'd given up smoking and put on fifteen pounds.

It felt as if I'd spent a couple of hours with, him but when he left and I checked my watch, I saw that I still had three and a half hours to go.

I spent the rest of the afternoon considering some of the words I'd found in Dr. Wyman's notes on David Mac-Donald:

> Anxiety disorder
> Anxiolytic medicine
> Anticipatory anxiety
> Systematic Desensitization

I had a long night ahead of me, one I looked forward to.

7

Around ten that night, I called Delia and asked her if she could help me out.

"Sure. What do I do?"

I told her.

"That should be easy," she said.

"I'd really appreciate it, Delia."

"Say," she said, just as I was about to hang up. "Guess who I ran into."

"Who?"

"My cousin Betsy. You know, the one with the big—"

"She still having trouble with her biker?"

"No. In fact, she said that they're probably gonna get married. I mean, he's agreed to start using deodorant and everything."

"No wonder they're getting married."

"But I told her about you anyway—you know, just in case it don't turn out too good—and she said that if she ever dumps him, she'd really like to meet you."

"Well, I'll be wearing her name on my lips."

"Huh?"

"Nothing. Just being a smart-ass. Look, Delia, I really appreciate all the help you've been giving me."

"No sweat, Bob. I just wish it'd worked out between you and Betsy."

"Maybe when we're reincarnated."

"You saw that Oprah show too, huh?"

I smiled. "Not that one. But I've seen a lot of others." She was crazy, Delia was, but relentlessly sweet. "Good night, Delia."

" 'Night."

8

Three weeks went by before Delia was able to find any pattern in David MacDonald's work life.

He always parked his splashy new Lincoln in a lot directly behind the office building he'd inherited from his father.

But as for when he arrived at work and when he left—he was usually erratic, no particular schedule being apparent to Delia.

Except for Thursday nights. Thursday nights, for some reason neither of us could figure out, he usually worked till around nine. A janitorial crew started cleaning the place up around three A.M.

Four different lunch hours, Delia drove me over to the office building so I could see what I needed to do.

I'd been in here before, back when I used to go up to see Sara when she was working for MacDonald, but I'd never really studied the place.

It was a nice building, built back at the turn of the century, defined by its curtain walls and its internal metal structure, then very fashionable. At least that's what the library book on local architecture had to say about it. And more: the soaring three-bay exterior is divided into three major sections; a two-story triple-arch base, an eight-story shaft of two tiers of projecting bay windows, and a crowning section marked by paired windows. Easy to imagine shiny black limousines pulling up here in the old days, and robber barons appearing in capes and squeaky black shoes.

The interior had been refurbished: pink marble and heavily rococo interior design. Your footsteps echoed on the marble floor, all the way over to and up the single elevator that ran up the very center of the building.

On my third visit to the place, an hour after work, I rode up to the ninth floor and went through a dry run of what I needed to do. I was in equal parts scared and excited. The run-through took twenty minutes. I managed to get through it without anyone seeing me—that I was aware of, anyway.

Back in the car, Delia said, "You're a mess."

"Thank you."

She laughed. "You know what I mean."

"It's messy work."

"And scary work."

"A little bit, I guess."

"You guess? You couldn't get me to do that in a million years."

"I just hope it works."

"Yeah," Delia said, putting the car in gear and pulling away from the curb, "so do I."

9

The following week, driving me back to MacDonald's, Delia said, "You scared?"

"A little."

"I'd be a lot scared."

"Well, I think that's more accurate."

"That you're a lot scared?"

"Uh-huh."

"Maybe it won't go the way you want it to. Maybe he won't—"

"I know."

"You could get killed, you know."

"I know."

"You're a lot braver than I'd be."

I laughed. "I'm not brave at all, Delia. I wish I were."

Her headlights swept the parking lot in back of the building, highlighting bumpers and fenders and license plates with cute personal statements such as: I'M CUTE. I doubted that anybody who had to brag about being cute actually was.

There was a cold mist and all the streetlights were haloed as I stepped from the car. We were getting winter in nickel-and-dime increments.

"I'll be saying prayers," Delia said.

"I'll need them."

"You'll be fine," she said in a way that suggested I probably wouldn't be fine at all.

"See ya," I said. I took my gym bag and left.

Some of the books I'd brought home from the library dealt not only with the structure of buildings but with the elevators they used. Starting in 1853, elevators of various kinds were introduced to the world. There had been steam elevators and hydraulic elevators and finally electric elevators. And it was on the electric elevator that I'd concentrated.

The dark front doors of the office building opened after I spent two hasty minutes working on them with a pick. The burglar alarm system had not been set yet. The janitorial service did that when they left in the middle of the night.

Once inside, I walked straight to the two elevators and rode all the way to the ninth floor. On the way up, I changed into the blue coveralls I'd stuffed inside the bag. I checked my watch. In the next fifteen minutes or so, if he was true to his usual schedule, David MacDonald would board this same elevator car on the floor beneath me.

I went to work. The first thing I did was hang an OUT OF ORDER sign on the second elevator and then rush back to the first car.

I punched the button to take the car to the eighth floor. On the way up, I opened the EMERGENCY phone box and ripped the two-inch receiver cord from its moorings. There'd be no calls from this elevator.

I left the car on the eighth floor.

I found the metal door with the FIRE sign above it and took the stairs down to the seventh floor, where I took a crowbar from my bag.

Everything was ready. MacDonald would board the car on the eighth floor. I'd give him a few seconds to start descending, then open the seventh-floor elevator doors with

44

a crowbar. The electric interlock would freeze the car right where it was—between floors—and I'd then run up to the ninth floor, where I'd again part the doors. Only this time I would step out onto the top of the elevator, which would be only a few inches below the ninth-floor elevator entrance.

I paced the seventh-floor hallway. The old building was filled with the ghosts of ancient plumbing and creaking floors. Every time one of them made a sound, I turned to the elevator. After several false alarms, I forced myself to calm down.

When he was finally there, one floor above me and putting his weight into the elevator car, I was daydreaming and didn't respond immediately. Then I had to hurry.

I pressed my ear to the elevator doors and listened for the eighth-floor doors to rumble closed. They did.

Then I waited to hear the whine of the machinery as the elevator began its descent. The car started to slowly descend.

I grabbed the crowbar and set to work.

In seconds I had the doors open. I heard the car stop. MacDonald shouted, "What the hell's going on here!"

I ran to the fire door and took the steps two at a time.

After six years and two months, after a prison term and numerous failed plans to prove that MacDonald had killed Sara, I finally had my best last chance to force MacDonald to tell me exactly what had happened.

All those fancy terms I'd found about him in his shrink file—anticipatory anxiety and anxiety disorder—meant one thing: MacDonald's lifelong claustrophobia had most recently manifested itself as a terror of the elevator in his office building. Over and over again he'd told his shrink about his nightmares—of being trapped in the elevator and suffocating.

He took medication, he did all the mental exercises his shrink suggested (this was where the term "systematic desensitization" came in), and he even considered moving his offices to a one-story building.

But none of that mattered now.

He was trapped on a very small elevator car, and before he left it, he was going to confess to killing my wife. And I was going to record it all on the hand-sized cassette player I'd brought along.

By the time I reached the ninth floor, MacDonald was screaming and pounding on the interior doors.

I got the ninth-floor doors open and stepped out onto the top of the car, where I knelt down and wrenched the T-handle straight up. This opened the emergency hatch. I looked down into the car at MacDonald.

He was aware of me immediately. He recognized me immediately too. "You sonofabitch, what d'you think you're doing?"

"The last time I broke into your office, MacDonald, you had me sent to prison. But I've learned a few thing since then." I stuck my recorder through the hatch and waggled it at him. "This time you're going to do all the work. And this time you're going to go to prison." I tapped the recorder. "You're going to tell me how you murdered my wife because after you were done with her you were afraid she'd turn you over to the district attorney for some of the scams she'd seen when she was your secretary."

"You think I'm going to listen to some dumb-ass ex-con?"

"You will or you'll never get off that elevator alive. You'll have a heart attack." I smiled. "You should've gotten on an exercise regimen a long time ago, MacDonald."

He was one of those men—you see them especially among male opera stars—who manage to carry an extra hundred pounds and still look handsome. There was a kind of baronial splendor to MacDonald, the long dark hair just now starting to show dramatic streaks of gray; the flowing dark suits meant to hide his girth and that somehow suggested a Victorian cape; and the masklike face, the cruel good looks of angry dark eyes and a petulant, crafty mouth. Sara had been pretty sensible. Or I'd thought so, anyway, until she got involved with MacDonald and his power games.

"You tore the fucking phone out, didn't you?"

"Guilty as charged."

"This time, asshole, you're going to go to the slammer and never get out."

The Moving Coffin

I smiled. "I'd try to calm down, MacDonald. You're going to be in there for a long time."

"Maybe not," he said, and before I quite realized what he was doing, a blued .45 appeared in his hand and he started firing bullets into the ceiling of the car.

I dove from the top to the ninth floor.

I let him fire, counting the shots as he did so. They echoed off the half-century silence.

He had one bullet left.

"It's not going to do you any good, MacDonald, that last shot," I said. "It's not going to get you out of that elevator."

The waiting started.

According to the books on phobias I'd read, what I could expect next were several outward manifestations of panic—shouting then screaming; pounding fists and then kicking as well; hurling himself to the floor and maybe even pounding his head against the wall. And pleading; earnest, savage pleading.

It sounded great.

Over the next forty-five minutes, at least according to the books, MacDonald had developed stomach cramps, lost his ability to stand up straight, probably wet his pants, had a difficult time swallowing, was terrified that he was about to smother to death, and could not focus his mind on any logical plan of escape.

That was when he began pounding the walls.

That was when he began shrieking.

That was when he began slamming at the doors with his fullback girth and his wounded-animal rage.

During this time, I snuck back to the top of the car, got my cassette player rolling again and shouted, "As soon as you tell me you killed Sara, MacDonald, I'll get you out of that car."

He couldn't help himself.

He was too far gone.

He'd planned to hold on to his last bullet until he really got a good chance to hit me—but he couldn't control his anger.

He fired his last shot up through the open hatch.

47

It ricocheted off the ceiling of the building, knocking loose some ancient dust, and then disappeared.

I closed the hatch again.

I had some more waiting to do.

This time, roughly twenty minutes later, he started sobbing. That was the only word for it. Wild, hysterical crying, and slamming his fists into the walls of the elevator car. The car shifted and shimmied beneath me; I look up the shaft at the cable. In the oily darkness, I felt the cable tremble from the terrible beating the car was taking.

I opened the hatch.

"You killed her, MacDonald, admit it and I'll let you out of here."

He spit upward, his oyster getting me on the forehead.

Without a whole hell of a lot of dignity, I withdrew my head from the emergency hatch.

Another fifteen minutes.

He started praying.

It was odd, hearing a man like MacDonald say the Hail Mary and Our Father, but he spoke them with his usual harshness, so they came off more curse than prayer.

Then he said, "Fuck you up there! I ain't gonna admit shit!"

After another fifteen minutes, I leaned into the emergency hatch and said:

"You didn't need to kill her, MacDonald."

"I didn't kill her."

"You didn't know her. She never would've turned you in. She loved you too much." The words weren't easy for me to say, but they were the truth. She'd told me that herself. "I loved her, MacDonald, and I would've taken her back and we would've moved away and eventually she would've forgotten all about you. You didn't need to kill her."

And that's when I realized how badly my elevator-phobia plan was going. MacDonald wasn't crying over Sara, I was. This was turning into a kind of therapy session for me: I was saying all the flinty things I'd kept in my stony heart during prison.

They needed to be said for me, not for him, and I didn't even give a damn if he listened or not.

I must've talked another ten minutes.

After an hour and a half, with Delia sitting out in the parking lot surely sensing that yet another of my plans had gone wrong, I started to wonder if MacDonald wouldn't beat me at his own phobia.

He phased in and out of terror, never getting quite so bad that he gave in to me.

Of course, then he'd erupt again, panic overtaking him, screaming, screeching, crying out for his mother, pounding and pounding and pounding the walls.

I needed one more thing that was one more thing too many—one more thing that—

I'd been crouching on top of the elevator, my recorder sitting on the edge of the emergency hatch.

My legs were dead from crouching so long. I needed to stand up.

And when I did—

Something fell, clanking, from my pocket.

And when I reached down to get it . . .

"You're dead, you fucker!" I shouted down through the open emergency hatch.

I was jubilant.

MacDonald was going to be confessing real soon now.

Real soon.

10

I didn't get out of the police station till much before dawn.

Delia was waiting for me in the freezing gray morning.

When I got in the car, she handed me an empty paper cup and poured some steaming coffee into it.

"So what did our fine friends the flatfoots make of the tape you played 'em?"

"They said that the D.A. wouldn't be happy that I got the confession that way but that it would still be useful in prosecuting MacDonald."

"So they are going to prosecute him?"

I nodded. "The cops hate him as much as I do. They've wanted to nail him for years. Now they think they can get him on a first-degree murder rap. They're very happy."

She looked over at me, her wise eyes gentle. "How about you?"

"Me?"

"You happy, Bob?"

"I guess."

"You really loved her, didn't you?"

"Yeah," I said, "in my imperfect way."

"Your imperfect way my ass. You're a good man, Bob, even if you won't admit it."

She put the taxi in gear and we pulled out of the lot.

When we were streaking down the street, pulling into a Hardee's drive-through for breakfast, she said, "You know, I was startin' to think you weren't ever gonna get him to confess."

I smiled. "Yeah, so was I. Then that lighter Sara gave me for our anniversary fell out and . . . Well, as soon I as started lighting paper and dropping it into the elevator car . . . Well, MacDonald started talking right away. Claustrophobia and pyrophobia is a pretty deadly combination. Of course, he's really going to have claustrophobia in that little cell of his."

"You want cheese on your eggs this morning, Bob?" she said.

"Yeah," I said, feeling almost ridiculously good about everything all of a sudden, "cheese sounds great."

Even seeing my parole officer Ralph DeConcini a few hours from now sounded great.

Hell, *everything* sounded great.

DOWN IN THE HOLE

Nancy A. Collins

(Based on an idea by William P. Myers)

I WAKE FROM UNWELCOME DREAMS, WRAPPED IN AN ENVELOPE OF cold sweat, the bitter taste of fear in my mouth. I look to my wife. She's still asleep. Good, I didn't wake her up this time. Coming out of a nightmare is bad enough, but feeling guilty for disturbing someone else's night makes it worse.

My wife is a wonderful woman. Very understanding. She tries to comfort me whenever I have particularly bad dreams—the ones I wake up from screaming. But I know it must be becoming wearisome to her. Lord knows, I find it annoying.

She recommended that I see a therapist about my— problem. But my father was a minister—one of the old-fashioned hard-line Calvinists—and he didn't hold with doctors who didn't cut you open. If something was wrong inside your head and heart, then that was God's province, not man's. Although I turned my back on my father's beliefs during college, old attitudes like that are hard to shake.

Besides, I don't need an analyst at one hundred dollars a hour, three sessions a week, to ferret out the childhood trauma that shaped my adult nightmares. I know all too well where my dreams come from. All I have to do is close my eyes, and it all comes rushing back to me—in way too much detail for my own tastes.

It was back when my family lived in Choctaw County. My father was assigned as pastor to the Methodist church there. I was six years old when our family first moved there—my brother Dale five. Seven Devils was a small, isolated Arkansas town located in the Mississippi Delta region. It was too hot in the summer and too cold in the winter. There wasn't much of a public library, and if you wanted to see a movie, you had to drive outside the county to nearby Monticello.

In some ways, Seven Devils's quietude made it the ideal place "to raise the kids up." On the other hand, in a town where there were as many liquor stores as brands of Baptists, teen pregnancy and alcoholism were through the roof. My friend Rich, who I attended school with all the way through high school, used to say there wasn't anything to do in Seven Devils "except drink beer and hate niggers."

It was summer when it happened. It was 1965 and the Beatles were in America, the Stones not far behind them. Vietnam was percolating away, and civil unrest was breaking out in cities both sides of the Mason-Dixie Line. However, none of this managed to penetrate the placidity that enveloped Choctaw County. In fact, nothing much in the way of social change had occurred since World War Two. I was playing with my brother, Dale, and our friend, Rich.

"You're dead!"

"No I'm not! You were dead a while ago!"

I clambered out of the tall yellow grass and lofted a thin bamboo stick at Rich. Rich ducked as the shaft drifted down beside him.

"You can't do that! That's your rifle, not your spear!"

Rich was only arguing for the hell of it now. We'd been playing War for a hour or so, and this was always how it ended. Dale appeared suddenly off to the right, standing up so his head and shoulders could be seen above the long grass. Dale and I may have been brothers, but our ideas about war were entirely different.

Dale preferred to hide out as long as possible without being caught, while I loved the tense thrill of a chase. The vacant lot behind the old church was the best place for either strategy.

Like I said, Rich was our best friend, although we often

got into squabbles as to whose best friend he really was. It didn't matter that Dale was a year younger than me; we couldn't remember a time when we weren't all doing something together. But that's how it was in Seven Devils. There were fewer than a thousand people in the whole town, all of them stranded in the butt hole of Arkansas. Friends had to last.

I leapt on my bamboo rifle-spear and pulled it out from under my foot before the others could reach it—just in case the game wasn't really over yet.

"I wouldn't have to spear you if you were playing fair!"

"Yeah, yeah, yeah!" Rich grinned.

I chased Rich halfheartedly out onto the gravel driveway, where Dale joined us. We stood around for a moment, unsure of what to do next.

Rich looked down the drive and nodded across the street. "What do you think Ray's been doing all day?"

Ray Burns was a big kid who rarely spoke to us, since we were just fourth and fifth graders. We didn't talk to Ray much either, since he never paid us any attention unless he was trying to pull some kind of gag. But there he was, bare-chested and sweaty, digging a hole where his neighbor's house used to stand.

Mr. Jennings had lived there, but then he died and the town tore down the old cabin he'd lived in all his life. It was weird seeing someone actually *doing* in our neighborhood. Nobody did much of anything, since most of the people who lived there were poor and old—except for Ray's family, who were just poor.

Mr. Burns, Ray's dad, spent most of his time driving trucks and left Ray alone on his own a lot. I thought that was kind of neat. I wondered what it would be like to not have someone telling you to do your homework, or telling you what to wear, or how to cut your hair, or when to go to bed.

"Maybe Mr. Jennings buried his money there?" Dale whispered. Dale was always interested in buried treasure—even more than War.

"Hey, I think he's coming over here!" Rich whispered anxiously. "Let's go!"

I watched the figure coming up the drive and tried to think

of what else we could do besides stand around like a bunch of dummies. "We'll just talk to him for a second and then go, okay?"

We shuffled our feet in the gravel and looked around uneasily as Ray crunched toward us. I didn't particularly dislike Ray. Sometimes I actually wished we could be friends. Ray was always doing things and he always seemed to have kids around him, but he never had any real friends. That was probably on account of his taste for cruel practical jokes. Like the time he "pantsed" that crippled kid at the roller skating rink. I wondered what would make Ray act so mean. Maybe it had something to do with him not having a mom.

Well, that wasn't exactly true. Ray *did* have a mom, but she was locked up somewhere. I once overheard my mother discussing Mrs. Burns during one of her bridge parties. She'd called Mrs. Burns a "dipso," whatever that was. Rich said that was another name for dork or wimp, but somehow I doubted that.

"Finished playing War? Who won?"

"Nobody," Rich said a little warily. "What're you digging for?"

"Nothing in particular. I just started finding stuff and kept going."

"So what'd you find?" I heard myself ask.

Ray cocked his hip and stretched his back. "Some arrowheads and pieces of an old gun."

Dale brightened with interest. Even Rich became curious.

"Can we see?" I asked eagerly, thinking of my own small collection of fossils and arrowheads.

Ray looked steadily at us. "Sure, but only if you promise not to tell anyone anything about it. Promise?"

We nodded, but Ray made us promise out loud before leading us down the drive and across the small asphalt road onto the old lot.

We climbed down into the neck-deep hole and started digging around. The earth fell apart in our hands like wet tobacco and smelt of dirt and cut roots. We looked around for a while, but the hole was no different from the ones we dug to play War—nothing but dirt.

"Where's the arrowheads and the gun?" I asked.

Down in the Hole

"Yeah, I thought you said you were finding stuff," Dale said accusingly.

"It's in the house. Just keep looking and I'll be back with the gun." Ray turned and left without waiting for a response.

We looked at one another, and when no one said anything, we went back to sifting the dirt with our hands. Soon Ray came back out of the house, wrapped in an old red blanket and sporting a leather headband with a dirty feather stuck in it.

Ray smiled and pulled the blanket tight around his shoulders. "You want to see the gun?"

Dale nodded.

Ray opened up the blanket and showed us a nickel-plated snub-nosed revolver. He held a bit of the blanket between the pistol grip and his left hand and had his finger around the trigger. In his other hand he held a bottle of cheap whiskey, which he hoisted for a drink.

I could whiff the sour smell of the liquor even in the hole. The space around me suddenly grew smaller and my mind started to scramble for the words that would get them out of this mess.

"You didn't find that gun here!" Rich blurted.

I didn't wait for Ray to respond to that one. "We gotta go, we were supposed to be home two hours ago." And the three of us rose as if the bluff would actually work.

Ray jumped sideways and pointed the gun at Rich. "No one leaves till Big Chief Red Feather say so! White man steal land, now white man pay! No move! Sit! If squaw want you, squaw come get you!"

Dale started to cry. I looked hard at Ray's narrow skull and wondered if there really was any Indian in him—probably not.

We sat quietly and waited for whatever would come next. Ray tilted back another swallow of alcohol and stared out across the rooftops. His eyes grew dull and emptied out into the distance, only to fill with a truly transcendent hate when he returned his gaze to us, huddled together in the hole like frightened pups.

"White man kill squaw and child! Only me left now! Now I kill white squaw and child!"

Dale was so scared he wet himself. Rich wiped at his eyes, trying hard not to let his lower lip quiver. I felt as if my lungs and heart were trying to jump out of my chest.

"Ray, we *really* have to go home. Mama's gonna get *real* mad if we're late for dinner—"

"Shut up!" Ray screamed, his spittle striking me in the face. "I told you my name's not Ray! It's Big Chief Red Feather! You understand me?"

I was too frightened to do anything more than nod.

"Then let me hear you say it! Say my name!"

"B-Big Chief Red Feather." My throat was so tight it felt as if I was going to choke on the words.

Ray smiled crookedly and sat down on the edge of the hole, dangling his legs over the side. *"That's* better." He took another long pull. "I hate this town." His voice had taken on a slur. He hefted the whiskey bottle, scanning the surrounding houses. "I really fuckin' *hate* it!"

I flinched at the sound of the F-word. In our house, nothing made my dad reach for his belt faster than cuss words. Especially high-octane dirty ones like shit, goddamn, and the Big F.

"Wassamatta, kid? Haven't you ever heard anyone say *fuck* before?" Ray sneered.

I squared my shoulders and tried not to look too scared. "Sure I have. I'm in the fifth grade."

"I'm so impressed." Ray pointed the gun at me like it was a shiny finger. "Yeah, but have you ever said it?"

"Said what?"

"Fuck."

"Sure. Lots of times."

"Then let me hear you say it."

Rich and Dale were watching me with huge, frightened eyes. Dale started to whimper.

"Shut him up!" Ray snapped, waving the gun at Dale. "He sounds just like a damn girl! It's bad enough I gotta sit here and smell his piss." He returned his attention to me. "Okay, let me hear you say fuck."

"I don't want to say it."

"Why? You too goody-goody? Afraid you'll go to hell if you say it?"

Down in the Hole

"I just don't feel like saying it, that's all."

Ray leveled the gun right between my eyes. "Big Chief Red Feather tells white man to say fuck or white man dies!"

"Fuck."

Ray cupped a hand to his ear. "What's that? Speak up!"

"Fuck."

"I can't hear yoouuu!"

"Fuck!"

The intensity of my shout made Rich and Dale jump. I met Ray's slightly out-of-focus gaze. The older boy nodded then looked away.

"God, I hate this stinkin' place." He was back to staring at the sky, although the gun remained pointed into the hole. "Ain't nothin' to do, nowhere to go, no one to see that you don't already know. Or think they know you. Everybody already got their minds made up 'bout how things are and how they're gonna be. Bunch of stuck-up jerkwads, that's all they are."

He peered down into the hole with angry, bloodshot eyes. "You should get down on your knees and beg me to kill you! Before you grow up and get like them! Like all the rest! I'd be doin' you guys a favor, y'know that?"

"What the hell's going on here?"

Ray jumped at the sound of an adult voice. The whiskey bottle and gun disappeared inside the blanket faster than a conjurer's doves.

"Uh, hello, Reverend Thayer! Me and the boys was just playin' cowboys and Indians, that's all!"

My father scowled at Ray over his spectacles. "Aren't you a little old to be playin' at that, Ray?"

Ray shrugged, careful not to dislodge the blanket. "They asked me, so I figured, why not?"

My father didn't look terribly convinced. He frowned down at Dale and me, cowering at the bottom of the hole. "What the devil are you boys doin' down there?"

"We was just playin'," Ray piped in. *"Right,* Mike?"

"Y-Yeah, Dad. Just playin'."

"Well, get on outta that hole! Your mother's about ready to have kittens! She sent me out looking for you 'cause she's afraid her tuna casserole's gonna go cold."

Ray was backing his way toward the house as we clambered out of the hole. He caught my eye and mouthed the words *Don't tell* while my father wasn't looking.

"Just look at your clothes!" my dad scolded. "Your mama's gonna be fit to be tied when she sees those stains!"

When they got back to the house, Dale started crying and couldn't stop. I told my father what had happened in the hole.

At first he got real quiet, then his face lost its color, then it came back—in spades. For a moment I thought my father was going to get his gun and shoot Ray.

"It's about time something was done about that boy! Emma, call Doc Sutter and have him come over and check the boys! Better tell him to stop by the Winters' place too, and see to Rich!"

"Honey, what are you going to do?"

"Don't worry. I'll see to it everything's taken care of."

My father went into his study and made a long phone call with the door shut. Mom made us wash and put us to bed, even though it was still light outside. Dr. Sutter came by and examined us later, although he wouldn't tell me exactly *what* it was he was looking for. Dale ended up getting a shot that made him sleepy because he wouldn't stop blubbering.

I sat on my bed and looked out the window in the direction of Ray's house. Just after it got dark I saw flashing red and blue lights and heard the sound of car doors slamming and men shouting. I'm not sure, but I think I recognized my father's voice. I wondered if Ray would tell about me saying *fuck* to get back at me for spilling my guts about the gun. My stomach knotted up at the thought of my father finding out.

The next day, I walked over to the empty lot next to the Burns house to look at the hole, only to find that it was filled in. When I asked my father what had happened to the hole, he told me not to ask questions that might upset people.

Not one in Seven Devils ever saw Ray again. A month after Ray disappeared, Mr. Burns signed on with a trucking company in Wichita and moved away. Three weeks later their empty house caught fire and burned to the ground.

When I tried to talk about what had happened in the hole with my parents, they pretended I was making it all up. Rich joked that my father killed Ray and buried his body in the hole, and that's why everybody pretended nothing had happened. I got mad and punched him in the nose hard enough to make it bleed. After that, Rich was Dale's best friend more than mine.

The months turned into years, and me and Rich and Dale grew older. Rich and Dale continued being close friends, even going so far as to going in together on an old car they drove to school and football games. I kept more and more to myself, preferring to sit alone in the high grass behind the old church, drinking contraband whiskey while contemplating the empty lot across the street and the secret it held locked in its dark belly.

Rich was first. We weren't even out of high school yet. He developed a serious drug problem while we in ninth grade. Crank. Downers. Coke. Whatever. He kept complaining about bad dreams.

His dad bought him a moped for his graduation. The week before commencement, he rode it straight into a semi.

They didn't leave the casket open at his service. It was so weird—like they were burying this box they said Rich was in, but there was no way of seeing if he was *really* in there.

Everyone thought it was an accident. Everyone but me. Rich had told me, a couple of days before he got run over, that he'd been having the weirdness feelings. Like wanting to steer his bike into the headlights of cars, like a moth to a flame.

The day after I graduated from high school, I packed my bags and bought a one-way ticket to Memphis.

No one in Seven Devils ever saw me again.

I struggled for several years, working any number of shit jobs while I attended art school. Then I managed to land a job working for an advertising agency, where I ended up making a lot of money.

Now I'm successful, moderately wealthy, and married to a wonderful woman. I'm light-years removed from the stagnant hellhole of my youth. But my dreams . . . my dreams are another matter altogether.

They always start the same way. I'm at work, desperately trying to sort out one of the bigger accounts. The intercom buzzes. It's my secretary.

"Someone here to see you, Mr. Thayer."

Before I can tell her I'm too busy to see anyone today, the door to my office swings open and Ray Burns walks in. He's dressed exactly the same way as the last time I saw him, except that the blanket is muddy and full of holes, and the feather stuck in his headband is muddy too. He reeks of cheap whiskey, and when he gets closer I can see that his face is smeared with dirt and the skin is flaking away, revealing the bone beneath. He grins at me and a worm crawls out of his nose.

"No one leaves until Big Chief Red Feather say so! White man steal land, now white man pay! Get down on your knees and beg me to kill you! Fuck-fuck-fuck-fuck!"

And then he pulls out the gun—the nickel-plated revolver —and points it right at my head and pulls the trigger. And I wake up just as the bullet enters my forehead. Sometimes I try to wake myself up before that happens—sometimes I succeed. But only sometimes.

They say that dreams reveal our deepest fears and hopes. If this is true, what do mine reveal? Am I frightened of failure? Am I worried that, should I not succeed in my business, I'll find myself back where I started? Doomed to spend my mortal span in Seven Devils, Arkansas? I can't help but feel that there is something else, something far more sinister at work here.

The last time I spoke to my brother was three months ago. It was late and he apologized for waking me up.

"That's okay, Dale. What's wrong?"

"Wrong? What makes you think something's wrong?"

"If nothing's wrong, why the hell are you calling me at two in the morning?"

There was silence on his end of the line. I could picture him chewing on his thumbnail, just like he used to do when we were kids.

"I'm having trouble sleeping. Dreams."

"Nightmares?"

"Kinda. Remember Ray?"

Silence on my end now.

"Mike? You still there?"

"Yeah. I remember Ray. What about him?"

"You ever read about 'delayed stress syndrome'? It's

usually used to describe Vietnam vets or hostages. It's when the events of something traumatic finally start to hit home, both physically and emotionally. Sometimes it can take years before the person starts to suffer the effects of what happened to them. And in cases where people have been made to pretend it 'never happened,' the side effects can be especially damaging. I'm thinking maybe that's what I have—delayed stress syndrome."

"Dale, maybe you need to see a doctor. . . ."

He laughed then, because he knew I had the same aversion to psychiatrists as he did. "Yeah, sure. Dad would really love *that.*"

"Dad's dead, Dale."

"You think he killed him?"

"Who?"

"Dad. Do you think Dad killed Ray?"

"Dad was a minister. Ministers don't kill people."

"Ministers aren't supposed to do a lot of things."

"Look, Dale, why don't you try and get some sleep? Try and relax—draw yourself a nice hot bath or something."

"Yeah, right. Talk to you later, Mike. 'Night."

Later that week, my brother Dale drew himself a nice, hot bath, climbed in, and opened his wrists. He was twenty-nine.

Now I'm standing here, staring out my bedroom window, frightened of returning to bed. Returning to sleep. Terrified that if I sleep, I'll wake up and kill myself. Just like Rich. Just like my brother.

I look at my wife, wrapped in her own private world of dreams. She frowns in her sleep and murmurs something. Maybe it's my name. I know she's been worried about me since my brother's death and the arrival of my nightmares. She has every right to be. As I watch her, I suddenly realize what my course of action must be.

I get dressed as swiftly and as silently as I can. As I write the note telling her not to worry, that I'll be back soon, I realize how crazy this all is. But it is something I must do. If I don't go through with it, I'll find myself eyeing the headlights of oncoming cars and contemplating the edges of straight razors very soon.

Seven Devils is a nine-hour drive from where I now live.

But first I must take a side trip, to the storage locker where Dale and I moved what remained of our parents' household after Dad died and Mom moved to the retirement community in Arizona.

It takes me a solid of hour of shifting boxes, but I finally find my father's tools. I take one of the shovels—one of the old ones—and place it in the trunk of my car.

It's noon by the time I reach Choctaw County. The town of Seven Devils seems to have dwindled even more than when I last saw it, twelve years ago. The buildings look more run-down, the streets emptier. It seems as if the town fathers are no longer bothering to pretend that this place has a future. It is dying, on its way to becoming a ghost town.

It takes me a while to find our old block, since all the neighborhoods look dilapidated now. I only succeed in locating it because I spot the Methodist church my father used to preach at. I pull up and stare around, shielding my eyes from the sun. I have to use my memory to try and place where the Burnses' house used to be.

I get out of the car and open the trunk, retrieving my father's shovel. I walk over to the empty lot. It has been twenty years, but I can still make out where the hole had been. I begin digging.

Although Seven Devils is a very small town, no one comes over to see what I'm doing or who I am or why I'm here. I dig for three hours, laboring under a sweltering delta sky. Sweat runs down my back and brow, making my eyes sting. Blisters blossom and burst on my hands. But I keep at it.

What was I expecting to find? Evidence of murder? Suicide? Ray Burns's worm-eaten skeleton, grinning up at me from its unhallowed resting place? All I found was a rotted leather headband, an old liquor bottle, and what might have once been a feather.

I stared at the detritus at the bottom of the hole. This was all the physical evidence that remained of the ordeal Rich, Dale, and I underwent two decades ago. Wherever Raymond Burns may have ended up, it wasn't in this hole.

I still don't know what made Rich and Dale kill themselves. Then again, I don't know what made our dad drink and why our mother spends her free time obsessing over her toy poodle—which she talks to more than any of her children. Maybe it was guilt. Maybe it was stress. Maybe it was unhappiness. Maybe it was from being raised uptight white Anglo-Saxon Protestants. Or perhaps it was the taint from being in such a soul-killing town as Seven Devils. I'll never know.

All I know is that within minutes of my finishing the hole, I fell asleep. And I dreamed. I dreamed about being in high school and being late for a test for a class I never once attended, and when the bell rang everyone came out into the hall and I suddenly noticed I wasn't wearing any pants.

It was the best dream I ever had.

THE LAYING OF HANDS

Shawn Ryan

GAVIN HATED THIS PART.

And he hated himself for hating it.

Pushing his grocery-filled buggy in front of him, making slow, measured steps, he approached the checkout lane at Safeway. Years of therapy helped him control the most obvious signs of his fear. Sweat no longer coated his palms or beaded his upper lip. His skin felt clammy, but he hoped it wasn't the pallor of cold, dead flesh, which it used to resemble at times like this. The beard he'd grown hid most of his face, precisely its purpose.

Nothing, though, could dispel the cloud of nauseating butterflies circling in his stomach. He felt its tingle start radiating up his chest. Once there, he knew he couldn't stop it from running through his shoulders and down the long, terrible nerve ways to his fingers.

Stop it, you wimp! Be a man! You've done this before! Show some balls and do it again!

The flavor of self-loathing was a bitch to lose once it was in your mouth. And when it latched its claws into your mind, it took psychological crowbars to rip it free. Gavin was familiar with the taste.

Haphephobia, the psychiatrists called it. Or haptephobia,

hapnophobia, aphephobia, haptophobia, thixophobia. They all meant the same thing. Fear of touching or being touched.

He looked at his watch to get his mind off the fear. Three A.M. He didn't enjoy shopping in the wee hours, but it was the only time he wouldn't be surrounded by people, others who might get too close or—God forbid—bump into him.

The night cashier stood at the cigarette cabinet. The padlocked Plexiglas door was open, and she stuffed cartons of Marlboros, Benson & Hedges, and Salems into their assigned slots. She turned slightly as Gavin walked behind her.

"Number five," she said in a bored voice.

Pushing his buggy between the rollaway metal racks filled with magazines and candy, he began unloading it. The cashier came around the other end of the checkout lane and grabbed a gallon of milk, dragging it over the laser scanner.

Gavin glanced at her and gave a slight smile. She offered only a tight-lipped grin in return. His shoulder-length brown hair partially covered his face as he pulled the items out of the buggy. Unloading the last box, dread clamped down on his entire body. In a few moments he'd hand her his money. Their hands would be very close.

He was thirteen when the initial stirrings of anxiety first occurred. He was at a reunion of the Menottes, his mom's side of the family. Since he was an only child, he was flooded by a never-ending river of aunts, uncles, cousins, and dozens of other people he'd never seen before, didn't know, didn't even want to know. They hugged him, tousled his hair, planted wet kisses on his face. The waxy smell of thick lipstick almost nauseated him, and he was certain much of it was forever ground into the flesh of his cheeks.

When he told his mother how he felt, she became exasperated.

"You're just being silly," she said. "Don't embarrass me."

As years went by, the anxiety about being touched continued to grow. By the time he was eighteen, he could no longer endure the agony of going to school every day, brushing against students in the halls, in class. In ninth grade shop class he discovered an aptitude for building furniture, and that's what he turned to when he graduated. With a loan from his father and his uncle Stan, he started a furniture-making business, a one-man operation that he ran out of a small, old building that once was a garage. He lived upstairs in a loft apartment.

The first few years were tough as hell, but he always was frugal, and not having a social life helped him save most of the money he made. When his mom and dad died in a car wreck ten years ago, the insurance money helped.

And he did good work. If it was wood, he could turn it into anything and make it beautiful. Eventually, word got around about Gavin Menotte and now he had more than enough business. In fact, in the fifteen years since he started, he'd saved almost thirty thousand dollars.

He'd have more except for the twenty thousand dollars spent on treatment for his affliction. After wading through a series of therapists, psychologists, psychiatrists, hypnotists, and anyone else he thought might help, he was intimate with all the buzzwords and explanations: fear of negative evaluation by his peers, fear of embarrassing public behavior, fear of making mistakes, of being criticized, of speaking poorly, fear of contamination, fear of sexual contact, abuse by parents. None of those fit his fear. He didn't mind talking to people, as long as they kept their distance. His parents never abused him, unless one or two well-deserved spankings were abuse. His phobia just existed. No reason for it. In the end, he simply learned to live with it. What else could he do?

His greatest regret was that he probably wouldn't have any children. He had sex when he was sixteen with a girl he met at a party, and while he enjoyed the sensations, the prospect of pressing his naked body against another person's for an extended length of time was too horrifying. But that didn't keep him from thinking about kids. He made trips to the park every Saturday to enjoy their squeals of laughter, experience their boundless energy.

Oh well, what good were regrets? he figured. Facts are facts. Sometimes life sucks.

"Forty-seven, thirty-eight," the cashier said. Gavin drew his wallet from the back pocket of his jeans and pulled three twenties from it. He gingerly held the bills out, making sure there was plenty of room for the cashier to grab them without getting close to his fingers. She took the money and punched the buttons on the register. Gavin remained taut, there was still change to be given.

"Freeze, motherfuckers!" a voice growled.

Gavin's head whipped to the right. Standing at the end of the register was a pasty-faced teenager, the 9mm pistol in his shaking hands darting back and forth between Gavin and the cashier.

"Oh my God!" the girl whispered.

"Shut up!" the boy hissed, his eyes red-rimmed but hard. "Where's the stock crew?"

"I-i-in the back, on break," the girl stammered.

"Okay, gimme all the money in the register," the boy demanded.

The girl did as she was told, holding out the money in both hands. The boy took a plastic bag used for ice cream and opened it under the cash. "Drop it in," he said.

She did, and he turned to Gavin.

"Gimme yer wallet!" he barked.

Gavin's wallet was still in his left hand and he held it out, his arm straight. He wasn't concerned about the money inside, although there was more than three hundred dollars in it. All he could think about was the boy's hand, the one now reaching toward the wallet. The hand looked huge, the fingers as big as fat, bloated sausages.

The boy snatched at the wallet, but as he did, his fingers skittered across the back of Gavin's hand. The touch was electrifying and Gavin squealed involuntarily, yanking his hand back and frantically brushing it off on his jeans. The wallet fell to the floor.

"You fuckin' pussy sonuvabitch," the boy said as he raised the gun.

For a brief second Gavin saw the black hole of the barrel pointing directly at his head. Then he heard a pop and his head snapped back. He staggered backward, slamming into the rack of candy and bubblegum, sending multi-colored packs flying in all directions. Slumping to the floor, he felt hot liquid running down the right side of his face.

How weird, he thought as he flopped onto the white floor tiles. It doesn't hurt at all.

* * *

Gavin opened his eyes, then quickly snapped them shut. The pain was excrutiating.

What had happened? Where was he?

He cracked his eyelids just enough to see through his lashes. An IV tube stuck in the crook of his right elbow, another stabbed the back of his left hand. He looked around at the dull, nondescript walls.

This was a hospital room, he realized. How'd he get here? Why was he . . . ?

He remembered. The gunshot.

Gingerly, he touched his right hand to the heavy bandage wrapped around his head.

The door opened and a middle-aged man in a white coat walked in, holding a chart in his hands. His eyes widened when he saw that Gavin was awake. Then he smiled.

"Well, hello there," he said in a rough, scratchy voice. "I'm glad to see you're finally awake. We weren't sure how long it would be before you came back to us."

"Who are you?" Gavin asked.

"My name is Dr. Brigman. I'm a neurosurgeon."

Brigman stopped and put his hand to his nose. His eyes squeezed shut and a vicious sneeze erupted from his mouth. He sniffed loudly, then took out a handkerchief and swabbed his nose.

"Ah God. Excuse me," he said as he sniffed again. "I've got a terrible sinus infection. It's all this pollen in the air."

He looked at Gavin and grinned through watery eyes. "Anyway, back to you. I'm the guy who operated on you."

"After I was shot, right?"

"Exactly. How much do you remember?"

"Everything before being shot. Nothing after."

"I don't doubt that. You were in bad shape when the ambulance got you here. But we managed to pull you through."

"How long have I been here?"

"Five days."

"Am I all right?"

"Well, I think so," he said. "The fact that you're awake and coherent is a good sign."

Brigman stopped talking and moved closer to the bed.

The Laying of Hands

Gavin tried to shift his body, to move himself away, but the pain in his head throttled him. He stayed still.

"Don't try to move too much," Brigman said. "You're going to be very sore for a few days. Right now, I want to look at your eyes."

Gavin nodded very gently. Even that hurt. He pushed his head slightly back into the pillow as Brigman drew close and gazed into his eyes, then shone a tiny penlight into them.

"Excellent," Brigman said, straightening. "Your pupil response is good."

"So what exactly did you have to do?" Gavin whispered.

"The bullet ricocheted off your skull and fragmented into three pieces," Brigman said. "They all went into different parts of your brain and they all went pretty deep, but we removed them and so far there doesn't seem to be any permanent neurological damage. Your vital signs are strong; your motor functions, at least the ones we could test while you were unconscious, are intact."

"So what do I do?" Gavin asked.

"For now, take it easy. You need to regain your strength. Meanwhile, we'll run some more tests on you, get a better grip on whether your brain activity has been affected."

Gavin closed his eyes. He didn't speak as shock and despair smothered him. All those people laying their hands on him. God, no. Brigman misinterpreted his reaction.

"Listen, so far, so good," Brigman said. "You're alive. Let's not think the worst. The human body is an amazing machine, capable of miracles."

Gavin didn't respond, keeping his eyes closed. He didn't see Brigman move closer until he felt a hand on his wrist. His eyes flew open and he jerked his arm away with a short cry. The IV needle in his hand yanked out and a small trickle of blood ran from the insertion hole.

"Don't touch me!" he screamed.

Brigman's eyebrows creased at the vehemence of Gavin's outburst.

"I was only checking your pulse," he said.

"Don't touch me," Gavin repeated. "I hate being touched."

"Okay," Brigman said slowly, "but I've got to put that IV needle back in."

He reached for Gavin's hand, and Gavin tried to block Brigman's wrist with his forearm. But the doctor altered his movement, trying to swing around Gavin's arm. Instead, however, Brigman's wrist slapped into Gavin's palm. Without thinking, Gavin clamped his fingers around Brigman. Instantly, something passed between them, something electric and hideously alive. Gavin felt a black burst of energy rip through his body and his head suddenly felt full, as if it were packed with hot, wet towels. His eyes itched, his nose tickled, and he felt an overwhelming urge to sneeze. Then the feeling dissipated like dust in a breeze, leaving only a lingering residue of darkness that made his stomach rumble slightly with nausea. Then that too was gone.

He opened his fingers and dropped Brigman's hand. "What was that?" he asked in a soft voice.

Brigman's eyes were wide and he opened his mouth to speak, but couldn't. He just shook his head.

"I . . . I don't know," he finally said, then stopped.

"My voice, it's not scratchy," he continued, bringing his hands to his face. "My head doesn't hurt anymore."

He took a deep breath through his nose.

"My nose is clear," he said. "It feels like the infection is gone." He stared down at Gavin. "What did you do?"

Gavin shrugged.

"What did you feel?"

"It was terrible. Like something moved out of you and through me."

"Through you?"

"Yeah, it's gone now. But it made me feel sick for a second."

Brigman didn't speak. He stared at Gavin for a moment, then spun on his heel and left the room, forgetting the IV needle that still needed to be replaced in Gavin's hand. "I'll be back later," he said. "I've got to check something."

"Waitasecond!" Gavin shouted, then the crack of pain in his head instantly made him wish he hadn't.

"What's going on? What's wrong with me?" he said more quietly.

But Brigman was already through the door. Dammit, Gavin thought, I want to know what the hell is happening.

The Laying of Hands

He reached for the nurses' buzzer and pressed the button. A woman's voice came back within a few seconds.

"May I help you?" she said.

"I want Dr. Brigman to come back here now," Gavin said.

"I'm sorry, but Dr. Brigman just got on the elevator."

"Well, get in touch with him and tell him I want to see him."

"I'll try, but I don't know where he's going," the woman said and clicked off.

"Yeah, right," Gavin said. He lay there for several minutes, but Brigman did not return. As he waited, anxiety wormed through him.

Oh Jesus, what was he going to do? More tests meant more people—nurses, doctors, technicians—coming into his room, touching him. All those hands, all over him. He shuddered and goose bumps crawled along his skin. No, he couldn't stand that. He couldn't just lay here. No way. He was leaving.

He raised his head off the pillow. The pain was enormous, but he quickly realized that if he moved very slowly, an inch or two at a time, the agony was bearable. It took him about five minutes to sit up and swing his legs over the side of the bed. It took another minute for the flashes in front of his eyes to cease and the nausea to subside. When they did, he stood up and shuffled to the closet. Nothing was inside. Gavin stood shocked momentarily, then realized the clothes he'd been wearing must be covered with blood. They'd probably been thrown away. Well, clothes or no clothes, he was hauling his ass out of there.

Creeping to the door and leaning against the jamb, he pulled it open and stuck his head out. There was no one in the hall, which stretched for about twenty yards in both directions. At each end, the hall stopped in a T intersection. To the left, Gavin could hear voices around the corner. He figured it must be the nurses' station. He didn't want to go by them. Maybe there were stairs or something in the other direction. He'd try that way.

Using one hand to grasp the rail that ran along both sides of the hall and the other to hold the back of his hospital gown closed, he staggered forward. Throbbing pulses tat-

71

tooed his head with each step. He wondered how much damage he might be doing to himself with this little jaunt, but decided he didn't care.

Exhaustion was creeping into his muscles as he reached the T intersection. This might have been a mistake, he thought, and knew he'd have to quickly find a place to sit down. He stumbled around the corner.

The wheelchair was just out of sight on the other side and Gavin couldn't stop. His shins banged into the metal foot rests and he pitched forward, his hands instinctively going out to break his fall. They landed on the bare forearms of the old man sitting in the wheelchair. For an instant Gavin's eyes locked into the man's. Blank eyes, flat and drained, with only the barest spark of life. They gazed into Gavin's without expression or even comprehension. They were the eyes of an infant, the eyes of Alzheimer's.

Gavin suddenly realized with abhorrence that he was touching someone. Before he could straighten, a blaze scorched into his hands, engulfing his mind. It was the same horrid feeling he experienced when touching Dr. Brigman, yet hundreds, thousands, of times worse. Touching Brigman was a firecracker compared to this nuclear volcano. It was all-encompassing, overwhelming, and evil. Yet it was mindless evil, a deadly, bleak force that attacked without conscience or knowledge. It didn't care; it didn't think; it simply was.

It grabbed Gavin by the brain and sucked his soul away. He flailed about, desperately trying to prevent the cosmic robbery, but the effort was useless. His mind vanished. He knew nothing, not even himself. He was terrified, but he couldn't tell anyone. He didn't know how.

Then it disappeared and everything returned. He was Gavin again. He righted himself and slumped into the nearby wall, looking again at the old man. Something had changed. A small flicker burned in the man's eyes. Understanding and intelligence and life began to fill them. They widened as the man lifted his hands to gaze at them. Happiness flooded his expression and a smile appeared on his mouth. He looked at Gavin and tears suddenly spilled out of his eyes.

"Thank you," he whispered. "Thank you. You can't

imagine how horrible it has been. I've been so alone in there."

He reached out to take Gavin's hands, but Gavin backed out of reach. "No, no, don't touch me," he said. "Don't do that to me again."

The man gazed at Gavin's beard and bandaged head. "Are you Jesus?" the man asked.

Gavin slowly shook his head.

"Then who are you?" the man asked.

"No one. Nobody. Nothing," Gavin said, walking backward. He turned and fled as quickly as he could back down the hall. At the other end was a door. As he got closer, Gavin could see the small sign on the door that said STAIRS. He pushed the door open and rushed into the stairwell.

He stumbled down one flight before his legs gave way beneath him and he collapsed onto the concrete landing. Only by holding tightly to the rail did he keep from falling flat. Panting, he leaned against the wall, tears of anger, exhaustion, and fear welling in his eyes. His mind whirled like a carousel. Panic raged inside of him and he felt like he was close to losing control.

Oh no. Oh no. Oh no. This couldn't be true. This couldn't be happening. How could this be?

Instantly he knew the answer. It must be the bullet. He couldn't do this before he was shot.

But it was so horrible. Not just the touching, which was repulsive in the extreme. No, it was the sickness, the disease, the blackness that took control of his body, of his mind. It was living, yet not alive. It was powerful, yet it operated without thought. He could never look at another sick person again and not understand what was inside them. He didn't want to know about such things. No one should know about such things.

Yet you have the power to help.

The voice inside his head shocked him. Not because of what it said, but because it was his own voice.

No! I don't want it. What good is this power in the hands of someone like me? I can't stand to use it, can't even stand the thought. Why me? What kind of sick bastard is God to pull a stunt like this?

Yet for all the awfulness, there was something wonderful

in watching life return to the old man. It was remarkable, a glowing, glorious thing to see. Reawakening. Rebirth.

No! It wasn't enough . . . was it?

Gavin sat on the floor for about fifteen minutes. A couple of times doors opened above and below him, but whoever entered the stairwell either went up or down, away from him.

He could try to go on with life and ignore the power, act like it didn't exist. No one said he had to use it. His fear of being touched forced him to be self-centered anyway, to look out for number one. This would just be taking that attitude one step further.

And who said this was a gift from God? Maybe it was just one of those freaks of fate. There probably was a rational explanation. He'd always heard that man only used ten percent of his brain. Who knew what the other ninety percent was capable of doing?

The gratefulness in the old man's eyes filled Gavin's mind. Their warmth washed over him. He raised his hands. They didn't look any different, feel any different. What was the Chinese proverb he'd once read? "Blessings never come in pairs; misfortunes never come alone." He was staring at a pair of misfortunes.

Oh Jesus. He had to get out of here. He felt the concrete walls staring down at him, slowly working their way toward him. The air was being sucked out of the stairwell. He couldn't breathe, couldn't think straight. He wanted to go home.

Getting up, pain once again assaulting his head, he gently descended the stairs. Three floors down, the stairs stopped at a solid metal door. Pressing on the bar, Gavin swung the door outward. A long, dark hall ran in front of him. The walls were cinder block, the floor poured concrete, and a series of pipes ran along the ceiling. Hooded lightbulbs threw spots of light on the walls every thirty or so feet. He was in the basement. Damn! He'd gone down one flight too many. For a moment he thought about turning around and going back up one floor, then decided it was probably safer to leave this way. Upstairs, he might run into nurses or guards or someone who would try to stop him. He trudged forward.

The Laying of Hands

At various points, halls led off to the right and left, but he kept moving straight ahead. About fifty yards on he could make out a door. He only hoped it wasn't locked. It wasn't.

The night air was warm on Gavin's face as he opened the door. A short set of steps led upward and he could see the dark sky and bright stars in the rectangular opening formed by the top of the stairway's walls. On the last step he stopped and looked around. Around him was in a small garden. Flowers, shrubs, and a few trees dotted the area. To one side, a wooden bench sat under a brightly blooming dogwood. The scent was heavenly.

A wrought-iron fence ran around the garden, the bars too close to squeeze through, but wide enough for Gavin to see the street beyond, traffic moving briskly along it. He shuffled to the fence and clasped it with his fingers, pressing his face into it, the metal cool against his cheeks. Here was something he could touch without fear.

"I don't think you can get out like that," a small voice said to his right.

He turned to find a little girl sitting in a wheelchair. She smiled at him and Gavin felt a tug of pain in his chest.

IV poles sat on either side of her, their tubes running into both of her bone-thin arms. She looked about nine, but it was hard to be sure. A stocking cap was on her head, but he didn't see any hair sticking out from under it. Her face was pale and drawn, with deep blue shadows under the eyes, which were blue and sharp.

Yet there was no doubt that she was dying. That was easy to see. As he watched, her face contorted with a brief flash of pain, then it returned to normal.

"You sick or somethin'?" she asked.

"No, I'm all right," he answered.

"Then why ya got that big bandage on your head?"

"I got shot."

"Really?" she said, her eyes full of excitement and wonder. "By who?"

"Someone trying to rob me."

"Oh, cool!" she blurted, then looked a bit ashamed. "Oh, sorry. I didn't mean it was cool that you got shot. But I never met anyone who got shot by a robber. It musta been real scary. Did it hurt?"

"I really don't remember much about it. It happened pretty fast. But I don't remember it hurting much."

"You're the first really neat person I met in a while. Usually all I get ta meet around here is other kids like me."

"Like you?"

"I got cancer."

"I'm sorry."

"That's okay," she said, then stuck her hand out. "My name's Cassandra. What's yours?"

"Gavin."

"Nice to meecha, Gavin."

Gavin stared at Cassandra's hand for what seemed like an eternity. Her tiny hand loomed in front of him like a mountain. The ultimate challenge. Or the ultimate shame.

He could help her if he wanted. He could take away her pain, her illness, give her back her life. She was so young; she had so much life before her. Was it fair that she was dying? Was it right? He couldn't see how. But he could make it right, make it fair. All he had to do was shake her hand. All he had to do was touch her. Right. That's all.

He stuck his hand out, but something stopped it only inches from hers. Gavin tried to will his hand forward, but it wouldn't move. His fear, the subconscious monster that controlled almost every aspect of his life, was holding it in an iron grip.

Let go! Gavin shouted inwardly. *Let it go, you fucker!*

"It's okay. Ya can't catch cancer from me," Cassandra said.

His hand remained still, balanced precariously between terror and release, between leaving things the way they'd been for years or perhaps changing things forever. By God! He was tired of letting fear be in charge. Just this once, if only this once, he was going to be in control. *I want to do this!*

With a Herculean effort, Gavin shoved his hand into Cassandra's. He grasped it firmly with his fingers.

He heard the girl gasp as the agony wave crashed over him, a tsunami of universal pain that knocked him to his knees. It flooded his body, poisoning every cell, turning them black with disease. It sunk into his bones, a devouring beast that drank life slowly and painfully. It was the most wicked creature in the universe. He felt death approaching on heavy, beating wings. It was very close.

Just as quickly, it disappeared, although Gavin knew he would never forget the feeling, it would cling to his nerves in a horrid embrace until he died. He released Cassandra's hand but remained on his knees.

"Gavin? Gavin? Y'okay?"

He opened his eyes and looked up. Cassandra was staring at him with a look of fear and concern.

"Yeah," he whispered. "Yeah. I'm okay."

He saw her begin to speak, then stop, only to begin again.

"Gavin, what didja do to me?"

"I don't know."

"The pain is gone."

"Good."

"Gavin, are you God?"

He stared directly into her eyes. "No. Just a man. Just someone trying to figure out the right thing to do."

"Am I cured?" she asked.

"I think so," he said, placing his hands on his knees and rising painfully. "But let's let the doctors test you just to make sure. You want me to wheel you back to your room?"

She nodded.

"Where's the door?" he asked.

She pointed to a glass door in a wall at the back of the garden. He pushed her back to her room, which was on the seventh floor. Sitting in a chair, he watched as she got out of her wheelchair and climbed into bed. She smiled broadly after pulling the covers up to her chest.

"That didn't hurt at all," she said. "I feel fine."

"I'm glad," Gavin said. He turned to leave.

"Gavin? Will I see ya again?"

"I'm not sure, Cassandra."

"Then . . . can I kiss ya g'bye?"

He stopped with his hand on the door. In his mind, he pictured her lips on his cheek. The image both terrified and repulsed him.

"Thank you, but that's not necessary," he said, and left.

This time he didn't even try to be sneaky. He was too damned tired. He simply took the elevator to the first floor and searched for the nearest door to the outside. It was late and he passed no one. Within a couple of minutes he found an exit door that opened onto the loading dock area. He walked out.

A block away he found a taxi. The driver almost refused to let him in since he was dressed only in a hospital gown. "Man, I could lose my license for somethin' like this," he said.

"I'll give you two hundred dollars," Gavin said.

"Where you hidin' it?" the driver asked. "Stuffed up your butt?"

"No, back at my place. You can come inside with me. Don't leave until I give it to you."

Eventually, after several minutes of talking and an agreement for three hundred dollars, the taxi driver pulled away with Gavin in the back.

He leaned his head back, staring at the stars through the back window. He felt miserable. He'd cured a little girl of cancer, taken the disease into his own body, yet he didn't have the guts to let her give him a peck on the cheek in gratitude. Now he had two forms of touch to fear, the outside and the inside. Both had their elements of horror. Not only would he have to steel himself to put flesh on flesh, he also had to prepare himself for the onslaught of their disease. He couldn't decide which was worse.

He held up his hands and stared at them. How powerful. How pathetic.

He knew what he had to do.

The taxi driver stopped outside Gavin's shop, then as agreed, followed him inside. While the driver waited just inside the door, but in full view of the entire shop, Gavin went to the safe in corner and took out the money.

"Thanks for the bizncss," the man said.

For a while Gavin wandered about, touching the raw wood and the finished pieces of furniture, running his fingers over the drills, the saws, the chisels and hammers. They had been his companions for years. He would miss them.

The last thing he approached was the table saw. He'd changed the blade yesterday. No, strike that. That'd be last week now. Its teeth were razor sharp. He looked at the blade then at his wrists. If he did it quickly, he might barely feel it.

The Laying of Hands

He reached down and flipped the on switch. The blade spun with a high-pitched whine. Gavin leaned down, placing his wrists side by side on the top and moving them within six inches of the whirring metal.

Unbidden, he saw the clear-eyed, happy smile of Cassandra. The smile was for him, because of him. It made him feel good. Cassandra's smile faded, replaced by the old man's bright eyes. Life radiated from them.

Two sick people and he had helped both of them, cured them, brought them happiness. He smiled too. He had made a difference. He'd truly touched these people, not just physically, but spiritually. There were preachers and priests who couldn't say the same thing. And now that he was away from the initial horror of the contact, was it really that terrible?

Yes, it was. There was no denying it.

But the effect. The joy, the wonder. He felt important; he felt special.

He felt worthwhile.

He sighed. Why couldn't life be simple? Why wasn't black always black and white always white? Why did there have to be so much gray? There was always bad to contrast with good. The question was: Is the good good enough to counteract the bad?

He didn't know. He just didn't know. And he was afraid to find out. But what he was contemplating would not only throw away the strange gift he'd been given, it would toss away everything he'd worked for his entire adult life.

What was he going to do?

Gavin looked down. Six inches away, the saw blade continued to spin.

THREE, FOUR,
SHUT THE DOOR

Kathryn Ptacek

ONE. FIVE. FIFTEEN. ONE. FIVE. FIFTEEN.

Dottie Brewster counted to each number. One. Then to five, and then to fifteen. Then up to fifteen, then to five, then one.

And repeat.

At the back door, she rested her gloved hand on the shiny brass knob, polished from many such sessions. She frowned. Was she counting to five or fifteen now? She'd lost track.

It didn't matter, she told herself.

Really.

It. Didn't.

But it did.

Her hand fluttered as she gnawed at her lower lip. One, two, three . . . all the way up to fifteen. Then she started over. One. One, two, three, four, five. And then the next sequence of numbers to fifteen.

She had to get it right.

Then she could open the door and go through it. Close it behind her. Go outside.

Had to get it right because nothing in her life went the way it was supposed to—the *right* way—when she didn't get the sequence correct.

After all, she hadn't been counting the day her mother and sister's car had been broadsided by a semi and they'd died in the flaming wreckage.

She hadn't been counting the day that Farron left her.

She hadn't been counting the day she got fired from the job she'd held ever since college graduation, the job she'd been groomed for during those four years of school and the two years of postgraduate work.

None of this would have happened, she told herself, if she'd been counting.

One . . . two . . . three . . .

Suddenly the lines from the old nursery rhyme drifted through her mind.

One, two, buckle my shoe.
Three, four, shut the door.

Damn.

She'd lost count again.

She leaned forward slightly, her forehead against the chilly glass of the door's pane, and closed her eyes. Tears trembled beneath her eyelids, gumming her thick lashes.

She hated this. Truly she did. With all her heart she wished she could get over it. But it wasn't like some virus where you got sick and went to bed with fever and chills, and after the illness had run its course, you got up and got on with your life.

Her problem didn't work that way.

One, two, three . . .

She knew she had a problem, had known that for some time, and she knew there were people who could help her, or at least try to help. She wasn't so sure they really could be of use. Psychiatrists, Farron had suggested, go see a psychiatrist or a psychologist.

Although she recognized the truth of his words, she'd responded angrily, telling him that she wasn't crazy.

"I never suggested that, honey," he said plaintively.

One, two, three, but she hadn't heard his apology, hadn't seen the look of anguish on his face, because she had been counting. Seven, eight, nine. Farron had tried to convince her that it was for her own good, but she wouldn't hear of it, couldn't hear his words. Thirteen, fourteen, fifteen.

A feeling of relief: good.

Time to start over.

Farron hadn't understood, she told herself, as much as he claimed he did. It wasn't the counting that was driving her bananas, not really, although that was annoying. It was the fear that she *wouldn't get the counting, the sequences, right.*

Don't get it right, and you screw up your life.

She had ample evidence for that.

Farron, her job, her mother and sister's deaths. There was her father's cancer too. She knew that was related. Somehow. It was her fault. Somehow her father had died because she hadn't gotten it right.

There were other episodes, other times from her early childhood, her teenage years, when she hadn't gotten it right and things didn't turn out the way they were supposed to. Her mother's closet alcoholism. Her best friend from childhood dying from complications of diabetes. Her boyfriend ditching her right before the senior prom. Her sister's botched abortion.

All these incidents were tied together with a thread that ran from her; she was the loom, and because she was coming unraveled—because she *wasn't getting it right*—the fabric had developed holes. And *it was her fault.*

Three, four, five, sang the litany in her exhausted mind.

Out of the corner of her eye she saw movement. She watched as a huge fly crawled across a food-flecked dish in the kitchen sink. Plates and glasses and saucepans, all dirty, piled high in the stained enamel sink. Something buzzed—a handful of flies at the window over the sink.

She wrinkled her nose, noticing for the first time the odor of sour milk, the sickening sweetness of overripe fruit. The stink of something else underlay all the others, and she wondered what it was. She couldn't identify it, not immediately.

She had to do something first.

One, two . . .

She should wait a bit before she went out. Yes, that was right. She could wash the dishes with really hot soapy water and dry them with some of her linen hand towels bordered with the fancy embroidery she used to have time for, and put them away in the cabinets, and then she would make herself a nice lunch.

Or was it dinnertime?

A sandwich . . . she could make that for either meal, and so it didn't matter *which* meal it actually was, because the sandwich would be for lunch or dinner.

No, she had to get it right. She looked out the window, saw it was still light, but couldn't see the sun's position. It could be afternoon. It had to be, since she was wearing gloves, which meant that it was cooler outside, which meant that it had to be autumn or winter or spring, and night came so much earlier then. Afternoon.

Or late morning.

One, two . . .

Buckle my shoe.

She almost giggled aloud.

In the last few months of her job she had grown increasing late. She had recognized that—she certainly didn't need anyone, much less Farron and her boss telling her—and so had started out of the house earlier and earlier each day. In the beginning she'd left on time, then that had graduated to twenty minutes earlier, then an hour earlier. Finally she was getting up at four-ten, so she could get out of the door and get to the university by nine.

It didn't take her long to get ready in the mornings—she showered, dressed, threw on her makeup, ate a quick breakfast. What took so long was the ritual of going through the door, because she had to do it right—*or else*—and every time she blew it, and she had to start over, and the ritual grew longer and longer.

Three, four, shut the door.

Five, six, pick up sticks.

Seven, eight, nine . . .

Thirteen, fourteen—

Why hadn't she chosen longer numbers? Something like a hundred would have been better. It would take more time to reach; but she hadn't selected the numbers. They had chosen her. Her mother had always told her to count to ten before responding when she was angry. She remembered as a child counting slowly to ten, and then over again because she liked the feel of control it gave her. She realized she could count, and even as she was doing that, she felt her anger or frustration melting away.

She didn't remember having a temper, but her mother always insisted she did, and her mother must be right.

She counted as high as she could go the first time her father put her in the closet and left her alone with the darkness. She had counted because she had nothing else to do. Counted. And eventually he had come back and let her out. He had said then that she was a good girl, not the screw-up she normally was.

She came to realize during the long hours when she was alone that it really was all her fault, and that she had better learn to get things right.

And the numbers had just popped into her head, and without warning she started counting—to one, to five, to fifteen, then to fifteen, to five, to one. She tried to draw out the ritual sometimes, tried to slow the counting, but it didn't always work, and so she would count over and over and over, and the quickness of it irritated her.

It had become her mantra. When she was angry, she summoned it; when she was tired or stressed out, she did the numbers. Knowing that somehow things would be right again.

Only the reassurance she obtained from it had decreased, and so she had increased the number of times she counted. Doubled the times. Then tripled.

Quadrupled.

Until the numbers bled together in her mind, jumbling—one, six, eleven, five, ten—and she had to start over from the beginning. Sometimes it seemed like every minute, every second, of her life was devoted to the numbers . . . to getting it right.

Eventually, even her boss had noticed, and he'd taken her into his office one morning and asked gently if there was a problem.

"What do you mean?" she asked, her voice trembling. She had been so upset that she forgot to count.

"You've been late six months in a row now, Dottie," Hal said. "I've looked the other way because you've been here so long and you've always been on time, but you're getting worse. You've got to do better. You've had a perfect record —and now this. And you're making mistakes in your work—you've never done that before. It's like your mind is on something else. Is something going on at home?" He had leaned across the desk, and for a moment she thought he was going to place his hand on her shoulder.

"No, there's nothing wrong," she lied.

"It's got to get better," Hal said.

She nodded.

Only it hadn't, and finally he had said regretfully that he must fire her, and they'd given her a generous severance check because of the years she'd been there, and she had gone home and sat in her living room and looked out the window at the dying flowers and counted.

To one, to five, to fifteen.

Too late now, she told herself, because she hadn't gotten it right.

She should have been counting more, should have slowed it down, made it last.

Only she hadn't.

The fear wrapped itself more tightly around her heart and squeezed.

The tears flowed freely now, and she brushed at her cheek with her other gloved hand, and left a streak there. She stared down at the dirt on her glove and wondered vaguely how it had gotten there. They had been clean when she put them on.

To one, to five, to fifteen.

One, five, fifteen.

She listened to the house, and heard nothing. Didn't hear the sound of the furnace, didn't hear the grandfather clock in the front hall, and wondered why. The clock must have run down, and she wondered when she had wound it last. Hadn't it been yesterday? No. Friday. No . . . before that. But when, she didn't remember.

Five, six . . . *seven, eight, open the gate.*

She told herself she would get through the door now. She had things to do. She had to get outside and get to—

Get to where? She frowned, wondering if she'd been

heading to the store or someplace else. Maybe a job interview? Yes, that was it. After she'd been fired, she'd pored through the classified section of the newspaper for jobs that interested her. A number of positions called for workers who stayed at home, which appealed to her. So she had called for an appointment, and she was headed for it.

Only . . . she frowned . . . only that appointment had been yesterday.

Or the day before.

She had blown it again.

One, five, fifteen.

She must have stopped the sequence somewhere, someplace, and she'd royally screwed up again.

She hadn't been counting last week when she'd been singing along with the old Bee Gees song on the car radio, and she hadn't seen the van in front of her stop abruptly, and so she had thumped into the back end of it. Her car had been more damaged than the other driver's, and she'd had to have it towed away, and she wasn't sure how she would get it back, because the bill was so huge and she was running out of money. Farron tried to help her with money from time to time, until she got on her feet and got another job. But she hadn't gotten another job. She wouldn't be getting another job if she couldn't get out the door.

Three, four, five.

One, two, three, four . . . thirteen, fourteen, fifteen.

She was so tired. So weary of the repetition. Over and over those numbers floated in her head, drifted through every waking thought. She was so tired of them. She should try them in foreign languages, she thought with a suddenly giggle.

Unos, dos . . . cinco.

It wasn't the same.

. . . three, four, five . . .

She yawned. She could lay down on the couch and take a nap for a while, and then when she woke up, she would be rested, and she would get up and wash dishes and she would go out the door.

Three, Four, Shut the Door

For whatever reason, she had to go out the door.

But first she had to count. And she had to get it right. Because if she didn't . . . she shuddered, thinking what might happen.

One. One, two, three . . .

She didn't count in her sleep. At least she didn't think she did. Usually she woke and, for the first few minutes of her day, didn't think about counting.

Maybe that was a mistake.

It had been morning, after all, when Farron told her he was leaving her. She had cried and screamed at him, and then fallen into a silence and simply stared at him. Why, she wanted to say, why? But every time she opened her mouth, all she could do was cry.

She had counted much too late then. She had counted to one, to five, to fifteen as he picked up the suitcase he had packed before she woke, had counted as he went down the stairs and she trailed after him, had counted as he walked out the door and she had stared out the front window as he got into the car and drove away, counted as the only man she'd ever loved left her.

Counted.

Too late.

She hadn't gotten it right.

Her father was right; she was such a screw-up.

The fear was in her veins, in her lungs, in her tissue; it permeated every bit of her body.

She wept then, loudly, forlornly, and she wanted it all undone. She wanted it to be all *right* again, although she never knew it would be.

Suddenly she felt a warmth in her groin, and then down her leg, and she looked down and saw the piss running there, making the pool at her feet even larger, and she recognized the foulness she'd been vaguely aware of, and realized then that she hadn't been there for a few minutes, she hadn't been there at the door even for hours.

She had been there all day.

Maybe all night. Maybe longer.

One, two.

Three, four, shut the door.

But how could you shut the door, if you couldn't even open it?

Seven, eight . . .

How long before you begin to decay? she wondered vaguely, and knew now why there were so many flies.

Nine, ten, do it again.

She *would* get it right. It was just a matter of time.

THE WISH IN THE FEAR

George Zebrowski

FRANK'S LEFT UPPER FRONT TOOTH HAD BEEN CAPPED IN 1970, after he had cracked it by falling flat on his face during a racquetball game. Earlier that year he had seen a man with a broken front tooth on the bus, and had wondered what it would be like to have a broken tooth. It was as if his future were casting a shadow into the past.

At least once a year since then he had dreamed that his cap had come off, because it seemed to him that every year beyond the first ten seemed too many for such a thing to stick to his filed-down tooth. Losing his cap was the one nightmare that continued to convince him of its truth, and he was always grateful to wake up to its unreality.

But this was only one of many trivial fears he would develop. Another involved sharp objects and the hidden nature of accidents. Were they fixed, waiting to happen at the appointed time? he asked himself as he idly imagined putting out his right eye with a pencil. Whether he could muster the courage to do so deliberately interested him, but the more frightening possibility was that a series of ordinary, even logical steps might lead to it surreptitiously, remaining concealed until it was too late. He suspected that there was some train of events that might make it happen, some arcane dovetailing of circumstances that would make it come out that way, or even worse, convince him that it was the necessary thing to do.

As a boy he had gone up to the cliffs that faced the apartment houses in the South Bronx just below the Grand Concourse, and had stood there on the edge of the loose slate piles with his back to the sheer drop, glancing over his shoulder at the empty windows to see if anyone was watching. He did not slip and did not want to, but it was hypnotic to imagine himself lying in one of the backyards below, his broken body motionless in a pool of bright blood on the paving stones. He could still see himself there, balancing on the balls of his feet.

Over the years he became adept at imagining that what he saw happening to other people might also happen to him. He was both attracted to and repelled by most of these reveries, but was unable to shake the foreboding that sooner or later some, if not all, would become realities for him. When he saw any kind of accident overtake someone, it was always a possible harbinger of his own fate.

But he lived a life remarkably free of mishaps. Instead he became a collector of other people's fears and phobias; and however terrifying they might be while he was in their thrall, nothing ever happened to him. He came to accept this as the way things were with him, and looked forward to the next one as people do to a concert, play, movie, or television show.

His most intense encounters with people stayed with him, becoming a collection of recurring dreams. Each new collision became a candidate for his growing labyrinth of shared fears and phobias. He sometimes suspected that the answer to what made one stay and another flee from his dreams was the secret of his life, the key that would open the door to himself, but he was content to hold it dear and unknown, hidden deep within himself.

He tasted the summer rain in his dream as the wind blew drops into the gazebo behind the pool. Everyone at the mountain resort had fled into their cabins and into the main building, but he had stayed out to watch the rain.

The Wish in the Fear

He heard the expected footfalls on the wooden steps behind him and turned to see Vera, still dressed in her white blouse, white shorts and sneakers, shaking water out of her shoulder-length blond hair as she looked shyly at him. He was nineteen and in college; she was just going on seventeen. She was here with her parents and brother, and they were all very protective of her developing sexual vulnerability, so he had kept his distance, content to watch from afar her stocky, athletic form filling out her well-pressed shorts and blouse.

"Hello," he said with a nervous breath.

"Hi," she answered, smiling angelically, and he felt once again that a hidden script was being revealed for him to speak, one line at a time, so he wouldn't know what came next, even though he had played this scene with her many times before. The words, expressions, and some of the physical movements varied, but the differences were unimportant.

She leaned back against the railing and took a deep breath. He came over, leaned back next to her and said, "Some rain. It might get cloudy for the next two weeks. That sometimes happens up here."

"Oh, no. I hope that doesn't happen."

He turned and gazed at her. She looked back as if searching his face for something, and he knew that she was afraid of being alone with him.

"I've seen you around," he said, glancing down at her pressed shorts, which stood away from her smooth, still slightly heavy but attractive thighs.

"Don't look at me like that," she said. "It makes me nervous."

"But I like the way you look," he answered gently, and saw her swallow, and knew that she felt pride and guilt about her emerging good looks. As she matured and gained her full growth, she would become a blond goddess and know power over boys and men; but for now she was still unsure, unable to consciously attract or humiliate, also following an ancient script that startled and intrigued her. "I think you're beautiful, but I couldn't tell you around your family."

She grimaced and smiled, then looked across the resort grounds as if her parents might see her from their cabin, but relaxed, realizing that they did not have a clear view of the pool. He began to gaze at her adoringly, but looked away as she became aware of the desire that was growing in him.

He moved closer to her and took her hand. She tensed, then blushed.

"You're very beautiful," he said.

"You're just saying that," she whispered.

"No—it's true," he said, leaning closer. She drew a deep breath and slid away from him on the rail, trying to smile knowingly, but it came across as sheepish, shy, and green.

He looked at her caringly, and something inside her seemed to break as he moved nearer and was about to kiss her. She took a deep breath and looked away from him.

"No," she said with a sob, "I can't."

"Why not?"

"Before," she mumbled, looking as if she might cry, and he felt pity and concern for her, and the impulse to protect her, to hold her, flattered that she was showing these feelings to him. He looked into her eyes and his gaze locked with hers, trapping him in a strange prelude to a dance that she would teach him.

"I went out last year," she started to say awkwardly, looking at him as if she had to expel feelings that were stuck within her. "He came to dinner at my house. My parents liked him, my little brother liked him, my friends. We went out for a month, and then he broke it off and it was . . . horrible." She choked on the last word and tears ran down her face. "And I couldn't tell anyone that he'd touched me and kissed me, and that I wanted him. I was so afraid. I'd thought he wanted to marry me, to be with me forever, but it was all a lie. I don't want that again."

She was silent, and he realized that it had been all or nothing with her, with no in between; and that this demanding familial finality had driven her first boyfriend away.

"It's okay," he said, putting his arm around her as she stopped crying, accepting the fact that there was nothing very interesting about her; not her white shorts and tanned legs and arms; not her blond hair or blue eyes. The silkiness of her fled from his mind before her raw need. She was hungry to swallow him. There was nothing personal about what might have been between them, only a role that she

The Wish in the Fear

expected him to assume; a hundred other boys would do just as well.

As he looked into her disappointed eyes, he saw her family lurking behind them, restricting her freedom, compelling her to think and feel as they did. She was imprisoned within herself. The realization horrified him. He was sorry for her pain, pitying her bonds, but glad that he had glimpsed them early enough to escape.

Are you going to kiss me and hold me? her eyes asked. And how long will it last? Then she saw that he was not prepared to pay the toll and moved away as if she had been betrayed again. He watched her flee from the gazebo and run across the grass in the rain, taking with her every fantasy he had nursed about her, leaving him with a conflicting sense of relief at having escaped arousing her feelings.

The pitiable terror that she had shown him stayed with him permanently, growing more painful whenever he recalled it. Not a month went by in the years since when he did not think about her physical lushness, the smell of her soap, the sexual grasp that he might have awakened in her in a vain effort to dispel the youthful horror that she had deposited in him.

He lay half awake, trying again to forget the dream of Vera, knowing that he would never lose it, then recalled Annette, the dark-haired girl in her twenties who had shared a cabin with two men that same summer in the mountains. He had watched her come out after lunch to sit by the pool, and her bikini-clad body had seemed exhausted from lovemaking. She had noticed him, he was sure, and he had felt that she was avoiding his eyes because she knew that everyone knew, but she didn't seem to care. She was imprisoned by her sexuality, and was giving herself to two young men in a vain attempt to burn it out, to quiet her soul. His very gaze seemed to arouse her, he had felt, and she seemed to cringe under his scrutiny as she tried to ignore him.

So you know, her glancing, dark eyes said. *So what. It's not your business.* And yet part of her seemed to say, *I'm a prisoner, I'm trapped, and I don't know what to do.* Visions of what they were doing in that cabin preyed on his imagination all that summer. The two men, both younger than her, always slept late. . . .

He sat up out of his dream and looked around his bedroom, wondering if it would be warm enough to go down and sit by the pool. After all, it was late May, and the temperature might get up to eighty, they had said.

He rose, went to the picture window and looked down five stories to the pool. The usual suspects seemed to be gathering at the patch of blue water, harmless types working for small businesses around town, dreaming of going to a big city for a job one day, but too insecure to ever do so. If they had any fears or phobias, they were buried deeply. He had nothing much to fear from going down among them.

He went to his CD player, put on some vintage disco, then went and did some exercises on his Soloflex. When he felt hungry, he went into the kitchen and stuck a complete brunch, coffee included, into the microwave, then wandered over to make sure his team of VCRs was taping the movie and Olympic events that he had set them to catch.

He dressed for the pool, reminding himself that he still had twelve days of vacation time left before he went back to the insurance office. Maybe he'd go somewhere for the last six days.

At poolside, he was dozing with his cap over his face when he heard Marianne, his neighbor from the fourth floor, say to her friend, "You're lucky, your boyfriend's your pal. You can talk to him." There was a short pause. "Either you're lying or just bragging."

"I'm bragging."

"I'd need an ass-lift to get a man like that. Don't deny it, I see how he looks at you."

"He's just fooling."

"He worships your ass," Marianne answered. After a moment of silence, she asked, "You know Alice who lives up front?"

"I've seen her."

"Well, she's terrified of being without a man. She almost gets hysterical about it. I don't understand it."

"Well," her friend said, "that's because you already have a

kid, and you've rid yourself of a bad guy. You see things from the other side. But doesn't she have a boyfriend?"

"Sort of," Marianne said. "He's a plump guy she doesn't seem to like much, but she lets him come over. He lives an hour away, somewhere south of here. He rarely stays over. I hear them arguing about it."

Suddenly the conversation was drowned out by splashing.

"Stop that, Mel," Marianne called to her boyfriend as he came out of the pool.

He laughed and said, "I heard you talking about chubby! What's up?"

"Chubby?" Marianne's girlfriend asked.

"Alice—he doesn't like her much." Marianne lowered her voice. "We were together at a bar, before I knew Mel, and Alice came on to him."

"Really?"

"Yup."

"Well," Mel said, "maybe she'd be good for a blow job."

"What!" Marianne shouted. "Don't talk like that."

"It's okay," Marianne's friend said. "Don't you ever listen when they're all together watching the game?"

"Who's gonna hear?" Mel asked. "Hey, Frank, are you asleep?" he called.

Frank decided to act asleep.

"Well, I'm going inside," Marianne said. "Coming, Estelle?"

"Sure thing," her girlfriend said.

Frank remembered Alice now. She wasn't all that bad-looking. Overweight, yes, but erotic in the way heavier women get when they're losing weight and looking hungry. He had seen her poolside in short white pants and a flimsy T-shirt, and she had looked attractive. He recalled smiling, and she had looked back gratefully. Rubens would have painted her with delight, even though she wasn't as full as his usual ones.

Frank dozed for a while. When he woke up and looked around, the deck around the pool was nearly deserted, except for Alice and her heavyset boyfriend coming out of the water. She was heavier than he remembered, and she looked tired today.

Frank sat up as they went by and his eyes met the boyfriend's. I'm here only to get laid, the man's eyes said apologetically, so don't think my taste is this bad.

Frank glanced at Alice. She shot him a look of defeat, and he wished that he had kept his hat over his face as her terror flooded into him—I'm going to be manless, without love or children. I'm going to die alone, an old maid. I've put out and gotten nothing for it, and I never will!

He lay back and covered his face, trying to regain his composure, but it was too late; she was inside him, infecting him with her fears.

He peered out from under his cap and saw her boyfriend smiling falsely at her. She smiled back more convincingly, but the turmoil inside her would not subside. At any moment, mantislike, she would reach out and tear off her boyfriend's head.

Frank felt a migraine coming on, and knew that this newest catch was going to be bad. He should have stayed in bed. He should not have underestimated his neighbors. Still peering out from under his cap, he could see that Alice was watching him, as if a way had opened between them and she could see into him.

It was nothing like that, of course. People imagined things about each other all the time, and the more clues they had, the more accurate their imaginings. People could feel each others' emotions because people were synchronous with each other, sympathetically tuned, because every human being was more alike than different, shading in and out of each other with no clear break anywhere. It was completely involuntary. Two people sucking each other's thumbs feel as if they are sucking their own thumbs. A man's next door neighbor sees a glum look on his friend's face, and from his years of conversation with him, suspects that he knows what's wrong. A man shows up at the local grocery when his wife is away, and the clerk imagines that the man's wife has left him.

The migraine was roaring in now. Frank got up and tried not to look at Alice. She was pitying herself, hungering and mourning at the same time, and he wished that he could stop her emotional bleeding. What he needed was to pick up something else to wipe out her fear and pain. He sat up and got to his feet.

"Hi, Frank!" Alice called, waving as her boyfriend lunged into the pool and made a massive splash.

Frank waved back and started for the gate. The migraine staggered him and he stopped, doubting that he would stay on his feet. It was his own fault for having come outside.

"Are you okay?" she called out.

"Fine," he said, then hurried through the gate and went into the building. The elevator door was open. He stepped inside and punched in his floor, already feeling better.

In his apartment, he looked out the window and saw Alice's boyfriend swimming across the pool. After one lap he struggled out and sat down in the chair next to her. She looked away. Frank watched them as they sat together, looking anything but together even from this height, settling for each other, afraid to be alone, and he knew that the boyfriend would not be with her long.

Frank turned from the window, sat down in his easy chair, and didn't know whether to laugh or cry, then looked around at his living room, noting that the carpet wouldn't need cleaning for some time yet. He examined his audiovisual system, with its two VCRs, wide-screen television, CD player carousel, turntable, and surround-sound speakers. The system kept him from having people over, because he didn't want to pick up their disdain for his stuff. The only thing he was sure of was that they'd admire his cherry desk. Who knew? They might like his whole place, but why take the chance? This worry had started when he had visited an old college buddy, Steve, and had picked up his fear of having his stuff dissed. The fear had been strong: don't dis my stuff, don't tell me, please, that it's second-rate, that there are better models. Frank had picked it up from Steve. He wished that he could simply pass it on, so that he could invite people again.

"You've always got *something*," Steve had said to him one day in their off-campus apartment. "We've got the same money, but you always have more stuff," he went on, pointing to Frank's then very modest stereo hookup.

"So? You get to listen to it."

"It pisses me off."

"Why should it? I only try to make the best of things, a little at a time, but it adds up."

"You're a pain in the ass. You never stop."

"Do the same, in your own way," Frank had advised him.

"And be like you?"

"In your own way, I said."

"You've always got to be in charge," Steve said, beginning to get aggressively strange.

"So what's your complaint?"

"You always have your own way with these little . . . additions of yours!"

"Look—things don't always go the way I'd like, but the fight is always joined, the victory real, however small. Your trouble is you don't fight, you don't struggle, and then you envy others. Cynical and skeptical, you poison your own life. And you'll never know what fortune might have brought you if you had been there to meet it. Any fool knows that when he goes to the track."

"You win at the track, Frank?"

"I've never been, but here's the difference between us. Fortune knows that I'm ready to be defeated *completely*, so there's not much it can do to me, except reward me enough to keep me playing, waiting for the moment of my ruin. But at that moment, I'll step aside and refuse to play."

"You'll see it coming?"

"I'll see it coming. I've seen it stalking me in countless small ways."

"You're a shark, Frank. That's all you'll ever be, but you hide it from yourself in a really nutty way."

"You really believe all this about me?"

"I'm not as sure of anything as you are. Maybe there's some kind of hope for you, but you'd have to fall flat on your face to find it."

"And that's why you'll never be anything," he had told Steve, "thinking like that. You're afraid of everything."

Today he could more easily see the bad stuff coming at him—especially when someone was ready to pass on a fear to him. They didn't know they were doing it, and they weren't really doing anything, of course. It was the small accumulation of information, the placing of three or more points on a piece of paper. Once there were points to connect, a line and a direction were established. With most people it was three scenes or more—situations or moments from their lives, enough for him to pick up the drift of their lives, maybe even sum up a life. They always had elaborate reasons for never becoming themselves. Dismay would flood through him, and shame for the other person, that they had fallen so low within themselves.

As for himself, he figured that insurance executive was about the best he could do; anything more demanding would be sabotaged by his ability to pick up other people's hurt. It had made him a good, sympathetic insurance salesman for a time, because he had a way of making people feel properly insecure about the provisions they had failed to make for their futures, before convincing them that his company would make things right for them—and keep it right for the rest of their lives. He had helped people to confront their fear of the future; but every sale had given him more than their signatures on the policy. With every "Trust me and sign on the dotted line" had come a new deposit from the damned.

Finally, after nearly twenty years, it was all he could do to control his flypaper innards behind the closed doors of a private office. He never went out into the field these days, and planned to retire by forty.

He got up from his chair and looked down at the pool again. Alice was now sitting alone, upright on the edge of the lawn chair, hands folded in her lap, and he guessed that she had just broken up with her man.

He lay down, grateful that the migraine had failed to blossom fully. Still fatigued by the poolside encounters, he tried to avoid fixing on Alice's terror of being manless. If he could somehow delay his reaction, the fear might die away.

He fell asleep and found himself standing on the second-floor porch of his first postcollege apartment, just as a group of homeless people came by and began to pick through his garbage. He went inside, but one young man came up the front stairs and opened his door.

"What do you want?" Frank called out.

"Ah, come on, Billy, let us in."

"I don't know you," he answered, going inside and locking the door behind him. He went to the phone and rang the police. When they were on their way, he opened the door and found the hall empty.

Rushing to the back porch, he opened the door a crack, peered out and saw that the man, the old woman, and two teenage boys were still picking through his garbage. The police arrived and began to move them along as gently as possible.

Frank opened the door wide, and the man who had come to his door looked up and shouted, "Thanks for the help, Billy!"

And Frank became Billy, betraying these homeless derelicts. The young man looked up at him reproachfully as the police told him to move along.

Later the cop came up and asked, "Did you know any of them?"

"No, officer," Frank said with a twinge of guilt, wondering if somehow he had known the man and forgotten, or couldn't recognize him now. "No, I don't know any of them. Who are they?" Suddenly he was afraid that the cop wouldn't believe him.

"We've been watching groups of them since this morning," the cop said. "They seem harmless enough. Good thing it's warm. The mayor doesn't want any of them to die while they're in town."

"Where will they go?" he asked, but the cop turned away without answering, and Frank woke up to Alice's fear of growing old alone, drying up and wrinkling, and decided that he would spend the last of his vacation as far away from home as possible, as soon as possible, maybe somewhere in the Caribbean.

He heard her speak his name softly as he lay on the beach in the Bahamas. Then she was whispering to him, saying that he could give her what she needed, that she wasn't unattractive, that she could care for a man deeply and for a lifetime, suggesting to him that she was startling in the nude, that she exercised and kept up her health, that she would

100

give him fine sons and daughters, that he should hurry to her now, before desolation ruined her for him.

He knew that he was saying these things to himself, but they were just as true as if she could reach into him and say them herself, as much as any human being could. He turned over, found his phone under the towel, and dialed his apartment building's switchboard.

"Henry, this is Frank. Connect me with Alice what's-her-name. You know who I mean?"

"Sure thing."

"Thanks."

The phone rang three times, then a fourth. He was about to hang up when she answered it.

"Hello, Alice?"

"Yes?"

"This is Frank. You know."

"Yes, Frank. What is it?"

"Well, I was wondering if I could come over and talk to you when I get back."

"Get back?"

"I'm in the Bahamas."

"And you're calling from there? What's this about?"

"Uh—I think it'd be better if I tell you when I get there."

She coughed nervously. "What's this about, Frank? You're going to make me wait and wonder—how long?"

"A day or two. It's nothing bad, believe me."

"Then tell me now."

He was silent, knowing that he should not talk to her over the phone, surprised by her alertness and suspicion. Her boyfriend had not left her in a good state.

"Frank?"

"See you soon!" he said, and pressed the button. He was out of breath, he noticed, and wondered why; usually, reaching out to someone calmed him. Then he realized that she had been confused by his call and that he had picked up some of her distress. But she had also been excited and intrigued by his interest, he concluded, and felt calmer.

She smiled at him when she opened the door. She was dressed in white shorts, a blouse, and leather sandals.

"Come in," she said, stepping back. She might have been Vera, years later, except that Vera had been pretty.

He came in and she motioned him to the sofa. He sat down. She took the chair that faced him.

Leaning forward with a drawn expression on her face, she asked, "What is it, Frank?"

He smiled. "You do know I like you, don't you?"

She seemed startled and sat back. "Do I?"

"I've been watching you. By the way, where's your boyfriend?"

"I'm not seeing him now. . . ."

"Good."

"Good? Why?"

"You didn't really like him."

She looked into his eyes, flooding him with her vulnerability and hurt.

"You're really interested in me?" she asked mockingly.

"Yes," he said, glancing at her thighs and feeling certain that he would enjoy her.

"Do you have eyes? I'm a well-groomed dog. Why should someone as good-looking as you want me except to play with? Is it a bet of some kind? Or are you a freak?" He could see that it was humiliating her to say the words, but she was determined to protect herself by exposing him before he could trap her. "Maybe you just don't have any taste," she said regretfully.

"No, no," he answered, appalled at how little she thought of herself. He could see her self-loathing turning outward toward him. And yet a part of her had to be hoping that it was true, that he liked her, that at last something good might happen to her, something happy and warm and forgiving.

He watched it all flash through her eyes like a vision of salvation; and then she rejected it, retreating behind her armor.

She stood up, and he felt her strength as she glared at him. "You're not going to use me. Go away. Get out of here."

"But why——" he started to say.

"Let me spell it out. You're too good-looking to want me, so I'm some sort of convenience—right? What are you curious about? You think I'll be so grateful, I'll do anything. Is that it?"

The Wish in the Fear

"No—" he started to say as he stood up.

"Get out of here!" she shrieked. "You filthy son of a bitch! You think that lying about calling me from the Bahamas would do the trick? What was that all about?"

She was herding him toward the door, her cheeks flushed with rage. He wanted to embrace her, quiet her, but she looked as if she would tear at his face.

He backed away, opened the door and slipped out. She shoved it shut after him, and he heard locks closing.

"You're wrong, Alice," he said loudly, hoping to calm himself.

The door opened a crack and she put her head out. "What are you going to do?" she said jeeringly. "Put a ring on my finger? Or just move in for a few weeks?"

"Couldn't we just get to know each other?" he asked meekly. The blood was pounding in his ears.

"No sex?"

"Sex would be nice," he said, not wishing to insult her, "but we could skip it."

"We? Who's this we? You're flapping out there, Frank."

"Why do you think I'm so terrible? I've never done anything to you!"

A fearful look came into her face, and he couldn't tell whether it was fear of him or panic. She was speechless, as if trying to reverse herself, to start over with him, because she knew that she could not afford to pass up the smallest chance. She had to be ready when fortune smiled; but it was too late.

He stood there and smiled at her, trying to look harmless.

"Is this the wise look you save for crazy females?" she said, then moved back and slammed the door. He heard her crying.

Putting his head to the door, he said, "I'm sorry, Alice. Couldn't we be friends?"

"I don't want your pity. Go away and find yourself some bimbo. It's what you really want."

"Alice—"

"I'll call the police!"

"I'm sorry I bothered you."

He felt her hunger reaching out to him, and trembled inside.

"I'm good enough to fuck, but not enough to love," she said suddenly.

"What? How can you say that about yourself?" he asked, impressed by the conviction in his voice, and felt a growing self-control.

"It's true. I've had it proven to me often."

"Alice, open the door," he said sternly.

"So you can be nice to me? What can you do?"

She was right. What could he do? Say that he loved her? That he would treasure her for always? That he would devote himself to making her happy? That's what she needed, but was he ready to do that? He didn't know. She was inside him with her pain, twisting. He was infected with her fear, standing on a cliff and unable to back away from the edge. In a moment he would be a bloody mess on the rocks below.

Back away, he told himself. Don't say another word. Just go away and forget it. He felt calmer.

"Are you there, Alice?"

Mercifully, she did not answer, and he breathed a sigh of relief as he retreated from her door.

In his apartment, he stood in the kitchen and considered going away again. Maybe to Hawaii. He could take another week off if he wanted to. Unable to decide, he stripped down to his shorts and went to exercise on his Soloflex, turning on a bit of Vivaldi on the way to drown out his thoughts.

After he had worked up a sweat, he stopped and lay there, cooling down as the Vivaldi went into a slow movement, and realized that the door to his life had had to stay closed. He lived outside himself, afloat in other lives because he had no life of his own. Nothing he had ever feared had ever happened to him—not disease, financial troubles, or lasting disappointments in love, because he had never loved anyone.

He got up from the machine, went out into the living room and looked out the window at the old wooden house across the street. It was a three-story, gabled structure that would soon be torn down because the landlord was unable to rent it. Suddenly he imagined that he had moved into the second floor with only a bed and a table, because he had lost his job and his possessions. All he had was a bit of money, the bed and the table.

He imagined sitting at the table, looking out through the curtainless window, looking back at himself across the street, wondering which of them was real, feeling his awareness switch back and forth like a swinging pendulum. . . .

I was something else once, he told himself, suddenly afraid of the wishes lurking in his fears. What did he want to happen? What had he ever wanted to happen to him?

He clenched his teeth, suddenly dismayed by what he had become, and the cap on his left front tooth slipped off into his mouth.

He held the cap in his mouth, rolling it around on his tongue, afraid to spit it out. The ground-down, naked tooth would look like the bottom of an ice cream cone and be discolored from years of being sealed away, someone had once told him. As he touched it with his tongue, he felt the sensitive tooth hanging there like a salty stalactite.

He looked at the building across the street again, and his phone chirped.

"Hi, this is Frank," his message announced. "You know what to do."

"Frank?" Alice said softly, and he felt her trembling self-hatred. "You can come over, if you still want to. Now would be okay."

The vision in his right eye went black; then in his left. Both eyes cleared, and he longed to escape into the bare room in the old house across the street.

"Frank?" Alice asked with a painful ache in her voice. "Please pick up."

The beeps cut her off, and he felt his stomach seize up into a solid mass of stone. His breath came with difficulty.

At any moment, if he didn't prevent it, the black, unforgiving nothing would invade his eyes again. He had to write her a convincing, heartfelt note at once, then go see her as soon as possible.

Desperately, he turned away from the window, went to his small cherry desk, sat down, pulled open the drawer violently, and began to fumble around in it for a sharp pencil.

DEXTER'S GREAT ADVENTURE

Randy Fox

Dexter's habit of people-watching was made all the more difficult by his fear of looking directly at them. He had solved this problem by always carrying some type of reflective surface with him. That way, he could watch all the people around him and no one would be the wiser. In the case of the butcher knife, that new dish detergent had made all the difference.

People were sure acting strange tonight. He noticed this as he walked down the sidewalk, watching their shocked expressions in the knife's blade as he brandished it in front of him, but that was the whole reason he liked to watch them. People were just funny.

As Dexter turned the corner, he nearly ran headlong into a surprised couple. He jerked suddenly as his eyes almost met those of the woman in front of him. She gasped loudly as he turned sideways to catch their reflection in the blade. The couple hurried away from him. The man drew the woman close to him as they scurried down the sidewalk. Dexter stood there watching the reflection until it bent and disappeared from the blade.

He was continuing on down the sidewalk when he heard

the sirens approaching from a distance. Quickening his pace, he headed back to his apartment. Sirens meant the police or some type of emergency crew was on the way. It was the duty of all responsible citizens to clear the streets and make the policemen's job easier. It always angered him to see the way so many people stayed out in the open, just waiting to gawk at the crime that had taken place. That was not for him, though.

Dexter did have to admit that the temptation to stay was very strong. The thought had crossed his mind on more than one occasion how he might catch a glimpse of his hero, Joe Friday. He knew that was a foolish thought, though. According to the television program, Joe was a policeman for the city of Los Angeles. There was not much chance that Joe would be operating with the police here, but there was still a possibility he might be on loan to the local police. He might be trying to solve a case that started in Los Angeles and then led to Dexter's city. It could happen, but if he did stay out on the street, he would not be acting as a responsible citizen. That would make Joe very disappointed in him.

Dexter turned into the alley that he used as a shortcut back to his apartment. The stink from the Dumpster was almost overwhelming as the smell of rotten fish filled his nostrils. The alley never smelled good, but he could save 847 steps on his way home if he took the alley rather than his usual route. At an average of two feet nine inches per step, that was a significant savings. Not to mention the time saved, approximately five minutes and 25 seconds.

Since the alley was empty, Dexter dropped the knife to his side and looked up. As much as he enjoyed watching others, it was nice to occasionally be alone outdoors. He knew his aversion to looking directly at people was not a phobia or any other type of psychological problem. At one time he had worried that he might be a victim of some type of mental illness, and he'd studied psychology texts extensively for some help. He had finally come to the conclusion that he did not have a problem. A phobia was, by definition, an irrational fear of a specific thing or situation. Since he had a perfectly sound reason for not wanting to look at other people directly, there was no phobia.

A groan rose from the far side of the Dumpster as Dexter

started to walk by it. Fearing that someone was on the other side, he raised his knife and continued walking. He held the blade close to his head and caught the men's reflections as he rounded the corner.

One of the men had his back to Dexter. He leaned over the other man, who was slumped against the wall. A cry of surprise escaped from Dexter's mouth when he saw the other man. His face and shirt were covered in blood. He moaned again. It was a wet, disgusting gurgle that escaped the man's throat. The other man spun around and saw Dexter standing there, the knife quivering in his hand.

"Shit!" the man cried out as he scrambled from the wall. Scooping up the wallet he had dropped, the man ran away quickly, his feet slapping against the wet blacktop of the alley.

It all happened so fast, Dexter was only now starting to realize what was going on. This was a crime, and he was the only witness. The man on the ground moaned again as he held his side and the blood continued to spread across his shirt. This wouldn't do, Dexter thought as the panic began to grow in him. He had responsibilities, jobs that had to be done; he had still not taken his measurements for the day, the department store ads still needed to be clipped from the morning paper and filed, and he was carrying specimens that needed to be catalogued. The man made another sound, and Dexter's eyes met the reflection in the knife's blade. The man reached up to him as he pleaded for help.

Dexter had to do something. The man could be dying. He hurried away as he spoke to the man behind him. "Don't worry, sir. I'll get you some help." Dexter dropped the knife to his side and raised his head a little as he ran down the remaining length of the alley. There was a telephone booth on the next corner. Dexter knew the number for emergencies was 911. It did not even require the usual twenty-five cents to make the call. Dexter was still glad to know that he had three quarters in his pocket, just in case the phone malfunctioned.

He quickly made the call and requested the police and an ambulance. It was hard talking to the person on the phone as he gasped for breath. Despite his daily walks, Dexter wasn't used to running, and his side hurt from the exertion.

Dexter's Great Adventure

Dexter hung the phone up, checked the coin return, and hurried back to the alley. The few people he encountered ducked quickly out of his way as he waved the knife in front of him. They obviously realized he was on an emergency mission, he thought.

The man was still lying by the Dumpster. His breathing was shallow and wet-sounding. He seemed to be unconscious as Dexter looked at his slumped form in the knife's blade. Again Dexter felt the fear and panic trying to overcome his excitement. He was not trained for this. His experience lay in research and observation, not emergency services. What consequences would come of his intervention in this event? Perhaps it would be better if he just left.

The other side of his mind argued back. What would Sergeant Friday say about his situation? A responsible citizen would do all he could to help another citizen in distress until authority arrived. Despite his fear, he had to stay.

The sound of a siren getting closer began to fill the air. Dexter hurried to the end of the alley to signal his location. At the street he raised the knife and peered into the blade to get a better view. A police car skidded to a halt in front of him, and two uniformed officers appeared from within the car. The closest drew his pistol and pointed it at Dexter. "Drop the knife!" the policeman yelled.

Dexter was astonished. The knife fell from his hand and clattered against the pavement. Perhaps the policeman was mad, Dexter thought, because he knew he'd been looking at him.

"Hands up! Get against the wall!" the policeman ordered, and Dexter complied. The other policeman ran to the Dumpster. Dexter still did not know what was happening. Didn't they know it was he who had called? He'd given his full name to the police dispatcher. Maybe this was all a part of protective custody. He had seen a criminal, after all.

Dexter could hear the other policeman talking to the man by the Dumpster. The alley was suddenly filled with the flashing red lights of an ambulance. Dexter kept his head down while he faced the wall. He could hear the flurry of activity that began to take place behind him.

The policeman started patting Dexter's legs and his sides

as if searching for something. "What's in your pocket?" the policeman asked.

"Bottles for specimens," Dexter answered cheerfully. He was glad to have the opportunity to tell someone about his research.

The policeman reached into Dexter's pocket and pulled out four small prescription bottles. One was empty and the other three contained, respectively: a broken toothpick, two pennies, and an unbroken cigar band. "I haven't catalogued these yet," Dexter said. "I was just on my way home to do so when I witnessed the crime being perpetrated."

"You saw what?" the policeman asked in a confused voice as he examined the bottles and their contents.

"Not from the very beginning, I didn't. I surprised the perpetrator and placed the call to the emergency number, 911."

"Joe," the other policeman said, "this knife's clean and there's no blood on our boy here."

"What was the knife for?"

"Why, for looking at people, of course," Dexter said, confused at the policeman's lack of understanding.

Dexter enjoyed the ride to the police station. The backseat of the car was very comfortable, and he noticed how safe it was. There were no interior door handles. No passenger could accidently fall out of this car. He was also fascinated by the wire grid that separated the backseat from the front. He counted 544 squares in the grid. The significance of this Dexter would have to consider.

The policemen held on to Dexter's knife for him. They even put it in a plastic bag so it would not get dirty. The only problem was that Dexter had a hard time watching the people around him without the knife. The only reflective surface he had handy was his watchband. The small rectangles of the band were not much use. They broke the picture up into tiny segments, and Dexter felt like he was looking through a fly's eye.

The police station was even more interesting, despite the limited view the watchband afforded him. While waiting to speak with a detective, Dexter noticed the ashtray. It was a round metal cylinder with a stainless steel top. He carefully emptied the ashes from the top and shined the steel with one of his emergency napkins. The view the ashtray gave was circular, as if he was peering down a long tunnel, but it was far better than the watchband.

Detective Owens, as he introduced himself, seemed very interested in Dexter's observations. He asked about the criminal Dexter had seen, Dexter's nightly walks, the specimens, and the knife.

"So, you say you were using the knife to watch other people?"

"That's right," Dexter said. He was sitting across the desk from the detective, his head down and slightly to the side as he looked at the reflection in the ashtray. "I always carry some type of reflective surface. I have recently been comparing different types to determine the best."

"Why can't you just look at people directly?"

"Oh, that would never do," Dexter said as he shook his head and the ashtray back and forth. "An observer always influences the outcome of an experiment. I'm sure you're familiar with Heisenberg's Uncertainty Principle and the Schrodinger's Cat Paradox. If I was to go around watching people directly, there's no telling what kind of effect I could have on their lives. I certainly wouldn't want to be the cause of some disaster."

"Uh, yeah," Owens said as he tapped his pencil on the desk.

It was almost ten o'clock the next morning when Dexter saw the reflection of Dr. Manning enter the squad room. Detective Owens had asked Dexter to stay for more questions, and although he was very tired, the excitement of assisting the police kept him awake. Dexter waved at Manning from across the room, and the doctor hesitantly returned the gesture.

Dexter had first met Dr. Manning at the state hospital while Dexter had been staying there, helping in important research. Manning still consulted with Dexter on a regular basis, and Dexter always found their talks illuminating.

Manning and Owens stepped into a side office and talked for several minutes. Dexter hoped Dr. Manning would not be upset over the valuable research time he had lost by being involved in this incident. Owens was surely explaining the situation.

After a talk which Dexter timed at seventeen minutes and 23 seconds, the two men left the office and approached him.

"Well, Dexter," Dr. Manning said, "from what the detective here tells me, it sounds like you're quite the hero. I'd say your observations were very beneficial."

Dexter lowered his head as he blushed. "I was just being a responsible citizen," he mumbled.

"It's true," Owens said. "The guy you found in that alley is going to be all right, but if you hadn't found him when you did, he might have died." He paused for a second and grinned. "I think even Joe Friday would be proud of you."

Dexter was so embarrassed that he didn't know what to say. He just stared at the floor, not even able to watch the reflections.

Dr. Manning gave Dexter a ride home. Detective Owens said Dexter could keep the ashtray if he promised not to use any more knives for watching people. Dexter felt proud as he marched into his apartment building with his police ashtray held high.

That afternoon Dexter went out for his usual walk. The butcher knife stayed at home just like he promised it would. He didn't need it anyway, not with his very own police ashtray. He could feel the admiring stares he drew from people as he walked down the sidewalk with his ashtray close to his face.

A few blocks from his apartment, Dexter watched as a black dog bounced happily down the street. He was fascinated by the dog's Brownian motion as it ricocheted from person to person. Dexter stood on the sidewalk watching the dog's reflection until it diminished from view. He turned and started around the corner as a girl came barreling into him.

Dexter and the girl hit the ground and the ashtray flew from his hands. It rolled down the sidewalk and came to rest against the side of a building. The two of them sat on the sidewalk, stunned for a second, before the girl spoke.

"Oh, I'm terribly sorry," she said as she stood up and helped Dexter to his feet. "Are you okay?"

Dexter looked at the girl. She fit the description of pretty, despite her odd clothes and hair. They were certainly not like the hair and clothes that women wore in the department store ads. Her hair was a purplish color and the short dress she wore was covered with bright, wild patterns.

"I'm really sorry," the girl continued. "I'm looking for my dog, Max. He got loose and I've got to find him. I just wasn't watching where I was going."

Dexter finished straightening his shirt to be in line with his pants and checked the specimen bottles in his pocket. From the girl's appearance, he concluded that she was a member of some youth subculture, probably at the nearby university. "Was Max a black dog?" he asked.

"Yeah, a black lab. Have you seen him?"

"Yes," Dexter replied as he pointed. "He was traveling in that direction."

"Thanks." The girl smiled. "Sorry about knocking you down like that." She took off running down the street in the direction Dexter indicated.

Dexter watched until the girl disappeared from sight. She had been very polite for a person that went around knocking people down. He hoped she would be able to find Max, the black lab dog. He retrieved his police ashtray and started back down the street. He was almost home before the thought occurred to him that he had been able to look directly at the girl.

BLACK HOLE

Nicholas A. DiChario

I STABBED AT MY POACHED EGG, NOTICING HOW HEAVY THE FORK felt between my fingers. If I didn't talk, Stephen wasn't going to say anything, but that was always the way with us.

"He's my father," I said. "Do you really expect me to let him die?"

No response.

I regretted having spoken first, hated myself for giving in, but that too was always the way with us. The ideal, New Age career couple had somehow fallen into traditional archaic roles, and I had let it happen. I, Jessica, the insignificant professional and the eternal maid-by-default.

But we had gotten along for nine years, his career and mine. His life and mine. A perfectly solid, albeit lopsided, dualistic marriage.

My hand unconsciously found my belly while my other hand busied itself strangling the stem of my fork. The kitchen smelled of wheat toast and all-natural, Valencia peanut butter.

"I never claimed to have motherly instincts," I reminded him.

"It's not fair, Jess," he said. *"Our* child, *our* decision."

Of course, Stephen would think of Stephen's loss, just as Stephen had always thought of Stephen's career. Unwritten law number one: A lawyer is more important than a public relations director. Unwritten article number one: Stephen is more important than Jessica.

"We didn't plan for this to happen. We've always agreed, no children."

Stephen rustled and snapped the morning edition. "Things change."

"Had I known you were a closet right-to-lifer, I never would have married you."

Stephen hid behind the newspaper. I didn't know how to deal with him anymore.

Mother, what would you do?

My mother died before I was born. A stroke during labor. The doctor had to rip me from her womb. Daddy raised me. Daddy took me to Little League when we mutually discovered that I was not cut out for ballet or Brownies. Even with my partial scholarship and my student loan, Daddy worked two and a half jobs to push me through Princeton. Daddy threw me a party when I accepted a position with Eastman Kodak Company that meant a year in Japan—and not just any party, a rent-a-hall, invite-the-world, surprise party, complete with an authentic tea ceremony and miniature Japanese parasols in the cocktails.

My father. Only fifty-nine years old. I could cure him. My fetus for my father. Would that be such a horrible insurrection?

Stephen continued to ignore me. He tapped the butter knife on the edge of his plate. *His knife seemed to descend slowly, like a pebble in a pool, his hands, his head, his lips seemed to move in slow motion.*

I thought of Elias Matthew Berry tapping his #3 pencil on the edge of his desk in the fifth grade, eyes downcast, searching for enlightenment on the pages of his older sister's physics book. I wanted him. Thick, chestnut hair; milky skin over exquisite lapidary facial features; long, spindly, unathletic body. Why the #3 pencil? Elias was left-handed and he didn't want the lead to smear as he wrote. My kind of guy.

We would spend afternoons together at the picnic table in his backyard. It surprised me how vividly I remembered Elias's lesson on black holes: "A black hole is nothing more than collapsed matter creating a space-time curvature. A supernova explosion. The core of a star crushed into a pulsar. Nothing can escape a black hole, not even light." He had read precisely, looking up at the clouds and chewing on his lower lip every third or fourth sentence. I suppose he really didn't need me there, but there was where I needed to be.

Stephen swirled the Minute Maid in his orange juice glass; the slow, circular motion of his hand broke the pattern of my thoughts, bringing me back. I was reminded of the old films I'd seen of the Apollo astronauts floating, swimming in space. "They drank Minute Maid, didn't they? The Apollo astronauts?"

"No, Tang," Stephen said, holding the newspaper stiffly between us.

"Stephen"—he wouldn't even look at me—"I want you to understand. . . ." But Stephen didn't want to understand anything. He would much rather hide behind his new psychological warfare weapon, a silent moral and intellectual superiority that served no purpose other than to raise the male brutality quotient to new and insufferable heights. Elias, always a man ahead of his time, had done the same thing to me twenty years ago.

I never should have tried to kiss him—Elias, I mean. He didn't have it for me, and it wasn't one of those mood-perfect spontaneous moments that all young schoolgirls remembered fondly for the rest of their lives. Spontaneity? Don't be silly. No practical application. Think it through, Jessica, it's smarter and safer to calculate the gains and anticipate the consequences of failure. Even in the fifth grade I knew about the Worst Case Scenario Theory, even if I didn't know it by name.

So I selected one day after school, a day when we were alone at the picnic table that had become our haven. *Now,* I told myself, *do it now,* and I leaned forward and kissed him quickly, clumsily, on the lips, not holding out for that consummate pause in the conversation, not waiting for the eye contact or the casual, unexpected yet longed-for brush of hands.

Things change.

That's what I had tried to tell Elias twenty years ago at the picnic table, but he refused to listen. He called me a bug pod from Venus, and said that he had never seen such childish behavior in his entire life, and then he moved away from me *in slow motion, so slow that every breath contained the pain of one complete lifetime in hell. . . .*

I still dreamt often of Mother. Often enough to concern my psychotherapist. In my nightmare, Mother would come to me naked, surrounded by black nothingness, and all I could see of her was her ghostly white skin and hollow mouth and eyes, and in a voice not her own, not anyone's, a voice filled with the dark emptiness of hollow space and an inexplicable terror, she would howl, *"Feeeeeeeeear* the black hole . . . *Feeeeeeeeear* the black hole . . ." and I would wake up drenched in sweat, panting, my legs pumping as if I were sprinting away from her as fast as I could.

"I've been doing some research. There's never been a recorded case of black hole phobia," my therapist had said, amused, trying to make light of it. He'd pulled his Latin dictionary off his bookshelf. "Let's name it . . . *ater,* black . . . *cavum,* hole. "You're suffering from *ater cavum* phobia."

I didn't find it funny and told him so. Sometimes I really hated him. As far as I was concerned, Mother was the first case, and she'd died from it.

"Seriously," he said with impatience—I wasn't exactly making progress at light speed—"a phobia is nothing more than a mind trying to complicate things. Instead of facing the real problem, we create a symptom and think we can escape the disease. In your case, the dream persists because you keep running away from your mother. Next time, reach out to her, touch her if your dream allows it. She might really be trying to tell you something important. Maybe it's something she never got a chance to say. Maybe she doesn't know *how* to say it. Just because she never knew you, Jessica, doesn't mean she never loved you."

And then he would say something like that and I couldn't hate him anymore.

Last week.
Dr. Patrice Maldanado's office.

Quoth the neurosurgeon: "There are neurochemical abnormalities associated with Alzheimer's/the mammalian central nervous system is nonregenerative/embryonic brain tissue grafts can be anatomically fused into the adult central nervous system/precise reconstruction of damaged elements is not required for the recovery of function/immature neural tissue can multiply and migrate and extend axons and dentrites/transplanted grafts receive inputs from the host brain/nerve cells won't reject without histocompatibility antigens/depletion of acetylcholine in the hippocampus/input from a cluster of cells at the base of the forebrain/disrupted synapses patterns/neurotransmitters/grafts/grafts/grafts/grafts . . ."

Dr. Maldanado reminded me of Elias, of course, the cream-colored skin, the gleam behind the eyes, the precision of movement and speech as if every word, gesture, and thought required a second surgical opinion.

Stephen leveled his ensiform courtroom glare at me, the one he normally reserved for jurors who refused to respond sympathetically to his diatribe. "Why do we have to use our own fetus?" he said. Neurosurgical gray matter could be easily translated into black and white as far as Stephen was concerned. Money had bought him everything, probably even me, so why not a fetus for the bitch's father?

"A genetic match is not necessary to obtain successful results," Dr. Maldanado said, "but the time it would take, and the legalities involved in securing a donor fetus—"

"I'm a lawyer, for God's sake. I'm aware of the legal complications."

Dr. Maldanado shifted her patronizing expression into one of impertinence, and I felt, quite illogically, that we had insulted her in some subtle way. "Alzheimer's is just one of the diseases that has benefited from our fetal tissue transplants. We've had success with Parkinson's as well as other serious neurological disorders. The results have been so promising that diabetes and cancer researchers are beginning to explore the possibilities. Even AIDS victims might benefit in the long run. All I can do is provide you with the facts. Do you want to be part of the success ratio? Ultimately it's your decision."

It would have been nice if my husband and my doctor had

been fighting for my best interests—me, Jessica, the insignificant professional—but they weren't. They were fighting over the child. The unborn child. My child. Mine. It had been the first time I had thought of the baby as my own.

Stephen pushed himself away from the kitchen table. *It seemed to take him forever. His distorted body wavered in front of me, nearly inert. And then he began to recede, slowly—twenty, thirty minutes might have passed before Stephen reached the door. Maybe an hour had passed, or a day.* I hated Elias for not loving me all those years ago. I hated Stephen for it now. I even hated Daddy for no longer being able to protect me, and Mother, of course, for never having the opportunity. I felt alone, abandoned, except for the baby growing inside me. My baby. *A second passed, or was it a millennium?*

I had read an article in *Scientific American* a few weeks ago about a young, distinguished astrophysicist named Elias Matthew Berry. He and a team of astronomers from Rice University had discovered the largest recorded black hole, one hundred billion times more massive than our sun, in a galaxy called NGC 6240.

Unfortunately, I would never get the opportunity to correct him.

This is what I discovered (me, Jessica, the eternal maid-by-default): The largest black hole has nothing to do with size. The largest black hole is the one inside the mind, the one that can swallow you whole and make you disappear, the one that binds you and at the same time sets you free. When you find it—this vast power that can crush a star into a pulsar—you realize no boundaries exist within it, no limitations, no time or place or reason or purpose. We all have this power. A treasure. Recognizing it, holding onto it, having the courage to pursue it, that is the challenge of a lifetime. Perhaps that's what Mother had been trying to tell me.

Power is terrifying.

Ater cavum. Black hole phobia.

I decided to stop running.

I moved my mind forward into the event horizon, into the disrupted synapses patterns of central-nervous-system space, swimming through the crushed gravity in my brain. A black hole is a theoretical object. And so, I imagine, am I.

Mother, was that your voice I heard in my mind? What's wrong? There's nothing to fear anymore. I'm here with you now. Why are you screaming?

RINGER

Pamela Sargent

CHERYL SAW THE TELEPHONE RING. THE CHIRPING SOUNDS exploded behind her eyes as a series of flashes. She pulled a pillow over her face, yearning for the dark silence to return. After months of nagging, she had finally persuaded Nick to get rid of their old black telephone with the rotary dial and the bell that hit her with the force of a lightning bolt, but this chirper wasn't much better.

The phone kept chirping. Cheryl prayed for it to stop, unable to bring herself to pick up the receiver. Nick was probably calling from his office, checking up on her, seeing if she was out of bed yet. She could tell him that she had gone out to a job interview. Pressing the pillow more tightly around her ears, she composed a possible story for her husband. Adele from Ronald Associates had called to tell her that the personnel manager at Trahel Engineering was looking for a new file clerk, had seen Cheryl's résumé, and wanted to interview her at eleven. That would be detailed enough to satisfy Nick, who would be delighted that she had miraculously managed to answer the phone and too busy to check on her story.

The phone stopped chirping. Cheryl peered out from under the pillow. The glowing numerals of the clock radio told her that it was almost eleven now. She had to get up. If she could pull herself together and go out on a few errands, she would not be here to answer the phone.

Years ago, when Cheryl was a small child, the sound of a telephone ringing had filled her with dread. She did not know why; it had always been that way. She had once thought that she must have picked up the receiver and heard something so frightening or upsetting that she had blocked it from her mind, recalling only that the telephone had carried the horror to her. But what could she have heard? Why had her parents known nothing about such a call? Surely she would have run to them, however emotionally distant they were, for comfort.

So, she had concluded years later, something else had to be at the root of her fear. Maybe it was the intrusiveness of the instrument, the fact that she was forced to pick it up without knowing who was calling or what she would hear. The chaotic outside world, the world her parents had tried to escape inside their neat orderly house in a dull small town, was always threatening to intrude through the phone. Cheryl could not know whether the call was from her best friend Marcy or from that creep Julie Colton, who always rushed to tell her what everybody was allegedly saying about her behind her back. She might be dreaming that Joe Wentworth, the best-looking boy at school, was finally going to ask her out, then pick up the phone only to discover that Mrs. Nance, her math teacher, wanted to see one of her parents for a conference on why she was doing so badly in that subject. She could answer to find that her life was on the verge of some precipice. The torment of wondering whether the voice at the other end was going to launch her into ecstasy or plunge her into depression was usually so great that she could not bring herself to answer the phone at all. The ringing would stop, and her life would remain as it was, placid and undisturbed, at least for a while.

She had supposed that the other kids, even Marcy, sometimes thought she was weird for being so abrupt with them whenever one of their calls did get through to her. Unlike them, she didn't mind when her mother or father picked up the phone first, and she usually hung up as quickly as possible instead of staying on for hours and hours to gossip. She could even feel relieved when her mother told a friend that she was doing her homework and could not come to the phone. She could not explain to anyone, even Marcy, how the ringing made her tense with terror.

By the time Cheryl graduated from high school, she could barely bring herself to say anything over the phone even when she was able to answer it. Sometimes words lodged in her throat, forcing her to hang up as she gasped for breath. Sometimes the disembodied voice at the other end of the line seemed alien and unfathomable, and she would find herself hanging up to escape the sound. "We must have been disconnected," she would tell the caller later. "Lots of trouble on this line lately."

When she went away to college, at a university only one hundred miles from her hometown, she did not follow the example of other students and plague her parents with collect calls. She never called them at all. Her mother sent her a short letter twice a month; Cheryl mailed a postcard back every six weeks or so. The lives of her mother and father remained uneventful, according to her mother's letters, and she sometimes wondered if they were secretly relieved not to have her living at home for most of the year. Even one shy and docile daughter had occasionally seemed more than the quiet withdrawn couple could handle. Her mother often looked vaguely distressed whenever any of Cheryl's friends dropped by on their infrequent visits, and her father seemed happiest when he was alone in his den with his books and records.

Getting through college without having to deal with telephones proved to be simpler than expected. Her roommates usually rushed to answer any calls first, and soon Cheryl had talked them into covering for her. The other girls took messages, called out for pizza, accepted dates, or turned down guys Cheryl wanted to avoid with excuses agreed upon earlier. As time went on, word got around the dormitories that any compulsive phone freak wanting to have a telephone entirely to herself ought to room with Cheryl Manfred. By the middle of her sophomore year, Cheryl was much in demand as a roommate.

During her senior year, she moved off-campus to an apartment with her friend Beth Terrence. Beth, as had her previous roommates, gloried in the opportunity to monopolize the phone. Because of that, Cheryl was surprised when, only two weeks before they were to graduate, Beth answered the loudly ringing phone, but insisted that Cheryl speak to this particular caller herself.

"Can't you tell them I'm not here?" she whispered, terrified as always.

"It's important," Beth replied, and then Cheryl noticed how pale her friend looked and how Beth's eyes refused to meet hers. "You'd better take this call."

Somehow she managed to hold the receiver to her ear and listen as Mrs. Redfern, her mother's closest friend, told her that both of her parents had died in a car accident. Mrs. Redfern's choked voice kept breaking as she spoke of rainslicked roads and of the car going through a guardrail and into a river swollen by late spring flooding. Cheryl knew then that all her terror of telephones, her fear of what might happen to her world if she responded to the ringing, had anticipated this incident, as if the future had been calling to the past through the telephone lines. Even through her grief, she felt a bitter satisfaction. Her fear, as it turned out, had been completely justified. She had been right to fear the phone.

Nick was pacing in the living room, talking to his mother over the cordless phone. Cheryl knew that her husband was talking to his mother because he was speaking in Greek and also sounded more tense than usual. He spoke to only two people in Greek, his mother and Mr. Vassilikos, the butcher who rented one of the commercial buildings Nick owned. In the three years she and Nick had been married, Cheryl had been unable to learn a single word of Greek, but she could tell to which of the two he was speaking by the tone of his voice. With Mr. Vassilikos, Nick sounded patient and resigned; with his mother, his voice was strained. Both Mr. Vassilikos and Nick's mother usually called only when they had complaints, one reason to dread their calls.

Nick's voice was rising; soon he would be shouting at his mother. They could not discuss even the most innocuous subjects without engaging in histrionics and high drama. Cheryl, out in the kitchen, tried not to listen. She hated it when he was talking on the phone to his mother, and speaking in a language she could not understand only made things worse.

Mrs. Christopoulos could be complaining about almost anything. She still thought of her mother-in-law as "Mrs. Christopoulos," since the woman was much too formidable to be addressed by her first name, and Cheryl could not bring herself to call her "Mother." She could endure Mrs. Christopoulos's annual visits, even if the two or three weeks sometimes seemed like an eternity. Usually her mother-in-law would keep herself occupied by watching soap operas while commenting on the moral degeneracy of the characters, and she liked cooking Greek dishes for her son that Cheryl had failed to master. When Mrs. Christopoulos was here, Cheryl did not mind hearing her conversing in Greek with her son; it saved Cheryl the trouble of having to talk to her. Whatever complaints the older woman might have, she usually kept them to herself in Cheryl's presence.

But the telephone, combined with a language foreign to Cheryl, gave Mrs. Christopoulos freedom to vent her feelings and say anything she liked to her son, and Cheryl could never know if her husband was sticking up for her or siding with his mother. She could sense her mother-in-law reaching through the phone lines from a thousand miles away, still clinging to the son who could never give her enough attention.

Cheryl, tearing at lettuce leaves, wondered what Mrs. Christopoulos was bitching about now. Nick should call more often, even though he called her at least once a week. He should talk some sense into his sister, who was almost thirty and still hadn't settled down. He could visit her once in a while, or even move back home instead of leaving her to rattle around alone in their old house, and it was about time he visited his father's grave, which he had not been to since the funeral. He could give up being Nicholas Christopher, as if Christopoulos wasn't a good enough name for him, and change his name back to what it had been. He could tell Cheryl that it would be nice to have her get on the phone once in a while and say a few kind words to her old and neglected mother-in-law.

Mrs. Christopoulos could be complaining about any and

all of those things, but Cheryl suspected that the lack of telephone conversations with her daughter-in-law was one of the complaints being batted around now. Nick had explained to his mother that Cheryl was shy, which had not done much good. Shyness was a concept that apparently did not exist in Mrs. Christopoulos's mental universe, where people were classified as either warmhearted or cold-blooded, and neurosis was considered self-indulgence. Cheryl tore up the last of the lettuce and began to peel a carrot, hating the sound of the Greek words she did not know, the words being drawn from her husband out along the telephone lines by his mother's voice.

Nick fell silent. She had put the salad into the spinner when he wandered into the kitchen. "Mom tried to call today, twice," he said.

"Must have been when I was out getting groceries."

"She tried at ten o'clock her time, and again at around two."

"Oh. Well, I had to go over to the mall to see if that screwdriver you ordered came in." She had decided to save her excuse about having an appointment with the personnel manager at Trahel Engineering for another time.

"You could have phoned the store about that."

"I was going there anyway. Benetton was having a sale. I don't know why she was calling anyway, when she knew you'd be at the office."

"Maybe she wanted to talk to you. Ever think of that? You are her daughter-in-law. It wouldn't hurt if you'd try to be a little friendlier to her."

"I do try. All she ever talks about is the soaps, cooking tips, what a fine little boy you were, and all those crazy people who lived in her village in Greece."

"They weren't crazy. It was just a different way of life. Look, I know she's a little difficult. She can drive me nuts sometimes, but she's not a bad person." Nick leaned against the counter and folded his arms. "You're not answering the phone again. I'll bet that's what it is. I never get an answer when I call home either."

She stared at the salad, unable to reply.

"I got rid of the old phone. I thought that'd help. I know that old ringer brought back some bad memories."

Ringer

He knew about the call that had told her of the death of her parents. That call, she had let him believe during the years he had known her, was the source of her inability to handle telephones; he did not know that she had suffered from her fear of phones since childhood. He'd been patient, making excuses to his mother and their friends and taking care of all their phone calls himself. Her anxiety still persisted, making her queasy whenever the telephone rang, even when he was there to answer it. Sometimes, unable to control her anxiety, she would find herself begging him to let it go on ringing and not to answer it at all.

"An answering machine," she said. "We can get an answering machine. It's about time we had one. Everybody else in the world does."

"You know I can't stand those damned things. It's bad enough having to have one at the office—I don't want one in my home."

Cheryl had never been enthusiastic about getting an answering machine herself, not wanting to dwell on anything having to do with telephones. Now she was wondering why she had not seriously considered such a device before. The machine could answer the phone for her. She could surely calm herself enough to listen to messages left hours before. The machine could screen calls, meaning that she might actually be able to overcome her phobia enough to pick up the receiver once in a while. An answering machine might even cure her.

"I used to feel the same way," she said, "but you know how it is. Once everybody else has something, you almost have to get it yourself in self-defense. I mean, people sort of expect you to have them, so they can leave messages if you're not around and not feel they have to keep calling back."

"I still don't see—"

"Look, if I get a job, we may need an answering machine. There wouldn't be anyone here during the day to take calls then." Not that there was much chance of her getting any kind of a job soon, Cheryl admitted to herself, although it eased things with Nick to pretend that she was looking for one. Too many jobs—almost all of them, in fact—seemed to require encounters with telephones sooner or later.

"You're not taking calls now," Nick said. "You've got to get over this, Cheryl."

"You're right." She turned toward him, trying to smile and look determined. "That's why we should get a machine. I'll be able to know who called, and if I can screen calls, so I know what to expect, maybe I can get into the habit of answering."

"I suppose it's worth a try."

"It is. I'm sure. I know it'll help," she said, wanting to believe that.

Cheryl had gone back home after graduating from college. The attorney handling the estate of her parents had told her that she was the sole heir, which was hardly a surprise. Each of her parents had been an only child too.

The details of the estate were as tidy as her mother's house had been. The mortgage was paid off, the house now belonged to Cheryl, and there was enough money from cautious investments and an insurance policy to give her a modest annual income. It had been surprisingly easy to move back home, and to tell herself that she might as well stay there until she decided what to do.

The house was still as quiet, as peaceful, as it had been when she was a child. Days would pass in which she got up late in the morning, ate her usual breakfast of cereal and fruit, took her early afternoon walk, and spent most of the rest of the day reading one of the books in her father's den or a volume borrowed from the town library. Occasionally people who had known her parents, or one of the few old school friends who still lived there, would invite her to dinner. When she was feeling especially adventurous, she would drive to Wellford, the nearest city and only a hour away, to shop in its new mall and see a movie.

Only the telephone disturbed her tranquility. She had grown so used to other people answering it for her that she could not pick it up herself or even bear listening to it after two or three rings. There was no reason for anyone here in town to call her. She always made the rounds during her morning walks, passing the houses and shops where she was likely to run into anyone wanting to see her later; the people in town knew her routine. She wrote letters to her college friends, although their responses were becoming less frequent. Soon she had turned off the telephone; the damned thing could ring all it wanted to as long as she couldn't hear it. There was, she realized, no reason why she had to have a phone at all while she lived here, but yet she could not bring herself to have it disconnected.

Somehow, she needed the phone there, much as she feared it. She would gaze at the telephone and think: If it weren't for you, everything would be fine. I wouldn't have anything to worry about then; I'd be content. It's your fault that I'm afraid. Such thoughts soothed her, reminding her that only an intrusive technology over which she had no control was responsible for most of her fears.

Eventually she would come to grips with her fear, Cheryl at times thought, maybe by forcing herself to make the occasional call to the local doctor or dentist for an appointment instead of dropping by to schedule one in person. She could work up to the occasional personal call and eventually to picking up the phone when it rang. But whenever she had such thoughts, her mouth grew dry and her body stiffened with fear. She would be hearing nothing but a voice, one created from electronic signals. There would be no visual cues to tell her what the unseen person might be thinking. She would be nothing except an insignificant, halting, hesitant voice herself, an invisible being that the one at the other end of the line could easily crush with only a few words. One call could destroy the peace she had managed to find.

The lines snaked down telephone poles, along streets, and through windows, then slipped into telephones. The world was encased in a web of shining wires and fiber optic cables over which voices babbled, shrieked, moaned, muttered, and screamed. No matter how many hallways she ran through and how many doors she closed behind her, she could not escape the tentacles through which all the world could demand her attention. Once she picked up the receiver, her thoughts would be drawn out of her, her soul trapped inside the wires.

Cheryl woke, afraid to move. The dream was a warning. The telephone was just waiting to ensnare her in its net along with everyone else.

The telephone on the nightstand chirped, making her tense. She gritted her teeth, knowing that the answering machine would take the message after four more rings. She counted them, then let out her breath when the phone fell silent.

At last she forced herself out of bed and went downstairs. Nick had bought an answering machine with a cordless receiver; the device sat on an end table in the corner of the living room, its light blinking at her. Two calls had come in already that morning; she had heard the phone ring earlier, before falling asleep again.

Cheryl lifted her hand, steeling herself to retrieve the messages. Her finger moved toward the "message" button, then froze. She could not know what was on the tape, what she would hear. The machine had not eased her fear, but had only compounded it. Nick had installed the machine three weeks ago, and she hadn't retrieved a single message. Even if she listened to the messages, she would never be able to return the calls.

Nick could listen to the messages later, not that this would solve anything. In fact, it would only make matters worse. He now had something else to hold against her; not only did she refuse to take phone calls, she left all the messages for him to handle.

The phone suddenly rang. Cheryl stiffened, knowing that if she did not pick it up, she would still hear the caller when the machine began to take the message. There was no escape. She longed to grab the machine and dash it against the wall.

Somehow she seized the receiver and pressed it to her ear. "Hello?" she squeaked.

"Hello," an unfamiliar male voice responded, "am I speaking to Mrs. Christopher?"

"Wrong number!" Cheryl screamed, then hung up and fled from the room.

Although Cheryl had welcomed a calm, serene life far removed from the turmoil of most of the world, she began to grow restless after nearly two years of living alone in her parents' house. She had taken on a part-time job at the local library two days a week, work that required her only to shelve volumes and arrange displays near the desk, but felt the need for more activity to fill her time. She did not see the people she knew here as often, and their conversations with her were more brief; their invitations to dinner came less frequently. Sometimes she could even feel that they were avoiding her.

While in Wellford one day, she picked up a flyer from the local branch of the state university listing evening noncredit courses for adults seeking self-improvement. During her next trip, she went to the small campus on the outskirts of Wellford to sign up for a course, knowing it would be impossible to register over the phone. Over the next two years, she took courses in calligraphy, conversational Spanish, Chinese cooking, and drawing. There was no need to call up any of the students in her courses, since they could easily get together after class for the occasional bull session, and she never grew close enough to anyone to worry that someone might try to call her. By now, she supposed, her phone would almost never ring, even if she turned the ringer back on. She was safe.

She met Nick Christopher after signing up for a course in macramé and going to the wrong classroom, where Nick was teaching a course on rental property management. He was a lawyer by profession and a stocky, energetic man with curly black hair and a wide grin. "Why don't you check out my first lecture?" he told her. "Maybe you'll want to switch to my course." She had been powerless to leave his class after that.

She never did master the intricacies of managing property, but Nick was soon taking her out for late dinners after class. He had a law office in downtown Wellford and owned two commercial buildings and two apartment complexes. He had reached that point in his life when he was looking for a nice woman to settle down with, someone who wasn't as driven and hard-edged and career-minded as a lot of the women he knew, someone who was more gentle and old-fashioned.

When Nick asked her to marry him, Cheryl quickly said

yes. The warm, kindly feelings she had for him had to be love, and he accepted her as she was. He had hoped to find a quiet soul, a contrast to his outgoing and vociferous temperament, someone for whom he could play the outmoded role of protector. He did not mind the quirks he thought of as her charming eccentricities.

"What do you *do* all day? Why can't you ever finish anything instead of just dabbling in one thing after another? Why can't you find a job so you'd at least have something to do? Why can't you even answer the goddamned phone and retrieve messages?"

Those were the kinds of questions Cheryl got from Nick lately. She no longer looked forward to having him come home in the evenings, when he was likely to destroy whatever serenity she had won during the day. What did he expect her to do with her days anyway? She did the housework and shopping, and would still have been doing all the cooking if he had not recently decided that he preferred cooking spicier dishes she didn't much like. She took a course at the state college every semester, her favorite ones lately having been anthropology, Italian Renaissance art, and the nineteenth century novel, and could not see why she had to limit herself to one thing in order to get another useless degree. There was no economic reason for her to get a job, one that would undoubtedly force her into confronting a phone.

Nick was on the telephone now. He had been on for almost half an hour, ever since the end of dinner, and now he had retreated to his study next to the living room with the cordless. She could hear him talking behind the closed door. Hearing his voice indistinctly through a closed door only made the call seem much more ominous. He had never gone to his study, closing her off, to take calls before. He was speaking in English, so he could not be talking to either his mother or Mr. Vassilikos.

Cheryl put her book down, got up from the sofa and crept toward the door. ". . . don't know," she heard Nick say. "It's driving me . . ." She leaned closer. ". . . try to get there by one."

She could not listen anymore. She would never be free of

the calls, the messages, the efforts of all these callers to wrench her from her refuge. Because she could not pick up a phone and speak to someone at the other end, her husband now considered her disturbed and possibly in need of help. He no longer saw her horror of telephones as a charming eccentricity; the day before, he had raised the possibility of counseling.

Maybe he was talking to a counselor now, the kind of person who would consider her healthy and normal if she went around routinely spilling her guts over the phone to all and sundry. Maybe Nick was complaining to a friend. He could hatch a plot against her with impunity over the phone. He knew she would be incapable of tiptoeing up to the bedroom and listening in on the extension.

The door opened; Nick came back into the living room and hung up the phone. He sat down in his chair in front of the television, picked up the remote, channel-surfed for a while, then turned off the set.

"We have to talk," he said. Cheryl stared at her book, refusing to lift her eyes. "We've had that answering machine for four months now, and it hasn't helped at all. It's probably made things worse. You're just using it as a barrier, something else to put between you and everything outside. I could put in one of those things that gives you the number of who's calling, and it wouldn't do any good, because your problem isn't just the phone—it's something more."

"You're wrong," she said. "You don't understand."

"I've been trying to," he said. "You can't say I haven't been patient. I thought you'd get over it, but it's becoming pathological."

How could she explain her fear to him? How could she convey her horror of phones? Having to speak to someone she could not see, having to fear that at any moment a call might come from someone she could not see or touch, with a message she could not anticipate—the thought was unbearable. Throughout her life, on those rare occasions when she had picked up a phone, she had imagined invisible callers listening to her stammered, uncertain words with mockery and contempt and indifference while feigning friendliness.

It was the interconnectedness of it all that got to her, the vision of a world hooked up and wired and always in contact, with fibers and cables and satellites carrying messages that no one could escape. It wasn't enough to put telephones in everyone's home; now people could carry pagers and drive around with cellular phones. They would all be sucked into the constant babble, the noise that would allow for no peace. There would be no solitude, no time for quiet moments; they would all be nothing but automatons reacting to the latest stream of messages. Nervousness, some might call it fear, or a speech problem, or a lack of interpersonal communication skills, but at last she knew it for what it was—her defense of her innermost self.

"You can't keep going through life," he went on, "without coming to terms with telephones. I mean, you can't escape them."

"Yes, I know," she murmured. "I know that only too well."

"I don't care how you do it. Go to a psychiatrist, or a group—if there is such a thing as a group for people like you—or just sit there and practice picking the damned thing up when nobody's calling, but you've got to get over this. I have to cover for you all the time. Even making a dinner reservation or calling back a friend is beyond you."

"I can't," she said.

"You can. You'd better."

"All *right,*" she said, because that was easier than arguing with him.

He picked up the remote and went back to channel-surfing. Cheryl stared at her book. He had not even told her who had called, something he had always done before, as if trying to reassure her that her fears were unfounded.

The telephone rang. Nick got up, muttered a greeting, then retreated to his office and closed the door.

There was no one Cheryl could turn to, no close friend or confidant who might offer her some sympathy. Acquiring and cultivating close friends seemed to require making telephone calls at some point. The people she met in her classes, or the couples who occasionally went out with her and Nick to dinner, remained only distant acquaintances. She had lost track of her college classmates, and would have to drive to her hometown to consult her few friends there.

Ringer

Nick was up to something. He had stopped nagging at her about counseling, and she had stopped lying to him about the psychologist she was allegedly seeing in Fensterburg, a small city one hour's drive from Wellford. He wasn't likely to discover her deception, since there was little chance of his running into her alleged psychologist. She had always taken a long drive on the days she supposedly had appointments, in case Nick checked on her mileage. The driving soothed her; she was enclosed in a protective carapace, away from chores and disturbances and telephones. Sometimes she would drive as far as her hometown. She still owned her parents' house, but Nick had rented it out to a couple with two young children; Cheryl could not even park near the house to gaze at it nostalgically without hearing the sound of ringing telephones through the open windows.

Nick seemed to be getting more phone calls than ever. He often spent most of the evening in his study, behind his closed door, taking one call after another. In the evening, before he came home, the light on the message machine was often blinking nine or ten times. He was doing it deliberately, just to annoy her. Sometimes she was sure she saw him smile whenever the phone rang, seemingly glorying in her distress before he went to answer it.

He was in his study now, speaking in a voice so low that she could barely hear him from her chair. He had been talking to his mother before; she had overheard an occasional shouted Greek phrase. She had also heard her own name spoken several times. Nick had not sounded as though he was sticking up for her. He had probably been telling his mother that there was no excuse for his wife's rudeness, that he had pressured her to make the occasional phone call to Mrs. Christopoulos until he was blue in the face, that he no longer knew what to do.

She got up and moved toward the door. ". . . sorry I ever got married," she heard before Nick's voice again fell. Cheryl crept back to her chair. So her suspicions were correct. With the telephone as his tool, he could call up anyone he liked and say whatever he wished, and her phobia made her powerless to stop him, to have any control over his actions.

The door to the study opened; Nick came toward her and

sat down on the sofa. "I may not be home for dinner tomorrow," he said. "There's a chance I'll have to talk to a colleague about a case, and I can't call you up later to let you know for sure, so just don't worry if I'm not here."

"Fine." She did not believe him. He was probably getting together with a friend to drink and commiserate. "By the way, didn't you mention a while back that the lease on my old house is almost up?"

He leaned back. "Yeah, I did. Almost forgot—the Ruddocks are moving out in three weeks. I was going to bring that up. I've been thinking . . ." He sat up again. "Maybe we ought to sell. I know you feel attached to it, but trying to rent it and keep an eye on it from here is kind of a pain."

"I know."

"It's your house, though. We ought to decide what to do with it together."

An inspiration came to her. "We shouldn't rent it out again," she said quickly. "We could live there ourselves. The town's quiet and safe, there's plenty of room for the two of us, and you could still get to your office here." This, she realized, was the answer to a lot of problems. Nick's business, and its potential disruptions, would be farther away. There was less chance his various tenants would pester him with phone calls about relatively insignificant problems if they had to call long distance, and his clients would have to leave messages at his office. Perhaps Nick would come to appreciate the virtues of a life without so many distractions.

"Absolutely not," he muttered, shattering her reverie.

"Why not?"

"For one thing, because I don't feel like commuting for two hours a day, and it'd probably take even longer in winter. Also because it'd be harder to tend to all my business from there."

Cheryl looked down. "Well, you could cut back on some of your business."

"No, I don't think I could." His hand was suddenly around her wrist, gripping her tightly. "Oh, there's one way I might manage it. I could get another computer for the house, and hook it up to a modem. I could put in a fax machine, and another phone line to handle any business calls that come there. I might be able to do more of my work at home, and drive into my office less often. How would you like that, Cheryl?" She lifted her head; he was smiling now, but his eyes glittered with anger. "Pretty soon everything'll be on the phone lines. You won't just be worrying about phones—it'll be more and more home computers, modems, faxes, TV, and God knows what else. What are you going to do then?"

She pulled her hand from his. "Stop it!"

"Don't you understand? I'm trying to help you, shock some sense into you."

She jumped to her feet. "Is it so wrong to want to be free of that damned thing?"

He gazed up at her. "You've got to do something about this, Cheryl. It's for your own good." He sighed. "I'll give you a month. That's about as patient as I can be at this point. If you can't answer a simple phone call by then, or ring me up for a couple of minutes at the office . . ." She waited for him to complete the threat. "You've got to put this phone bullshit behind you."

"We'll see," she said softly, then walked toward the stairway. Her parents had never raised their voices, she thought as she climbed toward the bedroom. She suddenly hated Nick for insisting that she change, for making a scene, for trying to frighten her with his talk of faxes and modems and all the other devices reaching out for her through the wires.

No, she told herself. I won't let them.

Cheryl parked her car a block from Nick's office and walked to the boutique across the way. Nick came out at six; a beautiful blond young woman was waiting for him in a blue BMW. The blond beauty looked familiar; Cheryl dimly recalled meeting her a year ago at a local bar association dinner. She had to be the colleague Nick was meeting for dinner. How convenient for him, she thought, to have to discuss business with such a babe.

A week later, when Nick told her once again that he had to meet another lawyer for dinner, Cheryl drove to his office once more. She was not surprised to see the same blonde pick him up again. There had been even more mysterious phone calls lately, calls that came in the evening and that Nick took in his study. The two were plotting against her, and the telephone was their ally.

She had tried to give Nick a refuge. She had thought that was what he wanted. How great it would have been if he could have come home to her and retreated from the outside, at least for a while.

She had known what was happening, long before she was fully conscious of the source of her fear. Telephones had only been the harbingers. The networks people had built to communicate with one another would soon flood them with so much babble that they would be unable to tell which thoughts and feelings were their own. They would become no more than receivers passing on the messages of the networks. Their most private thoughts would be overwhelmed by all the noise; they would call out to others through their phones and modems and microphones and never truly be heard. Solitude would be impossible.

The information lines were a growing nervous system, drawing her into itself, but she did not want to be part of it. She desperately needed to be apart, to be herself. She could not fight the system alone. But at least she could protect herself.

Nick was spending more evenings away from home, allegedly at business dinners. It was easy for Cheryl to pack some of her belongings each night and hide the suitcases and boxes in the basement before he came home.

She was ready to leave in a week. It was surprisingly easy to walk out the door with the last of her packed belongings and turn the key in the lock, having avoided an unpleasant confrontation. In a way, she was grateful that Nick had found someone else; that made it even easier to leave.

Her spirits lifted as she approached her hometown. The family in her parents' house had moved out; except for some crayon scrawlings on a couple of walls and worn spots on the living room carpet, the rooms were in good shape. She could sleep on the futon she had brought with her until she got a bed, and would drive to the electric company's local offices in the morning to get the power turned on. The Ruddocks had installed telephone jacks in both of the bedrooms and the kitchen, but had apparently taken their phones with them. The only telephone left in the house was her parents' old black one in the basement recreation room, and its receiver was off the hook.

Cheryl approached it hesitantly, then leaned down, picked up the receiver gingerly, and managed to put it back in its cradle. The telephone company would have disconnected this line by now. She could always drive over to the local offices to see about having it reconnected.

Assuming, of course, that she could come up with any good reasons to have the phone hooked up.

Nick came to the house two days later, just after the two men from the local furniture store had delivered her new bed. She managed to lock the front door just before he reached the porch.

He pounded on the door. "Cheryl! Cheryl! Open the goddamned door! I have to talk to you!"

"Go away!"

"You can't just walk out like this!"

"Oh yes I can."

"Cheryl!" He pounded on the door again, then stepped back. She could see him through the peephole. "Are you still there?"

"I'm here."

"Then I'll just have to shout at you through the door. I found somebody. He can help you. I've got it set up, he works with people like you all the time. He's actually kind of interested in your particular disorder. It took me a while to set it up, but he'll take your case on right away."

Cheryl said, "I'm not a case."

"Damn it, will you listen to me? You can beat this thing!"

"What do you care if I do or not? You've got that gorgeous blonde to run around with, that colleague who's been joining you for dinner."

He gaped at her. "Rita? You know about Rita?"

"You're goddamned right I know about Rita," she replied, wallowing in righteous fury. "I was outside your office. I know who you were meeting. Bet she was calling you up all those times too."

"Then you should have spied on me some more and

followed me to the restaurant, because her husband always met us there. You idiot! Rita had this massive phobia herself once, about airplane flights! She told me about this psychologist, the one who wants to see you. She helped me set it up."

She would not let him trick her into leaving her refuge, now that she was safe. "You wanted a quiet home," she said. "At least you said you did. You liked having someone around who wasn't competing, who looked after you, who just wanted some peace. I kept my side of the bargain. You're the one who's changed."

"Maybe you made me change." He thrust his face closer to the peephole. "If I'm ever crazy enough to get married again, I'll find somebody who's aggressive and loud and a workaholic and who's always on the phone." He wiped an arm across his brow. "You're not afraid of phones. You're afraid of life. You'll have to cut yourself off from everything to be happy."

"Go away."

"Cheryl—"

"Go away."

He turned around and left.

Nick did not give up right away. For two months he drove up every weekend to shout at her through the door. Because she knew he would come on weekends, when there were fewer demands on his time, she was prepared for him. Sometimes she came to the door to listen, although she never opened it. Sometimes she stayed upstairs and pretended she was not home.

At the beginning of autumn he arrived with an older man, who turned out to be another lawyer. Cheryl let them inside. Nick was ready for a formal separation, with the divorce to be final in a year. She would have her house, the money her parents had left her, the furniture and books they had taken from this house shipped back to her, and a cash settlement from Nick because he wanted to be fair. There was no point in contesting the terms. Nick was being more than generous, and for her to fight a long legal battle would inevitably require telephone calls.

Nick looked miserable when he left with his attorney.

Ringer

Cheryl did not know why. They had solved everything in a civilized, reasonable way, and he would get over her in time.

Her life was hers once more, Cheryl thought as she went upstairs to her bedroom. She had left the phone in the living room disconnected. She would no longer be plagued by the demands of others, by the need to make herself understood to them, by calls from the outside world. How odd it was that she couldn't feel happier about that. She had what she wanted; why did she still feel vaguely uneasy and afraid?

She went to bed early and fell into a dream. She was standing in an empty room with walls of glass. Through the walls she saw people pressing against the glass, calling out to her soundlessly. She knew what they were saying; they wanted her to come out. Nick was there, and his mother, and several of her college classmates. They wanted her to join them, to throw herself into the messy, painful, disorderly, unpredictable, and upsetting business they called life. She shrank back, afraid they might shatter the walls and drag her outside.

Cheryl woke up the next morning feeling drained, as though she had not slept at all, and glanced at the clock on her nightstand; it was nearly noon. Then she heard the sound, one she had never expected to hear again.

Two telephones were ringing in unison. One chirped at her; the other had the loud, jarring ring she remembered from her childhood. She could almost believe that the phones were right there in her room.

She quickly got out of bed. The telephones stopped ringing, then started up again.

Cheryl ran downstairs, then clambered down the steps to the basement. The black telephone in the recreation room still sat on a table in the corner. She had never had it reconnected; it could not be ringing. Yet the ringing went on, the chirping near her right ear, the more grating bell near her left.

The ringing stopped, then began again.

Chirp. Ring. Chirp. Ring. Chirp. Ring. Chirp. Ring.
Silence.
Chirp. Chirp. Chirp.
Silence.

Ring. Ring. Ring. Ring.

Cheryl found herself kneeling on the floor, hands over her ears.

Ring. Ring. Ring.

Chirp. Chirp. Chirp. Chirp.

The phones would never stop ringing, she realized, because they were inside her now, and they would never stop.

Ring, Ring, Ring.

Chirp, Chirp, Chirrrrrp . . .

THE MYSTERIES OF PARIS

Douglas Clegg

1

WE BECOME WHAT WE ARE MOST AFRAID OF, IT'S TRUE. I DON'T need to tell you the stories about the man terrified of fire who becomes a fireman, or the woman terrified of aging who grows old; neither do you really need to hear about the boy afraid of going bald, who, of course, grows up to lose his hair. Fear is often the crossing signal, the flashing light, before the train of inevitability; but fear is Cassandra, and she heralds what will be, and still we try to look the other way and pretend it will not come to pass.

But sometimes the lights are out and we cross the tracks unheeding.

Let me tell you about a town called Paris, not in France or Texas or in its dozen other namesakes with which you might be familiar, but Paris, Arizona, not far across the Colorado River from California. In fact, if you lived in this Paris, you might cross the state line just to get a decent Big Mac at McDonalds, or if you came through late one night, you might need to turn around just to get diesel if you owned an old shitkicker '83 Mercedes, which you bought for five hundred dollars not six months ago, from a mule skinner on his way to Mexico.

You learn all this when you stop for gas in Paris, and you find there is no diesel, and you are just about on empty.

But best of all, you learn the secret of fear.

2

"We been out of diesel for a week now, won't get filled up till maybe Monday afternoon. I tell you, there's a diesel place back in Blythe—maybe second, third stop back over the California line," the boy said—he was about seventeen, and heavily into the black leather look, which always made the man think of nerds he had known in high school, those who wore clothes to up their images. The boy looked at the dent on the front of the Mercedes in the fluorescent light by the pumps. He walked around the car. "Bad accident, mister?"

The man shrugged, craning his neck farther out the window. "Before I bought it. I got it cheap from this old desert rat who had to move to Mexico."

"What's cheap?" The boy asked.

"Five hundred."

"No shit? I don't believe you—no shit?" The boy blinked, and dug his hands into the pockets of his leather jacket. "Jesus, what I'da given for this. Four, five thousand, end of story. That's if I had it to *give*."

"Yeah, but the problem is, it's diesel. Hard to find these days, especially out here."

"Blythe's only twenty miles back."

The man shook his head. "It's on empty. I don't want to get stuck between here and there. Don't like dark roads. Makes me think of psychos and serial killers."

The boy half smiled and said, "This is one of their highways, apparently."

The man blinked. "What do you mean?"

"Well, you know, for some reason every damn serial killer seems to come through here at one time or another. Seems that way to me, anyway. I know this cop, and he helped catch one of 'em, not ten miles t'other side of town. Said the man had a woman helpin' him murder too, just like looking two rattlesnakes in the eyes, this cop said." The boy's mouth dropped from a grin into a straight line. "I don't like working graveyard because of it. This town's so dead, sometimes I think, when I walk home, that somebody's come right off the highway, someone like you, mister, even, and he's killed everybody in town, and I'll go home and my folks'll be dead too, and then I can't call nobody for help."

"Jesus," the man said.

The boy brightened again, giggling. "And then I think, Chad, you dick, you got the most active imagination and no serial killer'd even bother to stop in your sorry-ass gas station. . . . Look, I can give you a lift, mister. I get off shift at midnight. Cooter—he's graveyard—he sometimes comes in late, but no more'n half an hour. Look, I can give you a ride to Blythe, be back here fast, you got your gas, and I don't get my ass fried. End of story."

"I don't want to put you out. Really. That's a lot of trouble."

"It's either that," the boy said, "or you stay up with Cooter all night and drink coffee and wait for the three-fifteen bus from El Paso to come through for a fill-up and give the riders a place to pee."

"Well, to be honest, I think it might be a better idea if I just go get a room at the local Motel 6. In the morning I can either call Triple A or try and make it back to Blythe. I have this thing about night."

"The dark?" The boy leaned forward, placing his hands against the car door. He drummed his fingers on the metal.

"Not particularly, just night. Like you said, anyone can come off this highway. I heard a whole family got killed by a hitcher near Indio. And it was someone they knew. I just don't like thinking about it. It's always at night, those things. If I'm going to get stuck somewhere without gas, I'd prefer it be in broad daylight."

The boy added a bit of Arizona wisdom, "That's true everywhere else but here, mister. Here you don't want to get caught in the sun at noon, believe you me. This is the deadest place on the planet."

"I guess I'm just tired," the man said, not wanting to tell the real reason that he didn't want to ride with the boy. "I need a good night's sleep. I can figure the headache of diesel out in the morning."

The boy chuckled at the turn of phrase. "Headache of diesel, ain't it the truth. Oh. Yeah. That's a good idea. I mean, if you don't want a lift," the boy said, and pointed his thumb at the tow truck that was parked behind him. "We got a company truck and all, though, filled with gas, we can be in Blythe before twelve-thirty, and back before one. You could just keep on driving. I'd do it."

"Well," the man said, "thanks anyway. Can you point me in the direction of the nearest motel?"

The boy grinned. He was innocent in a way that the man had not experienced since maybe 1962, and this was '95, January seventh, and teenage boys of his age were supposed to be sullen and rude and helpless. But not this one; the man accounted for it by the small town. Paris, Arizona, and the sign had read (unless he imagined things) Population 65. Someone had crossed it out with bullet holes, a sign on the highway that was used for target practice. Population 65. Sixty-five people, living in a town with a single all-night gas station, a town of what appeared to be a smattering of one-story two-bedroom houses, vintage World War Two, with flat roofs and barracklike precision to the arrangement of the downtown area—the man had had to go through Main Street, all of three blocks, to get to the light of the gas station. And then this boy, like a beacon of innocence. The boy had squinty eyes and lots of dark hair, falling neatly on either side of his forehead. The man had always lived in cities, big cities like Los Angeles and New York, and found it refreshing on these occasional jaunts to find youth that seemed to harken back to his own green days, unaware of urban problems and of the difficulties of modern life. This boy looked as if his furthest horizon was Blythe to the west, maybe Phoenix to the east, and to the south and north, just the river as it snaked along. He probably had a nice nerdy girlfriend who was going to get pregnant before the winter was over, and he probably was going to pump gas for the rest of his life.

Not a bad existence, all things considered, the man thought.

The boy said, "We don't exactly have a Motel 6 or nothin',

but there's the Miller's Motor Coach Inn two miles up, just when you're leavin' town. It's usually pretty vacant because we don't get a lot of snowbirds comin' through, not the way towns right on the river do. I think it's about twenty bucks a night." He leaned into the window, close enough for the man to smell his breath, which was sweet, like he'd been chewing on orange blossoms all night. "I take my girl over there now and then. It ain't the best place, mister, but it does the job."

"Great, sounds good," the man said, and started his engine up again.

The boy in black leather stood away from the blue Mercedes and leaned against one of the pumps. He grinned again. "You see the lady who runs that place, you tell her Phil's boy sent you."

"Will do," the man said.

As he drove out of the gas station, he glanced in his rearview mirror, and noticed that the boy just stood there, watching him go, leaning against the pumps.

It was a circuitous route to get back on the highway, but he finally did, and saw the green sputtering neon of Miller's Motor Coach Inn—the sign was lit to read MILLE MOT R OACH IN. There was a buzzing yellow neon sign that read *Vacancy* out front, although he would've been more surprised if the place was full. The man wondered what he was getting into, but hoped it was a nice firm bed and maybe seven hours' sleep before he'd have to deal with all that called to him the following day. He parked near the small front office. The lights were down inside, but he got out of the car and went up and rang the bell by the door.

RING BELL FOR NIGHT MANAGER, the sign read. In fact, he noticed a sign plastered everywhere inside the dimly lit little office. He rang the bell twice more, but no one came. There were three cars in the parking lot, over near the rooms, so he knew that the place was operational.

Then the man got the strangest feeling. It was a feeling of being watched, not just by one person, but by several. The hairs on the back of his neck stood up, or it felt like they had. He glanced around the motel, and then down the dark street, lit with feeble lamps for only a few yards beyond the motel.

Headlights from the highway as several trucks passed by.

No one came to the office door, and he was about to go back to his car when the phone in the office began ringing. It was a bell-ringer, the kind of phone that the man missed, the kind that made a rather nice sound rather than the computerized electronic annoyances that phones emitted elsewhere.

So, he thought, someone will come to answer the phone.

He noticed a coffee mug and a half-eaten doughnut on the counter, and a ball of yarn sitting next to the phone.

The boy's words haunted him. *Somebody's come right off the highway, someone like you, mister, even, and he's killed everybody in town.*

The phone rang twelve times before it stopped.

The man had already gotten into his car. He was feeling uncomfortable, and he wasn't sure why. The place was so dead, he told himself, that was the problem. He had always liked cities, because there were always lights and people around, someplace, even if it was the train station, which was always open. Not that he ever ventured down to Union Station in Los Angeles at four in the morning, but just the thought had been a comfort to him. The thought that there was life and light. He swallowed. *Don't think about it.* Where to go next? His choices were to either drive back to Blythe, hoping that his gas tank would hold out, or sleep in the car.

Or go find that kid and get him to drive you to Blythe and back.

On a lark, he switched on the light in the Mercedes and drew the Triple A *Guide to Arizona* (from 1984) out of the glove compartment. He flipped pages to try to find Paris, and when he did, all it said was:

Paris, Arizona. Pop. 71

So, six smart people got the hell out of here.

He turned on the radio; nothing but static. Turned it off again—static and country music, all the way from Indio, and now just the idiot airwaves of confusion. *Like me.* Something about the static made him sweat a little. Keep it down, keep it down, he thought. Now, the man, if he could, would've kicked himself right smack in the butt. He owned another car, a good old Honda Prelude, but he had put it in the shop for repairs, and then, when this conference came up in Phoenix, he had thought: What the hell, take the Mercedes, even with the dent in it, it'll be a novelty for all those old farts with their spanking new Beamers and Porsches. Don't call the shop to get the Prelude back early, just drive the diesel, you moron.

 **3**

It took him ten minutes to get back to the gas station—he stopped every street or so in order to curse his sorry fate, and to calm down. The town was empty, the lights off in stores, even most of the streetlights were off. A few stores had GOING OUT OF BUSINESS signs up in their windows; others were too dark to see into. It was Thursday night, just about midnight, and this was a place where even the kids didn't run wild. Good lord, deliver me from small towns, the man thought.

The boy was sitting on a chair in front of the gas station office. He was leaning his head back, drinking a bottle of Yoo-Hoo. He looked up when the Mercedes pulled up and parked. He shook his head, smiling, and set the bottle down. He jogged over to the car just as the man got out, stretching his legs, yawning.

"Don't tell me that place was full-up," the boy said.

"No. Just nobody came to the door."

"That's weird," the boy said, "the woman who runs it, she don't sleep much, she's a what you call . . ."

"Insomniac."

"Thank you, and she usually is right up front where you can see her, knitting. Ain't that weird? I mean, it's been so silent tonight all over town too, now I think of it. She wasn't out front knitting? Weird."

The man remembered the yarn by the phone. "She was probably in the bathroom or something."

"How long you wait?"

"Ten minutes. But I rang the bell the whole time, and then the phone rang and nobody answered it."

"Ain't that strange, I was just, earlier tonight, talking to her, when . . ." The boy seemed briefly lost in thought, and then thrust his hand out. "Name's Chad Partridge, never introduced myself, my mama'd say where'd your manners go, young man, and I'da told her, after midnight, they always seem to go into hiding."

The man said, "Hello, Chad, I'm Bill."

"You got a last name, don't you?"

The man laughed. "Yes, I do. Mudd. People make fun of it, though, so I'm loath to admit to it."

The boy said, "That's a nice one. I sorta collect names, you know, when I'm workin' late, like I could tell you the name of everyone in Paris, backward, forward, I got that kind of mind, even though I ain't too smart in other ways. We got a woman named Hogg livin' here, and the great part is her first name and middle initials, Sue E. Pretty good, huh? And my uncle Jack, his last name's Coffman, and if you put those together, you got a pretty dirty joke, you was to ask me."

Bill Mudd laughed good-naturedly. "Amazing. Listen, is your friend—what was his name?"

The boy's expression changed. It almost looked like he was blushing.

"Cooter?"

"Oh," the boy sighed, "lordy, I didn't know what you meant for a sec, *Cooter,* he ain't been in yet, and it's"—the boy held his arm out in front of him and glanced at his wristwatch—"twelve-fifteen. Let me go call him, Bill, wait just a sec."

Bill went over to use the rest room while Chad went to make his call. The rest room was clean, and after using the urinal, Bill went to wash his hands and then his face at the sink. The soap powder smelled like Ajax, but it was nice to get some of the road stink off of his skin. He looked at his face in the mirror. *You stupid idiot, what the hell are you scared of? A nerd in black leather, a town on the edge of a vast nothing? Of all people, what the hell are you scared of?*

But he knew what he was scared of, it was a fear he'd had since as far back as he could remember. Totally irrational, but something that he'd had since he'd seen a *Time* magazine when he'd been seven, and in it a man had gone on a killing rampage. They'd showed the dead woman, one of the six, in *Time*. And then, growing up, how many others had he seen? Movies, too, that were totally unreal, and then he had been at a party and someone had mentioned another bout of . . .

He just didn't like naming it.

Unlike Chad, who could apparently name everything he'd ever come in contact with. (Like a collector, that boy was, only he collected the labels, and not what was behind them.)

He couldn't name it, and he knew everything there was to be studied about fears. Bill Mudd was no psychoanalyst, but he had spent his spare time reading every book, every article, he could get his hands on, about specific phobias, only he never found his, never precisely found the word that captured the fear he held inside, held on to tightly and could not deny.

He could put it in a phrase, of course:

It was a fear that someone near him was a psycho killer.

(He knew how inelegant and stupid that phrase sounded, but it was the best he could do.)

If they were in institutions, like Darden State, in L.A. County, it bothered him less, because then he knew. He *knew* they were psychos. He didn't need to second-guess someone on the psych ward. They had their labels.

But people on the outside . . . they were different. You couldn't always know. They could look just like a kid at a gas station who wanted to take you for a ride to get gas.

But what if a psycho killer, a serial killer in the making, looked just like anybody? Any ordinary person?

This was not precisely paranoia, but a close cousin.

It was a persistent fear for him, not a heightened awareness, but something that attacked him only in its most extreme incarnations. In Los Angeles he could read the newspapers and watch television—in fact, keep it on at his home 'round the clock—because he wanted to cure himself by glutting his life with information. What they looked like, their foreheads, their eyes, the way they walked, haircuts, clothes, everything . . . Bill wasn't stupid. (He could tell himself this a thousand times, but when he ended up in Paris, Arizona, at midnight with no gas and an empty motel, he didn't believe it.) Bill Mudd could spend days without the fear presenting itself directly to him, although it was there at the periphery of his existence, hovering, all the time.

Whenever he met a stranger, it was there.

He looked at the face in the mirror, drops of water under the eyes.

A knock at the rest room door.

"Bill? Mr. Mudd?" It was Chad.

"It's open," Bill said.

Chad opened the door and gave a nervous grin. "I don't like this john much. Makes me all weird."

"Oh?"

"A guy tried to get me in here once. You know. The way they like to do, those people."

"Oh." Bill didn't bother pursuing this further.

"Well, Cooter's not answering his phone, so I'm just gonna shut the station up for a while, and you and me, we can trot on over to Blythe and get back before he gets his sorry ass in here."

"Apparently, nobody's answering phones tonight," Bill said, drying his hands with a paper towel.

Chad brightened, clapping his hand together. "Not true, Bill, I called my girl, Betsy, and she picked up on the first ring so's her mother don't wake up. Let's go, hoss."

Something in the boy's manner made the man think that he could not refuse this offer.

4

Chad passed him a cup of coffee when he got in on the passenger's side of the tow truck. "It's on the house, a Little Debbie oatmeal cookie, if you want one. It's got cream filling, Bill, you might not want to pass on it." Chad held the large cookie in its wrapper up near Bill's face. "I love these things. Don't you love Little Debbie? With her little hat and her little smile. And then, you get to eat her cookie."

Bill took the coffee, sipped it, grimaced because of its bitterness, but drank some more.

Chad unwrapped the cookie before he started the truck. "Cooter's father owns the station, so Cooter gets away with murder sometimes, being late and all. He's the kind of guy who wipes his ass with a whole roll of teepee and then expects you to run get another roll for him. A practical joker, that dude is, always trying to put something over on someone. His name's actually Coolidge, his middle name, but he's been called Cooter since we was kids."

"You grow up here?"

The boy nodded. "All my life. All my life with everybody watching your every move and thinking whatever they like. You musta heard of Paris before? No? Hell, Mrs. Paladino, she ended up on Sally Jessy Raphael one time, using the name Crystal—which is funny since if you knew her, it's her little girl's name—she was on TV 'cause she was always terrified of things. Even Cooter used to scare the hell out of her."

"She's not scared of things now?" He was trying to make some polite conversation, but everything the boy said just made him sweat.

Chad shook his head. "Don't think so." He was silent for a moment, as he turned the truck out onto the narrow road that led to the highway. Houses were dark along the street. "She was a celebrity for nearly a month after she come back. I never want to be on TV, though, I mean, too many fags on TV, you ask me. That guy, what's his name, the guy on the show with the Mustang . . ." He mentioned the name of an actor, but not just his stage name, also his real name. "He's a fag, I think, at least he looks like one."

"What does one look like?"

"Oh, I can't describe it, but I know one when I see one. We're gonna take a little shortcut, Bill, is that okay?" Chad didn't wait for an answer, but steered the truck to the right at a railroad crossing, right up onto the tracks. He started laughing as the truck bounced along the tracks.

"Is this wise?" Bill asked, the last of his coffee spilling down the front of his shirt.

"Oh, I don't know 'bout wise, Mr. Mudd, but it's the best way to get you to pee in your pants—just joking, just joking, come on, how often do you get to see the desert from here?" Chad nodded his head at the passing scenery. "Look at it, it goes on forever."

"I can't see a thing," Bill said, his jaw tense, his voice

jittery from the bouncing of the truck as much as from nerves.

Chad laughed even harder. "Okay, okay, fun's over," and he spun the steering wheel to the left to get off the tracks.

The truck stalled.

Chad pressed his foot on the accelerator.

Bill was getting just a touch frightened by this, although he saw by looking up and down the tracks that no train was coming from either direction.

"Shit, Cooter told me this was gonna happen one day," Chad said, and beat his fist against the horn as if the noise would free the truck. "Looks like we got to get out and see what's the holdup."

The man and the boy spent the better part of an hour trying to get the tow truck off the tracks. Bill had to do most of the pushing, and Chad had a crowbar he was using to try and get the tire up from where it was caught, but nothing seemed to go. There was no flashlight in the truck, and only one headlight was working; it illuminated only the vast expanse of desert. Bill Mudd wasn't even sure in what direction the highway lay. Chad did a bad imitation of Stan Laurel. "This is a fine mess, you've gotten us into, Ollie."

Bill would've cursed and kicked the truck, but he knew it was futile, and he was starting to feel strange again too, something about Chad he didn't like, beyond the boy's foolishness at driving up the tracks. Something about the way he was acting, like this was planned, getting stuck on the tracks. Bill kept a false smile on his face and pretended the shivering was from the cold.

"It does drop at night, don't it?" Chad zipped his leather jacket up. "It can be hot as a griddle at noon, but come midnight, and you got yourself an icehouse."

"You're too young to know about icehouses," Bill said.

Chad face was in darkness. "We used to have one in Paris. It was kind of a train stop, this town was. Had a nice beer place, and a Harvey House. Or something like it. The old icehouse is just a pit now. My granddaddy, he used to deliver ice. He was a nasty man, though, used to whip me but good when I just was doing nothing wrong, mind you, just what boys do." He clapped his hands together. "But he's dead and rotting now, he is, end of story. Now, what say we walk back down the tracks—they'll take us into town and we'll get there fast if we hustle."

"Aren't you worried about the truck? I mean, what if the train comes?"

Chad giggled and came over to Bill, almost leaning into him. Again Bill smelled that orange blossom breath, only now it had a tinge of beer in it. *He must've had a beer when I went to check out the motel.* Chad whispered, "There ain't been a train through here since maybe 1962, which was a long time before I appeared in this one horse-dick town."

Bill stepped back. There was more than one beer in that breath; he was amazed he hadn't noticed it before. *Great, stuck in bumfuck with a drunk kid.* "I thought you said you were born here," Bill said.

"That's right, sir, my first appearance: birth. Son of Lolita Jane Hamer and Phillip Arthur Partridge, April first, 1977. An April Fool. Now, let's go, if we walk fast we can get to Cooter's place in fifteen minutes, twenty tops, and get his car so you can get your diesel."

5

"That's weird," Chad said, leaping off the porch and back onto the sidewalk where Bill stood. "Cooter's not answering. His old man neither."

"Maybe you need to knock harder," Bill said.

Chad, whose face was clearly distinguishable in the porch light, looked a little ticked off. "Maybe I need to FUCKING BLOW THE DOOR DOWN, BILL!"

Bill said nothing. The boy would calm down. He'd had a few beers and was probably all wound up worrying about his boss's tow truck. He was excitable, seventeen, wanted to go see his girlfriend. Didn't plan on spending Thursday night with some passerby who needed diesel.

The boy began stomping around the yard, reaching up and knocking his fists into his forehead. "That fucker Cooter, he's probably over in Blythe right now, with his suck-ass old man, doing inmates at Chuckawalla prison, that's where they are, damn it."

Bill began to walk up the street. If he walked fast, the boy might not notice him, and he might make it to the gas station within twenty minutes. He could take his Mercedes and get out of Paris, and head toward Blythe and maybe sleep on the side of the road if he made it at least ten miles out of this town, at least ten miles away from this kid. He was halfway up the block when he heard Chad shout, "WHERE THE HELL DID YOU GO, BILL?"

6

All right, he could admit to himself, it was an irrational fear, but that was the great thing about phobias, you knew you were overreacting, you knew your anxiety was more than a bit excessive. But that boy was really making him nervous, shouting like that so late at night, in such a small town, you'd think even the dogs would've been up and barking, but no such luck. The place was so quiet, and the boy's voice seemed to echo throughout the universe, that he wished *somebody* would open their window or go to the bathroom so there'd even be a flush, even the tiniest flush somewhere. He thought he heard the sound of footsteps, but he knew they were Chad's, and he really didn't want to deal with that kid anymore—he was bad news, and worse, he reminded Bill of some of the patients he worked with back at Darden State. He had been a psych tech for ten years, and the boy reminded him of what some of the patients must've been like when they'd been teenagers, before they'd killed their first human. A lot of the patients were doped up at Darden, but the newer ones, they were usually just like Chad, kind of stupid and bright at the same time, kind of sane too, the way they talked about how their wives and kids kept talking to them even after they'd chopped their heads off.

Bill Mudd vowed to do anything he could not to run into Chad again.

He walked a zigzag route through the narrow streets, hoping he was heading in the general direction of the gas station. The houses were flat-roofed and small, and the only trees in the town were tall palms, so it was not hard to find out where Main Street lay. The highway was to his right about two miles, so he knew that if he just kept heading east, he'd make it to his car. If the boy was still knocking on Cooter's door for another ten minutes before giving up, maybe he wouldn't even go back to the gas station yet.

You may even be wrong, Bill, he may not even be one of them, he may be an ordinary, high-spirited boy.

But something in Chad's grin had bothered him.

One window of one house had a light on, and just for the comfort of it, Bill walked by that house. He peered in the window, for it was facing the sidewalk, and what he saw made him stop.

On the other side of the window was a beautifully preserved Formica and chrome early sixties kitchen, in sparkling condition.

And there, on the kitchen table, a complete meal set out as if a family had, earlier, been sitting down about to have dinner. He checked each plate: it looked like ravioli, and some kale, and maybe apple sauce on the side. Two glasses of milk, an open beer can, and a can of Coke. Bill looked above the table, to the wall clock: 2 A.M.

Who would have their dinner this late? Two glasses of milk. Flies were wandering the edges of the plates. A Barbie doll next to one of the plates—a little girl's.

Flashing through his mind the images of: a little girl on the stairs, her face beaten in; a woman just beneath the window, inside, cut open from neck to stomach; a boy and his father, in the living room, still bleeding to death.

Chad's words in his head: *This town's so dead, sometimes I think, when I walk home, that somebody's come right off the highway, someone like you, mister, even, and he's killed everybody in town, and I'll go home and my folks'll be dead too, and then I can't call nobody for help.*

Bill tried to peer into the hallway, but it was dark.

And then someone touched his shoulder.

He turned and froze as Chad stood there with a flashlight turned on full blast into his face.

"Looky what I found," Chad said. "God, Bill, can you believe it? Just what we needed—it was in the work shed out behind Cooter's place—but why the hell'd you take off like that?"

Chad flicked the flashlight on and off, on and off, and then drew light-streak circles against the sidewalk.

"I just wanted to get to my car," Bill said. "I thought I'd get it and come get you and then we could maybe get help for the truck."

"No you didn't," Chad said, flicking the light off. The two stood in the light from the kitchen window. "You wanted to get in your car and drive out of here, because you're scared of me. End of story."

Bill said nothing.

He stared at the boy.

Chad stepped closer and tapped him on the chest with the flashlight. "Don't you be scared of me, I ain't gonna hurt you, not like I did that geezer in the john who kept wanting to . . . well, you know."

And then, looking over Bill's shoulder, at the kitchen window, Chad said, "Oh, my God."

Bill didn't glance back. He didn't want to take his eyes off Chad. He was trying to figure out a way that he could stop this boy from doing any harm to him. The flashlight seemed like a weapon now, as the boy tapped him a bit harder on the chest, and maybe it was only Bill's imagination, but it seemed like the boy was beginning to smell bad, like his body chemistry was changing.

Chad said, "The Bradshaws left their supper out. Ain't that weird? Jesus to Christ, ain't that like something out of *Twilight Zone,* Bill?"

While Chad was preoccupied with the window, Bill took the opportunity to grab the flashlight and hit the boy hard on the head; the boy reeled back for a second, and then came at him; Bill hit him with the flashlight in the forehead as hard as he could; the boy still kept coming, and pushed Bill down to the ground; Bill kept thrashing at the boy, and finally took his own fist and socked the boy in the jaw as hard as he could, and the boy slumped down on the sidewalk. Hit him one more time for good measure.

But he'd be up in just seconds.

Bill got up and just started running.

Funny thing was, what he was noticing as he was running was not his fear, or the houses passing by, or even that his feet ached because he was running in his street shoes, but what he noticed were the stars—on the desert, they were like optical illusions, there and not there at the same time, pinholes in the fabric of night. He thought he was going to die there, in that town, and his last memory would be nothing other than a starry night.

But he made it to his Mercedes.

And, even though he fumbled with his keys, he got the door unlocked and started the engine, and drove the hell out of Paris, Arizona.

7

The car came to a shuddering, shaking stop about seven miles on the road back to Blythe, and he managed to get it to the shoulder of the highway. He flicked the hazard lights on. Always kept a bottle of aspirin in the glove compartment. He retrieved it, opened it, and popped three in his mouth, swallowing them dry. It was 2:25 in the morning. Trucks went past him, blowing their horns, but none stopped. He locked the doors. Thought he'd get out and try to thumb down a truck, but what if it was another Chad behind the wheel? Who could be sure? What idiot would hitchhike at two in the morning anyway?

Bill tried not to, but fell asleep within an hour, and only awoke when someone was tapping on his window.

He awoke, sweating.

It was a highway patrolman.

Bill rolled down his window. "Officer?"

Morning hit him like the blast of a horn. He must've slept several hours. His clothes were soaked; his head ached.

"Are you all right, mister?" the policeman said. "Need some help?"

Bill coughed, and nodded. "I ran out of gas. Couldn't find any diesel."

"Paris is only five minutes down the road. They got one diesel pump. I'll give you a lift."

"No," Bill said, "I was there. I stopped there. The diesel pump was out of order."

"Mister, I don't know where you were, but I live in Paris, and I know for a fact that they got diesel because my son

159

works in the gas station, and my wife's family owns the place."

Bill looked at the policeman's eyes and noticed a resemblance. "He said it was empty."

"Cooter said that?"

"I didn't . . . meet Cooter. I met Chad."

The policeman shook his head, laughing. "Oh, mister, that boy of mine, Cooter *is* Chad. My boy been pulling your leg? I get after him about that all the time, and he still spends his time pulling folks' legs, boys will be boys, huh, mister. You got to forgive the boy, mister, there's only four families living in the whole town. He gets bored, I guess."

Bill remembered the sign: population 65. "But, I thought . . . I mean, all those houses."

"Oh, I know, all set to be condemned, we're gonna have to move back to Quartzite or someplace with a little more life to it. It was the work, it all dried up in the area—we used to have a lot of date farming, but it went a while back. The stores just went one after another. It's been the gas station and the motel that's kept us there. Oh, gosh, mister, he didn't do the thing where he sets a table to look like the Bradshaws still live in their—oh, no, I'm so sorry, mister, sometimes I think he belongs in Juvy. My wife got a shock when she tried that one on him, but he got a bigger one later on that night when he was grounded for three weeks. I will tan his hide, mark my words."

Bill was stuttering over thoughts and words. "I went there . . . to the motel. There was no one around."

"Well, last night, mister, my wife's sister, she had her baby over in Blythe, and we packed up and went over—Cooter had to watch the gas station, 'cause some of the truckers, you know, depend on us. So, can I give you a lift back to get gas? I'm sure Cooter owes you some kind of apology. I know, I know, in some places they'd strangle that kid, and in others, well, he'd be making millions coming up with commercials, or making movies or something. Hope no major damage is done? His ass is gonna be grass, you can count on that. Damn, but we were all boys once, huh. Jesus, what else is a boy supposed to do all by himself in a town like this? Didn't see him when I got back today, but it's only seven—he won't be off shift till nine. What say?"

The man named Bill Mudd sat there for a minute, staring at the highway patrolman, and wondered if he was still asleep.

Then he went with the policeman in his car back down the road about six miles.

8

It didn't surprise Bill Mudd when they returned to the gas station and Chad, also known as Cooter, was not there. Bill noticed that the diesel pump, indeed, did not have an out of order note on it. Cooter's father, whose name really was Phil, got a spare gas can and filled it with diesel, "on the house, and you come on back and I'll make sure my boy fills up your whole tank. If you hang on a sec, I'll just go in and use the phone and see if Cooter's up at his mama's."

The policeman took a set of keys out of his pocket and walked toward the glassed-in office.

Bill knew that Cooter was dead, lying on the sidewalk outside the Bradshaw's place where the boy had played a practical joke.

So, Bill thought, this is how my friends back in the hospital for the criminally insane start. It's just like they say, it's all an accident, you didn't mean to do it, not the first one, and then you do the second one because you need to make sure he doesn't find out about the first one. And then it just snowballs.

He looked at the patrol car, with the keys in the ignition.

The policeman with his hand on the phone.

What was the smartest thing?

He could just pretend he'd last seen the boy at midnight, at the gas station.

But there would be fingerprints on the flashlight.

Maybe he could just steal the policeman's car, and figure something out later.

But the policeman was on the phone. He might tell his wife to get someone else out on the highway to stop him, Bill thought.

The Big Question, the million dollar one, was how do you kill a policeman who has a gun on him?

Think, Bill, think.

And then he looked at the police car, with the engine running, the keys in the ignition, just waiting for him. The policeman would come out, not see him behind the wheel at first, and he would gun it.

And pray that the car would smash into Cooter's father before he could draw his gun.

End of story.

9

And so, you manage to drive out of Paris, finally, changing cars on the railroad track—Cooter was lying about that too, because the tow truck was not stuck. That boy had just tricked you so he could play his bizarre little game. You don't think too much about being tricked, neither do you think about your conference in Phoenix, because that's where everybody's going to think you're going. Instead, you head back to California, maybe you'll hide out in the hills, the Big Bear area. California seems to draw you back, as it does your brothers and sisters.

And you know the best part?

You're not afraid of them anymore, the psychos of the world or the games of life, because you know what the secret is, you've crossed the tracks of fate.

And you embrace the fears of this world with joy and gladness.

EYES HAVE IT

Dana Edwin Isaacson

THE HUBMANNS LIVED IN A GOVERNMENT-SUBSIDIZED TRACT house on the swampy end of the neighborhood. Mr. Hubmann was long gone and Ann Hubmann was frequently absent. Her days were spent as a junior high school science teacher, her nights at the Crystal Corner Lounge, third bar stool from the much-used Charlie's Angels pinball machine. Ann Hubmann's four children spent their days and nights relatively free from parental directive. They ate junk food and threw the wrappers on the wall-to-wall, where they would eventually be gnawed up by one of the many cats.

The Hubmann family were Ruby Kolpeck and Lars Tripp's favorite spying subject, their house one of the adolescent spies' most frequently visited sites. The four dirty Hubmann children, left to their own devices, made for eventful observations. They had séances, smoked their mother's Eve cigarettes, and had dramatic fistfights among themselves.

The neighborhood had the weak new trees found in any suburban development recently carved from a farm field. The houses were generally one-story, the driveways gravel. There were two basic designs, the difference being on which side of the front door the garage was placed. The house

163

where Lars and his mother lived was the exception. They lived in the farm's original house at the entrance to the neighborhood. It was a sturdy brick affair with three floors. There were real trees in Lars's yard, and tall bushes lining the fence, which hid the neighbors from Lars's mother's sensitive eyes.

Ruby lived with her parents and sister in yet another of the many aluminum-sided houses. Her house was a replica of the Hubmanns', although hers was on a slight hill, while the Hubmanns' plot was rather sunken and sodden. Her home was noisy. The empty, dusty mansion Lars shared with only his mother was eerily quiet. She wished they held their meetings at her place. She preferred its rowdier ambience. But Lars had set up their workshop in his basement. It had a separate entrance and exit through the cellar door, and at his house they could better observe the comings and goings on the road into the neighborhood. It made for more scientific reports, Lars argued, and she acquiesced.

Ann Hubmann was watched during the day. She was Ruby and Lars's biology teacher, and they relished the fact that they could analyze another of the family member's behavior in a different milieu. While both young spies had contempt for the Hubmann children, Ruby secretly pitied Mother Ann. The woman's yellowed fingers were testament to her nicotine habit. Her limp—also yellow—hair, cut in an unfashionable shag, needed a serious oil treatment. During her nonsmoking classroom hours, Ann continually popped tictacs. After checking a psychological reference book, Lars had determined that Ann Hubmann had an "addiction personality." As if we didn't know that already, thought Ruby. Ann's skin was a bit flaky. Ruby considered an anonymous gift of moisturizer.

Not that Ruby was a gentler soul than Lars. Although fully a foot shorter than Lars's ungainly six feet one, she was a willful, brittle little cookie. And few in the neighborhood would consider the pairs' spying activities harmless child's play. Both thirteen years old, they were too old to be sneaking about as they did. Both slightly bitter outcasts, they were forced by their outsider status into a covert netherworld of observation and analysis. Each read voraciously. They once had a nearly violent clash over George Orwell's *Down and out in Paris and London,* which Ruby disliked. Still, both found criminality appealing, and they would have been drug addicts had there been any opportunity or access to do so in their suburban world. Instead they searched out and devoured biographies of drug-addicted criminals and rock stars.

Getting into the Hubmann house was made both easier and more difficult by the many cats. At the back of the house was a high basement window, set in a well below the level of the ground. And set in the window was a cat flap allowing the cats to freely come and go. With Lars's long arms, he could reach in this flap and unlock the window. He was frequently scratched by one cat or another when doing this. Then Ruby and Lars could climb down to the cement basement through the window, oftentimes stepping on a yowling cat. This went unnoticed upstairs—the cats were always making a ruckus. They were wild.

It was because of the cat flap that there were so many cats, and it was because of the cat flap they were wild. Frequently perched threateningly atop the furnace was a fat calico tabby Lars called the Matriarch. Some time ago she was, Lars posited, the original Hubmann pet, who had ventured back through the cat-flap pregnant. She bore her kittens in the basement, where Hubmann children daily left bowls of milk and cat food. The kittens matured untouched by human hands. They became untouchable, uncatchable, gone in the flash of a lightbulb. These kittens then bore more kittens, some incestuously. The amount of food and milk was increased. The menagerie grew. Across the basement Lars and Ruby would move slowly, stealthily, carefully as through a roving mine field. They tried not to rouse or disturb the cats into noise or movement. And to avoid as many scratches as possible, they wore pants on these spying missions.

Lars crawled through the scrawny front-yard bushes and peeked through the living room's large window. All four children—slatternly Dawn at fourteen; bucktoothed Jim, twelve; plain eleven-year-old Colleen; and anemic Ginger, also bucktoothed at seven—were watching television. Lars recorded their seating arrangement in his notebook. He nearly yelped at a tug at his sweatshirt. "Don't sneak up on me like that!" he angrily whispered to Ruby. They crawled back to the side of the house and moved behind the neighbor's shed for a conference.

"Report?" said Lars. He pulled a scab from his elbow. It came off nearly whole.

"Gross," Ruby said in admiration. She showed Lars a fresh cat scratch on her hand, gotten minutes before while entering the Hubmanns' basement.

He ignored her, again demanding, "Report?"

"They're all in the living room," she said. Lars knew that. "I recommend we go back through the basement up to the kitchen. They may be observed from behind the plants on the railing into the living room. They're presently watching *The Flintstones.* She checked her watch. "No, *The Flintstones* are now over."

Lars pulled three objects from his bag. There were two identical stamps and a red ink pad. The stamps were identical: a simple outline of an eye. "I got these at Kresge's," he said. "Now wherever we go we can leave the mark of the eye. I propose we change our name to the Eye."

"Agreed," said Ruby. Before they ventured down the window well, each stamped the other's forehead with a red-inked eye.

In the basement, Ruby observed a new litter of kitties, including a cute white one, puny with pink eyes. "Oh look," she said and moved to pick it up.

Lars saw the Matriarch's fur rise. "Don't!" he snapped, urgently pulling Ruby from the litter. "We must not rile the Matriarch. And if you touch that kitten, you'll tame it. We shouldn't disturb the wild cats' ecological balance."

Ruby recorded the criticism in her notebook while they silently, step by careful step, ascended the stairs.

The next afternoon, Ann Hubmann puffed on a cigarette in a toilet stall in the staff women's bathroom. Alone at last. The school was a nerve-wracking zoo, and Ann's bathroom breaks were a much-needed relief from the relentless nagging of students and staff. Everyone seemed to want something from Ann Hubmann. Home economics teacher Jeanne Gerou constantly left notices of upcoming union meetings in her mailbox, then whined when Ann skipped them for the Crystal Corner. Principal Pearl Mutchler told Ann she could no longer smoke in the staff bathrooms. It was public space, even if the little monsters couldn't get in. That janitor with the one wandering eye seemed to follow her around with a broom and bucket, as if he might just one day sweep her up. She inhaled deeply and held it in, awaiting the rush.

Next period they were carving up fetal pigs in Eighth Grade Biology. That was the class with the two brats who lived in her subdivision. Ann suspected Ruby and Lars of various pranks and mishaps that occurred in her classroom, but she had yet to catch either red-handed. Still, Ann often (and judiciously) made the frequently tardy pair stay after school. She had them each write the Clorox formula five hundred times on the chalkboard. The odd teenagers acted as if they didn't even mind, could care less, showing no reaction even when Ann triumphantly erased their handiwork in front of them. She didn't look forward to this next period. The fetal pigs always got the kids overexcited. Was there time for another cigarette?

"Ann?" It was Pearl Mutchler outside the stall. Ann saw the principal's large legs bend as she crouched to get a look under the door. "Is that you smoking in there?"

Could she ever get some goddamn privacy?

Ruby lay on the Hubmanns' hallway floor, peeking around the end of the half wall into the living room, where Dawn was reading *Sassy*. Ruby winced as she heard the crack of the refrigerator door opening behind her. Lars was being too loud! Dawn looked up, her eyebrows raised in the anticipation that someone else was home.

Ruby scrambled backward like a crab. In one hand Lars held a casserole bowl. His other hand dipped in. Ruby moved quickly, quietly grabbing Lars and pulling him into the small bathroom off the kitchen.

She closed the door almost completely, then grabbed a peek through the slim opening just as Dawn slouched into the kitchen, looking about, then moving to the refrigerator.

"You idiot!" Ruby wrote on her notepad to Lars. "You were too loud, you fat cow!"

Lars looked stunned for a moment, then a devilish smirk lit his face. "Now what?" he wrote. "Stinks in here. Exit strategy?"

The bathroom had one window, now shut and locked. Ruby stole a peek at Dawn, seated at the Formica table gnawing on a tuna fish sandwich and some corn chips. She was staying put. Ruby began to breathe through her mouth. The smell was bad, the reason obvious: a kitty litter box was kept in this little-used bathroom. It had not been cleaned in some long time. The excrement was pungent, but worse was a dizzying ammonia smell.

Lars tried slowly, oh-so-quietly, to push open the window. It moved about three inches, then would not budge. Just the start of a further push made a threatening vibration of sound. They were stuck. Ruby and Lars both put their faces to the cracked window and inhaled the fresh, late afternoon air. They watched Jim walk by, to the back porch. They heard him enter the kitchen just a few feet away, behind the door. Lars moved from the window to hear the kitchen conversation.

"What's to eat?"

The pair had been in jams before, but Lars had a bad feeling about this. Despite his prematurely large stature, he had a frequent fear of getting beat up, even by Jim, a year younger than he. Lars had gotten beat up by other boys all too often. And when he thought about it, the last time had also been Ruby's fault. Then he had been made to eat leaves.

The effect of the chemical odor was not unlike a glue-sniffing high. The cheese noodle casserole from the refrigerator even tasted funny.

Ruby stamped the Eye across the cabinet mirror. For the next few hours, before Ann returned from her afterschool errands, Ruby and Lars passed accusatory notes between gasps at the cracked window.

Orange buses carried her scrutinizing students away from Ann. The fetal pigs were only half dissected. They would finish tomorrow. Meanwhile, Ann carried them one by one back to the storeroom. Cigarette dangling from her mouth, she imagined that the hard pale thing she carried was watching her. She didn't look down. If she did, she was sure she would see its eyes squinched shut. It was when she was not looking, Ann was nearly sure, the pig's eyes were wide open, watching her from its mutilated little body. She didn't look down. In the storeroom she saw another cigarette she'd left burning in her petri-dish ashtray. She set the pig down, perched on a stool, and smoked both cigarettes at once. Ann then thought she saw a little red eye in her petri dish. She looked away, puffed.

Later that afternoon she was unnerved that her bank had installed automatic doors. She jumped as they popped open at her unsuspecting step. At the counter, filling in her deposit slip, Ann grew conscious of the security guard watching her. He had a gun. And there were cameras recording her, she knew. It was perfectly natural, she told herself. She popped a Tictac. Usually Ann would have used the ATM, but her personal identification number didn't seem to work. To her relief, the bank transaction occurred without incident, even if she was sure the teller's smile had been faked. She wondered how familiar the teller was with her account. Ann looked around the bank, at the many busy employees moving throughout this hushed atmosphere. Any one of them could find out all sorts of information about her, and there was nothing she could do about it. Not a damn thing.

She pulled into the lane for the McDonald's drive-up window. At the free-standing speaker, a staticky voice said, "May I take your order, Mrs. Hubmann?" Ann was startled at the Orwellian recognition until she saw in the window ahead a still-pimply former student of hers, Karen Kortendick. The malnourished twenty-year-old wore a headset with a microphone to communicate with the out-door speaker. This is why I spend my days educating the ungrateful unwashed masses, thought Ann: so they can poison my own kids for four dollars an hour.

While Ann waited for the food, she listened to the news on the radio. A satellite had been launched that would substantially improve weather tracking. "You like your coffee black, right?" asked Karen.

At home, she drank the coffee and had a hamburger with her kids. The place reeked. Ann followed the scent with her nose. She forced the bathroom door open enough to stick her head in and made a horrible face. She then pulled the bathroom door shut to close out the stink.

"Will one of you clean that out tonight?"

"We ain't got kitty litter," said Colleen.

The place was a wreck, not like the days before her husband Ray had ditched her. One Saturday he took the truck, saying he was going for a lube job, and Ray Hubmann was never heard from again. On the hallway railing was a dried-up dead plant. Ann picked up the pot. Underneath was another red Eye. She silently placed the pot back again, then searched for her cigarettes.

She threw a few bucks on the table before leaving for the Crystal Corner. "Go to the store and get some litter," she ordered one of her kids, no one in particular.

Ruby and Lars had been terrified when Ann Hubmann came home, more so when she poked her head in their smelly prison cell. They had remained hidden, pressed against the bathroom wall behind the door. Still, Lars had managed to catch an amusing glimpse of Ann's grimacing face when she inhaled.

The kitchen was occupied at various times that evening by various Hubmanns. At the moment, Ginger was out there putting together a jigsaw. They were *so close* to escaping. Ruby had brought a large container of moisturizer in her bag, considering leaving it as a gift for Mrs. Hubmann and her terrible skin. Instead they slathered the metal window tracks with it, slopping it down into the cracks from above. It was working. The window was loosening up, Lars could feel it giving way.

They had been in the bathroom for over three hours. At one point Lars had to pee. He made Ruby turn around in the cramped space while he sat and did it almost silently. Her back and shoulders shook with suppressed laughter.

Ann had been gone about an hour or so when the window was finally silently freed. It was just getting dark outside. Lars went out first, slithering crawling back down the outside wall to the grass. Before he helped Ruby out, he made her retrieve the crusty, empty casserole dish. She gave it to him, eager for freedom. Ruby climbed out into Lars's hand-entwined foothold.

Eyes Have It

Outside, it smelled of grass and water. Lars applied the Eye on the dish and left it in the Hubmann's mailbox.

The night before had been a rough one for Ann. She had too many Manhattans at the Crystal Corner and had gotten into a drunken argument with her sorta friend Sally Depatie. After weaving her car down the streets home, she was dumbfounded by the casserole dish in her mailbox. When she saw the Eye, she tossed it into the front ditch. She checked to see if the bathroom had been cleaned. It hadn't, and there was a peculiar white ooze all over. And more Eyes.

She got the brandy bottle from the upper shelf of her closet. They got in bed together. She couldn't sleep for some time, her mind circling like a vulture over the recent meaty events. The Eye was everywhere, and everywhere she was being watched. She got out of bed and closed the venetian blinds. She left her room and went to every window and every door and locked and double-locked. Of course she missed one downstairs, but that was presently without consequence.

She could hardly keep her bloodshot eyes open the next day during classes. During the period with Ruby and Lars, Ann was being sustained by caffeine and Tictacs alone. When Lars stuck a wire in an outlet and caused a minor explosion, Ann worked herself into a fury.

"You little ingrates, ungrates, degrates!" Ann's face was scrunched up like it had been the night before in her bathroom. Lars remembered and laughed.

"You!" Without thinking, she rushed at the boy and slammed his face with her palm.

Pale but for the red mark of her slap, he was shocked, as was everyone. Then tears filled his eyes and he fled the room. A shaken Ann skipped her lecture and showed the students the only film she could find in her workroom, an obfuscating biology film supposedly about sex.

After Lars finished crying in the bathroom, he went to a pay phone and reported the Hubmann cats to the Health Department.

Bad to worse, from the frying pan to the fire, what other sayings like that were there? Bad to worst was more accu-

rate. They took away her cats. Then they took away her kids.
Who knew what they would do about her job? If no one
narked on her for slapping demonic Lars Tripp, she might
be okay in that department. But someone might tell. They
had given her pills because she had been listless. She'd
actually been just a little drunk, but she hadn't said anything. What they didn't know wouldn't hurt them.

Anyway, she was safe now because she had boarded up the
house. She had bought some lumber at the Farm and Fleet
and had nailed boards over the doors and windows. She was
alone. She had brought some old photos of Ray down in a
cardboard box from the attic and sat on her crumpled bed
looking at them. Lube job, she thought wistfully, looking at
his impish smile. She took a sip, then a pill.

Ruby was later proved right. She told Lars she thought
entering the Hubmann house would be a mistake. The house
had been dark and silent for three days. Still, Ann
Hubmann's car was parked in the driveway. She was long
gone, said Lars. This was an unpassable opportunity to
really investigate the house and see if some of their pro-
jected analyses had been correct. Ruby was somehow voted
down. If Lars went, Ruby went too.

He reached in the cat flap and unlatched the window. No
scratches this time. It swung open, and Lars lowered himself
through the window well. Ruby followed. On their foreheads were the Eye.

They moved across the barren cement floor to the stairs.

"It's sad without the c—" Ruby didn't finish her sentence, for at that moment, in a brown flash, the Matriarch
attacked Lars's left leg. He screamed and kicked, but the
starving, grieving Matriarch was beyond reason, clinging
with its claws to Lars's calf, gnawing at his pant-covered
knee. The cat's scream rang and echoed upon itself. Lars did
an insane dance of pain.

Ruby found a broom and beat the Matriarch's clawed
grasp free. The defeated cat retreated out the cat flap.

Ann heard the screaming downstairs but ignored it. She
wasn't about to go down there and get involved in somebody else's trouble. That was her problem, she was too
damn nice, just like Sally Depatie said. Wait, no, that wasn't

what she had said. Ann lay back on the bed, looking at the ceiling. She roused herself, finally realizing that whatever was downstairs could easily come up. Stumbling from the bedroom down the hall to the basement door, Ann heard and sensed movement ahead. She found the basement door ajar. Ann again sensed movement, from where, her drug-and-alcohol-ridden senses did not know. She did know, however, that they had come, that there was no safety from prying eyes. Ann felt some comfort from knowing that she hadn't been wrong: her fears were confirmed. At least she had that going for her. Ann swayed at the kitchen entrance, then went down the stairs to the basement.

In the living room, behind the couch, crunched against the wall, Lars wriggled off Ruby. Hearing Ann's clumsy approach down the hallway, they had piled behind the couch and, unfortunately for her, Ruby had been on the bottom. He had bled on her. Now Lars checked the front door and found it blocked by several two-by-fours. The windows were covered by thinner, large boards. Lars told Ruby to make sure Mrs. Hubmann didn't return up the stairs, while he investigated their escape strategy.

Lars thought maybe he could pry a board from the girls' bedroom window. First getting good leverage, he used both hands, pulling until a loud screech eked the nail free.

Ruby observed through the cracked stairway door. Ann stood motionless in a windowed square of light. Then the biology teacher began to spin in loose, erratic circles, like a warped pinwheel. Poor Mrs. Hubmann, thought Ruby, she's had some bad breaks lately, and she's lost it. Of course she should not have hit Lars like that, just because of a few sparks.

With the nail screech, Ann looked up. The upstairs door had swung open a bit and Ruby was exposed. At last Ann saw one of the Eyes, upon a surprisingly familiar face. She rushed the stairs.

Ruby slammed the door, but there wasn't a lock. "Lars!" she screamed.

Ann drunkenly pushed against the door, while the Eye tried to keep it shut. Ann Hubmann wasn't staying in the basement, why should she let her world get so much smaller so soon? Maybe later, she yelled. She wouldn't let the watchers have their way all the time. Sometimes maybe you had to compromise, but surely not all of the time?

Ruby was failing; the door was opening. Ann's hand reached around and swatted Ruby's nose. But then Lars arrived and bolstered Ruby's efforts. He pushed the door shut on the teacher's arm. She yelped and pulled it back. Lars wedged a kitchen chair under the doorknob.

Ann relented and merely yelled and beat on the door with her fists. While she continued her painful soliloquy—she knew there was no place left for her, she would accept the continual surveillance, although she could not pretend to ignore it—Lars, as usual, checked the refrigerator.

"Is this like *A Clockwork Orange?*" asked Ruby. She gingerly touched her nose.

Lars pulled a brown bag from the refrigerator, opened it, pulled a face, then said, "No." He found a jar of pickles and sat at the table.

"Are we in trouble this time?" asked Ruby. She was unsure of what would follow, just like after they abandoned the fire in the field. She hoped that now, like then, there would it be no real consequences.

Ann continued banging at the door. She had been foolish to think she could have been left alone and self-protected. There was no protection, no privacy, she yelled through the door. Not with that new satellite launched.

"Don't worry about it," said Lars. The pickles were bad. "I got a board loose in the bedroom. If you wanna go, we'll get out of here."

They couldn't leave Ann Hubmann alone.

The earlier psychological evaluation determining the paucity of her parenting skills had noted a mild paranoia. When the same psychologist evaluated her barely a week later at County Mental, she was amazed to find heightened obsessional reactions previously unnoted. Ann Hubmann feared telephones and radio waves, envelopes and pigs. Everyone, every *thing* even, conspired to keep her in check. She trusted no one.

She preferred to keep her eyes shut tight. Then no one could see her. They could see her body, yes, but they could not see *her*. She didn't want to open her eyes because she would only see them watching her right back. During the long days, she sat on the edge of her bed in the plain hospital room, awaiting nightfall. And at night she lay down. Sometimes she slept, and even then she was not free.

Of course, Ann Hubmann was right. She had always been right. They were watching her, now more than ever.

Few people ever saw the Matriarch, she moved so fast and mostly at night. She fought raccoons for garbage, and had field mice for dessert. And under the stars, she yowled on the fence below Lars's sleepless room, and he wondered if he was imagining things.

STOMACH TROUBLE

Ron Dee

THE FIRST TIMES THEY MADE LOVE, SHE DIDN'T TELL HIM. THAT was before they got married, before her pregnancy made them decide they really *were* in love.

It seemed so stupid.

But a few weeks after the honeymoon, she woke with a scream from that nightmare of the past, slapping him and rolling to the other side of the mattress so fast she fell off onto the floor, bumping her left kneecap too solidly. It had swollen so badly, Mark nearly called an ambulance, and she was relieved that he had gone along with her desire to see if using an ice pack might be enough instead, even more relieved when her knee returned to nearly normal size the next day.

In the hospital they stuck you with *needles*.

A week passed before she answered Mark's constant question of why she'd awakened so frightened.

Amy shuddered in that all too near memory, rubbing her knee, which ached only a little now. "You touched my . . . my belly button. It . . . startled me."

Mark laughed. "So?"

She didn't smile back.

He gulped with the rise of his thick eyebrows. "Look, I didn't mean to. I was just kidding around, you know?"

Stomach Trouble

She swallowed, wanting to tell him.

Not wanting to tell him.

"Amy, come on, it wasn't like I was—"

Closing the past from her mind, she hid the shiver that wanted to shake her. "It hurt!"

He rubbed the sparse stubble on his chin. They were both so young, and she guessed they'd just been lucky he hadn't gotten her pregnant before her high school graduation. She looked at his soulful brown eyes, which had first attracted her to him. They were blank in curiosity now.

"Hurt?" Mark chuckled wryly. "You're barely three months along. . . . Is it the baby?"

"Not that," she hissed, regretting her admission. "Look, just forget it, okay?"

He grinned and reached to her stomach.

"No! Don't touch my stomach, okay?"

Now a frown grew on his forehead. "Are you crazy? What's—"

She realized she really didn't want to tell him . . . or to remember it herself. It was always there, in the back of her mind, but that was no reason to bring it into her present thoughts. "Look . . . I just don't like anyone touching me around there, Mark. It really *does* hurt . . . and you prefer my other parts more anyway, right?" She batted her lashes purposefully.

He rubbed his jaw again, then scratched his long nose. "I don't understand what the big deal is."

"You don't need to," she assured him, then put her hands on his shoulders and kissed him quickly.

And then it was okay.

For a while.

But Amy couldn't help but notice the way he stared at her tummy now when she was naked, instead of her breasts . . . instead of her legs and the reddish triangle of hair between them. They never spoke of how she had reacted, but she could feel his fascination and confusion in the secrets she kept from him.

It had always been so hard to live with—even watching TV could jar her. Especially the soft-core movies Mark sometimes rented so often now to get her in the mood. It didn't always work, because sometimes the women wore rubies and diamonds in their navels. The sight of them brought it all back and made her hurt.

Yes, it hurt . . . worse even than the sight of people getting hypodermic shots in other movies, though that affected her too. Horror films were especially bad about those latter kinds of scenes, and those instances frightened her worse than the images of Dracula tearing open a throat or the hungry living dead devouring their human meals.

Amy had been bitten by a rabid dog at the age of five, a time of her life so long gone she barely could recall the particular moments of it . . . except for those endless seconds when that stray she'd innocently gone to pet had turned and come toward her, growling low. It had been a short-haired, tan mutt with wandering, sad eyes. She even remembered her giggles at the funny dog that was lathering its white foam like it had just gotten its mouth washed out with soap . . . the way Mom threatened to do to brother Billy when he said bad words.

Her smile and cheeriness at the sight of the silly dog had ended immediately as the animal's eyes narrowed into flashing fury and its growl grew deep. Its mouth opened to show the white knives under its lips . . . and it *attacked*. She'd cried out and searched for help, but no one was near! A muggy heat had flushed over her and drenched her in sweat, and her own screams had filled her ears and made her throat ragged as her wrist became a torn, wet median of hideous pain—

Then everything was a void until she had awakened in the hospital, her hand bandaged. Through a sweaty fog she'd seen Mom and Dad looking down at her with concern and worry.

They'd reassured her, but none of their words had gotten her ready for the suffering and apprehension of the doctor and nurse when those white-suited figures brought in the hypodermics and turned her abdomen into a pin cushion.

Life had changed in those hours. She'd been so alone then too. Even knowing that Mom and Dad were close by didn't help. They'd been almost as near when the dog—

It wasn't *fair!*

But Mark was careful not to put his hands anywhere near her stomach anymore. It made their increasingly infrequent

Stomach Trouble

lovemaking more like an medical operation itself. He'd become so cautious . . . the sudden couplings of their first days had turned into rehearsed rituals.

The feelings that had surrounded Amy and Mark, the attraction they held for each other, seemed to falter.

All because of that wretched, ignorant moment from her past! Her father and mother had come to save her from the lunatic dog too late. She'd been so alone as those fierce teeth had clamped deeper than just into her flesh.

Into her very soul.

Five months after she first warned Mark away from her stomach, it was so large that she began to wonder if maybe he only stared at it for that reason, not because he wanted to touch her untouchable spot. Maybe that was why he'd seemed to be gazing at her belly button all those times before—in his own amazement at the life inside of her, a mixing of theirselves in the love they'd created.

She tried to believe that, but dreaded the thoughts of having to go to the hospital to have their child. The doctors and nurses would use needles to give her shots to . . . *relax* her.

When Amy looked at her bloated, naked body in the mirror, she was unable to think of anything but the terror that wasn't only in her past. Her belly button, once a chug hole into her soft flesh, had become a soft, protruding mound . . . almost a target. When she embraced Mark, he couldn't help but brush it with his own body, and Amy had to struggle against recoiling from him each time.

As she did now as he came home from classes and entered the front door, pulling her to him.

"Don't," she moaned, pushing him back.

This time, a frown ringed his apologetic eyes. "Damn it, Amy, I just hugged you. Not even very hard. Hell, I love you—it's an expression of affection!"

She stepped farther back, staying out of his reach as he tried to touch her again. She had finally told him why her tummy was so sensitive, one night after making a tepid love. He'd just gazed at her softly rounding stomach miserably afterward, and she felt so sorry for him she'd tried to make him understand.

But she knew he hadn't. He couldn't! "If you loved me, you wouldn't want to hurt me!"

The weeks of their increasing distance, both emotionally and physically, became suddenly wider in her words, and she saw that effect in his grimace, and knew she'd nearly cut their fledgling union completely asunder. Already, after only five months of what should have been newlywed intimacy.

Amy felt the closing inner walls of a new pain and despair—of losing him. The worry of him walking out on her and leaving her to endure the hospital's needle horrors on her own: It was a pain that she knew would be far worse than the agony of birth, because again she'd be in pain . . . alone.

But she had already decided that she didn't want to accept the anesthetics they would offer her.

Mark's thin and handsome face, now half obscured by his thickening beard, twisted like her emotions. His hand stretched out toward her, but didn't come nearer. "Look, Amy . . . this is really driving me crazy! You didn't used to be like this. God damn it, you're like a prize vase I'm afraid to touch!"

She so wanted to lose her distress of him touching her. It had grown inside her so that even when he didn't get near her navel, she couldn't enjoy his attentions, fearing that he would forget, or accidently brush her there, like he just *had*. For some reason, that center of her body had become the center of her frustration too. "You knew," she said hoarsely, "that there would be things about me that you wouldn't like, Mark. There are things about you that bug me too. I hate the way you leave your shoes all over the place . . . the way you sound like a foghorn when you're blowing your nose—"

"Yeah? Well, I hate the way you leave out your dirty dishes for me to clean up . . . the way you tie my socks together—"

"At least I do the laundry!" she flared, but wanted to take back those words with the new lines gripping his face.

For a moment Mark said nothing. He moved his eyes from her to the wall covered with his movie posters, then walked past her into the mobile home's living room. She watched him hulk to the couch his folks had given them and sit down, staring blankly at the coffee table and a stack of old magazines. "I really thought we loved each other enough to make it work for a lifetime," he muttered dully.

His tone pinched her. Amy took a deep breath, dreading his thoughts, which had been her own. "I . . . do love you, Mark. I really do. I just . . ."

"You just don't want me to touch you."

Amy didn't want to admit it, but it was true. She had more alarm from his touch and proximity than she felt from even an ugly stranger, because Mark rubbed her too fondly, with too much familiarity. He touched her without thinking, and that thoughtlessness ended all too often in these disasters.

"That's just what I thought," he said when she kept silent. "How can you say you love me and not want me to even be close to you, Amy? What kind of love is that? If we're going to stay together, you have to get over this."

Timidly, literally walking on the eggshells life had become, Amy went to the other end of the couch and joined him, leaving a good two feet of space between them. "I'm trying to get over it," she said. It was true to a degree, but she knew that the only way out of her fear, if there was one, would be to face it completely, and she wasn't sure how to do it.

And didn't know if she wanted to know how to do it.

He shook his head. "We have to get used to each other, sure. We have to learn to put up with and ignore the things about each other that we don't like, but this is something more than that, Amy. It's not normal for a married couple not to touch each other . . . to worry about touching each other like this. I mean, hell, you can touch me wherever you want."

"I told you," she said, "I'm doing the best I can to overcome this, Mark. It's not so easy."

"You need a psychiatrist."

Although his tone wasn't condescending, the statement rubbed her as if it were. She clenched her fists on her knees. "I'm . . . not crazy, Mark! I told you about that dog! I told you why—"

"So what?" He leaned back and studied the ceiling now, keeping his eyes from hers as though he was afraid that even looking at her might be getting too close. "Look, remember my car wreck? It practically killed me, Amy. I was in a coma for a month and they had to cut a hole in my gut to siphon out the blood. I had broken bones too." Now he did turn to her, and his eyes were like hard nuggets of coal. "But I'm not afraid to let you touch me where I got hurt, am I? I've got scars all over me. I'm not even afraid to drive in a car."

"That's a lie," she said. "Getting into a car still makes you nervous, I can tell."

Another silent moment went past. He relaxed his lips and jaw, forcing a smile. "All right . . . I admit it. But the point is, Amy, I still do it. I could just walk or take a bus, even, so driving isn't something I have to do, but I know that the best way to get over my nervousness is to deal with it by facing it."

Facing it.

"I know," she said, her voice thick.

"I'm trying to deal with this too, Amy . . . not touching you. But, goddamnit, I love you! Touching the person you love is part of it all!"

"I thought you married me for myself," she murmured, trying to hold on to her own logic and to deny his. "If I'd of known that all you wanted was a teddy bear to hug, I would've bought you one and saved you the disgrace of finding out that that's not what I am!"

Colored by a red blush now, Mark's grimace turned nastier. "You really do want me to leave, don't you?"

Amy's new fright crescendoed. She swallowed, trying to find patching words to mend this moment, but only a sob came from her heart. A wet trickle from her eyes.

The sound of cars from the street outside roared in Amy's ears as though they were right inside this room. Her deep breaths pulsed with her heart, and her skin seemed covered by the same sad mugginess under her eyes.

"I can't take this shit," Mark whispered, standing up abruptly. He paced back and forth, from the TV at the other side of the room to the coffee table, then glared at her with a hateful anger she'd never before guessed in him. Not for her.

"Mark—"

"Listen," he barked, "if you weren't just about due, I'd probably pack my things and get out for good, but I do care about you, Amy. I think I still love you, but you're driving me up the fucking wall. You don't know what it's like to have to go through this kind of rejection a dozen times every week! I have to get out for a while at least. Damn it, I have to be around someone normal right now . . . who doesn't mind me touching her."

Her lungs seemed empty, and she couldn't push up the air for her question. Instead her lips moved soundlessly. She wanted to jump up and hold him, apologize.

"If you need me, call Ralph." Mark rubbed his damp eyes and sniffed, showing Amy he shared some of the emotion she was feeling.

But not her fear—no trace of comprehension for that. She stopped trying to form words as she focused on his refusal to understand.

His refusal of loving her enough to understand.

Then his feet slapped the floor loudly and he was out the door, slamming it hard.

Amy gulped.

He just didn't understand.

Outside, the car's engine cranked and roared, and Amy flinched at the squeals as Mark tore down the street, away from their mobile home.

Away from her.

The tears ran freely now, released by his absence, and she trembled with the sobs that broke from her now filled lungs. She remembered their first meeting on the school stage as they'd tried out for their high school's production of *Boy Meets Girl* two years before. She had teased him over his flubbed lines, and after they were cast as the show's lovers, she'd kissed him more earnestly than acting required during that single scene.

They seemed to have so much in common, and their relationship had soon continued off the stage boards in warmer and more clinging dates.

Soon, hot and sweaty . . . naked. The love of their conversations had become physical, and she'd wanted to keep that sense of love even though their soon frequent unions bothered her more and more in their touch of flesh.

Now, he was gone.

But he said, promised, he'd come back. He'd cool down.

Maybe he would accept this, and maybe she could somehow learn to overcome—

Rising with the jitters flushing through her body, Amy went to the TV, started to turn it on, and walked away instead. She stared at the front door, remembering his hurt voice, the slam and the sound of urgent tires.

She wished he were back.

She wished that she had tried harder.

That she'd never been bitten by that rabid dog.

Maybe Mark was right and she should go to a psychiatrist. But even if she agreed to it, they had nowhere near enough money to afford those treatments.

That might not work anyway.

The tears slid down her cheeks. She thought of his thinly veiled threat to find comfort in another woman's arms, a knot in the pit of her stomach that felt as large as the baby. Their baby. She hoped the threat was empty. "Oh, Mark," she moaned, trying not to think of the way her life had changed since meeting him, especially not how it might change without him.

But then, she wouldn't have to worry about him touching her, would she?

Still, going back to the TV and turning it on this time, returning to the couch, she didn't smile. Solitude surrounded her despite the false video laughter.

At midnight Mark still hadn't returned. The hours since his departure had been more than any day since they'd wed, and even though she'd often felt they were spending too much time together, she missed him.

Amy went to the small bathroom at the other end of the trailer and stared at herself in the mirror there. Even in her biggest blouse and stretch slacks, she looked like an over-blown blimp, a monstrosity of what she'd been only three months before, as though she were seeing herself in some horrible, funhouse mirror.

Even so, Mark still told her he loved her. Still wanted to hug and fondle her.

The dampness crept back to her eyes, rimming the lids. She unbuttoned her blouse and slid it off, her breasts like oversized cantaloupes under the tight bra. She bit her lip at the sight of the red stretch marks that had appeared on her stomach, hissed her own reproach at herself as she removed the bra and saw the thin stretch lines marking her breasts now too.

He didn't just love her for her body. How could he?

Then her eyes dropped to the flesh of her outward belly button and she trembled. Bringing her fingers to her distended stomach, she crept them toward it from either side.

No. She couldn't even bear to touch it herself. She hadn't cleaned it since it had gotten like this, not even dragging a washrag over the bump when she bathed. Right now, it hurt her to just look at her swollen abdomen, and the memory of the doctor sliding needles into her made her face pale.

Mark had carefully obeyed her rule to keep his hands away from that inflamed area, but it hadn't been enough. The terror of his stroke that long ago morning had dug deep into her mind, removing her thoughts of pleasuring him or herself.

Her lower lip, thick and pouty in a way that Mark once gushed over, shivered with the chill of what that long ago childhood incident had done to her. A mindless dismay she had never before tried to control. There had been no reason to overcome it in the past, and she had nearly relished it, liking the originality of her trauma. Other people were disgusted or frightened by snakes, spiders, or watching grisly events, and she was nearly unique.

But now, her special, bizarre apprehension had turned on her. It had become nearly an addiction, interfering with other parts of her life.

Peeling down her slacks and rubbing her abdomen gently, Amy felt the same disgust for herself as for dope addicts— those who let their desires become needs that destroyed their health and existence.

Surely, for Mark's love, she could overcome this fear?

Again she stroked her thumbs upward, to the now offending center of her body, pretending they were Mark's, hesitating. She closed her eyes and felt them as though they were his fingers, rubbing her gently in love and the desire for her.

In the vows they'd repeated to each other, she'd promised to love him . . . till death did they part.

Closer. Her left thumb nudged the outer circle of her

navel and she tried to pretend her new shiver was one of unadulterated lust, like she'd felt those first times they'd lain together.

Then the onrush of memories. The dog. Mom and Dad. The doctor and nurse.

The needles.

Wasn't it really just the needles she was afraid of? Was her abdomen really still so tender after so long?

She had always pretended it to be so. The needles hadn't even touched her navel, but somehow her fears had chosen it as their hideout.

Reopening her eyes, Amy saw her flushed, sweaty complexion in the mirror, barely believing the starched countenance that stared back.

"It's . . . my body," she told herself. "N-Nothing to be afraid of. My fingers . . . his . . . *aren't* needles!"

But as her left thumb brushed into the tender skin once more, she nearly shrieked, only jerked out of it at the sound of a car slowing outside.

Mark!

Nearly tripping over her pile of clothing, Amy hurried to the bathtub and the window above it. The short green tub ran the length of the room's far wall, and she had to step into it to pull back the plastic curtain and stare out, but her heart sank as she saw the glowing red taillights pass down the street.

"Goddamnit!"

Where was he?

He'd told her that if she needed him, she should call Ralph. Amy had only met him once, when Mark had brought him by for an introduction. They were in two of the same classes together. Mark was getting a head start on her own education this semester, while she had the baby, intending to take a lighter schedule next semester and to trade care for their new baby while she began school too. Her classes would be paid for by her scholarship, and he still had some money from the nearly disastrous car accident that had laid him up for so long.

Maybe the fact that he'd been so compensated for his trauma had been what had helped him get over it. Amy wondered at that and stepped back out of the tub, passing the mirror but trying not to look at herself this time.

She'd gotten nothing from her accident but pain and dread. The dog that had bit her had been a stray. The toys and goodies Mom and Dad treated her to for weeks after hadn't had the same effect on her as the money Mark had gotten relieved him. He'd been a lot older too. A child's psychological scars were much harder to lose than an adult's.

Her dread of being touched wasn't her own fault. Nor Mark's. He'd done it accidently, but there was no one to blame but him, the doctor, the dog.

Maybe Mom and Dad, for not watching her more carefully that fateful day . . . for not warning her about sick, rabid animals more directly.

Or maybe the dogcatcher of that city was to blame for not doing his job . . . or maybe God for allowing diseases to exist and for creating dogs and people in the first place.

Knowing this kind of thinking was useless and served no benefit, she shook her head, entering the main bedroom and finding her yellow robe on the bed. She looked at the two pillows and wondered again where Mark was.

Maybe he really *had* gone to another woman's arms. Some pretty, unpregnant, unscarred schoolmate who had flirted with him in class. For the first time, Amy really wondered if the streamlined versions he'd told her of how his days on campus went were true. He rarely mentioned talking with any young women or making friends with the opposite sex, and the only friend of his she'd met here had been Ralph. Her own friends were all going to other universities, and as often as they came to visit and she talked with them on the phone, she hadn't really felt any desire to go make new ones. There really wasn't much opportunity for that out of her own classes anyway.

But the thought of Mark with another woman sent a new charge of queasiness through her, adding to the constantly irritable near-illness of being pregnant. Amy sat on the bed, touching the briefly squirming mass under her tight flesh, gasping as she always did each time the baby got near to poking her belly button from the inside.

She looked down at the dirty, brownish bulge of it again. In a lot of ways it was really her own point of origin as well as the focal point of her fear—the mark of the lifeline that once attached to her own mother, just as the baby inside her was attached to her.

It had been so sore to touch after the needles had injected a serum to prevent insanity and death, although they'd bitten lower. They had raped her, saving her life and sending her mind into this hell.

Mark had left her.

He would be back.

Amy's hands continued to stroke their baby through her slick skin, and she didn't like the frustrated thought-images that preyed on her. Mark and some beautiful, unsaggingly big-breasted coed, in her room at a dorm, maybe. Maybe kissing, or maybe well past that point. Mark wasn't at all bad-looking, even better now in his new beard. He'd had a lot of girlfriends before her.

Tears again. She felt the hot splashes on her legs and abdomen, her stomach, her . . .

Hands.

Flattening her lips to her teeth, Amy dared to stare at the atrocity she'd committed to herself without even realizing it. Her fingers, unconsciously, subconsciously, whatever, had moved on their own into the former indention of her belly.

Her navel.

It didn't hurt. She hadn't even noticed. Although now, knowing, the familiar pangs tried to rise up and flood through her brain, but she knew they were completely false. Purely psychosomatic, as the doctor had once told her. He'd told her disbelieving ears that one day she would get over it.

Maybe the doctor had been right.

Suppressing the distress she'd once coveted for attention and was now despising, she continued to probe the long unfelt part of her body. It had only taken the blame for enduring too much, too young. She trilled the hoarse giggle from the back of her throat.

If only Mark could see this!

Her eyebrows slanted and she gritted her teeth harshly as she thought of him again, cutting through her own new joy.

Stomach Trouble

As her thumb poked down on her button's bulge, as the baby pushed up on it as the same instant, giving her a thrill instead of nauseated disgust, she felt so angry at Mark for leaving her tonight.

To go wherever he'd gone, to do whatever he was doing! She was cured! Where was he?

But then her mind fell into an earlier trap. If Mark hadn't left, bringing her jealousy, she might never have lost her fears enough to learn how unreal they were at all.

But—

She stopped the endless trail before the ideas could go on in their circular journey, and reminded herself how much Mark loved her. How could he have told her he loved her so much and then gone out like that to find someone else and be untrue?

He couldn't. He wouldn't dare.

Amy walked to the phone on the bed's other side—*his* side of the mattress. She glanced through the listing of phone numbers Mark had written on the phone book's cover and found Ralph's, then raised the receiver and punched the numbered buttons. She tried to lose this new dread of Mark's unknown activities in her desire to tell him that her phobia was becoming a thing of the past.

"Hullo?" answered a sleepy voice.

Amy's heart almost stopped beating as she suddenly pictured Mark in bed with Ralph.

Naked. She shuddered and fought that vision away fast, knowing it couldn't be true.

"Hello?" the voice asked again, more alert this time.

"Ralph?" She paused, hearing his yawning grunt. "Hey, this is Amy Streeter, Mark's wife. I . . . he told me to call you if I wanted to get hold of him tonight. I thought he'd be back home by now, and I need to talk to him, is he there?"

There was a long pause, and Amy tried to halt her wicked imagination of Ralph turning to Mark as they together lay on sweaty sheets.

No. Not that. Not Mark.

"Amy?" Ralph yawned again. "Sorry . . . took me a second. Are you in labor?"

She frowned at his question, not expecting it. "Look, I just want Mark to come home. Is he there?"

Ralph sniffed self-righteously. "Not for a couple of hours. We partied hearty awhile with some friends, but I got a test in Logic tomorrow and had to crash. Mark told me you might call. Are you ready, uh, to deliver?"

"That's not any of your business," she said coldly, wondering what the hell was going on.

Where the hell Mark was.

"What I mean is, are you ready to go to the hospital?" Ralph paused again, and now his voice seemed a little cheerful. "Look, maybe it's none of my business, Amy, but Mark told me you guys were having a pretty nasty fight, and he said he didn't want to talk to you unless you needed him to take you to the hospital."

Her round chin quavered. She clutched the receiver tight, as though it were Ralph's throat. She squeezed, almost hoping for a burst of his surprised pain from the line's other end. "Look, Ralph, it's none of your business that Mark and I are having problems. I want to talk to him, okay? He's my husband!"

"Is he?"

Her hold loosened a little and she fought a dizziness. "We're married, you know that."

"Again, none of my business you'd say, but it sure doesn't seem like you two are married from what Mark told me. I mean, hell . . . you don't even want him to touch you?"

Amy's mind flared. Mark had no right to have said that! But she kept her voice as even as she could: "You're right that it's none of your business, mister. Look, just tell me how to get in touch with Mark, okay? It's really important."

Ralph yawned again. "I'm sure it is. Look, I'll call him, okay? He'll call you if he wants. Right now, I need to get back to sleep. Please, don't call again unless you're ready to have the baby, okay?"

"Fuck you, Ralph," she whispered. "Where the hell is he?"

Laughter. "I don't think you want to know," Ralph said, and hung up.

She listened to the hollow dial tone, the harsh chuckles still loud through its echo. Her thumb dug more deeply into her navel but she barely noticed it.

Where the hell was Mark?

Stomach Trouble

Who was he with?

Shuffling her bare feet on the carpet, back through the narrow hall to the living room, sitting before the still-playing TV and sitting on the couch in the moving shadows the TV's lights created, Amy now tried *not* to imagine. She had heard the dripping undertone in Ralph's voice, and she suspected that he was right, that she *didn't* want to know where Mark really was.

What was he doing to her? Was this his form of a shock treatment to destroy her fears of his touch?

That thought made her feel a little better. Maybe Mark had suspected the twisting of emotions his leaving would put her through, hoping it was the answer. Maybe he *was* right there, snoozing on Ralph's couch, not knowing that his plan for her had already worked. It wasn't much different than the games she and her girlfriends had played on boys to get their attention in high school.

If that was the case, surely he would call soon. If he was there, and knew what Ralph had said to her, surely he wouldn't let her stew and wonder about his fidelity for long.

A half hour later the TV station signed off, and since they didn't have cable, Amy couldn't find another that caught her interest. She shut it down and went back to the couch sleepily, constantly fingering her navel the way Mark wanted to, and enjoying the amazement she still felt doing it and not hurting.

Hours later she awoke from a dream of Mark licking her pregnant tummy and her protrusion. She sighed, her panties damp, peering through the darkness uselessly, knowing he still wasn't back.

"Mark?" she hissed, her new desire for him turning sour. She wished the contractions would start. If they did, maybe she wouldn't even call him, but a taxi instead, going to the hospital to have the baby on her own. He'd be so sorry when he found out.

But the idea of the needles still disturbed her, and she drew her fingers back from her navel as it stung a little with the reminder. She didn't let the terror overcome her again, though, reasoning it out logically, making herself believe there was no pain.

The pinch was now only in her heart, at the thought of

Mark, God knew where, sprawled between some unknown bitch's thighs as she made love to him.

"You bastard, Mark," Amy breathed.

The gripping knife of the hurt he was putting her through was worse than the needles, even. More pain than she had ever experienced, even though she knew it was only inside her. Just the thought of him breaking his vows to her while she was nearly ready to have their baby.

Sitting up with difficulty, Amy wondered if maybe she should call Ralph back and tell him it was time. It would bring Mark back, and then she could just tell him the pangs had stopped and that it was a false alarm.

Amy could barely believe that all this mess had occurred just because of that damn dog all those years before!

She watched the VCR's clock tick by the minutes. She was no longer sleepy at all. Sick, cruel notions spun through her thoughts of hurting Mark back for this . . . from the ridiculous and jarring notion of severing her navel from her flesh and wrapping it up as a gift for him, to divorce.

An hour later he still hadn't returned, and although she stared out the window at each car that passed, none of them slowed or stopped.

Could Mark have really left her for good, over something this small? How could he really love her and do this to her? She was alone, just like before, just like when that dog attacked her . . .

Despite her shivers, Amy's eyes drooped as another hour passed, and just before five, she tried to force herself into solid wakefulness as she heard a motor cut off outside. A door slammed. She knew it was him, and didn't bother to look this time. His limping step was so familiar even now, but it didn't give her the joy to hear it that it might have earlier.

He'd played this game too long.

She touched her navel and pulled her fingers back fast, but not from the old pain. This was a new pain. The hurt that Mark had given her tonight.

The door opened. She waited, glancing up at him as he entered the living room and gazed at her.

"Hey, Amy, I'm sorry. I had no right to do that . . . to leave you—"

Stomach Trouble

"Where the hell were you?" she sniffed, her voice as wooden and cold as she felt. "Have fun?"

"It . . . it's not what you think," Mark said lowly. "I went to Sandra's place. . . .She's a girl I met at the first of the year, and she really likes me a lot. I thought I wanted to . . . you know." He made a whistling sound through his teeth, lowering his voice still further. "But I couldn't, Amy. I love you . . . I want to work this out. I . . . I'm sorry I blew up like that."

She wanted to reach out to him and draw him near, hug him the way he'd tried to hug her hours before, but her navel really hurt her now . . . more than ever. Not the pain of the dog and needles.

This was the agony he had willingly put her through.

Mark stepped closer, touched her immobile hand.

Her slitted eyes blazed in the darkness and she drew a deep breath. *"Don't* touch me."

"Amy, I'm sorry. Look, I told you—I didn't do anything!"

"Yes, you did," she breathed. The endless hours of her solitude were like lava in her mind. "You did plenty. If you'd come back earlier, things would have been fine, Mark."

"I . . . I'm back now."

Those years ago, her parents had come out in the yard too late to save her from the bite of that mad dog. She'd been bitten and infected with rabies, and only the needles had saved her from death. Now Mark had infected her with a madness too.

"Don't touch me," Amy said.

Working his jaw, she knew he was thinking of leaving again.

But he didn't.

But it didn't stop the new pain. Nothing could, but at least the hospital needles were no longer as much of a fear to be dreaded.

Unless she were alone, and she knew she would be.

HE KNOWS WHEN
YOU'VE BEEN
SCREAMING

Harold Schechter

1

BY THE LAST MONDAY IN NOVEMBER, THE CHRISTMAS SEASON had already arrived. The Thanksgiving decorations—the grinning turkeys, brimming cornucopias, and caricature Pilgrims clutching blunderbuss rifles—had been stripped from every display window in the city and replaced by the trappings of Noel.

Heading to work that morning—a day so bright and balmy that it could have augured bunnies and baby chicks instead of jinglebells and reindeer—Kenny Stevens paused before the Hallmark store on Fifth, his eye caught by something in the window. It was a box of his favorite Yuletide accessory—the ever-popular, plastic Santa pin, the kind with a tiny red bulb for a nose and a little pull cord dangling from its bottom. At the sight of this trinket, Kenny's face lit up as if some tender hand had given his own little dangler a friendly tug.

Staring into the window, Kenny heaved an inward sigh for the lost days of his boyhood, when a ninety-eight-cent novelty item could bring him a rush of the purest joy. Within seconds he had made his decision. Disappearing through the revolving door, he exited two minutes later with one of the plastic Santa heads pinned to his lapel.

Standing on the sidewalk, he tweezered the little pull cord between his right thumb and index finger and gave a gentle yank. When the nose bulb beamed, Kenny felt a corresponding surge in his heart. Ah, he thought. Nothing like getting back in touch with the inner child.

Of course, he was aware of another, less guileless motive for his purchase—one related to pleasures he had only discovered since falling from the prelapsarian world of his Flushing, Queens, boyhood.

He knew that the Santa pin would endow him with a charmingly childlike air that no woman could possibly resist. Quickening his pace east toward the Metropolitan Medical Center, he chuckled through his nose. The babes'll eat this up, he thought, like pussycats lapping cream.

Sure enough, no sooner had he entered the hospital lobby than Donna Caputo—arguably the only female in existence who could look like the winner of a wet T-shirt contest while wearing a freshly starched nurse's uniform—came sashaying up to him. With one gaudily manicured fingertip she stroked the little pull cord while purring, "Oooh, Dr. Stevens. Can I turn on your light?"

"Anytime, Nurse Caputo," Kenny leered.

A moment later Kenny watched in a rapture of gratitude as Nurse Caputo's traffic-stopping ass receded down the hallway. Silently, he offered a fervent prayer of thanks to the Heavenly Creator of All, whose divine ingenuity had resulted in little plastic Santa pins with illuminated, battery-operated noses.

The elevator door slid open, revealing a vacant car. Kenny stepped inside punched 14, and leaned his back against the rear wall, whistling a jaunty rendition of "Santa Claus Is Coming to Town" as he ascended.

Five floors up the elevator stopped to admit another passenger—a trim-looking blonde, maybe twenty-three, twenty-five years old by Kenny's estimate. There was nothing flashy about her. On the contrary, she seemed dressed for concealment, wrapped in a long cashmere coat, her eyes hidden behind black Ray-Bans. Even so, Kenny could tell she was a looker.

At first, though Kenny was the only other person in the car, she seemed oblivious of his presence. After a moment she gazed up and gave him a faint smile. Her face was suffused with an infinite sadness. She might have just come from an all-night vigil at the bed of her dying mother.

Here's one pretty lady who could use some cheering up, thought Kenny. Flashing her his trademark lopsided grin— the one he believed gave his features an irresistibly Kevin-Costnerish cast—he reached a hand to his lapel and tugged the little pull cord on his Santa pin.

Two things happened simultaneously: Santa's nose light clicked on. And the elevator car exploded.

At least, that's what it felt like to Kenny. In reality, it was the woman who exploded—in a burst of such sudden, violent hysteria that the shock made Kenny's heart seize up like a vapor-locked engine.

Shrieking wildly, the woman flung herself backward, smashing into the control panel and hitting the big red emergency button with a shoulder blade. The car jolted to a stop that sent Kenny staggering, while the alarm went off in frenzied clangs. Sunk to the floor, the crazed woman waved her arms frantically, as though trying to fend off an attack from a knife-wielding rapist. "Getitaway!" she screeched. "Getitaway!"

Cowering in the opposite corner, Kenny could hear people on the landing above, pounding on the metal doors. A moment later the motor whirred to life. The elevator rose and stopped, the door slid open, and two orderlies burst in. Sizing up the situation at a glance, they grabbed the woman by her arms, wrestled her out of the car and hustled her down the corridor. Several nurses came hurrying at their heels, one of them wielding a big hypodermic and a bottle of sedative.

Kenny, his legs shaking so violently that he had trouble standing, groped his way out of the elevator. As he emerged, his buddy, Dr. Max Sternberg—a hotshot young behaviorialist in the psychiatric ward—came running by. "Go wait in my office," called Max as he disappeared in the direction of the hysterical woman and her attendants.

When Max got back to his office fifteen minutes later, Kenny's hands were still quivering so badly that, though he would have killed for some coffee, he couldn't trust himself to manage a cup. He was sunk into the little sofa that stood against one wall of the office.

"You okay?" Max said. He gazed down at his friend, brow knitted in concern. Suddenly, his eyes widened slightly as he spotted the pin on Kenny's chest. "Jesus Christ," he muttered.

"What?" asked Kenny.

"No wonder she went bonkers. Trapped like that in an elevator."

"What are you talking about?"

"That woman—Sarabeth Masters. She's a patient of mine."

"Yeah? Well, what the hell's her problem?

"Acute clausophobia."

"Then what the fuck was she doing in an elevator?" yelled Kenny, his voice shaking. He was still very agitated.

"I didn't say claus*tro*phobia," Max answered softly, his gaze returning to Kenny's lapel. "I said claus*o*phobia."

It took Kenny a moment to notice what his friend was looking at. When the realization struck, his mouth dropped open. "You gotta be fucking kidding," he said.

Max shook his head.

Kenny barked an incredulous laugh. "She's phobic about *Santa Claus?*"

"Santa Claus, Santa's elves, Santa's goddamned reindeer," said Max. "In fact, everything to do with Christmas."

Kenny shook his head slowly. "Let me guess," he said after a moment. "She suffered the ultimate Oedipal trauma of childhood. She snuck out of bed on Christmas Eve and saw Mommy kissing Santa Claus."

Max gave a humorless snort. "Not exactly."

"So tell me," said Kenny.

"She can tell you herself," said Max. Stepping over to a storage cabinet behind his desk, he ran a finger along a row of plastic audiocassette boxes and plucked one off the shelf. "I taped her diagnostic interview the first time she came to visit me a few weeks ago. She had just been released from the, ah, facility. Been there for almost fifteen years."

"Facility?"

"Where they sent her," Max said, seating himself behind his desk. "After it happened." He popped the tape into his machine. "Got a few minutes?" he asked, index finger poised above Play.

"You kidding?" said Kenny. "This I *gotta* hear."

"Take it away, Sarabeth," said Max, and gave the button a decisive punch.

2

"Cold? No, no. It's very comfortable in here. I'm just a little shaky, that's all. On the bus ride over here, it suddenly struck me—just three weeks to go before the madness starts. You know—the *holiday* season. Some holiday. Gives me the creeps just thinking about it.

"It's funny—you can avoid it completely for almost the whole year. Shit, I'd be in *real* trouble otherwise. I mean, you ever see an image of Santa in, say, February? I don't know—maybe I should just move to Williamsburg for a couple of months, live with the Hassids—you know, like what's-her-face, Melanie Griffith, in that crummy movie a few years ago. Probably the only place in the country where you're guaranteed not to have goddamn Christmas shoved up your ass.

"Don't suppose you've got an ashtray? Didn't think so. Amazing how much has changed since I went away. No place anymore for a smoker except out on the street. Not that *I* indulged in cigarettes back then, needless to say. Not even chocolate ones. Little Miss Goody Two-Shoes. Nah, don't bother looking for one. I can go cold-turkey for an hour. Probably just drip ashes all over myself anyway, the way my hands are shaking.

"Okay, enough beating around the bush. Time to get down to it. Begin at the beginning and all that crap. Sorry, don't mean to sound flip. It's just, you now, I'm a little nervous being here.

"So when did it start? That's easy. On the day he became an adolescent.

"I don't mean on his thirteenth birthday. In that sense, it's a little hard to pin down. But it really did seem to happen overnight. One day, he was my big brother—you know, protecting his kid sister from bullies and all that crap. The next he was a totally different person, like he'd been taken over by an alien being. Not a monster exactly. But definitely scary. And very, *very* weird.

"Who knows where it came from. I mean, my family wasn't any more or less—what's the word you hear all the time now?—*dysfunctional* than average. Believe me, one thing you do when you're put away for fifteen years is spend lots of time in front of the tube. So I've seen enough *Oprah* and *Geraldo* to last a lifetime. And absolutely nothing went on in my family like you see everyday on those shows. I mean, Christ, nowadays you don't feel *normal* unless you've been sexually abused by at least one family member.

"But that's not the way it was in the Masters household. My mom was a standard-issue suburban matron, maybe a little more tight-assed than usual, but basically your average perky Stepford wife. As for Dad—okay, so he wasn't the warmest, most sensitive guy in the world. But, hey, hang around Grand Central any weekday morning and you'll see a million just like him stepping off the trains—jut-jawed Type-A's with their Brooks Brothers topcoats and *Wall Street Journals* tucked under their arms.

"True, both of them were maybe a *teensy* bit out of it. For sure, they didn't seem to notice anything weird going on with Tod. Not until they were staring it in the face, that is. Very literally. After that—well, I haven't spoken to them in a few years. Fifteen to be exact. But I imagine the whole experience was a real eye-opener for them. Oh yeah. I bet it made them see all kinds of things they'd never been aware of before. Things they'd never even *dreamed* about. Not even in their worst nightmares.

"Hmmmm? Yeah, right, *weird*—I know. I keep using that word to describe him. How weird? Well, that's a good question. He was weird in, well, in a weird kind of way. Not your usual adolescent weirdness—you know, where Little Johnny Cub Scout suddenly comes home one day with a nose ring and a neon-green Mohawk. Nothing like that. No, my big brother Tod was an original. I'll give him that.

"Let's see, how do I explain this? Okay, you know the book *The Catcher in the Rye?* Yeah, of course—I mean, who doesn't? Okay, so you know how like everyone in the world, no matter big an asshole they are, identifies with Holden—you know, thinks they're these lovable, deeply sensitive human beings surrounded by jerkoffs and phonies? I mean, Christ, the psycho who murdered John Lennon thought he was goddamn Holden Caulfield!

"Okay, so my brother, Tod? *He* reads the book, and guess what? He thinks *Holden's* the total asshole. And why? Because Holden can't stand the idea that his kid sister, whatever-the-hell her name was, is going to grow up and discover what a miserable, depressing world it really is. It drives Holden *crazy* to think that this sweet little child is going to lose her innocence in a few more years.

"My brother, on the other hand, sees things the exact opposite way. He looks at *his* kid sister—yours truly, Little Miss Moppet—and it makes *him* crazy that I don't see the truth. The truth being that the world is a total shithole, full of horror and misery and man's-inhumanity-to-man. You know, life's-a-bitch-and-then-you-die, that kind of crap. So Tod becomes totally *obsessed* with setting me straight. It becomes his goddamn mission in life, curing me of my innocence. Rubbing my nose in life's shit.

"What I'm saying, see, is my brother was Holden Caulfield in reverse. Like his evil shadow or something. You know how Holden has this fantasy where these kids are walking through a field, and there's a high cliff they can't see, and Holden's going to stand at the bottom and catch them when they fall?

"Well, my brother Tod had the opposite dream. He *wanted* me to fall. Couldn't *wait* to push me off that cliff. And he ended up doing it too. Oh yeah. Right over the fucking edge.

"Examples? How many you want? Okay, how about the

time he introduced me to the concept of death. This was
right after my grandfather Robertson died of colon cancer.
Of course, I had no idea he had died of colon cancer or
anything else for that matter, because my parents, in their
infinite wisdom, decided I was too young to be told the
truth. So they made up this bullshit story about how
Grampy had gone off for a long vacation in California, and
how he might stay there forever if he liked it, which they
assumed he would.

"Needless to say, I was a tad upset that Grampy never
even bothered to say good-bye to me. I really adored him.
Still, the fact that he had gone somewhere beautiful and
warm, where he could just lie out in the sun all day and feel
good—that made me pretty happy.

"Then Tod took it upon himself to set me straight. Oh
yeah. Treated me to quite a little lecture on the horrors of
terminal cancer. He had real talent, my brother. Could have
been another Stephen King. Seriously, I can still remember
how graphically he described my grampy's wasted body in
the final throes of an agonizing malignancy. Not to mention
filling me in on all the details of funeral procedures. You
know—a step-by-step explanation of the entire process,
from embalming to burial. Complete with a final, unforget-
table description of my grampy's corpse being turned into—
what was the expression he used? Oh yeah—'worm chow.'
Yessiree. Made quite an impression on me, I can tell you
that.

"Needless to say, I got pretty upset and ran screaming to
Mommy. She was a bit disappointed in Tod. Gave him a
firm scolding. At that point, of course, she couldn't exactly
deny the truth about Grampy anymore. But she tried to put
the best face on things. That was a real specialty of hers. You
know those little smiley-face buttons? Stick a blond, bouf-
fant hairdo on one of them and that was my mom. So she
tells me that yeah, it's true, Grampy's dead—but all that
means is he's gone up to heaven where he's happier than
ever, and if I look up at the clouds and wave, he'll be able to
see me.

"So right away I go looking for Tod to gloat at him. You
know—'Nyah, nyah, you said Grampy's worm chow but

he's not, he's in heaven smiling down at me.' So Tod listens to this and then basically laughs so hard he almost wets his pants. Tells me heaven's just a load of crap. 'But let's say it's not,' he says. 'Let's say there really *is* a heaven—that means there's the other place too. And what makes you so sure old Gramps wasn't sent down *there?*' 'What other place?' I ask. You can tell how innocent I was. So Tod proceeds to tell me all about hell and the various torments of the damned— having your flesh roasted and your fingernails yanked out and hot needles driven into your eyeballs for all eternity. That kind of thing.

"That was one of his favorite pastimes, in fact— describing unspeakable tortures to me. Yes indeed. Gave me a real education in the Spanish Inquisition and Nazi medical experiments and the martydom of Catholic saints. Oh wow, I just flashed on this memory. God, I haven't thought of this for *years.*

"I'd been watching some old cowboy movie on TV, I forget the name, where this tribe of hostile Indians attacks a wagon train or something. So at dinner that night I'm sharing this with my family and my mom says, 'Well, dear, you know the Indians were treated very badly too. And you must never refer to them as "savage redskins." That's very insulting.' So she goes on to tell me a little about the way the United States government kept breaking all these treaties and taking away the Indians' land. Naturally, I start feeling very sorry for them.

"So that night, it's beddy-bye time, and I'm all tucked in beneath my 'Rainbow Brite' comforter with my teddy bear and stuffed kitty. And my bedroom door swings opens and in walks Tod. He just wants to fill me in on a few facts about the poor, mistreated Indians, he says. You know, a couple of details Mom left out. 'Sure, they got the short end of the stick,' he says. 'But it's not like they were these poor gentle lambs.' To prove his point, he describes a favorite form of torture that the Iroquois liked to perform on their captives. Whew. So much for *that* night's sleep.

"Hmmm? Oh, right. I forget—not everyone had a big brother who was an expert on Indian torture. Okay, what the Iroquois would do is, they'd take a captive and make a little incision in his abdomen, then pull out one end of his small intestine and nail it to a pole. Then they'd make him run around the pole until his intestine was completely wound around it.

"Where'd he learn about this? Books mostly. He was very well-read—at least in certain subjects. He just loved sharing his knowledge with me too. Oh yeah. I learned all kinds of interesting little tidbits. Like, for instance, I bet you don't know what a 'one-and-a-half' is. Nope, it has nothing to do with figure skating. It's sideshow slang for a kind of freak—a person with a little, half-formed twin growing out of his body. I know this because Tod thought I needed to learn something about human birth defects. So he shows me this book on freaks, full of all these amazing pictures: pinheads and living skeletons and children born with these fingerless flipper hands.

"Let me tell you. Once you've seen some of those pictures, you *never* forget them. I mean, I still have bad dreams from time to time about Tiny LaVonda. She was this sideshow freak with no body below her waist. Believe it or not, she got married—to a circus clown named Alva Evans. She even had a baby—don't ask me how—though it was stillborn. See what I mean? My head is full of this shit, thanks to my big brother Tod and his private tutorial program.

"Why? Hey, you're the shrink. You tell me. What he *said* was that he was doing it for my own good. That I needed to see the real deep-down truth, not just the sugarcoated surface. He wanted me to know the kind of 'shithole'—that was his favorite word, 'shithole'—the world really was. So while my friends were busy playing with their My Little Ponies and Malibu Barbies, I was learning all about serial killers and starving African babies and Hawaiian leper colonies and the Holocaust. 'Life's dark underbelly,' was the way Tod so poetically put it.

"Oh Christ—'underbelly.' That makes me think of another famous Tod-related episode. It was the time my pet hamster, Seymour, died. I still remember, it was a weekday afternoon, I had just gotten home from school. So I walk into my room and there's Seymour, belly-up on the bottom of his hamster cage. Little paws sticking up in the air. I can tell *something's* wrong with him, but I don't know exactly what, so I reach into the cage and lift him out, and he's all limp and floppy, with this creepy blue film over his eyes.

"So I begin to blubber, and Tod comes sauntering in. 'What's up?' he asks. I hold out Seymour. 'He's broken,' I sob. Tod totally cracks up, like he's never heard anything so hilarious in his life. *'Broken?'* he says. 'You think he's some kind of windup toy? Like there's springs and wheels and cogs inside him? Here, let me show you something.'

"So before I know it, Tod hurries out of my room and comes back a few seconds later with this dissecting kit he uses in his high school bio lab. He pulls out a scalpel and this little pair of scissors, lays Seymour faceup on my desk blotter and starts slicing and snipping away at his belly. 'See?' Tod says. 'This is the truth, Sarabeth. It's not make-believe. Not some kind of cutesy-pie *toy.'* By now his voice is rising until he's almost shouting. 'It's the stinking, rotten reality. The real nitty-gritty. And it's what's inside *you* too.'

"And meanwhile he's using this long tweezers—a forceps, I guess you'd call it—to yank out Seymour's insides, his heart and lungs and these slimy, wormy little guts.

"When he started in on Seymour's eyes, I bolted into the bathroom and puked up my whole lunch. Yuck. Still makes me queasy to think about it.

"Hey, look, can we take a break for a minute? I need a glass of water. Bad."

3

"Whew. Thanks. So where was I?

"Oh yeah. Tod's motives. Who knows? As far as *he* was concerned, he was doing me a favor. 'The sooner you get rid of your illusions, the stronger you'll be.' Yeah, he actually said that to me one time. Probably some truth to it too. God knows, what finally happened took a fair amount of strength—a helluva lot more than you'd expect from a ten-year-old girl. Guess there was all this stuff building up inside me. Even Tod must have been a little, ah, surprised when it came out.

"What made it even more surprising was that, to look at

me, you'd think I was just kind of wasting away. I wasn't sleeping much, wasn't eating well—thanks to Tod. I mean, *you* try polishing off your dinner after watching someone pry the eyes out of your pet hamster.

"Even my Mom, out-of-it as she was, started getting worried. Of course, she refused to face the truth—that Tod was tormenting me to death. As far as she was concerned, I must not be getting enough nutrients. That was her big thing, nutrients. So her solution was to double my daily dosage of 'Flintstone' vitamins. Talk about denial—but I guess I don't have to tell *you* about defense mechanisms, huh?

"So anyway, this stuff with Tod has been going on maybe five, six months, and it's getting harder by the day for me to hold on to any of my illusions. Except for one, which I'm clinging to for dear life. You guessed it—the jolly fat guy in red.

"Funny. Just thinking about Santa now gives me—here, look at my hands. Ever see anything like it? It's like I'm having an epileptic seizure or something. Back then, though, Santa was this incredible comfort to me. In fact, now that I think of it, it was kind of like believing in God.

"You know what I mean—there was just something intensely reassuring about the idea of this enormous, apple-cheeked guy with a big white beard watching over me. Like in that song—'He knows when you've been screaming, he knows when you're awake.'

"Huh? I did. You're kidding. I meant *sleeping.* Jeez. Talk about Freudian slips.

"Well anyway, starting right after Thanksgiving, I would pray to Santa every night before bedtime. I still remember—I had this flannel nightgown I loved, it was creamy white and very fleecy. And I would get down on my knees and put my hands together and tell Santa what a good little girl I'd been that day. Then I'd say, 'So I hope you'll remember me when Christmas time comes around.'

"To show you what kind of a kid I was, you know what I'd always start out asking for? That Tod would start treating me nice again. That Santa would bring back the brother I loved.

"Kinda makes you want to puke, doesn't it? I mean, I'm

telling you, I was *such* a Little Goody Two-Shoes. Still, I don't want you to think I was this totally perfect, selfless little angel. I mean, I was as greedy as the next kid come Christmastime. There was one thing in particular I was *dying* for Santa to bring me. A doll called—what the hell was its name again? Oh, right—'Baby Lookalike.'

"You know how it is—you come home from school, have your milk and cookies, then cozy up in front of the tube to watch your favorite cartoon show. And—zap!—you get bombarded by about a zillion commercials for Mattel's 'Baby Lookalike.' And after a couple of days, you feel that you absolutely *cannot* survive without it.

"And she *was* pretty neat too—with this soft, downy hair and big twinkling eyes. The really special thing about her, though—she was made of this incredibly realistic stuff. I guess it was rubber, but it felt just like flesh. It made her seem totally alive. Boy did I want that doll.

"So there I am, on my knees every night, praying to Santa—'And please, even if you don't bring me a single other present, *please* bring me a Baby Lookalike.'

"And there, lurking outside my door, listening to every word I'm saying, is my big brother Tod. And what he's hearing is absolutely driving him *nuts*.

"So he comes barging into my room and begins ranting in his usual way—'How can you believe that crap? Don't you know it's all bullshit? There *is* no Santa Claus. The presents come from Mom and Dad. When are you going to grow up? Blah, blah, blah.'

"So finally, after a couple of nights of this, I go running from my bedroom in tears to find Mom. I still remember this part so clearly—she was in the kitchen preparing some kind of casserole for the next day's supper, chopping up onions with this enormous kitchen knife. So I tell her what Tod's been saying, how mean he's being, how he's completely ruining Christmas for me. And for the first time since all this shit started, my mom finally gets angry. I mean, *really* pissed.

"So she calls Tod into the kitchen and starts reprimanding him. 'How can you be so cruel? What's gotten into you? Why are you trying to destroy Christmas for your sister?' She must have gone on like that for five minutes. Finally, she says, 'Now I want you to apologize to Sarabeth, young man. And I expect you to behave with the proper holiday spirit from here on in.'

"Tod looks at me with a little smirk and says, 'Sorry,' but in this very sarcastic tone of voice—you know, in that obnoxious way adolescents have. So I just stick my tongue out at him and go marching back to my room.

"For the next week or so, he lays off a little bit. He still makes sure to hover outside my doorway and let out a few snorts while I'm saying my nightly Santa prayers. But at least he refrains from his usual shit. As for me, I do my best to ignore him. He'd been making my life an utter misery for months—I wasn't going to let him spoil Christmas too.

"Or so I thought. Pretty ironic, huh? I mean, here I am with this awful Christmas phobia, all because of my god-damn brother. I wonder what he'd say if he could see me now?

"Oh well. Guess we'll never know, will we?

"What happened next is a little hard to describe. My memory's kind of fuzzy in places. Actually, more like a total blank. I still remember the first part, though. Bright and clear.

"It was Christmas Eve. It was still pretty early, maybe seven, eight o'clock. Mom and Dad had gone over to our neighbors, the Simons, for a drink. I had hung up my stocking, put out a plate of oatmeal cookies for Santa, taken one last look at our tree—a big balsam pine all sparkling with ornaments and lights. Beautiful angel on top with white, gauzy wings.

"Then I hurried up to my bedroom, threw on my fleecy white nightgown, said one final Santa prayer, and hopped into bed. I couldn't wait to fall asleep. I just knew that when I woke up, I'd find my own Baby Lookalike waiting under the tree.

"No sooner had I snuggled under my comforter than Tod pops his head into the room. 'Going to bed so early?' he asks in this very innocent voice.

"'Yes, Tod. I want to fall asleep as fast as I can, so when I wake up, it'll be Christmas.'

"'Hey,' he says, 'before you sack out, there's something I want to show you.'

" 'No, Tod. Go away. I want to you to leave me alone.'

" 'Come on,' he says in this pleading way. 'It'll only take a sec. You'll really find it interesting. I swear.'

"So I heave a sigh, and swing my legs out of bed, and stick my feet into my fluffy pink slippers, and follow him.

" 'Where are we going?' I ask in this impatient voice.

" 'You'll see,' he says. But I can already tell where he's taking me. To Mom and Dad's bedroom.

"As soon as we step inside, he heads straight for their closet, yanks open the door, then moves away so I can see inside. And what I see, of course, is that the floor is piled with Christmas presents.

" 'Well, well,' says Tod in this mock-surprised way. 'What have we here?' And he reaches in and starts pulling out the boxes and opening them. 'Gee,' he says. 'I guess Santa must have come early and stored all this stuff in Mom and Dad's closet, huh, Sarabeth? I mean, I don't suppose there's any possibility that Mom and Dad bought this stuff themselves. Oooh, and look here. Here's a box from Toys 'R' Us. I guess Santa must do his shopping there, huh, Sarabeth?'

"So I'm standing there and watching this, and the terrible truth is starting to hit me— *Tod was right!* And I can feel the tears start to well up in my eyes, and my lower lip is trembling uncontrollably.

"And then Tod reaches in and pulls out the last present of all. And I see through my tears that it's a Baby Lookalike.

"Tod opens the box and pulls out the doll. Then he grabs her by the hair and starts waving her around. 'Look, Sarabeth,' he says in that same jeering voice. 'Look what Mom and Dad—oh, excuse me, I mean Santa Claus—got you.'

" 'Stop!' I scream. 'You're hurting her!'

"Tod stops and stares at me like he can't believe what he's hearing. 'Jesus Christ,' he shouts. 'What is *wrong* with you? Why can't you face up to reality? First you think your hamster's a toy. Now you think this stupid toy is alive. Here, let me show you the truth!'

"And with that, he grabs one of Baby Lookalike's arms and yanks it from the socket. 'See!' he shouts. 'No blood. No screams.' Then he pulls off her other arm. Then he grabs her by the neck with one hand, digs the other into her face and twists and tugs and strains—and tears off her head.

"That's when something happened to me. Something very strange. You'd think I would have gotten totally hysterical. But I didn't. I mean, something snapped in me, all right. I could hear it, an actual noise—like a wire snapping inside my head. But I didn't scream and shout. I got totally quiet. I must have looked weird, though. There must have been something in my eyes.

"Whatever it was, Tod saw it. And it scared him.

"His voice suddenly got very quiet. 'Look, look, it's okay, Sarabeth,' he said in this panicky way. 'I'll stick her back together, okay? I'm sorry, I'm sorry. Don't tell Mom and Dad, okay?'

"And that's the last thing I remember.

"See, this is where my trouble all started. I'm convinced of it. That's why I'm here. They never really helped me at, you know, the other place. Just kept me medicated most of the time. But now that I'm out in the world again, I've got to find some way to get back to normal. I mean, I can't go through the same hell every Christmas. I keep thinking, if I can just recover the memory, relive it, no matter how painful, it'll free me from the torture.

"The next thing I remember? Christmas morning. And even here, I can't really recall things directly. The only way I can deal with it at all is by imagining how my parents must have felt. To see it through their eyes. I guess it's a way of distancing myself from it. From the horror.

"I see them rising from their bed early Christmas morning, putting on their bathrobes and slippers and hurrying downstairs. I picture them coming into the living room, expecting to see me and Tod opening our presents. Neither one of us is there. And something is very strange about the tree.

"I imagine the looks on their face as they stare at the tree—first surprise, then utter bewilderment, then a kind of stunned incomprehension as they struggle to make sense out of what they're seeing.

"That gross-looking pair of ornaments, for instance, like a couple of poached eggs dipped in ketchup. Christ, if you didn't know better, you'd think they were eyeballs. And those flesh-colored icicles dangling from hooks. Damn if they don't look just like fingers. And what in God's name is that slimy pink rope strung around the tree? Jesus. It could almost be a length of uncoiled bowel.

"And—wait a minute!—that mangled mannequin's head stuck on the top where the angel used to be. Who the hell put *that* there? They squint for a better look at the awful thing. Its eyes and ears and tongue are missing—but it's still recognizable.

"'Tod,' croak Mom and Dad in unison.

"And as whimpers of raw, animal terror emerge from their throats, they suddenly become aware that another person has entered the room and is standing beside them. Their angelic little daughter, clutching an object in one hand—an enormous kitchen knife with a reeking blade.

"She is dressed in her favorite, fleecy nightgown. Only it's not spotless white anymore. It is horribly spattered and sticky. And red as a Santa suit."

... FOR I HAVE SINNED

Jerry and Sharon Ahern and Samantha Ahern

BITS OF BONE, FLECKS OF SPITTLE, AND DROPS OF BLOOD stirred in a crude wooden bowl by a pagan witch, the dregs of tea leaves read from the bottom of a blue willow china cup by her aunt. Portents. Kellie studied the little white object she had just taken from her urine stream, almost spatula-shaped, a rough-edged pink line at its center, the color only confirming the fear that had gnawed at her soul for the last two weeks. She'd missed her period, lying to herself that she was merely late. But she had never been more than a week or ten days late. So, she had purchased the home pregnancy test; but she waited three days before getting up the nerve to use it. The missed period, the pink line, omens of destruction all.

Tears filled her eyes as she studied her reflection in the bathroom mirror.

She could choose to lose her life or sacrifice her immortal soul, birth the baby and die or have an abortion and be damned for eternity.

Kellie disposed of the physical evidence of her doom, then washed her face, brushed her hair, lipsticked, and left the bathroom.

Dean was mowing the lawn. She could hear the mower as it alternately hummed and sputtered. Kellie crossed the bedroom, deliberately stopping to look at the bed, then left the bedroom, taking the steps down to the first floor.

She went to the kitchen, placed ice in a glass, filling it the rest of the way with sweet tea, replacing the pitcher in the refrigerator. She carried the glass out into the yard, waving at Dean as he rounded the oak tree. He waved back, stopped the mower, and walked toward her. The oak tree was very old and too near the driveway, the concrete always needing patching, as the tree's roots did their destructive work without stop.

Like most men, Dean looked somehow bigger, stronger, handsomer when his face and arms gleamed with sweat.

Touching her gingerly, his hands grasped her shoulders and he kissed her lightly on the lips. "Thanks." He took the glass from her hand and swallowed half its contents in a single gulp.

"Can you come inside for a minute?"

"Sure, honey. What's up?"

"Something I have to ask you about."

"Right," he answered, nodding his head and swallowing the remaining tea from the glass. "Most of the grass is cut."

Kellie took his empty glass, walking beside Dean toward the sliding glass doors.

He was always gentlemanly, in the two years they dated before marriage and in the six years since. He followed her inside, closing the doors, sealing out the July heat.

Kellie stopped just inside the doorway, turned and faced him, watching his pretty blue eyes. Instead of telling him what she dreaded telling him, she asked a question. "Why did you go to the doctor the day before yesterday? Is there anything wrong?"

"No, uh, what's wrong?"

He had always been able to turn conversations. Most men could, domination something that was perfectly natural to them. But she couldn't let him do it this time. Both hands wrapped around the condensation-dripping glass, she asked again, "Why did you go to the doctor, Dean?"

Dean started fishing in his pants pockets, looking for his cigarettes, she knew. He lit one, biting his lower lip in the instant afterward, as he always did when he used lighting a cigarette as a delaying action. "I was worried."

"About your health? You never said—"

"No, I, uh—when you didn't start your period. Have you started?"

Dean was trying to maneuver the conversation again. She couldn't let him. "What did the doctor say to you?"

"You know, don't you?"

Kellie nodded, casting her eyes down to the glass in her hands. The ice was nearly melted, a quarter inch or so of water in its place.

"What did he tell you, Dean?"

Dean walked over to the counter, leaning heavily against it, bowing his head as he flicked ashes into the sink. There was a soft hissing sound for an instant. He spoke, his voice low. "I don't know how it happened. I was sterile ever since I got hurt. But I was always afraid that somehow something would go wrong. You missing your period and everything? I got spooked, I guess. Had myself checked. Dr. Koch said my sperm count's almost normal. Are you—"

"I'm pregnant."

"Damn, Kellie. But, well, maybe—"

"I'm going to die."

"Look," he said, still not looking at her. "I know how you feel about babies, about kids, but just because you've always been afraid of becoming pregnant doesn't mean—"

"The baby will bring about my death," Kellie told him, squeezing the glass so hard that it nearly shattered, slipping from her hands instead and breaking into razor-sharp shards at her feet. If she picked one up, raking it across her wrists before Dean could stop her, then it would end now.

But suicide was a mortal sin. . . .

Kellie waited her turn, then entered and knelt in the darkness before the screen, hands folded in prayer tight against her abdomen. She heard the familiar scratchiness of the wooden panel sliding open, so fearful a sound when she was just a little girl and would be momentarily unable to remember any of her sins. Kellie began to recite the Act of Contrition.

"What troubles you, my child?" The deeply melodious

voice was unmistakable: Father Andrew. He was young, handsome, new to St. Jerome's.

"I'm pregnant, Father."

"From the tone of your voice, I gather this news doesn't make you happy. But you should be happy that you carry God's gift of life within you."

"I don't want to be pregnant, Father. I never, ever wanted to be."

"Are you married, my child?"

"Of course, Father!"

"Then why do you feel as you do? Our Blessed Mother accepted God's Will; so should you."

"Dean and I only got married after he assured me that he was sterile. He was injured when he was in his late teens and it left him that way—sterile, I mean. I never wanted a baby, so Dean's condition was perfect. I knew it would be a sin to get my—get myself fixed or something, or to ask the man I loved to sin for me and get a vasectomy. And birth control is a sin too, Father. I loved Dean so much and I still do, but I never would have married a man who could make me pregnant, any man, even Dean."

"Then the child you carry is another man's child? Is that it?"

"No, Father! Dean's condition has reversed itself." Her voice trailed off.

Father Andrew laughed softly. "Then Our Lord in His Infinite Wisdom has chosen you for a miracle, my child, the miracle of life. You should thank Him for this chance He has given you and your husband." The confessional box was old and smelled dusty, her throat dry, but her nose was runny still from crying. "A child is a gift of love, not only from God, but between husband and wife."

"I'm afraid, Father."

"It is difficult for a man, priest or layman, to understand the feelings which you must be experiencing, but as a Catholic, you can take great comfort from Our Lady, knowing that she has endured what you will endure, as did your own mother before you—"

Kellie began to cry.

"What have I said?"

"I, ah . . ."

"You can tell me, my child."

Kellie bit her lower lip. Getting up from her knees, she ran from the confessional, her eyes streaming tears. . . .

On the edge of her bed, naked except for her panties and bra, Kellie stared at her abdomen. Abortion was a sin, and so was suicide. The instrument of her destruction grew within her womb, nourished with every breath she drew, every ounce of food, every sip of liquid, growing stronger until one day the child would do what she knew it would.

The doorbell rang.

She sat there for a moment longer.

The doorbell rang again.

Dean shouted up from the kitchen where he had been grading some math papers, "I'll get it, Kellie!"

She got off the bed, walking over to her closet and taking down a pair of jeans and a T-shirt. She stepped into the jeans, pulling them up along her thighs, then zippering the fly without having to inhale. Soon the baby would be pressing against her, straining to escape into the world; then, not even her loosest fitting pants would close over her abdomen. She had several belts that fit the loops sewn into the waistband of the jeans, but she could never cinch a belt tightly enough to strangle the child.

Barefoot—and pregnant, as the old saying went—she left the bedroom and walked downstairs. Unborn babies could die if their mothers-to-be took a fall down such a flight of stairs. But unless she should be fortunate enough to have such an accident, to deliberately hurl herself down these stairs would be murder. That was a mortal sin. That was how Stephen killed her mother.

Father Andrew waited in the living room, tall, straight, a worried look beneath his bushy brown eyebrows. He wore a blue windbreaker, with the black clerical shirt and its white collar beneath. Dean stood beside him.

"I recognized your voice, Mrs. Strauch, but only after thinking about it for a while. So many new people to meet since I took over for Father James. I may not be the most experienced priest in the world, but I've never had somebody run out of the confessional on me before. Your husband was kind enough to let me in. He has no objection if we speak alone."

"There's nothing for us to talk about, Father Andrew."

"Look, Mrs. Strauch, I don't mean to make things awkward, but I was worried about you. Please? I could always come back, but somehow I think we should talk about things now. And it can be like an extension of the confessional. Trust me on that. Or, if you like, the three of us can talk, and whatever we say will still be held in confidence."

Father Andrew smiled. As he did, a heavy, auburn curl fell across his forehead.

"May I get you something, Father?"

"Nothing. Perhaps later. But thank you."

Dean, lighting a cigarette as he spoke, suggested, "Why don't we all sit down?"

Dean sat in his easy chair. Kellie walked over to perch on the little hassock near it. Father Andrew sat on the couch.

"The reason I came, Mrs. Strauch, is that I suddenly realized that perhaps the fear you spoke about concerning your pregnancy wasn't the physical ordeal of childbirth."

Kellie clamped her hands over her knees, licked her lips, waited for him to say something; but he did not. At last she spoke. "You're, ah—you're right, Father."

"Then what is it that troubles you, Mrs. Strauch?"

For once in her adult life Kellie wished that when she had tried cigarette smoking as a teenager she had kept up the habit, but she would have to give it up in any event. To willfully cause damage to the unborn child (considering the warnings on cigarette packages) would be a sin. "I'm afraid of having children, Father, not afraid of being pregnant. In college, in my psych class, we talked about phobias. That just put a name to how I'd felt ever since I was ten."

"A phobia? You mean like being afraid of cats or the dark or—"

"Yes, but in college the professor taught us that most of the time a phobia is rooted in something you've forgotten, that you just transfer the fear to things that are similar to the situation that made you afraid in the first place. But I know why I'm afraid."

Dean cleared his throat, stubbed out his cigarette in the

pedestal ashtray beside his chair. "Anybody want a drink? I mean a real one?"

Father Andrew looked at her, then at Dean. "Yes, please."

Alcohol could damage a fetus. "Nothing for me," Kellie told her husband.

"Beer, scotch, blend, what, Father?"

"Scotch'd be great, Mr. Strauch."

"Water? Ice?"

"Ice and a little water."

"Right."

Dean went to the kitchen.

Father Andrew asked, "Are you sure that you feel comfortable in this situation, Mrs. Strauch?"

"It doesn't matter."

Dean returned with beer for himself and a tumbler of scotch for Father Andrew. Kellie put out coasters on the coffee table, then retook her seat.

"So, we gonna tell him, Kellie?" Dean asked after a moment.

She closed her eyes, shrugging her shoulders. She looked at Dean, then at Father Andrew. "I have a younger brother that I haven't seen since he was six and I was ten. He was locked away in an institution. After he was released, I never wanted to see him again. I don't even know if he's still alive."

"And you're afraid that whatever his illness is, it might be hereditary . . ."

He was just like Dean, finishing her thoughts for her rather than letting her say anything. "No. That's not it exactly. It might be hereditary, but I don't think so. I just know that if I have a child, the child will bring about my death."

Dean seemed to want to talk, so she let him.

"You see, Father Andrew, what my wife's trying to tell you is that she's afraid the child will actually bring about her death."

"Deliveries these days are much easier than in your mother's time, Mrs. Strauch."

Kellie just looked at Father Andrew's handsome face. He didn't understand. Did Dean? Or had her husband just humored her ever since she'd told him that his then sterile condition was a blessing to them, and because of it, not in spite of it, they could be married?

She closed her eyes again, beginning to speak. "When she was delivering—my mother, I mean—and Stephen was coming out, for some reason he turned. It was a Catholic hospital. He knew that somehow he would be saved at the cost of her life. Except my mother didn't die then. She was sick for a very long time, but she recovered."

"A baby can't will itself to change position in the womb, let alone the birth canal, Mrs. Strauch." That soft, musical-sounding laughter again, but humoring her now, as if she were a fool.

"Stephen did. Whatever you say, I know he did."

"And that's—"

"That's not all of it, Father," Dean said, slugging away his beer.

She stared at Father Andrew, hoping that maybe he would see in her eyes that she was not making this up, not hysterical. "We lived in a big house with high ceilings and a second floor where all the bedrooms were. When Stephen was five years old, he filled the first stair at the top of the staircase with marbles. I saw him laying them out very carefully, filling the entire surface of the stair. Then he went down the stairs halfway and laid himself down, so it would look like he'd fallen. He started yelling and screaming and crying. My mother came running. She would have died then, falling, but I screamed at her and grabbed her. She pushed me away. I grabbed for her again. I thought she was going to fall over the railing. But she caught herself and fell to her knees. She saw the marbles, and then she started crying."

"There's more," Dean said as Father Andrew started to say something.

Kellie wished now that she'd taken a drink. "I don't know what Mom and Dad talked about that night, but I heard some shouting. Stephen went to live with my mother's aunt Rose for a few months.

"When Stephen came back, I could see that Mom was frightened. It was just before Christmas, a week before. Dad took me with him to get the Christmas tree. We never decorated early, because we always kept the tree up until Epiphany, when the wise men came to see the baby Jesus. And it would be Stephen's sixth birthday on January sixth.

"When we came home," Kellie went on after a moment, her voice barely above a whisper, "Dad's arms were loaded with the tree. I rang the doorbell and nobody answered. I remember Dad looking at me, putting the tree down and telling me, 'You guard the tree, kiddo, okay?' and putting the tree down on the porch. He took his keys out of his pocket and let himself in. Dad didn't come back for a long time, and I went inside.

"The basement door was open. I heard my father crying. I walked to the basement doorway and looked down the steps. Mom was at the bottom of the steps. I guess I realized it just looking at her. She was dead. There were Christmas lights strung at the top of the steps, but the cord was broken. Stephen sat on the basement floor, playing with the light strings. He was smiling."

"My God," Father Andrew murmured.

Kellie could no longer speak. Dean cleared his throat, lit a cigarette. "They took Kellie's brother to a psychiatrist. The psychiatrist said that Stephen needed to be put away, that maybe an institution could help him. He admitted that he'd killed his mother deliberately, just because he'd wanted to."

"And you're afraid that somehow your child will be like Stephen," Father Andrew said, stating what to her had always been obvious. . . .

Kellie agreed to psychiatric counseling, in order to rid her of her fears, make her view them as groundless. She endured amniocentesis, ultrasound, and every possible examination and test. Almost grudgingly, she felt some sense of relief when she learned that the child she carried was not a boy. Because it was her moral duty, as both a Catholic and a mother, she did all that she was told to do concerning prenatal health, never touching a drop of alcohol, getting Dean to give up cigarettes in order to avoid the hazards of secondhand smoke, exercising, watching both her diet and her weight, preparing healthy drinks that would nourish the child growing within her.

Margaret Lucille Strauch was born without incident the following spring. . . .

Father Andrew, a little gray visible in his wavy brown hair, kissed the stole as he lay it across his neck, then opened the prayer book. He began administering Extreme Unction.

The hospital room was gray, what little light there was filtering through the closed venetian blinds.

Kellie looked into his eyes. She could not speak, only watch and listen. Lucy's sixth birthday would be in three weeks. The world was coming alive again with the life of spring, yet in this room there was death.

A death she should have prepared for.

But Lucy was always so good, so sweet, so loving in every way. How could she—Kellie—have known?

The room seemed to be getting darker.

It was harder to hear Father Andrew as he recited the Last Rites of the Dead.

It was all very simple. Lucy climbed up into the big oak tree and started screaming that she couldn't get down. She started crying. Dean had been up in the tree pruning away some dead branches, so the ladder was already erected. It was simply a matter of climbing up to get Lucy down.

As loving, parental hands reached for little Lucy, Lucy pushed against the ladder with her feet, using all the strength in her little body. Kellie screamed. The ladder fell backward to the driveway surface. Kellie remembered seeing the look of fear vanish from Lucy's face, laughter taking its place.

Father Andrew made the Sign of the Cross.

Dr. Koch shook his head, whispered that there was nothing he could do, then began to lift the sheet.

Kellie walked out of the room and into the corridor.

Lucy sat there, a nurse beside her. "Is Daddy dead yet?"

Kellie nodded.

Lucy laughed.

SUNPHOBIC

Nancy Kilpatrick

"SHE *NEVER* GOES OUTSIDE?"

"That's what I've heard. Anyway, *I've* never seen her."

"She could use some sun."

Their whispers reached Lena like light waves singeing the air, hoping to find a solid object, preferably human skin, to land on and penetrate. Of course she heard those two graphic artists. Did they think she was deaf? Or stupid?

Lena *hated* having to come here once a week to pick up and deliver work. At least the copy department was located in the middle of the floor—the offices with windows were reserved for the big cheeses.

The elevator door closed on Lena, the lone occupant, and the box descended. God, she was angry! Those two creatures would probably be congratulating themselves, thinking they were the first ones who ever thought she was weird. But refusing to venture out into sunlight unprotected was a case of better safe than sorry. They'll learn, Lena assured herself. When it's too late.

The elevator door swooshed opened and she darted into the underground concourse beneath the office building that housed the ad agency she wrote copy for on a freelance basis. The labyrinth was as familiar as the blue veins bulging on the backs of her pale hands.

She made a quick stop at the health food store that sold organic fresh food. Picking through the produce, she ignored most of the nonroot vegetables, and turned her nose up at the potatoes with a greenish tinge—the skins had gotten too much light and now they were poisonous. The romaine had scorched edges, but it wasn't bad; she bought a head anyway. At the drugstore they were out of zinc oxide and she had to content herself with a tube of extra-strength sunblock. Finished, she hurried along the concourse toward the subway entrance, battling the rush-hour crowds through the turnstiles.

The density of fifty stories of concrete and steel overhead felt reassuring. No sunlight would ever penetrate down here. Or in the subway tunnels. At least the powers-that-be in Toronto had had the sense to build connecting underground links through most of the downtown. They did it because of the severe winters, but Lena had benefited in a way they hadn't anticipated. She was a canary, recognizing the dangers of sunlight while others walked complacently beneath those damaging rays, inviting disaster.

The subway train arrived and she found a seat along the aisle. A young couple sat next to her facing the front of the train. They thumbed through a glossy travel brochure advertising foreign lands composed of dazzling white beaches and perpetual sunshine.

"We should go to the Caribbean again," the redheaded woman said. "God, I love sunbathing down there!"

Sure, Lena thought. With your freckly skin, you'll develop a melanoma by the time you're thirty-five.

And she should know. All those years as a child, summers spent on the beach at Wasaga, her fair skin scalding beneath the deadly sun, flesh red as a tomato, never tanning. Then painful white blisters, followed by peeling, long strips of translucent skin that left vulnerable new flesh. Over and over. And why? Because her sun-worshiping mother and father, who tanned easily, could not believe that Lena would not. It was a stage, they said; Lena would get over it. They were naturalists, even dragging her to nudist camps, until she got old enough to protest. She'd felt like a guinea pig. Their constant experiment. A failed experiment. And she had suffered for those failures.

Sunphobic

"Hey, maybe Rio!" the fiery-haired woman cried. "I could go topless and get rid of my tan lines."

Lena turned her body away in disgust. The movement sent a sharp pain through her lower back. Lately, her muscles, or maybe it was her joints, had been acting up. Probably a summer cold coming on. Everybody seemed to have one. It was a good thing she'd stopped the vitamin D supplements. Being lactose intolerant, and the fact that she didn't use milk products, vitamins had seemed the only alternative. But that theory she'd read in one of the healthy-eating magazines, about supplements making the immune system dependent, had convinced her. She'd only started on the D because she'd read somewhere else about how lack of sunlight would cause a deficiency. That was the trouble, you read this, you read that. There were too many "experts," all with opposing views; who could you trust? In the end, only yourself. Well, she was living proof that after four years of not venturing outdoors even once in daylight unprotected, nothing bad would happen.

She scanned the backs of her hands, then her palms. Her skin was pale and unblemished, free of sunspots and dark pigment, the damage from childhood healed. She had the energy of five, more energy in fact than the vast majority of naive human beings who risked cancer and immune system depletions from those intense solar rays.

The couple next to her continued chatting. They discussed which resorts had the best beaches and pools. Foolish, that's what they were. Couldn't they see what was going on? The ozone layer was breaking down at an alarming rate, and ultraviolet rays scanned the earth daily like alien eyes searching for research subjects. Well, Lena thought bitterly, I'm not going to be a victim again. Suddenly she felt depressed. Alienated. Why couldn't people *see* they were in danger?

Once the train reached her stop, she halted on the platform and began the ritual. She squeezed the last of the zinc oxide from the tube and spread the cool white cream over the dried layer already coating her exposed skin. There wasn't enough and she was forced to open the new tube of sunblock 39. Then she coated her lips with sunblock 17 lip wax. She fumbled in her purse for the dark glasses that blocked UV rays. She would not risk the tiniest bit of light.

But all this made her angry again. She'd been more charged than usual lately. It was summer, the air warm, but still she was forced to wear polyester pants, thick boots, a long-sleeve polyester blouse, floppy hat and gloves, all so any stray sunbeams couldn't penetrate the plastic clothing to her vulnerable hide. Her large purse held a polycotton ski mask—the best blend she could find—but today was so hot she couldn't bear to put it on.

A smell wafted down the stairwell and into the station—fish. From the lake. With it came the flash of a memory.

She was ten, boating with her parents. Yellow light, silver glint on water. White sails snapping. The small cabin cruiser skirted Lake Huron. Hot breeze. Skin warm. Lena stood at the helm, rocking gently from side to side with the pull of the water, piloting the craft for hours. Heat unbearable. Her head throbbed. Vision blurred.

Sunstroke. Severe. She'd been dehydrated, weak and nauseous for days afterward. Exhausted. Her flesh suffered second degree burns. Her mother and father didn't say anything to her directly, but from their intense whisperings, she knew they were angry. She had been a disappointment and a bother. Again.

Lena resented all this paraphernalia she had to wear. It was *their* fault, the ones who polluted the air, who didn't bother cleaning up what they excreted. They were like some alien conspiracy, bent on destroying everything through overexposure. They forced her to protect herself from what was natural—sunlight—because they had ripped away the filter that was so necessary. But she knew their game. She would never again risk exposure to what was deadly.

She hurried through the turnstile and stopped. Cement steps led up to the dangerous outdoors. Stifling air and killing light reached down like metallic tentacles. She took in a deep breath, popped open her large black umbrella, and ran up the stairs. Halfway to the top, sunlight struck.

Lena felt light-headed. Noise, people, all the scents packing the air dimmed as she focused on the cage of harsh light. Her brain *knew* the coatings and clothing would protect her, but her cells reacted to the violation.

Sunphobic

She ran a block and a half, frustrated when the traffic light turned red, causing seconds of delay. The heat was unbearable. The weather report was wrong, as usual. They said 78. Obviously it was more like 98!

The moment the light flashed cool green, she sprinted across the wide street, over the pavement, and dashed up the steps of the house where she had recently rented an apartment. The overhang provided little protection. She fumbled with the ring for the right key.

Finally the door was open. She raced down the stairs to the basement.

Lena stood before her apartment door panting. Her leg muscles spasmed, the bones beneath them ached. Oh no! She *was* under the weather. It had been those damn supplements! The article warned there'd be withdrawal symptoms, even up to a year later.

She slammed the door to her apartment behind her and, with a sigh of relief, snapped the dead bolt. The small windows at the top of the walls had long ago been blocked with black oilcloth. The apartment was as black as space.

Her cheeks and forehead felt like a mask of hard grease. She peeled off the nonporous clothing and stood nude in the cool darkness, catching her breath.

Finally! Safety. Even after all these years, she still felt grateful to have braved that fireball again and survived.

The basement was refreshing, and she decided to stay undressed, as she did many summer nights. She had blocked the air-conditioning vent, not wanting to contribute to the global warming problem. Mrs. Edwards, who owned the house and lived upstairs, said there was no way to turn it off just for her. Mrs. Edwards was angry Lena had taken the initiative, deciding, based on nothing, that blocking the vent would damage the system, if not overload the electrical system.

She felt only a little cooler naked; she'd better take her temperature.

Navigating through the one-bedroom apartment to the bathroom couldn't have been easier if she'd been a mole burrowing through familiar underground tunnels. She didn't bother turning on the light, but washed the zinc oxide from her face and hands in the dark. There was only one item on the shelf above the sink. She pressed the dispenser. A glob of soothing cream filled her palm. She applied a liberal coat of aloe vera over her entire body, letting its healing properties repair any damage that may have been done. Suddenly she didn't feel so hot; no need to take her temperature. Obviously it had been just the heat of the day.

She thought about her constricted life and how necessary that was. Working freelance meant she didn't need to go out often, and her apartment was safe; the only threat was that one passage where she exited the subway. It was like a chasm. A tear in the fabric of her universe. Fury surged. Why were her options so narrow? It was because of *them!*

Lena wasn't hungry, but thought she should eat something. By the light of the refrigerator she prepared brown rice and a salad of raw green beans and lettuce, after she'd stripped the head of the burned leaves and dumped them into the kitchen composter beneath her sink. Research had encouraged her to tailor a vegan diet to her own needs. The diet had kept her healthy so far. Apparently she got all the vitamins and minerals she needed.

Getting rid of the radiation-emitting TV had been a smart move. Over dinner she read with the aid of a candle flame the latest research in *Scientific American* on ozone depletion. Her hips ached, for some reason, and when her calves began to throb and feel as if they were turning inward, she decided to make it an early night.

Lena awoke to a noise. It sounded like her mother's voice, calling her name from down the beach, the sound traveling through the hot air and high over the crashing surf.

She lay on her bed naked, uncovered. Boiling. Her body slick with sweat in the stifling darkness. Her heart beat erratically. She turned toward the clock for the time—there was no time. Again a sound. Movement through her apartment!

She tried to get out of bed. Slowly, painfully, she sat up. Her body was so stiff, the muscles sore, the bones they encased felt weak and light and on fire.

Whoever was in here was at a disadvantage. *She* didn't need light to get around, but *they* did. Carefully and quietly she crawled along the floor to the half-closed door and listened.

A peculiar sound. A hot sound. A red sound. Sizzling. No, it was whispering. My God, there were two of them!

She heard a male voice say "Overload," and "Damage." Then, "Maybe irreparable."

A beam of concentrated light scanned the room, she saw two dim shadows flit through the living room.

She was stark naked, exposed. Her robe lay across the room, but she could not risk getting it. Her sanctuary had become a trap. She had to escape.

On hands and knees, like a child, she crawled soundlessly along the carpet toward the apartment door. Her hand climbed the door frame, then to the left. In seconds she touched the knob.

She leaned back, trying to get from her knees to a crouch, but for some reason her legs were resisting. Pain shot up through her shins to her thighs. Her pelvis felt twisted.

"Too close to the source. Can't cool down," a male voice said.

"It's her fault. Well, she'll have to pay," a woman answered.

Lena forced herself back, despite the pain. A joint snapped loudly. The voices paused. She had to get out! Now!

Lena turned the dead bolt, threw open the door, then raced down the hallway. A voice behind—"Lena. My God! Wait!" But she was up the stairs and outside under the blazing sun before she realized.

People stopped and stared, mouths agape. But it wasn't the fact that they saw her naked that sent her out of control. The door to the house had locked behind her. She pounded on the glass, screaming, crying. Her legs gave out beneath her and she collapsed on the steps and fell down them to the sidewalk.

It wasn't long until the police arrived. Lena tried to tell them about the sun, and how it killed, slowly, painfully. And Mrs. Edwards was there. "Emergency . . . knocked . . . didn't think she was home . . . let the repairman in to unblock the air conditioner . . ." She heard an ambulance siren growing louder.

"She's so pale," the policeman said, and the female office found a spare shirt in the cruiser and covered Lena with it. But it only covered some of her body. She lay helpless in the light of day, most of her skin exposed to the yellow fire searing down and into her, forcing her into submission to its brutal will.

When Lena awoke, she lay in a bed in a hospital room. A window beside her allowed sunlight free access to her face and arms. A needle was embedded in the vein on the inside of her left elbow. Her right leg was in a cast, elevated. She felt weak. Drugged. She struggled to move her hand, to cover her head with the blanket. Her entire body ached and the slightest movement caused pain.

Two doctors walked in. "How are you feeling?" The woman took a pencil from her pocket and made a notation on a plastic clipboard.

Lena tried to speak. Her lips felt dry, burnt. "The sunlight," she managed. "The window."

"Yes, you could use some sunlight," the male doctor said. "There's plenty of vitamin D in sunshine, and you've got a serious D deficiency. Your body hasn't been absorbing calcium. Your bones have been affected, and you've sustained a bad break in your right femur."

The woman told her, "If you hadn't been treated soon, you'd be crippled for life, if not dead."

Lena recognized she had no choice; she had to place herself in the hands of these two. Maybe they would take better care of her than her parents had.

"Have you been suffering from depression, irritability, hysteria? Aching bones and joints? They're classic symptoms of a deficiency."

Symptoms? Of a deficiency? A smile twisted Lena's mouth. She felt the skin on her cheeks swell upward as if it had become one large and painful blister. "All my life," she whispered.

READY OR NOT

Alan M. Clark

A NIGHTMARE FROM MY PAST RETURNS TO HAUNT ME, BRINGING with it the ghost of insanity. I call the ghost Malcolm S. Mulheney, or just plain Mal.

We were best friends in Vietnam during the war. But that was before he killed a couple of my good friends in the jungles of Quang Tri Province. I tried to forget him and the pain he'd shown me. Truth is, I never really got him out of my system and I've never been able to get close to anyone since.

For reasons that are unclear to me, I have boarded a flight to go see him in the hospital where he's been kept ever since the killings. The flight attendant says something about this airplane being a DC-10 and how he hopes I'll have a good flight. Right now, that's the farthest thing from my mind.

It was what—day before yesterday—that I got this call from a doctor named Cutlip at the Tucson V.A. Domiciliary; Mal's home away from home. The doctor had asked me what I knew about what happened to him.

"His universe was pulled out from under him," I had said. "I told you guys all I knew about Mal back when you owned me."

But the doctor kept talking, telling me that he was the new

229

head of psychiatry there at the hospital and that, having read all he could on the case, he had some hope for Mal. I didn't want to think about it, but I was polite and I listened.

"You were the one who subdued him when—"

"Hey, I just tackled him," I said. "And the other guys all piled on to keep him from swinging his M-60 around."

"Yes," he agreed. "But it says here in the report that once you got him into the helicopter you kept him calm by talking to him, and that for a short time before he lapsed into catatonia, he seemed quite lucid."

He told me that lately Mal has been more responsive to the staff and has been heard to say my name. Cutlip had a whole lot more to say, so I listened, not understanding everything. But I could see that the guy had his heart tuned properly, and before I knew it, I heard myself agreeing to come visit Mal.

F-15. I locate my seat wedged between a fat man chewing gum with his mouth open and a silly-looking woman wearing too much makeup and fun-in-the-sun apparel. The woman makes little effort to tuck in her legs so I can get by. The fat man has spilled over into my seat. He gives me a look of disgust and lets his breath out sharply as he moves his briefcase and coat so I can sit down. I must not dress and groom myself the way he would like me to. This is typical of the crap I've gotten from people ever since I came back to the States.

I got home from the Nam five years ago and I'm trying to build a life in the real world. It's not much of a life yet—eight jobs in the last three years alone, no good friends, and no place to live that I'd want to call home. After what happened with Mal, it's difficult to trust anyone. I had a lover for a short time, but found myself beating on her and decided to cut the relationship short. I can't seem to get comfortable anywhere or with anyone.

And it looks like I'm not going to get comfortable here either. Damned seat's too small. The fat man and the silly woman are using all the armrests, and I have to sit with my elbows in my lap.

As we taxi to the runway, the captain is making garbled noise at us over the intercom.

Smells damned strange in here. Someone ought to come

up with just one perfume to put in all the toiletries for men and women, so if people wanted to stink themselves up like that, at least they'd all smell the same. Then there'd be none of these weird-ass odor combinations, like the smell of the fat man's hair grease mingling with the five different perfume aromas wafting my way from the five nearest women.

Now that the plane is taking off, I'm stuck with these strangers for the duration of the flight. And they're getting stranger all the time as I breathe their breath and watch their every move.

Some of these smells trigger memories of places and things I'd rather not recall—experiences in the Nam. Remembering the war, I'm becoming more and more uncomfortable with the tightness of my current surroundings.

Claustrophobia—I guess this is something like the way Mal felt in the jungle. It was hot and humid, had the most God-awful insects I'd ever seen, and the animals screamed at you wherever you went. But to hear Mal talk, it surrounded and touched every inch of him, closed over his mouth and nose and tried to suffocate him.

See, Mal was from Arizona, where, he told us, it got hotter than the Nam ever thought of being. "The air's dry, though," he said. "The heat don't follow you around. Even on the worst days, you stand in the shade and you can cool off."

He complained about the jungle getting into his fatigues and boots. I thought he meant the bugs. But he said it was the air itself, all full of warm moisture and the smells of the jungle and its people.

He had this nervous habit of swinging his arms and that damned M-60 real wide and shrugging his shoulders for no reason. He'd just be walking along and make these weird gestures like he was checking his elbow room or pushing with his shoulders against the air around him.

He tried to tell me about his claustrophobia—said it started when he was about seven or eight playing a hide-and-seek game called Sardines with some neighborhood friends. I'd never heard of the game myself. He explained that the one who's It hides and the others try to find his hiding place and hide with him. The last to find the hiding place is It for the next round.

When it was his turn, he'd hidden under a rickety loft behind some boxes of newspaper in a run-down garage. Junk was stacked high and carelessly on the rotting frame of two-by-fours. As the other kids crammed into the narrow hiding place, everything got pushed out of shape, and down came the loft and all this dusty garage shit on top of them.

The other kids got out all right. But Mal was pinned. The framework of the loft had landed on his legs, breaking the left one. A wooden crate on his chest had broken several ribs and punctured a lung. He was fighting for air and at first didn't have the wind to cry for help.

The others were all laughing. Rage and panic overwhelmed him. It was as if he had been swallowed whole and there was no air in the belly of the monster garage. He couldn't move. He felt that if he didn't get out immediately, he would never move again—he would be a fossil embedded in crushing stone, a fossil with terrible pain!

Eventually, he passed out. The other kids finally caught on to what had happened and began to dig him out of the wreckage. The loft was too heavy for them to lift and they had to find grown-ups to help. After forty-five minutes Mal was free. But the terror of that experience would strike him unexpectedly, again and again, for the rest of his life.

Claustrophobia—I never experienced it until I heard Mal describe it.

Now that we're airborne and the no-smoking light has gone out, the silly woman to my right lights up. The way she holds her cigarette, the smoke rises straight into my face. She pretends not to notice. I won't say anything, won't give her the satisfaction of knowing I don't like it.

The Sarge wouldn't let anyone smoke while we were out on patrol. The enemy could smell it a mile away, he had told us.

The game we played in Vietnam was hide-and-seek of the deadly variety. Mal and I were part of a platoon involved in reconnaissance patrols in Quang Tri. Our squad of about eight men hiked deep into enemy territory counting enemy strengths, directing artillery fire and air strikes and generally collecting information for the brass. We followed the dirt trails that crisscrossed Quang Tri, trails punctuated frequently with booby traps.

Ready or Not

The Sarge had us all taking turns on point. When you were leading the way like that, you had to know what to look out for. If you missed just one booby trap, you might find yourself missing a whole lot more. Or it might miss you, and then you'd be missing your good buddy who was walking along behind you.

I remember the Sarge real well—name was Howey Rhodes. He honestly believed in that war, and since I didn't know what to believe and needed a role model, I followed his example.

Besides Mal, I was closest to Blue Boy. He was young and looked like the guy in the painting. He and a guy we called Rampage were the funny ones. The more frightened we were, the harder they tried to get us to laugh.

Spook was quiet. He had this uncanny way of just all of a sudden being there. You wouldn't hear him approach. But you'd turn around and there he'd be. It would startle the shit out of you until you got used to it. He was the best at sneaking up on the enemy, and he loved doing it.

It's hard to remember some of them, especially the ones that didn't last long—like Igloo. All I remember about him was that he kept all to himself. The guys said it was like he had a wall of ice around him. Others, like Hairball and The Evangelist, an irritating baptist from Tennessee, weren't around long enough for anyone to get to know. Seemed like a core of the squad stayed intact for a long time while our replacements just kept being replaced.

One night we were all bedded down in a small clearing. We knew we wouldn't be hitting the red zone until late tomorrow morning and so we were feeling remotely secure —all but Mal. He wouldn't eat, wouldn't talk to us, just fiddled with his gear, rubbed his photo of his girl (he said this brought him luck) and mumbled to himself. When I looked over at the photo, I could see that her face had been rubbed clean off.

Then, when everyone was asleep but me, the watch, and Mal, he turned to me suddenly with this look on his face like he'd just shit a poisonous snake and wanted me to help him get rid of it before it bit.

"I've got fifteen days left. And the closer I get to going back to the world, the more this place crowds me. It's closing in like it's going to hold me down and keep me here. I've got the worst feeling that I'm not getting out of here alive—worse than ever."

I didn't need this shit. Everyone was scared of not making it. But it was the way he put it—I could feel what he meant. I'd always had a problem with that; somebody tells me something they feel, and it's like I'm right there in their shoes, in their skin, looking out through their eyes. It caused me a lot of pain. Every time I saw someone catch a slug or a piece of shrapnel, it was like I took the impact and the pain along with them. And sharing Mal's mental anguish was just the same.

He had been talking like this on and off for some time, and it was really getting to me. I wanted to keep my distance, but he was my best friend. We'd survived together.

The next day we were trudging down this trail through a broad, grassy area. I was on point and it had been pretty painless. One bouncing betty was disarmed and we caught sight of a shitload of pungi sticks before they caught us.

When my turn at point was up, the Sarge tapped Mal on the shoulder and said, "You're it, Mal. Take point."

I fell back and Mal shrugged his way forward. As he passed me I could see his eyes changing like they were becoming wide-angle lenses, taking in as much as possible. He might be nuts, I told myself, but he was not likely to miss anything. He was giving himself instructions as he moved along, and the Sarge had to remind him to maintain noise discipline. He turned and flashed this fierce look at the Sarge and began to mouth his words silently.

We were approaching a slight rise and Mal saw a bush making very unbushlike moves. He signaled with his hand and we all dropped. Suddenly, silently, trees on three sides sprouted teenage boys complete with tennis shoes and guns to play army. Except these were grown men who looked about the size of fifteen-year-olds to me, and their rifles weren't toys.

Mal took a slug through the upper left arm and Igloo got one in the back. We were all scrambling for the brush. All but Mal, who stood and started pruning the trees with his M-60. The human clippings were falling and he was screaming at them like he knew them by name and they'd pissed him off.

The rest of us were firing and doing our best, but it was Mal that cleaned up. He took another slug in the thigh before he was through with them. But once they were all down, he didn't stop. He turned his weapon on us, nearly cut the Sarge in two.

I was up now and I tackled Mal. With the wounds he had, he went down easy, but he was still thrashing around firing his weapon. Blue Boy got one in the head. The others, Spook, Rampage, and a new guy whose name I don't remember, all grabbed a piece of Mal. Hairball got the M-60 away from him.

And just like that, it was all over and everything was quiet, even Mal. I felt the tension go out of him. His muscles relaxed and tears began to puddle up in his eye sockets as he lay there on his back with his eyes closed.

We called for Medevac and returned to base. The Sarge, Blue Boy, and Igloo were dead. Mal was packed off to the States and locked away. Two good friends were dead and Mal might as well have been.

I've never known how to feel about this after all these years; much less how I feel about Mal. I do know that I'm angry and I want someone to pay for what happened. But I haven't found anyone to pin the blame on, not even Mal.

I get these bizarre urges when I think about it. Like right now, I want to take a rifle and see how many of these passengers I can take out before someone can stop me. There are maybe a couple hundred of them. With them strapped all snug in their seats and me running up and down the aisles with an M-16 . . .

I'm not that nuts, though. Not like Mal.

The captain says we're beginning our descent. That's just how I feel—the closer I get to seeing Mal, the further I descend into the pit of my angry imagination. Mal made that descent and hit bottom. The difference between him and me is that I'd always been able to pretend that it wasn't real, just a bad dream.

But now, reliving some of this shit, I stumble on fears that I should have dealt with. They're like the booby traps in the jungle. Instead of denying them, I should have disarmed them long ago.

I know that no one is out to get me, that's my rational side, but my feeling is that everyone *is* out to do me harm. As I look around this plane, I can find it in subtle things the people say and do. A lot of the time it isn't easy to distinguish between what I believe with my rational mind and the crazy ideas that come from what I feel.

I am home from the war and I'm safe. I know now that it cannot follow me, but in many ways I feel it has. The war is in me, and I feel shame and guilt for what I've done. I've done the job I was asked to do—a job all of the passengers on this plane counted on me to do—but no one here could accept me if they knew what the job involved. These people don't know that, because the squad didn't have the man-power to carry wounded prisoners, I shot them in the head rather than leave them behind to alert the enemy to our presence and strength.

I have this fear that it shows in my face, that people can see that I'm a killer, and that one day someone might decide to do something about it. So I'm careful to watch everyone, to see if anyone catches on to who and what I am.

Knowing that this is paranoia doesn't help.

So why am I going to see Mal? Fuck, I don't know. Maybe it's because he was my friend and we survived together.

Shit, that's a laugh. Neither one of us survived.

Or maybe I'm partly responsible for what happened to him. If I'd made more of an effort to talk to him when he was slipping . . .

The fat man wants to get by me. "The plane has landed, buddy," he growls. "You gonna get off, or what?"

What will happen when I see Mal? Will he give me a big hug? Or is he so nuts he won't even recognize me?

And what about me? In trying to help Mal, am I seeking some sort of atonement for whatever it is that I think I've done wrong?

"For the most part, Malcolm has been in a catatonic state for the past five years with little response to the staff."

Dr. Lealand Cutlip is a round, red-faced man, kinda nervous and not much like the friendly voice I heard over the phone. His words are as dry and clinical as his office. There isn't anything in here that isn't functional; no gewgaws, art, or decorations of any kind, not even curtains, just open blinds letting in the harsh, white, Arizona sun.

He's telling me about Mal's condition and there's only so much of it I understand. His description of catatonia gives me the impression that Mal is holed up inside his own head, that he can't be a part of the world for fear of his capacity for violence. Sounds like another tight space, one in which he has trapped himself.

"Periodically," says Cutlip, "Malcolm comes out of it and becomes agitated, even violent. There was an incident shortly after he was brought here in which he attacked an orderly and nearly killed him. And then here recently, he became violent again. An orderly stooped to retrieve a fallen food tray and the sudden movement must have disturbed Malcolm. He brought his knee up into the orderly's face. When the poor fellow reeled back, Malcolm struck him in the throat. If one of our nurses hadn't performed a crude tracheotomy, the man would have died."

"Isn't he locked up? I mean, strapped down or something?"

"Oh, no." The doctor is a bit surprised. "That would be cruel. This is not a hospital for the criminally insane, and his is not considered a criminal case in spite of what happened in Vietnam. That was ruled a friendly fire incident."

"So, how can I help?"

"Well, to start with, let's just see if there's any reaction when he sees you."

"But you said he's almost always out of it."

"Oh, he's perfectly aware of everything going on around him. It's just that he's not always able to respond."

The doctor rises, motions toward the door, and we exit the office. In the corridors there is nothing to excite the human mind. Maybe that's intentional. The light coming through the windows dims. A cloud must be passing in front of the sun.

I hear the echoes of our footsteps, a typewriter clacking, a door opening or closing with a squeak, and, far away, a sound halfway between a chuckle and a sob. At an intersection whispered voices come from the corridor to my right. "He won't be leaving today," is all I can make out.

Are they talking about me? Have they prepared a room for me here?

My palms hurt from my fingernails digging into them. I should take slow, deep breaths and try to relax. Cutlip must see how nervous I am. Why doesn't he say anything?

The doctor pauses, his hand resting on the handle of a door. "Malcolm may look very different to you," he says. "He's been inactive for many years."

I nod and my stomach feels like it's just turned a flip.

He opens the door and I see a man leaning against the wall inside the room; an orderly, I guess. Another man sits in a chair, leaning forward as if he's studying the pattern on the tile floor.

It's Mal. But he's gotten so thin. His head is balding, and the little hair left has turned gray. Cutlip motions the orderly over toward Mal.

"Carter, please help Malcolm to sit up."

The orderly crouches and pulls Mal upright. The eyes look vacant. My gut is full of restless worms and my skin prickles all over.

"Position yourself in front of Malcolm," Cutlip tells me, "so he can see you."

Now, face-to-face with Mal, I see no recognition in his eyes. His face remains slack. Slowly, his eyes focus on me, a slight tremor runs through him and a wet sound comes from his open mouth. I want to hide. His face twists into a childish look of pain as if he's going to cry. My name comes crackling out of his throat and he begins to reach for me. I shrink away and the orderly pulls Mal back by the shoulders.

His face quakes with anger and Mal drives his right elbow back into the orderly's ribs. There is an audible crack and the man stumbles back and falls to the floor holding himself.

I'm up and headed for the door. Cutlip is moving toward me and we collide, head-to-head—a hard metallic jolt like an electric shock. And now blackness . . .

I have to move through it, through the flashing honeycomb patterns in my eyes. I must get out!

I stumble on something—Cutlip on the floor.

Why was he trying to stop me?

Ready or Not

I'm up and through the door and I hear Mal behind me. He's grabbing for my shirttail! Nowhere to go but straight down the corridor. Doors could lead to dead ends or no telling what, and windows, no time to get one open.

I'm screaming for help but I don't see anyone.

An intersection—move to the right—have to make it to the stairs.

Mal is screaming now. Looking back, I see him bounce off the wall, miss a step and stumble. But he's on his feet and still coming.

I grab a door frame and swing into the stairway and I'm moving down the winding steps, taking three and four at a time. Above me I see Mal spring over the railing and drop an entire flight.

I hit the stairway door hard, stunning my left arm and shoulder. But I'm out and I see people and I'm shouting for help.

The door behind me slams open against the wall, and I turn and there's Mal with a hungry look on his face and he's coming on with incredible speed. I turn away from him and run right into an orderly and knock him on his ass.

And there's the admissions desk and the front door.

There's a shout and, looking back, I see that the orderly on the floor has grabbed Mal by the leg. Mal fists him in the side of the head and the man slumps. Another orderly rushes to intercept him. Mal sweeps the guy's legs out from under him and the man goes down with a crack when the back of his head meets the floor.

And I'm out the front door and running across the courtyard toward the front gate. Reaching it, I turn to see Mal just coming out of the building. With his long legs, he's faster—I'm just across the road and he's already at the gate.

He's got to tire out before I do. He's so thin and he's not used to this.

There's nowhere to go—just a plowed field! Across the field there are trees; I could hide in them or climb one and defend myself from higher up.

The plowed dirt is so loose, I can't get my footing—like running in a dream, I can't seem to get anywhere. I stumble on over the clods and soft spots.

He's right behind me. I feel his fingertips, his breath!

My heart is a tight, cramping fist, lungs dry and raw, and my vision swims.

My foot—caught between heavy clumps, and I'm going down. The dirt bites into me. I know what's coming, have to turn over and face him.

But now it's difficult to move; the limp arms and legs of Dr. Cutlip tangled about my own. Struggling, I turn to see the orderly just beginning to rise, his arms cradling his injured ribs.

A shaft of sunlight breaks free from the clouds and spills in through the window, illuminating the dark form that closes in on me.

Shaking the honeycomb pattern from my throbbing, aching head, I look up at Mal. The glow, the relief and sanity that shines from his face, is the final insult. The world does not approach as it surrounds and suffocates.

He raises a pale, bony hand—reaches down and taps me gently on the shoulder.

"You're it," he says.

THEY KNOW

Brad Strickland

AL RICHARDS SAW OLD MAN GARLAND STANDING ON HIS lawn beside the paper box, and the first thing Al thought was that the old coot was there to complain. No matter that Al delivered the Abington County *Informer* to the whole rural north third of the county; no matter that years might go by without a single skipped subscriber or late delivery; no matter that he knew every soul on his paper route as well as he knew his own family. Toss just one on the roof, forget to stuff just one Sunday comics section, and you caught high hopping holy hell.

Al slowed his clattering Chevy down. Normally he didn't even have to stop, just got down to a crawl, slipped across the vinyl-covered front seat, and chucked the paper into the box without aiming, then moved back under the wheel as the car regained speed. But Old Man Garland looked like he had something on his mind.

"Afternoon," Al said, putting the car in park and sliding over to offer the paper to Garland.

The old farmer took it with a hand ropy with veins, knobbed with knuckles, spotted with age. "Thanks."

"Nice day," Al said.

Garland grunted.

"Well . . . these papers ain't gonna deliver themselves."

Al slipped back across the seat, out of range of Garland's odd, pale eyes, irises so milky blue that they almost faded into the whites.

The old man hunkered down on his heels and clamped his free hand on the window frame. "Listen," he said. "You know anybody got some puppies? Or grown dogs, even?" Those pale eyes, their pupils startlingly black, pinned Al down.

Scratching his left arm where the June sun was hot on it, Al thought. "What kind of dog, Mr. Garland?"

"Big one. I don't know. Shepherd, pit bull."

"Looking for a guard dog?"

Garland opened his seamed mouth, a mouth shriveled like a pale prune, closed it, swallowed so that his Adam's apple bobbed in the cleft of his blue chambray work shirt, and said, "Yeah."

Al scratched his head. "Well, let me see. The Victors out on Poplar Springs Road are fixing to move, and they can't take their old Randy with them. Randy's a German shepherd, full-grown, good-sized dog. He's pretty old, though."

"Mean?"

Al shrugged. "Don't know. He never bothered me any, but I never get out of the car. I'll ask the Victors about him if you want me to. They won't be going until end of the month."

"Yeah. Ask them. I'll see you here tomorrow."

Al caught Old Man Garland in the oblong of his right rearview ("Objects are closer than they appear"). The old man, paper under arm, stooped and picked up something—a rock—and threw it with a vicious sidearm cut. Al actually flinched, expecting the stone to crack against the rear window.

It didn't. It punched into the spirea hedge a little ahead and to the right of the car, and something gray darted out, too close, too fast, for Al to hit the brake. The Chevy lurched and crunched. He stopped the car on the shoulder a few feet farther along and climbed out. Old Man Garland was stalking toward him, his seamed face set in fury.

"Didn't mean to hit your cat," Al said. "The rock must've scared her, and she run right out—"

Garland stopped fifteen feet away. "Wasn't a cat."

They Know

Al looked at the gray and red ruin, registered the ratlike body, the naked tail. "Oh," he said. "A possum."

"Give you five dollars to carry that down to the bridge and throw it away. You take five dollars to do it?"

Al swallowed. "I guess. You know if they carry rabies?"

"Don't know. Never heard tell of one with it."

"Well, anyway, get me a sack or something."

Garland went into his house and came back with a plastic cinch tie garbage bag. Al puzzled over the best way to go about the job, finally turned the bag partly inside out, mittened his hands with the plastic, grabbed the body, pulled it back and in, and then tied off the top. Garland handed him a five-dollar bill.

That and pausing to toss the bag off the bridge into the river slowed Al, so he made the rest of his rounds at a little more than normal speed. His thoughts kept going back to the hapless roadkill, to the look of concentrated fury in Garland's pale eyes, to the sick, slick feel of fur, warm flesh, and bone through the plastic of the bag. It wasn't me at all he was mad at, Al realized at last. He wasn't even looking at me when his face was so mad.

He was looking at the possum.

The dead baby possum.

A week later, after finishing his route, he drove back from the Victors' house with their German shepherd, Randy, sitting in the passenger seat. Randy had that moody, worried look that all shepherds wore, and his big body swayed to the curves. He was a good car dog, though, and except for occasionally moving his paws for better purchase on the vinyl seat, he made no stir. Now and then he would whimper softly, and Al would speak to him: "That's a good boy. Good fella."

He parked in front of Garland's house, went around and opened Randy's door. The dog looked up at him apologetically, not sure what to do. Al stooped and retrieved from the floor the chain lead the Victors had given him. He snapped the lead to Randy's collar, and the big dog jumped out with a surprising delicacy, barely jangling the chain. He walked beside Al toward the house, his tail curled under, his head low, his nose working.

Garland came out before they reached the house, came down the steps, knelt in the grass to welcome Randy. The dog sniffed tentatively, gave a slight wag of his tail, and the old man reached out to ruffle his ears, to slap his shoulder. Randy ran his tongue out, and Garland laughed like a boy.

Al cleared his throat. "They had some dry food they wanted to give you. I'll bring it up."

He handed the lead to Garland, who didn't look up, and then went for the food. It was most of a twenty-five-pound sack, and he slung it up on his shoulder. He grinned as he headed back. Garland had taken the lead off Randy's collar, and the big dog was on his side, grinning, tail thumping hard enough to raise dust. Some people just had a way with dogs, and Garland was evidently one.

The old man straightened up. "What do I owe you?"

"Not a thing, Mr. Garland. I'm glad to see old Randy has a good home. Where you want this food?"

"Just put it on the porch beside the front door. I'll take care of it." Garland grinned, showing white dentures. "Tell you what. You come in, I have a couple of beers in the fridge, we'll crack 'em and drink to Randy. Okay?"

It was a long speech for him. Al nodded in genial agreement. "Sounds good to me."

The inside of Garland's home was neat, almost obsessively tidy. The kitchen was small but orderly, and the two tall bottles that Garland took from the refrigerator were dark brown and unlabeled. "Brew my own," he said. "Hope you like it." He popped the tops and handed one cold bottle to Al.

Al tilted it back. The ice-cold beer had a nice sharp tang, with a deep, smoky, nutty undertaste. "Good," he said.

"Well—here, let's set at the table."

They sat across from each other, an expanse of red-and-white-checked tablecloth between them. When the beer was half gone, Garland said suddenly, "I hate possums."

Al had been about to drink. He paused, the bottle tilted toward his lips. "Come again?"

"Possums," Garland said. "I hate them. They scare me." He took a long pull at his bottle, his Adam's apple bobbing. Then he belched softly and said, "They look like something from hell. They're . . . I don't know, ancient and evil. I used

244

to kill every one I saw, made my old woman mad. Let God's creatures be, she used to say. I still killed 'em, and when she'd see a dead one, I always told her dogs got it. Some people eat 'em. I'd sooner eat a devil from hell."

Al took a long drink, ready to leave now. "Well," he said, "not many people cook possum nowadays."

"Listen," Garland said, his cracked voice intense, "do you know anything about being afraid of things like possums? If maybe there's a medicine you could take for it?"

Al shook his head.

With a sigh, Garland said, "They know. They ain't got minds like a cat or a dog, but minds from way back, from dinosaur times. They're predators, what they call 'em. What's the word? Carnivores. Ever seen one at night, eyes shining like hellfire in your headlights? They know we've come along and replaced their kind, and they'd like to see us all die. They know."

Eyes in the headlights. Al had seen his share, all right, his share of night-running, speed-bump possums, eyes on fire but brains too dumb to flee a car. He'd crunched his share too—ba-*dump!* ba-*dump!* front wheel and rear, and a smear on the blacktop behind. They'd never bothered him, though, and he'd felt no more remorse for their deaths than for those of the late-flying moths suddenly cracked like eggs on his windshield. He swallowed the last of the beer and couldn't resist asking, "What do they know, Mr. Garland?"

The milky blue eyes looked haunted. "They know when they got you scared," he said.

Another week into hot summer, and twice Garland asked Al to dispose of small bodies in plastic sacks. The second time he protested that he couldn't do this anymore, that it was probably against the law to dump them off the bridge anyway. Garland thought a minute. "Come tomorrow," he said. "Help me dig a trench for them."

A blazing Saturday, the sun pressing down like a physical force. Randy lazed in the shade nearby, big, confident, a strong dog, while the two men worked with pickaxes and shovels to chisel out from the red clay a three-foot-deep trench, five feet long. "That ought to be enough," Garland grunted at last. He covered over the trench with a sheet of plywood, covered the mound of upturned earth with a tarp weighted by bricks all around the perimeter. "Have a place to put 'em now." He straightened, his back creaking audibly. "Have a beer or two with me?"

They sat outside, under a sycamore, Randy at Garland's feet. "They keep coming," Garland said. "Randy, he knows when one's around. You'd think they'd be a-scared of a dog that big, but they keep coming at night. I heard one up on the roof a couple of nights ago. Randy didn't get that one. I don't know. Maybe it was the big greasy one he killed yesterday, but he didn't get it that night. I think it was trying to find a way in to get at me."

Al swatted at a buzzing fly. "Might have been a squirrel," he said.

Garland set his jaw. "A possum. They know, I tell you. They know. They come by ones and twos now, but more often. I worry. What if they come by fives and tens? By the hundred? What could Randy do? Or me?"

The beer was as good as ever, sharp and welcome to his parched throat. The sweat on his shirt was cooling in the slight breeze, making his armpits clammy. "Mr. Garland, why are you afraid of them, anyway?" Al asked.

The old man sighed, looked away. "They're killers," he said. "They're made for it. Seen the teeth on one? Not like a dog's teeth, or a cat's. More like saw blades. Learn killing from when they're babies, never forget it. And when they've killed something, they don't eat it, not right away. They leave it out to rot for a while first." He shivered despite the heat.

Randy got up and shook himself, sending out a light cloud of red dust and yellow grass clippings. He trotted off across the neatly cropped lawn and through the garden patch, disappeared between rows of growing corn. "Maybe you can get over it," Al suggested.

"I'm seventy," the old man said. "I can't remember not being afraid of them. And they know when you're afraid."

"Wouldn't you like to get over it?" Al asked.

The old man glared at him but said nothing. Al tilted the bottle again to escape the angry gaze. The corn rattled violently, and Randy's deepthroated growl rolled out. Both men jumped to their feet, but at the garden patch Garland held back. Al pushed on into the corn, its sweet grassy odor cloying in the heat. Randy was there, his back to Al, shaking something hard. "You, Randy!" Al yelled.

The dog dropped the thing it had been shaking and turned. A couple of fine lines had been scored in blood along his muzzle. Randy trotted past Al, back to Garland. It was a grown possum this time, a long-snouted body gone almost white, shaggy and disreputable, one ear long torn away, patches of fur long missing, scars of ancient battle showing that it had been a fighter. Randy had broken the neck clean.

"One for the trench?" Garland asked.

"Yeah," Al said, his muscles remembering the labor of hacking into the red clay subsoil. "One for the trench."

The next Thursday Garland asked him to help dig another trench. "Already?" Al asked.

"First one's full," the old man said.

A Sunday afternoon. Al knocked on the door, and Garland opened to him. The air inside the house smelled of disinfectant. Randy lay on a round throw rug, whimpering. His nose was scored, his ear slashed deeply, one eye swollen shut. "They're coming more and more," Garland said. "A pack of three of them before sunup. Didn't have no fear at all, just went right for Randy. What you got there?"

Al cleared his throat. "I went to the county library the other day," he said. "They had this. You can borrow it if you want to read it. I thought it might help." He held out a thin book, wrapped in a plastic-protected gray and black dust jacket.

Garland took it and held it at long arm's length, squinting. *"The Treatment of Phobias,"* he read in his creaking voice, painfully bringing the word out broken-backed, one syllable at a time. "What's that mean?"

"It's a book about being afraid of things," Al said. "A psychologist wrote it. He says there's no medicine for phobias, but there's treatments, psychiatric things you could do. I took a look at it, and I couldn't understand all of it, but—"

The old man's face flamed. "Damn it, a book ain't no good!"

For a second Al thought Garland was going to hurl the book at him, but he didn't. He simply handed it over. "They tore up my dog. I got to take care of him," he said, kneeling beside Randy. An open bottle of peroxide, a bottle of iodine, and a tube of antibiotic ointment lay on the rug beside the dog's head, along with some squares of gauze stained with red blood going brown.

Al let himself out.

That week, or maybe the one after, he began to dream about them. He saw Old Man Garland's house from the outside, possums of every size and weight on the porch, on the lawn, millions of them, all watching him with that cold killer stare as he drove past. Possums were on the roof and hanging by their tails in the trees, in the paper box even. And though Al did not stop to deliver the *Informer,* did not even roll down his windows, he sensed something in the backseat, felt something leap to his shoulder, felt the piercing clench of fangs in his throat—

Al woke up, sweating, and switched on the light. Late at night, unable to get back to sleep, he read the phobias book himself. It convinced him that he did not have a morbid fear of possums, or of anything else for that matter, but the nightmare gave him a glimpse of what Garland's every waking moment must be like.

He did not stop to chat with Garland anymore, mostly because the old man gave him no opening. The dream never returned, and once when driving late at night, Al caught a half-grown possum sprawled on the asphalt, mouth open, eyes glaring that mad green reflective glow at the oncoming car. He swerved and missed the creature, and afterward he thought about it only briefly. Saving it made no more difference to him than killing it would have—one possum in the world more or less, no big deal.

Still, Al never paused at the Garland place, just slowed down to thrust the paper into the box, then sped away again. From time to time he saw Randy outside, looking haggard and eventually limping, favoring his right front paw. Through many days, the old man kept to himself.

They Know

Then one Monday, Al saw the Sunday *Informer* still in the box. He crammed the Monday paper in too.

And then the Tuesday one.

The Wednesday one had to be dropped to the ground beside the box.

Thursday, at last, he stopped. With all the papers under his arm, he knocked on the door, but got only the hollow echo sound that empty houses have. He dropped the papers, the earlier ones yellowing already, beside the door.

It was high August, sweltering, with the chirr of cicadas rattling away, the sound of summer frying itself toward fall. After hesitating at the foot of the porch steps, Al swallowed and walked around back. The first trench had all but vanished under unkempt new grass. Beside it was the second, and a third, a fourth, a fifth, the last one not completely filled in. The backyard grass needed cutting, and the garden patch looked a little neglected, not badly overgrown, but sprouting with the odd weed, some tomatoes overripe and sagging. It was not the garden of a neat man, not any longer.

A whiff of corruption came to him, and it seemed to Al its source was somewhere in the corn patch. He didn't want to walk into the green silence, but he did.

Randy lay there, ripped, gutted, bloating, buzzing with green flies. Dark oily stains had leached into the earth around the body. Al started back, hearing in his mind Old Man Garland's implacable voice: "When they've killed something, they don't eat it, not right away. They leave it out to rot for a while first." Al turned, gagged, and lost the coffee and pie he had eaten for lunch.

He staggered out of the corn patch. Something stirred in the tall grass beside the back steps, the steps that had beneath them a dark, cool place ideal for concealment. Al walked carefully. It could be a snake.

It wasn't a snake.

A nine-inch-long baby possum, snow-white but tinted pink from the redclay dust, came trotting out from the black recess under the steps, holding a dangling gobbet of something in its jaws. Al edged around, not taking his eyes off the little animal.

The possum looked at him, an antediluvian idiot stare.

They know, Al thought, fighting an urgent need to urinate. The possum opened its mouth to hiss and lost its rotting morsel. An oblong, irregular ball, it popped onto the grass, rolled almost to Al's toes, and came to rest. Al felt that his muscles were frozen. He couldn't take his eyes off the thing.

It lay in the dust, glazed, dirt-coated, but recognizable, staring up at him with a milky blue gaze.

THE BACK OF MY HANDS

Rick Hautala

THE BACK OF MY HANDS STARTED LOOKING LIKE A MAN'S, BACK when I was—oh, maybe ten or eleven years old.

I remember how fascinated I was by the curling, black hairs I saw sprouting there; how amazed I was when I flexed and unflexed my hands and watched the twitching blue lines of veins, the tendons as thin as knitting needles, and the bony knobs of cartilage and knuckle. Sometimes I used to constrict the flow of blood to my arms—you know, like a junkie—to make the veins inflate until they fairly bulged. The bigger they got, the more "manly" I thought my arms and hands looked.

It might seem laughable now, but I still believe that hands are a God-given miracle. They let us touch and manipulate the world outside of ourselves. Sure, scientists say that vision is the only sense where the nerve connects directly to the brain, but hands are the only things that let us reach out to touch and explore the world. They allow us to *feel* love and to *create* what we know and feel, both internally and externally.

They're our only *real* connection with what's "out there." Our other senses—sight, sound, taste, and smell can all deceive us. They trick us into thinking we're experiencing something that might not really be there.

But when we touch something, when we hold it in our hands and caress it, we have no doubt whatsoever that it truly exists.

When I look at my own hands now, though, I can't help but be filled with revulsion, with horror.

Yes, *horror!*

That's probably an overused word these days, but there's no better word for what I feel.

These hands—*my* hands—have done things so terrible, so hideous, that I can truly say they are not mine. They've acted as if powered by a will of their own—a will with a dark, twisted purpose. And in the process, they've ended the life of someone—of the one person I've been closest to in my life, the one person I should have cherished the most.

Okay, let me start at the beginning.

The easiest part was killing my twin brother, Derrick.

No problem there.

I'm serious.

It certainly wasn't very difficult to orchestrate. You'd think I was a musician, talking like this, but when it came time to actually do it—to aim the gun at him and pull the trigger—I didn't flinch or have the slightest hesitation.

And I've had no qualms about it afterward either.

Why should I?

Look, Derrick had it all. Everything. He *was* everything I wanted to be.

I know, I know . . . sure, he worked just as hard for it, maybe even harder than I did; but everything seemed to come so easily to him, almost as if it fell out of the sky and landed in his lap.

And it never came to me. Certainly not as easily anyway. And no way near as much.

You see, he was the one who was born with all the talent. I couldn't help but think that because that's what I heard my whole life, growing up. All through high school, Derrick was it—an honor student, popular, handsome, smart, talented. In college too, he graduated at the top of the class, married a gorgeous woman, had a wonderful family—three kids, and

The Back of My Hands

a beautiful house in the country, about two hours north of Portland.

Far as I could see, he had it all.

And what did *I* have?

Nothing.

The leftovers.

Sloppy seconds, if you'll excuse such an inelegant expression.

All my life I had to listen to teachers and friends' parents—even my *own* parents—exclaim with surprise that sometimes bordered on absolute shock how Derrick was so amazingly gifted, and that I was so . . . well, that I didn't quite measure up to the standard my brother set.

The worst of it was when people would question, sometimes even to my face, how identical twins could be so . . . so "different." Oh, we looked enough alike so anyone who didn't know us well couldn't tell us apart, but it seemed as if all the intelligence, personality, and talent went into his half of the egg, and I was left with . . .

Well, with sloppy seconds.

Maybe that really was the case.

I used to wonder about it, mostly late at night as I lay in bed, staring up at the bottom of Derrick's upper bunk. I still lie awake at nights, wondering. Now I have plenty of time to think about such things. Back when we were kids, I could hear my brother's deep, rhythmic breathing coming from the top bunk, as if even sleeping was something he simply did better than I ever could.

It didn't surprise anyone that Derrick and I both entered the field of art. Ever since we were kids, we'd both shown unusual talent for the visual arts, although, as usual, Derrick's paintings and drawings—hell, even his throwaway sketches—always seemed to be several notches better than anything I could ever produce.

Not that my stuff was bad, mind you. I have quite a bit of talent.

After college, we both landed jobs within our chosen field. Derrick started right out as a painter—an "artist" with a capital A. Within a year or so he was having one-man shows of his work at galleries in Boston and New York. The "art scene" had apparently taken notice of him, and within a year or two his paintings were selling for astronomical amounts. Personally, I thought they weren't worth the price of the canvas they were painted on, but there's no accounting for taste.

And what about me?

I went to work pasting up ads for a local giveaway newspaper, all the while trying to convince myself of the worth a steady paycheck held while I concentrated on my own art on evenings and weekends.

I think—hell, no! I don't have to lie about it anymore, do I? I *know*—that's when the full measure of the resentment I felt toward my brother began to blossom.

Until then it had always been there, festering inside me—maybe even since before we were born; but it had always been . . . you know, buried deep, like a seed in the soil that was struggling hard to push its way up to the sunlight. It was only after college, once we were out there in the real world, settling into our respective careers and trying to make a living, that I finally allowed the seed to break through the surface. Over the next few years, as I watched my brother accumulate success and wealth and fame— everything I wanted and felt I deserved—I watered and nourished that seed of envy and hatred. . . .

Yes, *hatred!* I hated Derrick, sure enough, and I cursed the fate that I had been born to, wondering why. What cruel, uncaring God could do this to me?

Why couldn't I have been given at least *something*—just one goddamned single thing more than my brother?

But Derrick had it all, and I had . . . much less.

That's when I started planning to change all that by killing him.

You know, one person I talked to a few days, maybe a few weeks ago, now, I'm not sure—but anyway, she said she thought I never *really* wanted to kill Derrick, that what I really wanted was to kill myself. She said that by identifying so closely with my twin brother and by envying his success so much, I was turning all my pent-up anger against myself. She used all sorts of fancy terms like "transference" and "guilt projection" and "displacement"—stuff like that— but I'm pretty sure she was wrong.

The Back of My Hands

I *really* wanted to kill Derrick.

I *had* to kill him.

The way I saw it, there was no way around it.

Getting to do it was much easier than I thought.

Derrick and I live—I should say "lived"—about two hours away from each other. I have a place here in Portland, and he lives up near Fryeburg. Driving up there was no problem. Last March, I knew his wife had taken the kids to Orlando for a week at Disney World. I thought he'd be there alone, no doubt working on some paintings for a show or something. I wasn't expected or anything, but I guess I was lucky that no one saw me or recognized my car. Just to be safe, though, I stuck to the back roads. It added a little time to the drive, but then again, what did I care?

Derrick lived in a fairly secluded area—a development with a lot of fancy-ass houses spaced pretty far apart. He didn't have any security or anything—no bodyguards or locked gates, so getting into his house was easy.

Hey! Who'd want to kill a famous artist, right?

It turned out I was right. When I got there, he was home . . . alone.

Before I got out of the car, I pulled on the two pairs of rubber gloves I'd brought at the pharmacy. I'd seen something on a cop show, I think it was, about how a detective lifted a fingerprint even though the burglar or whatever had been wearing rubber gloves. The rubber, you see, was so thin that it still left an impression—at least enough to identify the culprit.

So I wasn't going to take any chances.

Just shooting him wasn't going to be enough, though. I had to even the score a little bit too.

But like I said earlier, killing him didn't bother me any. I just aimed the gun at him and pulled the trigger.

Pop.

Of course, before I got to the house, the whole time I was driving, I couldn't stop thinking about *why* I was doing this. I came up with a whole shitload of excuses, but I knew they were all bullshit.

The real reason was quite simple.

Even I can see that now.

He had more talent than I did, and I knew why.

It was all in his hands!

The only time I felt even a tremor of nervousness was when I got out of the car and walked up to the door. Mostly, I think, I was just scared that some neighbor might see me going in. I suppose once he was dead I felt pretty excited too. I'll tell you one thing—I was glad he was dead because otherwise, trying to cut off his hands with that ax, and missing the way I did, would have really hurt.

Once I had what I'd come for safely rolled up inside a plastic trash bag, I left by the same door I'd come in, being careful to close and lock it behind me. I looked around to make sure there wasn't any activity at any of the neighbors' houses, then got into my car and drove away.

So that was pretty much it until I got home.

I guess I was still a little bit nervous when I got back to my apartment—you know, kind of jittery. I knew the cops would come around sooner or later and be asking all sorts of questions. I didn't have a solid alibi, but I figured they weren't going to suspect me much. Hell, Alice and the kids were going to get whatever inheritance was coming, and I'm sure there was plenty of that. I might get a little something, but not enough to make anyone suspicious.

Besides, who'd even think I'd want to kill my brother?

All I had to do was act like I was real broken up about it, and I was sure they'd let it slide. Besides, I already had everything I wanted from Derrick.

I had his hands.

In case the cops came around, I didn't do anything with them right away. I put the trash bag in the freezer and tried to forget about them. Of course, that didn't work because I knew they were there, and I knew sooner or later what I was going to do with them.

I waited until the next day. My hands were shaking, I was so excited as I took the plastic bag out of the freezer and defrosted the hands. The skin was as pale as polished marble. What I did was throw them into a pot of boiling water, like a couple of albino lobsters. You have to understand, I had no idea if what I was planning to do was going to work. I mean, I figured it would because skin is so tough, but you never know until you try something.

After boiling the hands for quite a while, I took them out and peeled the skin right off, turning it inside out like I was removing a glove or a dirty sock. Of course, there was no blood involved, and I had a little problem with tearing around the fingernails, but it wasn't anything serious.

When I was done and turned them back right-side out, I had two pretty close to perfect gloves made out of my brother's hands. I put them down on the counter, and I swear to God I thought they might start moving around on their own or something.

My biggest concern was that they wouldn't fit—that Derrick and I were still exactly the same size; but with a little bit of tugging and a few tiny slits here and there to loosen them up, I was able to pull them on over my own hands.

I could barely contain my excitement as I raised my new hands up in front of my face and looked at them. I flexed the fingers, thrilled by the taunt, elastic pulling of my new skin.

Let me tell you, it was exquisite beyond belief!

My hands—Derrick's hands, really—were trembling as I reached out to touch something . . . for the first time . . . with someone else's hands.

Think what it must've been like for me!

I can't tell you how excited I was, but I stopped myself because I knew I had other things to take care of first.

Unrolling my new skin gloves, I carefully laid them aside while I cleaned up. Then I took my new hands—because that's the only way I could think of them—and went into my work room.

I tell you, I was so excited I just about fainted. I felt like I was drunk or tripping or something as I pulled the skin gloves back on over my own hands and wiggled my fingers to make sure everything fit perfectly.

Custom made.

Once I was ready, I picked up a pencil, tacked a clean sheet of drawing paper to the drawing board, and began to draw.

For the longest time I couldn't stop staring at the back of my hands. Just like when I was a kid, I watched the skin shift and slide across my muscles and tendons, amazed at how the skin felt so supple, almost alive. I could practically feel it bonding with the flesh of my own hands—my goddamned less-talented hands.

This is it! I told myself. *The moment I've been waiting for my whole life! I'm going to draw what I see inside my own head with someone else's hands!*

But it didn't work out quite as I planned.

The sketch I started working on that night still seemed somehow flat and uninspired. The spark wasn't quite there. I had to tell myself that I was too excited, that I was distracted by watching the way my new hands moved; but deep inside, I already was starting to feel this gnawing worry that I still didn't *have* it. The picture looked like it was being drawn by . . .

Me.

It'll take time, I told myself, hoping I could calm down enough to concentrate.

That made sense.

I couldn't right off the bat expect to be able to feel and touch and control things that way Derrick had. I had to adapt to his way of feeling and manipulating the world.

After all, art doesn't happen overnight.

After trying for an hour or so, I carefully peeled the skin gloves off my hands. I wasn't quite sure what to do with them afterward. I knew if I left them out, they'd start to rot. Plus, once the cops came around, I wouldn't want anything like that hanging around. I wondered how to go about drying them out, to cure them. I thought maybe I'd tan the skin—you know, like leather, so they'd retain their suppleness.

While I was wondering what to do, the phone rang.

It was Alice, calling from Florida. She had just gotten a call from the Maine State Police, informing her that someone had broken into the house and killed Derrick. I wondered who had found him, but of course didn't ask. I tried my best to sound upset and supportive when she told me that she was flying back in the morning. I even told her I'd pick her and the kids up at the airport.

What a guy, huh?

After I got off the phone, I toyed with the idea of wearing Derrick's hands when I picked Alice up at the airport. I was curious to see if she'd recognize her husband's touch when I hugged her, but I decided that wouldn't be such a good idea. I had no idea what else to do, so I put Derrick's hands back into the freezer for the night.

The next few days were tough, if only because I had to act a lot more upset about Derrick's death than I actually felt. As expected, the cops came around and asked me all sorts of questions about how Derrick and I got along, about where I was the night he was killed, and was there someone who could corroborate my whereabouts—things like that. They pushed me pretty hard, but I held up perfectly, I must say.

One time, I think it was the second day after Derrick died, I was heading down to the police station to be interviewed again, and I did wear Derrick's hands. The whole time, I was pretty self-conscious about them, but no one seemed to notice.

But every night, when I put them on and sat down at the drawing board, I started to get some pretty unusual sensations. My drawings didn't seem to be any better than usual, at least not to me, but there was a feeling inside the gloves, inside my own hands when I was wearing the skin, that was . . . well, kind of strange.

I had finally come up with a method of preserving the skin. Every night before I began to draw, I would take fifteen or twenty minutes to rub hand cream into the skin. I didn't scrimp either. I bought the most expensive kinds of hand cream available, and spent a lot of time working it into the thirsty pores. Night after night it seemed as though the new skin—my new hands—were becoming increasingly supple and sensitive. Touching things—anything—became a thrill. Vibrant ripples of pure energy tingled from my fingertips, up my arms and neck, all the way to the center of my brain.

Let me tell you, it was exhilarating!

Intoxicating!

I could barely concentrate on my drawing because I spent so much time simply touching things . . . feeling them as if for the first time. That's exactly what it was like—for the first time in my life, I felt like I was really *feeling* things. And I kept telling myself, it was just a matter of time before I could translate what I felt onto canvas and paper. It would come, and soon enough I would have it all—my brother's talent and maybe even the fame and fortune I deserved!

But gradually—and I'm not sure when, maybe a week or so after Derrick died—something happened. It seemed as though my own hands inside the skin of Derrick's hands were changing. At first all of the sensations were pleasant— warm and moist, kind of tingly, but comforting . . . almost as if this was my real skin. But after a couple of nights the feelings turned more intense. The gentle warmth got steadily hotter, until it began to feel like there was a slow-burning fire smoldering deep beneath my skin. Every time I flexed my hands and watched the veins wiggle beneath the extra layer of skin, I gloried in the way the outermost skin—and I no longer thought of it as Derrick's skin—stretched and pulled.

These were *my* hands!

The skin had become *my* skin!

One night while I was drawing, lost—as always—in watching the way the skin on the back of my hands moved, my hands suddenly felt like they had burst into flames. At first I tried to ignore the pain and kept drawing; then I tried to endure it; but after a while I couldn't stand it any longer. I threw down my drawing pencil and started to roll one of the gloves off, the one on my right hand. Over the past few weeks, I had treated the skin so well that it usually rolled right off, but this time, when I lifted the top edge, it caught. I tried to pull it down, but the skin on my wrist lifted up and then started to rip.

Let me tell you, I panicked.

It took a great deal of effort for me to sit back, close my eyes, take a few deep breaths, and then try again. I sure as hell didn't want to damage the skin. Where was I going to get another pair like this? I thought maybe it was just a matter of decay, but when I took the edge of the skin on the other hand and tried to lift it up, I once again felt my own flesh pull up with it.

This can't be happening, I told myself.

Someone—I think it was that lady shrink I talked to— told me I must have imagined all of this, that Derrick's skin had rotted away to nothing by then, and that I was pulling at my own flesh. As if I'd want to skin my own hands! I listened to her, but like all that transference bullshit she'd been talking about, I knew she was wrong.

I lowered my drawing light and shined it straight down onto my hands, looking closely as I tried several times to peel back the skin. Each time, I got the same result. The skin wouldn't roll down. It was fused to the back of my own hands. Hell, I can't deny it. It looked like it had *become* my own skin.

I'm telling you, I was scared some at first, but the more I thought about it, the more I started to accept it.

Hey, this ain't so bad, I told myself. In fact, isn't this exactly what I'd wanted all along?

Why have hands that I have to put on and take off?

Why not make them permanent?

Didn't I want to feel the way Derrick had felt, and be able to control pencils and brushes the way Derrick had controlled them?

I had wanted Derrick's hands, had coveted them so much that I was willing to kill him to get them. So what was so wrong if his skin became permanently attached to mine? We'd been twins in the womb. Other than the women in our lives, we had shared everything, right down to our chromosomes. There wasn't anything we *hadn't* shared!

The only problem was, no matter what I did—whether I massaged more hand cream into them or held them under a steady flow of cold water—I couldn't make that maddening, burning itch go away. It penetrated all the way to my bones, bringing tears to my eyes. I told myself that I'd eventually get used to it, that this was just a stage as Derrick's skin and mine fused, but believe me, I didn't sleep very much that night.

The pain—yes, the pain!

It was a pure, silver, singing pain inside my hands, and it never let up! Even when I did sleep, I could feel it.

That next morning I was supposed to be at a memorial service being held in Derrick's honor at one of the art galleries in Portland. I forget the name, but I'm sure the invitation is still on my desk, back at my apartment. Everyone was going to be there—a lot of important people in the art community as well as Alice and Derrick's three kids. I've been trying to feel bad for them, losing their father like they did, but pity just doesn't seem to be inside me.

When I got out of bed that morning, hardly having slept a wink, I considered calling the gallery and canceling. I was supposed to say a few words about my brother, but I hoped Andrew—he's the gallery director—would understand that I couldn't cope with doing something like that.

Before I dialed the gallery, though, I started thinking how suspicious canceling out might look. Sure, the cops had stopped asking me questions, apparently satisfied that I'd had nothing to do with my brother's murder, but I couldn't be sure. They might still think I *had* done it, and they might just be waiting for me to slip up so they could nail my ass. Maybe they had recognized Derrick's hands that day!

So I determined, no matter how bad the pain in my hands got, that I'd go through with this farce of a memorial service.

The problem was, I had no idea how bad it could get.

Even before I walked into the gallery that morning and saw how many people had gathered to honor my brother, my hands were clammy with sweat. I shook hands with as few people as possible, but couldn't help but notice the startled reactions most of them had when we clasped hands.

Being one of the guests of honor, as it were, I had to sit in the front row along with Alice and the kids. Every wall in the room was adorned with Derrick's paintings. None of them were very good, I thought.

Andrew spoke first, a bit too long, I thought, about how he had been one of the first people in the "Art World" to recognize Derrick's extraordinary talent, and how we and all of humanity had suffered a great loss in such a senseless, brutal act. I could hear people sniffing back their tears, but I

The Back of My Hands

hardly paid any attention to them. I couldn't stop looking down at my hands. They felt like they were on fire.

I tried rubbing them, scratching them, folding my arms across my chest and pressing them against my sides—*anything*—but nothing would stop the pain and burning itch. It got so intense I thought I was going to scream.

I didn't notice when Andrew stopped speaking, but after a moment or two I noticed that the room was filled with a hushed expectancy like just before a thunderstorm hits. I glanced around the room and realized that everyone was staring at me.

A boiling blush raced up my arms and across my face. My heart was slamming hard inside my chest when I realized that Andrew must have already introduced me. I shifted uncomfortably in my seat, preparing to stand, but I wasn't even sure my legs would support me, much less carry me all the way to the podium.

The crowd was utterly still.

A steady, low, throbbing sound filled my ears as I inhaled and held my breath. I took a single step forward. My shoe scraping across the carpet made a sound like the rough scratching of sandpaper. Cold sweat broke out on my brow and trickled down the sides of my neck.

I wanted to scream, I tell you, but as I made my way up to the podium, I noticed a glass pitcher and several clean glasses on the small table beside the podium. The pitcher was filled with ice water, and that gave me an idea.

With each halting step forward, the agonizing sensation in my hands grew steadily worse.

Intolerable!

I had no idea what to do with my hands, whether to shove them deep into my jacket pockets so no one would see them, clasp them behind my back, or shake them wildly above my head and start screaming.

That's what I wanted to do—scream . . . scream until my throat was bleeding.

The thought crossed my mind that if I fell apart completely, everyone in the room would be sympathetic. They'd be understanding and think it was simply an outpouring of grief over the loss of my brother.

But my throat felt like it was closing off, and my chest and lungs were so constricted I could hardly breathe, much less scream. I was suddenly afraid that, if I opened my mouth and tried to say a few words—something about my dear, departed brother—deathly cold hands would clasp my throat and begin to choke me.

I was suddenly fearful that I would no longer be able to control my hands. The skin—Derrick's skin—had long since dissolved into my own hands, fused with my hands and become part of me. I glanced down at my hands and was suddenly quite convinced that I didn't even recognize them.

They were someone else's hands!

Derrick's!

Yes, I know that isn't possible. You're not the first one to tell me it was all in my mind, but even if it was, it was nonetheless true to me!

The silence in the room continued to pulsate. When someone toward the back of the room cleared his throat, it sounded like a distant cannon shot. Somehow, though, I made it to the podium. Leaning forward and gripping the edge of the podium with both hands, I forced a smile, but I could tell by the way the skin stretched around my mouth that it was more of a grimace.

Glancing to my left, I once again noted the pitcher of ice water. More than anything, I wanted to plunge my hands into that water to try to soothe the pain, but I just stood there, frozen.

I could see that the audience was getting restless, maybe feeling a bit embarrassed to see me so obviously distraught, but it was just as obvious—to me, at least—that they didn't see the real reason why I was so upset.

I nearly fainted when I lowered my gaze and looked down at my hands. The backs of my hands were discolored a sickly yellow and were wrinkled like an old man's hands. For a dizzying instant I felt as though I was looking at my hands through a huge magnifying glass. Every hair, every pore and blemish, every vein and tendon, stood out in frighteningly stark relief. The feeling that these were not my own hands—that they were Derrick's—grew terrifyingly stronger. I thought that, somehow, maybe Derrick was still alive and standing behind me, reaching around and manipulating things for me.

I tried to push these thoughts away and cleared my throat. With great effort, I began to speak.

"I want to . . . thank you all for . . . being here today."

I forced my grimace to widen, hoping it looked like a smile. I locked eyes with Alice, sitting there with her children in the front row. Her expression as she looked at me was soft, sympathetic. I could see that she was on the verge of tears, but she nodded to me, offering me her silent support.

The choking sensation in my throat grew steadily stronger. When I reached up to loosen my collar, I was suddenly fearful that my hands—Derrick's hands—were going to grab me by the throat and start to squeeze until they choked the life out of me.

I lowered my eyes and shook my head, taking a moment to compose myself. I wiped my forehead with the back of my hand, but it was like striking a match against a sunbaked sidewalk. A line of flames seemed to erupt across my brow.

It was intolerable, I tell you!

I wanted to say something, anything, just a few words about how much I mourned my brother, what a tragic loss his death was, but I couldn't focus on the few notes there in front of me. All I could think about was the burning pain that was flaming inside my hands and spreading up my arms.

I looked again at the pitcher of water and knew what I had to do. You see, I knew then—or if I had known it before, I finally admitted it to myself then—that these really *weren't* my hands.

They truly *were* Derrick's!

His dry, desiccated skin may have rotted away weeks ago, but some part of him had become fused with me, and this small part—the one small part I foolishly thought I could possess and control—was *not* under my control and never would be!

Maybe I would have been better off if I had killed myself then and there, had strangled myself in front of that crowd.

It would have ended it all, and maybe the people gathered

there would have thought that I had been unable to contain my grief and had finally snapped.

But that's not what happened.

And I didn't plunge my hands into that pitcher of ice water either.

I had tried that before, and I knew that it wouldn't work.

No, what I did—well, you probably read about it in the papers, but what I did was take that water pitcher and smash it against the side of the podium. I don't remember hearing the sound of breaking glass or feeling the cold dash of water. I sensed some immediate reaction from the crowd, but not much. I was lost inside a cocoon of silence where there was just the raging roar of my own breathing and the unbearable burning knowledge that my hands were not my own.

Holding the shattered handle of the pitcher, I turned the jagged edge around and began to slash and saw at the back of my hands.

"These aren't my hands! These aren't my real hands!"

I remember shouting something like that, but I can't remember exactly what because I was lost in a blind frenzy of panic as I cut and raked the broken glass repeatedly across the back of my hands. Suddenly an unnerving sensation swept over me, and I felt like I was somehow outside of myself—that I was floating above it all, watching what I was doing as if it was a movie or a play.

I felt no pain whatsoever, but I could see the thin strips of raw flesh I was scraping off the back of my hands. There was blood everywhere, but no matter how much I tore at the skin on my hands, it didn't stop the burning sensation inside them. It continued to spiral higher and higher until it was the only thing I knew. The mere physical pain of tearing flesh from my hands was nothing . . . literally nothing.

Every other sound in the room was muffled, but I sensed a rush of motion behind me as someone—it was probably Andrew—ran to help me . . . to try to stop me.

Then I heard a sizzling crackle. Trailing white sparks filled my vision, and then everything went black.

I woke up here in the hospital sometime later. I realize now that I must have grabbed onto the microphone and, because I was standing in the water I had spilled, had gotten one hell of an electric shock.

Not enough to kill me, mind you, and—well, the emergency room doctor said that, thankfully, I hadn't severed any arteries, so I didn't bleed to death. I could have, you know.

The most horrible thing about it all, though, is that I didn't get rid of Derrick's skin. It's still here, on the back of my hands.

See?

It's still growing. Maybe you can't see it, but that's because it's inside me now too, growing . . . and look at this. See? It's spreading up my arm like a fungus or something. Pretty soon it's going to cover my whole body!

I swear, it's true.

Look! Look at my hands.

What do you mean you can't see it?

It doesn't matter anyway, because the worse thing is, I still can't control them either. My hands! Even with these bandages on, I've been doing a little bit of drawing while I've been here, and as you can see, I'm not drawing anything very good. And it's certainly not what I want to draw.

Look at these sketches. Every single one of them depicts something from that night when I killed my brother.

See here?

This is him lying on the floor, leaning up against the wall. Don't you think he looks sort of like a puppet whose strings had been cut?

Well . . . doesn't he?

That's *exactly* what he looked like that night!

And check out this one.

This is the design the splash of blood made on the wall behind him, after I'd shot him. You'll have to take my word for it, but it looks *exactly* like the bloody smear on my sheet of notes. The exact same shape!

And look at this one.

See?

It's a close-up of Derrick's face, once he was good and dead. He looks really relaxed, doesn't he? Don't you think it's amazing how much he looks like me? I also did a couple of sketches of what his arms looked like after I'd chopped off his hands, but I had to throw them away. I didn't like the way they were coming out even though I always used to be pretty good at drawing anatomy.

The problem is, you see, I'm not the one who's doing these drawings.

Derrick is.

He's using my eyes and memory to record what happened to him.

His hands are doing this!

The police never would have even found out that I had killed Derrick if his hands hadn't started drawing these pictures.

That's how they finally got me to confess. They wore me down by telling me that no one except the murderer could have done these sketches, not with such exact detail. They even showed me a couple of photographs taken that night at Derrick's house. I don't remember if that was before or after I drew these pictures. They've got me pretty confused here. I think they're drugging me—you know, to confuse me.

And yes, the backs of my hands still burn like hell. I don't even like looking at them anymore. Sure, they're healing up just fine, but the burning sensation just keeps getting worse, day after day. I tell you, it's driving me fucking crazy! Even when the nurse gives me a shot of something, it doesn't really stop the pain. And I know, sure as shit, once these bandages come off, it won't get any better.

Oh, no.

It'll be worse. That's why I asked you to come up and see me again today, Doctor.

I know we talked about all this before, but I'm positive that I want you to do it.

Why do you keep saying you won't?

I know you can! You have the equipment here, don't you?

Look, even if these *are* my hands, you have to cut them off. We can't take a chance that they'll do something else even more horrible!

JAMIE'S DEMON

Nathan Eliot

JAMIE WOKE UP SCREAMING.

Perspiration soaked the sheets, forming a warped silhouette of the young boy's body. Ripping off the covers, Jamie leaped out of bed and darted for the door that adjoined his stepbrother's room. Navigating through the darkness as if by instinct, he dived into Dwayne's bed, shrouding himself with any exposed blankets in reach.

Awakened by the jolt, Dwayne turned quickly. "What the hell is going on?"

"It happened again," Jamie gasped. "The dream." He turned toward Dwayne and began sobbing softly.

"It's a good thing Mom and Dad ain't here tonight. They said they'd send you back to Creekview if your nightmares continued."

"Dwayne, don't tell 'em. *Please.*" Jamie whimpered and pressed closer to his stepbrother.

Burrowing his hand beneath the covers, Dwayne caught Jamie's waistband with his thumb; his fingers touched the moist fabric below, then quickly withdrew. "You're wet again. Geez."

"I was scared," Jamie whined as he pulled the blankets up to his neck. "Please let me stay here with you."

"You're wet." Dwayne was adamant. "Get out—before you stain *my* sheets."

Jamie tugged at the fabric matted beneath his waist and drew them down. Reaching down to his feet, Jamie grabbed the moist material and dropped them on the floor.

"They're off, Dwayne."

Dwayne probed beneath the covers to confirm the absence of the soiled fabric. Jamie pressed his hand gently atop Dwayne's, but his stepbrother pulled away.

"Great. Just great. Not only do I have a twelve-year-old brother who still wets himself at night, but now he also sleeps naked with his older brother. If the guys hear about this, I'll be the laughingstock."

"I'm sorry, Dwayne. Really." Jamie glimpsed eye contact, and forced a smile. He knew it was too dark for Dwayne to notice. "I won't tell anyone. I promise."

"All right—this time," Dwayne sighed, "but it's *got* to stop."

"It will, Dwayne, really," said Jamie as his anxiety began to cease. "I'll do better next time. Just don't let them send me back." He pulled closer to Dwayne and shuddered at the thought of Creekview.

Dr. Pelle, the psychiatrist at Creekview, had told Jamie's parents that it was a simple phobia—an irrational fear that kids his age commonly experience. "Sometimes, though, kids can actually hurt themselves trying to convince others that a phobia is real," the doctor had said, then paused in contemplation. "We need to evaluate James in the hospital for a few days."

A few days of evaluation turned into six months of treatment. Fear turned to anger, then hate—first toward his parents for leaving him there, then to the shrink who never took him seriously. He valued the little warmth left to him from his brother's body and recognized a new, emerging feeling. He had begun to hate himself too.

Jamie stretched his hand across the covers to touch Dwayne, but he had already rolled over and gone back to sleep. Jamie listened to the whirling blades of the ceiling fan and hoped his demon wouldn't follow him here.

* * *

Jamie's Demon

Until Billy Malone and his big mouth, none of the other kids knew why Jamie vanished to the hospital for most of last school year. The principal had thought that Jamie's parents had beaten him up real bad the day he came to school with bruises all over his face and neck. The school even called the police to talk with Jamie. The next day he was gone. Then Billy, who didn't even know Jamie until he was admitted to Creekview for stealing his dad's Corvette, told everyone at school about Jamie's demon.

"Everything you say in this group is confidential," Dr. Pelle had explained. "That means that anything you hear in this room stops at the door. Understand?"

It was the same opening line, day after day. Just once, Jamie thought, I'd like to shake my head no and see what happens.

The doctor glanced at the six young patients sitting on beanbags about him. One by one his stare forced a nod of affirmation.

"It's important that each of you participate in group. You can say whatever you think or feel. You can even curse and not get in trouble. Only by sharing your innermost feelings will you get well enough to go home."

"Either that or your insurance runs out," Jamie interjected with a smile.

"What if I don't want to go home?" an impish boy named Greg asked. "My mother beats the fuck outta me when I get a bad grade—what if I try to kill her again?"

"Sarah?" Dr. Pelle asked. "What would you say to Greg in this situation?"

Sarah stared silently at the doctor, then at Jamie. "You're cute. What's your name?"

"Better watch out now," Billy warned with a smirk. "She wants you."

Dr. Pelle quietly jotted down notes while giggles pervaded.

"She wants to get in your pants. Don't'cha Sarah?"

"Lay off her, Billy!" Jamie shouted as he rose in protest.

"You're just jealous," Sarah teased back at Billy, "'cause you're thirteen and *still* a virgin."

Billy stood and kicked the chair away from him. "I

suppose getting fucked by a demon counts," he screamed at Jamie. "That's what happened, didn't it?" Flushed with rage and indignation, he bolted for the group room door.

Dr. Pelle pressed a small intercom button. "Dr. Strong to room two, Dr. Strong to room two."

What a stupid emergency code, Jamie thought. If I were in charge, I'd just call *loony loose in room two.*

Billy shoved the door open. Two orderlies stepped in and grabbed him.

"Let go of me, you fuckin' perverts, or my parents will sue. Let go of me or I'll hurt you so fuckin' . . ." Billy's screams trailed off as the orderlies dragged him into the seclusion room.

Jamie smiled inwardly, imagining them tying Billy down to the four posts of the steel bed frame within. He knew the routine all too well since being placed in "four-point" restraints the day he arrived for picking a fight with a nurse over not taking his medication. His wrists were red and raw from the leather straps. He'd never resist again. He never had.

"Demonophobia," Dr. Pelle said. "You simply have an irrational fear of demons."

Jamie wondered why it was irrational to fear a demon; a minister once told him in church that everyone should fear them. "Not all demons—just one," he finally piped in.

The doctor's eyes narrowed in mock interest.

"I—I mean, I've only known one demon. But I'd rather not see it again."

"Ahhh. I see."

"Is that all right?" If it had been a demon that he loved and worshiped, would he be any better off?

"Sure it is, James. Anything you say is all right."

He stared at the doctor in disgust. *My name is Jamie, asshole.*

"Now then, please close your eyes and let's try once again to visualize the demon you've experienced."

Dr. Pelle made him repeat, in detail, everything he could recall about the demon: the beast's sharp claws, coarse and heinous voice, putrid stench, and piercing crimson eyes.

Jamie's Demon

Jamie was able to tell his story by rote; its every vile action imprinted in his head as clearly as his own name. Every few weeks they would add a new diagnosis, change his medications, and try to convince him that his demon was the result of one disorder or another. They made him swear he understood it was just a nightmare. Jamie knew it was real.

Jamie woke the next morning and called out for Dwayne. Nothing. A Post-It note on the headboard read, "Gone to soccer practice. Back after lunch." Dwayne's writing was almost undecipherable. Jamie had the house to himself for a while, and he was glad. He felt safe in the house during the day. The demon *only* came to him at night.

He soaked in the tub for a while, contemplating what to do if the creature returned. His parents wouldn't be back until tomorrow afternoon, and Dwayne was *not* going to let him share his bed again. He flinched at the thought of the demon's return. Even the thought frightened him. Only once had he ever considered fighting back.

Jamie had struggled as the demon clasped its talons rigidly around his neck. The beast tightened its grip, then choked him, ripping its sharp claws into his shoulders. Jamie gasped for air. Its acrid smell made him retch. Dizzy, coughing, he gave up and felt the cold hands of the creature touch him.

The phone rang, jolting Jamie out of the disturbing memory. Grabbing a towel, he wrapped it around himself and darted for the phone. It was Dwayne.

"What took you so long to answer?"

"Nothing." He was glad to hear Dwayne's voice.

"It's two-thirty in the afternoon. I'll be by in ten minutes and we'll go out for some pizza. My treat. Okay?"

"Okay, I guess." He hung up the phone wondering what Dwayne was up to. Pizza, his treat?

He caught sight of the photographs of Dwayne and himself on the dresser. Dwayne was tall and muscular, with jet-black hair and a moustache in the works. Having just turned seventeen three weeks ago, he had bought himself a used Camaro he'd been saving two summers for. Jamie then stared at himself in the picture. Five feet in height, blond hair, and features that were nothing compared to Dwayne's.

A horn blasted in the driveway. He raced out the door and hopped into the shiny red sports car. They drove to the local pizza joint and ordered Jamie's favorite, pepperoni.

"Look, kid, I need ya to do me a favor."

"Sure, Dwayne," Jamie said as he wiped a string of cheese from his chin. "Shoot."

"I got invited to a party tonight that I really want to go to—and I can't take ya with me."

Color drained from Jamie's face. "But you told Mom and Dad you'd stay with me. I don't want to stay home at night alone."

"I know, kid. That's the problem. If you stay over at the Clarks', or have Eric or Steven sleep over, you know Dad will restrict me from the car for at least a month."

"Please don't leave me." Jamie looked at the pizza and lost his appetite.

"Don't have a cow over it." Dwayne put his hands over his stepbrother's shoulders squeezing tighter and tighter until Jamie's trembling gradually ceased. "Tell you what. I'll be back by midnight, and you can stay up until I get home."

"But what if you're late, or Mom calls, or—"

Dwayne interrupted as he pulled a five-dollar bill from his wallet. "Midnight, I promise." He stuffed the five into Jamie's right hand and signaled to the waitress. "We'll take the rest of this to go."

Jamie followed Dwayne back to the car.

"Hell, two kegs and no parents don't come just every Saturday night."

"B-But—" Jamie stammered.

"It's settled, okay?"

Jamie broke into a nervous sweat, his heart racing as the sidewalk pitched at an awkward angle and began to spin. Dwayne opened the passenger door and guided Jamie inside. Jamie flinched as Dwayne touched his shoulder.

The ride home was silent. Jamie dug his fingernails into the leather upholstery as thoughts flew across his mind. Maybe I could try to prevent Dwayne from going. I could sabotage his car. Nah. If Dwayne gets drunk again, like he always gets at parties, he won't be able to protect me. Why doesn't he understand that?

* * *

Jamie nuked the remainder of the pizza in the microwave and stretched out in front of the television to think about the night. He had to be prepared in case the demon returned before Dwayne got home. If there was a gun in the house, even a BB gun, it would have been snatched up as his weapon of choice. Not that he'd ever shot, or even handled, a real gun—he was just sure he'd seen enough movies on TV to figure out how to make it work.

After an hour or so of MTV that he barely watched, Jamie went to the kitchen and rummaged feverishly through the drawers of silverware. He grabbed the sharpest knife he could find—a double blade with no handle. Studying the notch at the base of the blade, his eyes rose to the electric carver plugged into the wall near the can opener. Grabbing it from the charger, he locked the blade in place and slid the on switch up. The motor whirred as the blade shifted in and out so fast it almost appeared to be still.

Jamie closed his eyes and imagined the knife racing across the demon's throat, a thick stream of blood spurting across the room. The mere thought of revenge excited him.

Carrying the knife like a sword at his side, Jamie shut off the TV and returned to his room. Dwayne would be pissed if he wasn't undressed and in bed when he came home. Lying awake, he stuffed the weapon under his mattress so he wouldn't look so foolish when Dwayne checked in on him. Almost twelve, he thought.

Staring at the digital clock, Jamie counted out loud each second past midnight; at two thousand he stopped. Slowly rising from his bed, Jamie crept into Dwayne's room. Maybe the creature might be fooled by his empty bed and leave. It was worth a try. Jamie jumped into his stepbrother's bed and nested beneath the spread. Within minutes he fell fast asleep.

"Noooo!" Jamie bolted upright, eyes open. The dream again. His eyes scanned the room. No demon, no monsters —no Dwayne. The digital alarm clock caught his gaze: 3:40 A.M.

Shit! Where the hell was Dwayne?

Jamie closed his eyes and took a deep breath. An unearthly numbness came over him without warning—the demon's stench was in the room.

"Please don't . . ." he called out to the darkness. It was too late. The creature's claw cupped his mouth, pressing him firmly to the mattress. Jamie thrashed wildly, then kicked up as hard as he could.

The demon ripped the spread from the bed and threw the full brunt of its weight on the boy. Jamie opened his mouth to scream, and felt exposed flesh from the creature's claw fall between his teeth. He bit down as hard as he could.

The beast let out a shriek as it clutched Jamie in its claws, then hurled him off the bed. He hit the hardwood floor with a resounding thud.

The beast grabbed Jamie like a toy and lifted him from the floor, then carried him back into his room and tossed him on his bed. A sharp claw ripped at Jamie's underwear. Jamie tried to scream, but the creature's hand pressed his face forcefully into the pillow.

It was always the same. Jamie would succumb—and survive in self-hatred. If only the beast would just kill him. Then it would stop, and Jamie could finally sleep.

He clenched his fists around the mattress edge and fought back tears. His left hand caught something sharp. He had forgotten about the knife. Jamie withdrew it from beneath the mattress and turned it on. The whirring sound surprised the beast.

Self-hatred turned to anger. Jamie arched his back suddenly and rolled to the side, catching the demon squarely in its face with the pulsating blades.

The creature staggered back and bellowed, then struck at Jamie fiercely. It lunged at the boy, sharp talons ripping at his chest while hind legs pounded his abdomen. This was unlike before. The creature was killing him.

Jamie tried to scream, but could only muster a whimper. He gasped for air. A claw closed over his mouth—pinning it shut.

Still clenching the knife, he thrust the blade upward, gashing the creature's flesh. A thick, warm spray burst across Jamie's face as the beast pulled away. It stumbled backward into Jamie's dresser with a crash, then tumbled to the ground, stilled.

The demon was real. He had proof. Jamie only wished Dwayne was here with him now. His stepbrother was the only one who had ever believed in his demon. He crawled back under the covers and knew that he could finally sleep.

"'Morning, darling," his mother said in a cheerful voice. The sunlight hurt Jamie's eyes.

"Now don't you move," she sang, "I've got breakfast coming right up."

He turned and checked the clock: 8:03 A.M.

"Hey, Mom! I'm going to be late for school."

She placed the tray on a small table next to the bed. The familiar smell of his favorite dish made him smile. Jamie peered over to the dresser. The picture of Dwayne and himself was gone.

"Eat up! It's been months since I made my signature French toast."

"Where's Dwayne?"

She turned away and leaned on the door frame for support.

"Mom, where's Dwayne?" His pulse began to race.

She walked quickly from the room. He knew she was crying. Jamie strained to sit up in bed; his muscles ached. Only then did he notice the dressings on his chest and legs. He ripped the bandages off, revealing deep lacerations and many small wounds. He slowly stood and followed her down the hall.

She was in her bedroom, kneeling by the bed. The photo of his stepbrother crinkled in her hands, collecting tears.

"Is something wrong with Dwayne?"

She shook her head without lifting it from her hands.

"Mom, what happened?" He could not recall how he got so badly cut. It was far worse than the bicycle accident he got into last summer.

"I'm so sorry we went away for the weekend," she sobbed. "We'll never do it again."

He gently lifted her head from her hands. "But what happened?"

"The police are still trying to sort things out. They say someone broke in and attacked Dwayne and you."

She burst into tears again. "D-Dwayne's dead, honey. We

buried him yesterday. You've been asleep now for a few days. The doctor gave you some strong medication so you would rest. He said you might not remember much at first."

Jamie grew queasy. He felt like he wanted to throw up, but his stomach was empty.

"The doctor wanted you to stay in bed," she said, looking at her son. He was bleeding. She put her arm around Jamie and walked him back to his bed. "After you eat, I'll redress your boo-boos."

He gave her a hug. Jamie hadn't heard that expression for a long time.

"Dr. Pelle said he doesn't expect your demon to ever return."

"I'm not afraid anymore," he said, crawling back into bed. He closed his eyes and tried to recall a dream he had last night.

Huge and muscular, he was a great bird of some type. Strong. Unafraid.

Piercing red eyes.

Razor-sharp claws.

Diving in on his prey.

He smiled. Things would be different now. He already knew how to kill.

HOOVES

Lucretia W. Grindle

IN HER DREAMS IT WAS ALWAYS THE SAME. SHE WAS STANDING, her feet welded, lead and locked to an earth that she could not see. Around her the darkness was thick and total and it pulsated with their breath. She could feel the damp heat of them against her skin, sense them surrounding her, pushing in on her, suffocating her with their huge, warm, breathing presence. She would like to raise her arms, hold out her hands to push them away, but even if she could, it would be useless. They would still surround her, still press in on her until, finally, they would shriek and scream in their half-human voices, rising up to crush her, to beat her down with the rapid swinging darkness of their hooves.

She had told Dr. Whitney about it. Told him repeatedly while sitting in the white armchair and staring up at the white ceiling of his blue office. It was, she found, easier to talk to him, easier to tell him about the horses, if she looked up. As if she could totally recreate them on the blank whiteness of the ceiling. Dr. Whitney had only been with her for three months. The horses, of course, had been with her for years. For years and years they had been her constant, tormenting companions. She thought, now that Dr. Whitney had forced her to think about them, to actually

279

consider them, that they had in fact been with her ever since she married Robert.

She had never really intended to marry Robert. It was not something that had been part of her plan. But then again, thirty years ago, when she was eighteen, she probably didn't have a plan. She thought it was possible that she might have had dreams. It was a long time ago and hard to recall. But she thought it unlikely that she had had plans. Life had stretched ahead of her. She had all the time in the world. Why would an eighteen-year-old waitress worry about having plans? What she worried about, if she remembered correctly, when she dared to remember at all, was what color to paint her nails, what movie to go to on Saturday night, if she could save up enough tip money for a new dress or a new pair of shoes or a new coat with a fake fur collar and outsize cloth-covered buttons. It amazed her now that the creature that gazed out of the high school yearbook, the slightly doughy-faced girl with the large eyes and fifties curled hair, the one who had been voted "most friendly," could actually have been her. She hadn't worried about the horses then. She hadn't even thought about horses then, barely considered them other than, she supposed, things that grazed in fields, like cows, or were on pictures on the top of calendars. But that was before she met Robert.

Robert came into the diner. Without even thinking about it she could remember the day clearly, totally, as if it were a film that rolled through her head. As if it were romantic. As if it were love.

He wasn't especially handsome. He was short and powerfully built. Like a bull. His eyes were green or blue, depending on the day. Depending on how you looked at him. He was loud and he was charming, at least that's what people had said. He sat at the counter and he wore jeans and smelled earthy and warm, like the stables he worked in. And he told her about growing up on his parents' farm and riding his pony to his first day of school when he was five and about loving horses. And he looked at her through his hooded blue-green eyes as if she were devourable, a doughnut or a piece of the slightly jellied meringue pie that sat, served up on its doily, under the cracked plastic pie dome.

When she got pregnant, which seemed, in her mind, to

happen almost instantly, he said that he would marry her. He announced it, just like that, shrugging as he leaned against a broom in the stable aisle, the horses hanging their heads out of their stalls and watching with their bulging eyes, blowing their breath into the winter air. She didn't think to argue or ask. Looking back on it, she supposed that that must have been what she wanted. After all, in those days it was what you did. And afterward, after he said he'd marry her, well, she supposed that that was what you did too, right there in the barn with the horses watching. He didn't even bother to undress her that time, didn't even bother to take his jeans off. He just backed her up against some bales of hay and pulled her skirt up. She could remember the feel of him, clinging to his back and looking over his shoulder as he did it, meeting the wide eyes of the horses as they stared back at her, opening their mouths and smiling, laughing at her with their even white teeth and long pink tongues. They closed in around her, watching as he did it, as he pinned her back against the rough wood of the wall and the prickling of the hay. They watched her as he came, grunting, and then lifted himself off her, not even bothering to speak, turning away and reaching for his broom as he zipped up his jeans, leaving her sitting there with her skirt around her waist. After all, they were getting married. She was his now, until death did them part.

Dr. Whitney was playing with a pencil. He balanced it on the edge of his ashtray, rolling it back and forth across the rim with his index fingers. He did this without looking at the pencil, which fascinated her. While never taking his eyes off of her, while listening to every word she spoke, or did not speak, while giving her his undivided attention, he rolled the pencil back and forth with the regularity and hypnotic quality of a metronome.

Before she had married Robert she had not known words like "metronome." She did not learn it from him. Oh, no. Metronomes had nothing to do with horses, and horses were all Robert ever talked about. Robert had become famous. Riding horses, he had represented his country in the Olympic games. Selling horses, he had earned enough to give her the life she might once have dreamed of. Back when she might have had dreams, if she could only remember what they were. And teaching others to ride horses, he had acquired admirers. Many of them young. And many of them female. And yet, none of that had anything to do with words like "metronome." Or, well, she thought, watching the pencil as it rolled evenly back and forth between Dr. Whitney's well-manicured index fingers, perhaps it did. Because words like "metronome" were the sort of thing that she'd learned in her courses.

As Robert became more famous and spent more time at the barn and therefore had many more late night meetings that he had to attend, she went to courses. In the courses she learned about music appreciation, the history of the chateaux of the Loire, Amish quilt-making, and gourmet cooking. It was, she sometimes told herself, called "having a life of your own." For a while, when the baby was a baby, she had him. But when he was five, Robert bought him a pony. Robert brought it right up onto the front porch of the house on the morning of her son's fifth birthday, and after that the horses took him away. In her mind she would see it sometimes, when she was at the supermarket, or driving in the car or brushing her teeth. Her baby, her sweet, downy-smelling baby, would be sitting on a horse and he would be receding, disappearing into a deep green landscape of trees, a tangle of undergrowth. She would try at first to follow him, but after only a few steps she would lose the path and the despair would wash over her, leaving her standing, rooted to the earth in that dark place, left with only the sound of hooves as her baby moved farther and farther away.

At dinner, on the nights when Robert did not have a late night meeting, she would listen to them talk. Robert and her son, who was now no longer a baby, but a grown man and a business partner of his father's, would sit at the table, hunched over their food, and talk about horses. Loading the dishwasher, standing in the kitchen, listening to them, she began gradually to feel that she could not understand them, that the language they were speaking was no longer even English or anything remotely familiar to her. Looking at them, they would seem utterly alien to her, their eyes bulging slightly, their nostrils flaring in breath that would, she knew if she could feel it, be hot and damp.

She tried, as precisely as she could, to explain this to Dr.

Hooves

Whitney. Tried to explain how, in the first year of her marriage to Robert, the horses had contented themselves with periodic visits into her sleep. There they would snort and stamp and stare and surround her until she woke, sweating and terrified, next to the snoring shape of Robert. Then, eventually, as her son grew older, the horses got pushier. They were no longer content to limit themselves to nighttime or solely to the bedroom. Now they began to creep into the day and into the thick verdant woods that surrounded the newly landscaped garden of their newly built ranch house.

She knew what they were up to. At first she couldn't always see them, but she knew that they were there. As she weeded and planted the herb garden that she was learning about in her "gardens to grow by" class, she could sense them watching her. She could hear their breathing, just glimpse their eyes staring out at her from behind the screen of trees and thicket that edged the property. Sometimes they whispered. But she closed her ears. She knew better than to listen to what they had to say.

When she asked Robert to put a fence around the garden, he was puzzled. But she knew what she was doing. The fence would keep the horses out, and she knew that Robert would comply. He'd had a lot of late meetings at just around that time, and she'd learned over the years that he was always willing to give her things when he had to work late. She explained this to Cara. Cara was the girl who came to clean the house once a week. She was a student at Robert's barn and she cleaned houses for money for her riding lessons. Of course, she didn't explain to Cara about the horses and the fence, because not everyone knew about horses the way she did. No. She simply explained to Cara one August afternoon, as they stood in the new glass kitchen watching the new fence go up, that her husband always gave her things when he had to work late so much because he missed being with her. Because she was the center of his life. Because he loved her so. Cara had looked at her for a moment and then she had given her a funny little smile and left the room. Outside, the workmen had hammered and hammered on the new fence until the noise they made sounded for all the world like hooves.

The fence, however, was a disappointment. She had made one fatal error. She had forgotten that horses could jump. They didn't do it at first. It took them a couple of months. But after a while, right as rain, they jumped right in.

She heard them before she actually saw them. She was standing in the kitchen, alone, one evening when she heard them. She heard their tails swishing and their soft, insistent snorting as the dishwasher ran, washing the pots and pans that she had used to create watercress soup and coq au vin that had gone uneaten because Robert had forgotten to tell her that he had a meeting. Shortly after that, Cara stopped coming to clean the house, and as a result she spent much more time inside. The horses stared down at her from the pictures of her husband and son that lined the living room walls, and she could hear them breathing and snuffling as she ran the vacuum cleaner back and forth across the already spotless rug. It was at about that time, she thought, but could not be altogether certain, that the episode with the car had occurred. The episode that, as she thought of it, brought her Dr. Whitney.

Rolling the pencil back and forth between his index fingers, smiling at her gently as he did so, Dr. Whitney asked her to tell him about the episode with the car. She leaned back against the head rest of the white Naugahyde armchair and looked at the white ceiling. A crack ran across it diagonally, zigging and zagging from one corner of the fake wood molding to the other. It had been a bright February day, the sort of day that lingers between winter and spring. The sort of day when it is possible that there could be either a snowstorm or the sight of the first crocus. The sort of day, in short, that would be filled with possibility, is she had still believed in the idea of possibility. Which, as far as she could remember, she did not.

She had gone to the supermarket, the large new supermarket on the outskirts of town. The one that had a parking lot the size of a football field, or a pasture. In the supermarket she had wheeled her cart up and down the aisles, filling it with packets of tea and spices and bunches of organically grown vegetables and colored pasta. They could afford these things now, these expensive, peculiarly colored gourmet foods that she would never even have thought of back in the days when she served meat loaf and Boston cream pie and tuna-bake at the diner. Back in the days before she had met Robert, when she still thought about lipstick and life and possibility. Before Robert had vowed to love and cherish her. Before the horses. She was picking her way through the vegetable section, carefully avoiding the carrots, when she saw Cara.

Cara was some way away from her, her back turned, also standing hip-deep in the sea of Egyptian artichokes and French green beans and Californian petit-pois. She knew it was Cara at once from the color of her hair, which was a rather peculiar deep purplish shade that was supposed to pass for red and had nothing whatsoever to do with the forces of nature. She had always thought that it was rather garish and cheap, and had even remarked as much to her over dinner one night, on one of the few nights that Robert was home to eat the stuffed trout almondine that her class had featured as dish of the week. Robert had looked at her and blinked with his odd-colored eyes and said nothing. For some reason, she thought of that now as she watched Cara, who still had not seen her, turn and begin to push her cart away up the aisle toward the fruit. There was something odd and yet decidedly familiar about the way she moved, the way she walked with a slight waddling roll to her hips, and as she turned her cart away and headed toward the checkout line, she realized what it was. Cara was pregnant. Not particularly noticeably, but pregnant nonetheless. It was something women recognized in one another, even from a distance.

She didn't have time to think any more about Cara or being pregnant. The line was progressing and the frantic rush to empty the cart onto the checkout belt had begun. The tea, the fresh coriander, and the cream flew out of her hands to the accompaniment of the cashier's rhythmic clicking and bleeping. A nice young boy helped her with her grocery bags, loading them into the hatchback and wishing her a nice day, and before she knew it she was sitting behind the wheel. She started the car and began to back up and then it happened. One moment she was steering out of the parking lot, and the next she was surrounded with them. They were everywhere, their eyes bulging, staring in at her, dwarfing the tiny car, their breath steaming up the windows and windshield. She couldn't move the car forward or backward. They surrounded it, pressing their hairy hot bellies against the glass, staring and snickering until she covered her ears to block out the noise, the horrid noise that she knew would, must, come next. The noise of their hooves as they reared, raining blows, one after another, onto the roof of the little car Robert had bought her.

That was three months ago, and since then she and Dr. Whitney had discussed the horses many times. He had asked her what she would like to do when they surrounded her, when they pressed in on her, snuffling their hot breath onto her cheeks. And little by little she had been able to tell him. It had taken some time before she could actually formulate the idea, and some more time still before she could tell him about the desire that lay within her, dormant, like a dream or a hope, the desire to raise her arms and spread her hands and push the horses away.

And the car? He had asked her about the car. She was angry about that, she remembered. Angry because she knew that the horses' hooves would dent the roof and the fenders and the shiny new paintwork of the little car that Robert had given her. And what would she like to do about it? Dr. Whitney had asked. And slowly, very slowly, she had been able to first think and then say that those damned horses had made her so mad that she'd like to just accelerate right through them.

After that, after she'd said that, she thought about starting to drive again. She even went to the supermarket, but she didn't see any more horses. They were scared now, perhaps because they knew that she was angry, that the whole episode with the car had just been one step, or perhaps one hoof, too far. She didn't see them as much in the house now either. Occasionally she'd hear them snuffling and snorting in another room, but she'd become firm with them. She opened doors and looked for them, and several times she had found that the noise was not, after all, the horses, but Robert snoring in his black leather chair in front of the television.

It was Dr. Whitney who suggested that she should visit the barn. He suggested it slowly, gently, as he suggested everything, as he had suggested that she raise her arms, hold out her hands, push the horses away. At first she rejected the idea absolutely. The barn was Robert's domain. In it he had his office and his fax machine and his secretary and the letter of commendation, in a frame, that he had received after he had not won a medal representing his country at the Olympic games.

Robert would not like her coming to the barn. She knew that, even though he had never actually said so. Instead he said that it was dirty. That it was where he worked. That she was the clean and precious flower of his life. That she would be happier at home. Or at one of her classes. But, Dr. Whitney pointed out, wasn't her son also at the barn? Well, of course he was. He rode at the barn and taught at the barn and worked at the barn all day long. Wasn't it silly, Dr. Whitney said, to stay away from the place where her family spent so much of their time? Wasn't she ready, perhaps, to see the horses in their stalls and realize that they only ate hay and oats and stood around in their rather large and harmless way? She and Dr. Whitney talked the idea over several times. He brought it up gently, persistently, rolling his pencil. She promised to think about it.

She did think about it. She liked Dr. Whitney and would have felt badly if she had broken a promise that she had made to him. So she thought about going to the barn. And as spring moved away and summer came closer and the nights became softer and the evenings longer, she thought about the barn more and more. She rarely saw the horses now, and with their absence life seemed quieter and less confusing. An alien sense of peace sometimes snuck around the edges of her consciousness.

One evening, while she sat waiting for the six o'clock news to come on, she thought about Dr. Whitney. She thought of his white ceiling with the crack in it and of his number-two pencil and his ashtray, and she thought of his kind smile. She had an appointment with him the next afternoon, and suddenly she thought of how very much she would like to do something nice for him, something he would be proud of that she could bring him as a gift of thanks for all of the hours he had spent listening to her talk about the horses. She decided to go to the barn.

Robert had called to say that he had a meeting and would not be home. Her son, she guessed, was still at the barn. Perhaps she could meet him there. How surprised, how happy, he would be to see her. She could see his face now, his sweet baby face, smiling at her as he turned toward her and away from the staring eyes of the horses. As she got in her little car and started down the road toward the barn, she felt a slight prickle of fear. Resolutely, she stepped on the accelerator. The horses might not want her to come to the barn, but she was angry with them now. They could no longer tell her what to do.

The evening was still half light, and a slight mist rose from the edges of the road. The barn was at the end of a long drive that was bordered by woods. She knew that the woods were laced with paths for people to ride along, and for half a moment she thought the idea might be almost pleasant. As she drove into the parking lot of the barn she noticed that there were three cars there. One belonged to her son, one belonged to Robert, and one, an old gray Camaro that resembled a batmobile, was vaguely familiar to her, though she couldn't think why. As she got out of her car and walked toward the office door, she felt a wave of dizziness, of the old churning nausea of her dreams. She told herself not to be silly. After all, she probably wasn't even going to see any of the horses. She was just going to go into the office and see her son and then perhaps they could go somewhere for dinner. As a kind of celebration. As a new beginning.

She opened the office door and stepped into the reception area where, during the day, Robert's secretary sat with her fax machine and her two-line telephone. The door to Robert's office was closed, although the light was on. She paused, wondering what she would say, wondering at her son's surprise, his delight in seeing her here unexpectedly. She wondered whether she ought to knock or whether she should just go in, and as she did, she heard voices. Well, not really voices as much as sounds. Sounds that sounded like the horses. A kind of snuffling and snorting. A light sweat broke out on her forehead. She began to feel dizzy again. She raised her arm up, pushed out with her hand as if to knock, took a deep breath and called her son's name.

She wasn't really certain, but she thought there was a kind

of pause, a silence and then some scuffling. She felt a wave of fear. She could feel the eyes of the horses, they were looking down at her from the pictures that lined the walls of the office. She turned to get away from them and banged into the secretary's desk. The two-line phone went crashing to the floor. The clatter sounded dreadfully like horses' hooves. The door to Robert's office swung open and Robert was standing there. As she bent to pick up the phone she babbled an apology, looking down to the grab the receiver which had fallen off the hook and gone under the secretary's chair. As she did, she noticed that Robert had no socks or shoes on. His pudgy, high-arched white feet looked odd against the dark green of the indoor-outdoor carpeting of the office.

She wanted to tell him why she'd come, to explain, but she couldn't think how to begin. Instead she asked where their son was. Robert pulled his office door shut behind him and took the phone from her hands. He told her that their son was still out riding in the last of the summer light. He suggested, almost kindly, that she go home now. That he and their son would be there soon. That they were looking forward to one of her nice dinners. She nodded, wanting only to get away from the barn, from the eyes of the horses on the wall. She turned to go, and as she did she saw, through the gap in Robert's not quite shut office door, something purple. A head and a flash of naked shoulder. Hair that could never really pass for red.

She backed toward the door and fled, running for her car, the horses pursuing her, calling her name in their laughing, snuffling voices. She started the car and turned out of the parking lot. She wanted to get away from them as fast as possible, away from their laughing and their staring and their breath, which rose into the road like mist. As she turned down the drive she thought that perhaps they were not following her after all. She took a deep breath and realized that she had not turned her headlights on. She almost laughed at herself. She leaned down to the dashboard to turn the switch, and as she looked up, there, suddenly, in the drive, right in front of her, was a horse.

It just stood there, staring at her, and it seemed to represent every trap, every dead end, of the entire life that she had allowed Robert to lead her into. She felt a kind of horror and then a terrible rage. She knew that if she let this horse stop her, then it would be over forever. They would be back in the house, back in her dreams. She would be paralyzed, crushed, trampled under the endless stamping of their hooves. Even Dr. Whitney would not be able to save her. She would be imprisoned by the horses forever.

She jammed her foot down on the accelerator, and only at the very last moment did she have time to realize why it was that this horse had struck her as different. It was because this horse had a rider. A man was sitting on the horse, and as he raised his arms and screamed at the car bearing down on him, she saw, for one brief moment, the sweet, smiling face of her son.

A GOD IN THE HAND

Wayne Allen Sallee

I T WAS WELL PAST MIDNIGHT WHEN MODINE CAME BACK TO THE house with the man dying of brain cancer inside. He stood in the driveway on that first day of 1991, mildly surprised that there was little traffic along the interstate. It struck him that I-64 was what people drove to leave town, not to go to New Year's Eve parties on Nolan Pike. This was where Modine and his cousin Danny had been the last several hours.

An ominous water tower, green by day, was a black spot blocking out the stars on the horizon to the east. It was a sad thing, this black spot that made Modine think about the tumor in his uncle Melvin's head. A leech on his brain, the way the city, Chicago, took away the individual stars one by one. You could barely discern the Big Dipper anymore, and it wasn't just because of the high-intensity sodium lights.

"Well," Modine said to his cousin, simply to get his mouth moving. The air burned his nostrils. The dying man was only his cousin's stepfather, but both of them stood there angry at the randomness of death. The two of them had taken down the Christmas lights earlier that day, before leaving for the party.

They had not committed themselves to taking down the lights, the tree, or removing the presents, until Melvin

Melone chose, while in a stupor, to come home from the hospital. For he knew, even though the pain bit into his rationality, that there was no sense in staying.

There had been no way for the two men to get out of attending the party. Just like second guessing, it wouldn't have changed anything. And there were others in the dark and quiet house with the dying man. A blue light flickering through the living room window, which yesterday would have been obscured by the Christmas tree, meant that the television was still on.

The doctors at the cancer hospital said that Melvin had two weeks to live, if he was lucky. With his cousin gently opening the door, Modine let his breath plume into the sky, and wondered if God gave a shit about luck.

They walked quietly into the living room, and Modine saw everything with the familiarity of . . . well, this house on Hill-N-Dale Road might very well have been a summer house for him. Someplace he would go to write his stories and not be disturbed.

That is how well he had come to perceive it over the past two decades. His auntie Dorothy had moved back to Shelbyville after her first husband had died, also at home. Died from a heart attack while he was dressing for work, in their two-flat on Crystal Street. His auntie's first husband, William Szostak, had been young, just older than Modine was now.

Everyone was young back then. Bobby Kennedy was still alive, and there was no reason for South Park Boulevard to be renamed Martin Luther King Drive. The concepts of moon walks and space shuttles were dreams.

The room itself, back on Hill-N-Dale. His cousin had plopped into a chair. The television was not showing some musical party to ring in the new year. What he saw was a black and white movie involving young children playing pranks on an old man.

He thought of Father Time, but only briefly.

On the top of the television there was a lace doily, and on top of that was a plasma-colored lava lamp and one of those water-filled things where you make the sand fall down by flipping it over, making a new landscape. Modine did not think about these conversation pieces at all, but knew that they were there because of his familiarity with the house. Even in complete darkness he would be able to walk to either bathroom without knocking over picture frames. Graduation photographs of every cousin, wedding photos, baby pictures with backgrounds of wooded areas and autumn-blue skies.

There had always been time in this house.

He glanced around to see who was awake. Who was keeping vigil. Danny's sister, Denise, was not there, she had fallen asleep in the other bedroom. Denise worked at King's Daughter Hospital, and Modine often asked her for correct descriptions for his Chicago stories. She had been born when he was three, brought back to Crystal Street from Lutheran Deaconess, and Modine had been told that he'd tried to push her from her crib, because she was getting all the attention, but he could not remember this, being three at the time.

Sitting on the couch was Denise's roommate, Paula Sparrow, her dog beside her. The two women lived in Louisville; Danny had only recently moved back home. Paula came from a town smaller than Shelbyville. She worked for a police publication in Louisville; yet another source for background material. The dog wagged her tail happily at the newcomers.

Modine knew that Paula had stayed there that night because she felt a kinship with the family.

"I feel like we're blood," she told him fifteen days later, after the funeral. It would be raining then, her lavender trench coat soaked; President Bush's deadline for war having passed, the bombing of Baghdad would not start until later that evening.

There was much more rain than snow that winter, he remembered.

Paula mentioned the evening briefly, said how Melvin had slept off and on. His stepuncle and auntie slept on a water bed near the end of the hall, but in the days to come, he would sleep on a special bed in the living room. Where the Christmas tree and presents had been.

Modine never asked anybody if his auntie had slept in that special bed with her husband at any time during those final two weeks. He did know Melvin was fed blue-green morphine in a spoon, much of it dribbling down his chin. Denise later told him that his stepuncle spoke clearly and severely to a spot near the ceiling during the last days.

Now that the men were home, Paula went down the hall to Denise's old bedroom to go to sleep. The room's wall was now lined with memorabilia: guns, and a hatchet and helmet from the dying man's days and nights as a firefighter in Jefferson County. Long since retired, he had driven a school bus part-time. Just before leaving that job, the cancer entered his body, in his left foot.

Danny had fallen asleep in a chair near the door. He was tired, having been at the hospital early that day and for most of the weekend.

Modine had come down from Chicago on Greyhound. He'd called home from the bus depot on Jefferson and Des Plaines in Indianapolis, saying that the bus was way behind schedule because of the floods caused by early December rains. The bus had left the interstate and was averaging only 35 mph along Indiana Route 31.

He recalled his auntie telling him years before what it was like to travel between the three states when there was no interstate. Amtrak still doesn't carry a direct route between Chicago and Louisville.

When the AT&T operator put him through to his sister's apartment in Burbank, she told him to expect most everyone to be at the cancer hospital. Evidently, his stepuncle had been acting increasingly strange since Christmas Eve, talking about building a shelving unit and losing his balance more than once.

Others in the family had shown similar signs before corrective brain surgery was needed.

The Greyhound finally made it into the Sixth Street station in downtown Louisville, phone calls were made, and his cousin, now gently snoring in the chair, picked Modine up at ten o'clock on December thirtieth. The hospital was within shouting distance of the bus terminal.

The town of Shelbyville is about thirty-five miles southeast of Louisville. Not much was said as the two men drove in darkness down the Gene Snyder Freeway and away from the city lights that reflected off the low cloud cover.

A God in the Hand

The bone cancer had gotten into Melvin's spinal co. Modine was told.

He saw his stepuncle the next morning at the hospital, television game shows murmuring in the distance. While Melvin Melone's immediate family, including his sons from his first marriage and their wives and children, discussed matters, Modine tried to memorize the names of the patrons of the hospital who had donated money over the years.

On the afternoon of New Year's Eve, he and his cousin moved the furniture, and in the evening the women took down most of the Christmas decorations. He had regained a semblance of objectivity by then.

The only time that he found himself blinking away tears was when they were driving in the yellow El Camino down U.S. 60, on the way back from chopping firewood at their grandmother's farm in Eastwood. Melvin had always been the first to volunteer to chop the wood for Busha, since Grandpa Frank had become increasingly more infirm. At times, Modine was surprised that so many people he knew had made it into the 1990s.

He had been staring out at the sighing wheat fields, the trees, the gray sky, when a particular song came on the radio. Modine was always bad with titles, and it wasn't until May that he learned from a video on TNN that the song was entitled "Pink Houses." John Cougar Mellencamp, another midwesterner, singing over and over, "Ain't that America . . ."

Listening to the music, the smell of the cordwood still in his jacket the way nicotine sits in the fabric after just an hour in a tavern. Seeing the horizon, hating the fact that he loved people down here way too much. His lip quivering. His cousin had looked over once, then back at the road, allowing him the moment. That was something Modine would always remember and appreciate.

He thought of all this, awake in this house filled with time and people in various states of consciousness. The first day of a new year. The first day of a different way of thinking.

He had never been very religious, and had always said that you could only rely on yourself. What was going to

...ing to happen. End of sad song. No deposit,

...would say that if you relied on yourself, you were
...g so with God's help. "Let Go and let God" was one of
those phrases the people who made wall plaques pulled in
the bucks on. Or the one about the single set of footprints,
the man denying God's help, God telling him that the
footprints were His with a capital H, when the man,
lowercase m, was too tired and generally fed up with life to
walk by himself.

This was so much crap, and the situation in that house
filled with time about proved it. God was the individual,
and Modine did not think of this in the religious sense.

His auntie was witnessing another husband dying, too
quickly, too suddenly. If there was a God, then He was
playing as fair as anybody down the street back in Chicago.
Even if you paid attention, you'd still lose at three-card
monte. Modine mused about that conclusion, and decided
he liked it.

God on a Halsted Street bus, tossing over cards to a
gullible and bored crowd. The black queen. God in the
cards. God in the hand of the hustler who knew the odds
because it was the hustler who created the odds.

A God in the hand.

So many ways that this could be defined.

A gun. A knife; or salad fork, for that matter. Hell, his
penis could be a god if he wanted to get sacrilegious about it.
Whatever gets you through the night, so the saying goes. For
some people, praying gets you through the night. Your hands
do have other uses.

So, for some, it is other things.

On this night, technically still the last night of the
previous year, Modine stood in the kitchen, not ready to
surrender to the night just yet.

He might have been afraid of what his dreams would be
about.

On the mantel between the refrigerator and the entrance-
way to the kitchen was a small blue box. Next to the box was
a portrait card of St. Peregrine.

A neighbor had brought over the blue box earlier in the

day. It was a monitoring device; Modine had seen son
thing like it advertised on television before the holidays.

It didn't beep, didn't hum, nothing like that. It was more
like a gigantic listening device, disguised as a potential
alarm clock. The box allowed you to hear if a dying person
in another room has died. Simple as that.

Modine stood there, his own breath becoming more quiet
and reserved. The sounds of the television faded the way
unwanted elevator talk can be made to fade away.

He listened to the box. He could distinguish between his
auntie's breathing and that of his stepuncle's. But he had
always been able to do that.

He closed his eyes and imagined the light blue he always
associated with brain waves, even when he saw the opening
credits of *The Outer Limits* in his youth. The waves became
ribbons of interstate highway as he drifted up into space.

Not floating to heaven. Modine was weary thinking about
God. And at that moment, he could care less.

The breathing in the other room continued, through the
speaker. He heard more rapid breathing then, and almost
smiled when he looked down to see Paula Sparrow's poodle.
Dogs are always happy to see that someone else is awake
when they are. Modine supposed that this was the reason he
liked dogs more than he liked cats.

The dog pranced under the table, her nails clicking
against the linoleum, and, perhaps understanding the enor-
mity of the moment, she cocked her head, in that special
way dogs do. Then, wagging her tail, she went back into the
other room.

Modine thought it best to take some aspirin before lying
down on the couch, and walked over to the kitchen counter,
because he knew where everything was in this house. As he
was tapping two gel capsules into his palm, he saw the four
plastic champagne glasses. They were placed in a square,
faceup, on top of a paper towel.

Because they were not facing down, he could not tell if the
glasses had been used, if a toast of any kind had been made.
His cousin Denise later told him how the three women and
Melvin had shared a small drink at midnight.

Modine was not drunk, nor had he been at any point that

His head hurt simply because he was thinking

the tap water run into one of the champagne s. Dry-swallowed the gel capsules. Then raised the ass in a silent toast to his auntie and stepuncle as he listened to their breathing through the monitor.

When Melvin Melone died two Sundays later, he was taking three breaths per minute and was fed nothing but blue-green morphine in a bathroom cup. The Gulf War started, and everybody thought that it was going to last much longer, and that many of the GIs would die. All the way home from the funeral, all through Indiana, there was no music. The same news about Scuds and sorties and the bombing of Baghdad played on every radio station.

Modine thought of a time just half a month before, driving down a similar road and weeping as quietly as possible. That entire spring he believed that from New Year's Eve on, Shelby County, Kentucky, would remind him of a man he always wanted to talk to, boys dying in a desert across the world, and hugging people in the rain.

In June he was back in Shelbyville, as he had been for every Father's Day since he was born. If anybody was talking about his stepuncle's absence, he wasn't around to hear it. He liked to think that down here you moved on, but his cousin Denise later told him that it wasn't so. In Chicago, impending and recent death was a litany the populace mouthed daily on the streets as if it were the sole way of getting on with their lives. Counting off names and diseases on their withered fingers. Those who will outlive us all litanizing the most.

He saw his Paula Sparrow again at the house on Hill-N-Dale, and made unexpected plans to watch her care for a horse at a stable near Shelbyville. She picked him up the next morning at seven-fifteen. Eating bread and drinking milk in that same kitchen, he had time to think about the past winter. About how he would like his memories on the subject to end.

These were painful memories, always the awkward kind

for him, and he had told Paula that he knew earlier that year how it would end, that it was simply a matter of writing it.

Modine gathered his thoughts one last time as he watched her walk the horse in widening circles, her ponytail bobbing, the air thick with kicked up dirt.

They stood by the car, the sky an endless blue. He had told Paula, as achingly beautiful as a midnight bus ride when you were the only passenger awake, that last winter he had felt there was no longer any reason to hope for anything. A man was responsible for himself and no one else.

The hell if anybody saw that as being selfish. It was the way he felt. He had always suspected that most people simply prayed for themselves anyway.

A god in the hand, was all it was. A play on the phrase "the hand of God." A gun, a knife, a bottle of wine. A phone; answering machines like confessionals; 900 numbers having similar uses.

A man's life was in his own hands, or in someone else's. God had nothing to do with it; it all depended on the neighborhood.

Someone might find him one day with a litany of hesitation marks on his arms, a rusty razor blade in his mouth. Or they might come across his corpse in an alleyway, a sucking holy wound in his chest, killed for dope money or the color of his clothing.

Forever and ever, amen.

More frightening than a brain tumor was the simple fact that you could die at any time, in any number of ways. And the world would simply keep on keeping on.

This Modine told Paula as she finished her work and let the horse run free in the field outside.

GRAVE PROMISES

Jill M. Morgan

I'VE ALWAYS BEEN AFRAID OF GRAVEYARDS," SAID CYRUS
Emmons.

The old man was frail as a sapling, thought Dr. Schaefer.
He would be ninety in a week, and caring for him at this
facility put a strain on the staff. This wasn't a nursing home.
It was damn depressing waiting for Emmons to die. The
nurses hated coming into his room. The smell alone was
enough to turn back all but the most hardy.

Still, Schaefer reminded himself, he was a doctor. It was
up to him to see if he could prolong the man's life a little
while. Though what good it did anyone, he didn't know.

"I suppose you don't like to think about dying," he said,
responding to the man's comment.

"Oh, it isn't that," said Emmons. "I know more dead folk
than I do the living. I'll be ready enough when my time
comes. It's graveyards that scare me."

"They scare a lot of people, I think," said Schaefer, trying
to drop the subject. Emmons was his last patient on rounds.
When he left this room, he'd be free to leave the hospital and
go home to a nice dinner with his wife. They had a new
baby, eight weeks old.

It had been three months since Schaefer had slept with his
wife. The last month of her pregnancy, she'd been too

uncomfortable. Since the baby arrived, they'd both been too tired. Tonight, he was thinking about doing something about that—if he could get out of here early.

"I can see the graveyard, over there." Emmons pointed in the direction of the north-facing window. "When these nurses put me in my wheelchair, they sit me by the window, and that's what I see for hours, a graveyard full of standing stones. Like it's waiting for me, you know?" Emmons spoke with a slight Irish accent, one he hadn't lost even though he'd lived in the States for sixty years.

"I'll talk to the nursing staff about giving you a different view," said Dr. Schaefer. He understood Emmons's concern. He wouldn't want to be staring at his future final resting place all day. It was insensitive of the nurses to park his wheelchair in such a spot.

"Why did they build a hospital by a graveyard, anyway?" asked the old man.

The doctor knew why. The facility was put where it was because the land had been cheap. Businesses wouldn't touch it. Nobody wanted to build their homes near the place. But a hospital couldn't afford to be as choosy as businesses and homeowners. A hospital needed one eye on the budget and the other eye on ways to cut expenses even more.

"I think they were offered a very good deal on the land," he told Emmons.

The old man shook his head.

Schaefer stood, intending to leave. If he got out of here now, the gift shop downstairs would still be open. He could pick up some flowers to take home to his wife. It might help to set the mood.

"Have I ever told you what happened in the graveyard when I was a boy?"

"I don't think so," said Schaefer. "Maybe the next time I'm here—"

"I won't be here when you come back tomorrow," said the old man. "You'd better hear my story now. It's not long. Sit down, Doctor."

Damn, thought Schaefer. If he were rude, like Cooper or Burton, he'd just walk out, as if he hadn't heard the old man. He'd seen the other doctors do it, and the nurses. And he'd despised them for it. He hadn't gotten into medicine to ill-treat people. Besides, he felt sorry for Emmons. No one ever came to visit him. He must be lonely.

"All right," he agreed. "I'll stay a minute or two." He settled back in the chair.

"Pull your chair closer," said Emmons. "I don't want anyone else to hear this."

Feeling foolish, Schaefer scooted the chair closer to the hospital bed. "Please," he said, "I have to be leaving soon."

"In a hurry, are you? The young always are."

Schaefer sighed.

"I was in a hurry that day, I remember," said Emmons. "I was eleven, going on twelve that month. My mother had sent me on an errand for buying the fixings for our supper that night. Being young, I'd played the time away, not noticing the hour until it was nearly too late to reach the store before it closed for the night. Then would my mother have been mad, and my dad too."

Schaefer tried to think of an excuse to get up and leave. He had to put an end to this. He could tell the man was winding up for a long, long roll. "I really can't stay," he said. "My wife's expecting me home."

"Oh, I know how women are when they expect you back at a certain time. That's how it was with my mother, exactly so. She had a temper, and I was afraid of her, old as I was."

Emmons struggled to be more comfortable in the bed. His hands worked at trying to lift himself higher on the mattress, not making any progress, but laboring with hands braced on the mattress and knuckles bent in effort.

"Here, let me help you," said Schaefer. He put his arms around the old man's back and lifted him higher in the bed, bolstering the position with two pillows.

"Is that better?"

Emmons nodded, catching his breath. "Much better, I thank you."

It occurred to Schaefer that he could leave then, and Emmons might not remember there had even been a story to tell. The old were forgetful as children. He could walk out of the room and—

"It was because I was late for the store that I dared cross the graveyard as a shortcut," said the old man. His blue eyes stared at Schaefer, as if willing him to stay.

Resigned to it, he sat back in his chair.

"I made a pact that day, with myself, and with whatever fear it was I had in me. I bargained my way across that ground of the dead. It was a boy's promise, no doubt. But a promise is a promise, even so. I hadn't bargained for having to keep my word. Not then. I was young, not much more than a petticoat child."

"Petticoat child?" Schaefer had never heard the expression.

"It was how mothers dressed their children, in dresses and long curls, till they reached a certain size and age, even the boys."

"Really? I've never heard of that." He smiled, trying to imagine Cyrus Emmons in petticoats and curls. It was quite an image, with the man's bristling mustache and grizzled beard.

"So, you made a promise?" asked Schaefer.

"I did," said Emmons, "then never thought of it again, not through all the years between that time and now. But lying here," he said, "knowing what's to come, I've thought of that promise again, and remembered every word of it."

"I wouldn't worry about such a thing," said Schaefer. He could see the old man was worked up over this. He wanted to put the man's mind at ease. "Children say a lot of things. No one expects—"

"No, a promise is a sacred oath. I made it to them in the graveyard, and they listened."

"Surely, you don't think . . ." He tried to be tactful, respectful of the old man's fears. "You don't believe in ghosts, do you, Mr. Emmons?"

"No, not ghosts."

"I've never seen one in all my years of medical practice, and I've seen people die," Schaefer said.

Emmons's breathing was heavier, harsher-sounding. Schaefer could hear wheezing in lungs that had sounded clear before. The old guy was giving himself an attack, thinking about all this.

"Stop this, now. Let me get you something for your chest, to help you breathe easier."

"I promised they could have my body on the day I died. Not my soul, mind you, but my body they could have. It was

303

a foolish thing to offer, but I was young and told myself I had the rest of my life before me. I thought it better they take it at the end than at the beginning. You see, don't you?"

What he could see was how agitated Emmons was getting. He reached across for the old man's wrist and took his pulse. It was rising. "Listen to me," he said. "You're all right. You mustn't let yourself get too excited over this. In the morning, I'll have one of the pastors come and talk to you. Would you like that?"

"Ministers?" Emmons shook his head. "I've no need of them. Settled those accounts long ago. I have a need to tell this, Doctor," he said, "and you're the only one who's left to me. Let me finish."

"You're making yourself ill, Mr. Emmons. Now, I want you to lie down and rest. If you don't do this willingly, I'll have to order an injection."

Emmons seemed to slump at the threat. "You would not take what time I have left from me? I'm ready, as I've said, but I'd keep the few hours I own. Don't be robbing me of them."

Emmons sounded more Irish by the minute, as if the weaker he became, the more pronounced was his accent and dialect. He was slipping back through time, back to his years as a young man and the days of his childhood. Schaefer was a witness to the process, as though ninety-year-old Cyrus Emmons were growing younger.

Growing back in time to his eleventh year.

Schaefer's skin rose gooseflesh at the thought. Everything Emmons had said was childish and without any rational reason for fear, and yet . . . Schaefer didn't want to see the graveyard when he left the hospital. He didn't want to ever see it again.

"They had me, you see," said Emmons. "I was alone and vulnerable. What could a boy do against so many? Which one of them wouldn't have taken my body for his own? So many."

As they'd spoken, it had grown dark in the room. Schaefer moved to turn on the light. When he stood, the graveyard was in view, the stones casting their shadows over the grass . . . long shadows, like bodies climbing from the graves.

"You believe what I'm telling you, don't you?" asked Emmons. "I was in their keeping, a living thing in a field of the dead. There was not another living soul I could call to for help. Who goes to the graveyard at the close of day?"

"Look, could we talk about something else for a while?" said Schaefer. He knew he couldn't leave his patient like this, the guy was getting worse by the minute, but he sure as hell didn't want to keep digging up the ruins of old Emmons's graveyard.

"I've been watching, every day as I sit by the window. I've seen them notice me. They'll be coming for me tonight. I can feel it."

"Cut it out," said Schaefer.

"I don't mind the dying so much," he said. "Everybody expects that. It happens to all of us. I just . . ." He looked scared. "I just don't want them taking me before my soul's gone, you know?"

"Aw, Jesus," said Schaefer. He stood and glanced through the window. It seemed like one of the stones had moved.

"You've got me seeing things in that cemetery."

"What's your given name, Dr. Schaefer?"

"What?" He was staring at the stones. One really had moved. No, that was crazy. Still, he didn't want to look away from the window.

"Your given name," Emmons asked again, "what is it?"

"Oh, William." He could have said Bill, that's what Sharon called him. So did everyone else who'd known him for any length of time. The nurses called him Dr. Schaefer. It was hospital policy, not his. He called them by their first names, and they called him Dr. Schaefer. And now, when one of his patients had asked him, he'd called himself William, not Bill.

"William," said Cyrus Emmons, "stay with me until I'm gone."

He thought Emmons meant until he went to sleep.

But then the old man added, "Don't let them take me before I'm dead. I don't mind what they do after my soul's gone, but stay with me till then, I'm asking."

"You're not dying tonight," Schaefer told him.

He should have gone home earlier, should never have let the man start talking this way. How long had he been sitting

305

here? At least an hour. Cooper or Burton wouldn't have put themselves through all this. They wouldn't let it go on a minute longer.

And neither would he.

He decided. Things were rapidly going downhill for the man. If he didn't do something quickly, he might lose a patient tonight.

"I'll be right back," he said. He stood and walked out of the room.

"Don't leave me!" cried Emmons. "They'll come before it's time. Have pity on my soul. Don't go!" he pleaded.

Schaefer steeled himself against the sound. He moved away from the room and down the hall. It would only be a few minutes. He'd draw the dose into the syringe himself, something to quiet the old man and settle his nerves. He'd give him the injection, wait with him until it took effect, then get out of here.

Damn hospital. Shouldn't have built it next to a grave-yard. Didn't they care what patients would think? Didn't they know sick people would look at those stones and wonder if the next one put up would be theirs?

He felt a chill shudder through him. It seemed to touch through to his heart, blood, and bones. Like a cold breath, it touched his soul.

Oh, God, he thought. Shouldn't have left him alone.

Schaefer hurried, running along the corridor, loaded syringe in his hand. He called out so Emmons could hear him. "It's all right. I'm coming. Here I come."

How could he have left him like that, with the old man pleading? Begging? How could he have—

Schaefer grabbed the door frame with one hand as he rushed inside.

The room was empty.

"Emmons."

He went back. Looked at the number on the door.

"Emmons," he called again.

The bed's sheets and blanket were wrinkled, as if someone had recently been lying between them.

"Emmons!"

That was when he looked to the window, found himself

walking across the room to stare out the glass. It was hard to see. Night had settled like a veil of death over the land.

And yet . . . The moonlight held a shadow of tree branches blown by the wind, or a flurry of leaves and debris cast high by a powerful gust, or something racing over the grass of the graveyard, between the stones. Something running, followed by a flittering of movement behind it, like spirits in the night.

And in the midst of this dark mass, as if captured by the wind or by whatever whirled around it, a glimpse of something seen only in a flash of moonlight turned and stared up at the window of the hospital where William Schaefer stood. It was the face of Cyrus Emmons. Schaefer saw him. Then, as quickly as he recognized the image, it disappeared.

Schaefer stepped back from the window. Shaken, he stumbled to the chair, staring blankly at the old man's bed. The blanket and sheet had been thrown to the floor. He didn't want to touch them. Didn't want to move.

Something terrible had happened; he knew it. Something beyond his understanding. What did he know of an old man's promises? Only his fear, he'd known that.

A sudden cry came . . . hollowed by the wind, like the piercing scream of a child.

Schaefer heard, covered his ears with his hands and groaned. A crack of lightning sealed the sound. For a moment all was silence, broken only by drops of heavy rain splattering the window, like fingertips beating at the pane.

He didn't want to, but looked at the glass. Nothing there. Again, a rapping of fingertips beckoned from outside the hospital window. Rain broke in torrents, sheeting over the water-distorted glass. As if summoned, Schaefer walked to the window.

Below him was the graveyard, rain soaking between the stones and the earth beneath . . . seeping into the ground, touching the concrete grave liners, some broken . . . seeping between the cracks in the seams, into the fissures of broken concrete, broken wood . . . rain touching the decomposed bodies of the dead.

In the next flash of lightning, Schaefer saw what he was

meant to see, the old man surrounded by a scattering of shapes. Not tree branches. Not swirling leaves. Shapes, tall and menacing. He saw and knew, whatever fear Cyrus Emmons had carried for all the years since his childhood in Ireland had finally come to claim him.

Don't let them take me before I'm dead . . . stay with me till then, I'm asking.

But Schaefer hadn't stayed, despite the desperate plea, the final prayer. He'd left the old man alone. He'd let them come and take him.

"Emmons!" Schaefer cried, tearing from the room as if he could stop what he knew was already happening.

"Dr. Schaefer, what's—" a nurse asked.

He didn't hear the rest. Couldn't, as he ran along the corridor to the fire stairwell. Didn't matter. Nothing mattered, except getting there in time . . . getting to the graveyard before whatever force that held Emmons collected on a boy's terrified promise.

He couldn't wait for the elevator, but took the steps two at a time. He was young and strong, jumping over the rail, hurrying down four levels to the ground floor, to a back door leading from the hospital's temporary morgue to the connecting grounds of the adjacent cemetery.

Rain hit his face when he stepped from the building, hard pellets of water striking like needle points. The downpour blinded him, but he ran. He knew the direction, followed the rise of ground to the high ridge at the back corner of the cemetery. That's where he'd seen them circling the old man. That's where he'd seen the lightning flash outline a glimpse of tall, menacing shapes surrounding Emmons.

As he ran he heard them. Not the howl of wind, nor the scrape of stone on metal, but unearthly sounds of converging evil. He ran toward the ground's rise, not thinking of what he might do if he got there in time, or what his fate might be. Thinking only of a small boy, alone and afraid, crossing a darkened graveyard after nightfall.

Something rent the air around him—a scream, a smothered cry, he couldn't be sure.

"Leave him alone!" Schaefer yelled, but the wind carried away his breath and the sound of his voice.

He felt a shudder run through him, and knew. At that instant he knew it was over for Emmons. Too late.

Dr. Bill Schaefer, William, slumped to the sodden ground, devoid of strength, breath, and courage. The rain pummeled; he felt its weight upon him like dancing death.

He felt as if he sank, body and soul, into the depths of this rain-soaked ground. It was more than losing a patient, more than watching a man die. *I should have been there to save him,* Schaefer condemned himself.

William, stay with me until I'm gone, the old man had asked.

But he hadn't. And now . . .

A stir of movement over the ground startled him, like cracks opening along the seams of earth, like tall, formless shapes drawing toward him from a swollen concentration on the hill. The lands of the dead opened from doorways of shifting gravestones.

He felt them coming for him. A rush of adrenaline threaded through his veins, pumped in his heart and into his brain. He tried to run, legs trembling, arms pressing at the dark in terror, but it was too late. He was caught.

Schaefer knew them. Not faces, bodies, or even recognizable shapes, but he knew them as the demons of his nightmares. They were what all people feared, beings without pity or soul. He was a grown man, not an innocent boy, but he trembled, even as young Emmons must have.

He knew what they wanted.

"Don't take me now," he bargained, knowing there was nothing he could do to keep them back. So many. He felt them move closer, like a breath of wind over his wet skin. "Take me later, when I'm old. You can have my body then, I promise."

A sudden chill swept over and through him. Another flash of lightning seared an image into his mind, one he would never forget as long as he lived—an image of ravenous, gaping maws, without a spark of life.

At the clap of thunder, the image vanished.

Schaefer was left untouched by the bolt of lightning that struck the graveyard, cutting down trees, sheering off stones. Untouched, but not unharmed.

William Schaefer went home to his wife that night. When she asked what was wrong, he told her he'd lost a patient. Like the good wife of a doctor, she didn't press him for more. She was thoughtful, kind, always forgiving.

But he couldn't forgive himself.

He carried that harm inside him, a wound that would not heal. He remained a doctor, but couldn't treat this affliction deep within him. Over the years, it grew.

He couldn't go on working at the hospital, not after what had happened. The memories were too real. Couldn't stare at the graveyard from the window of the fourth floor and not be haunted by what he'd seen. He told no one of his experience. Who would believe him?

With his wife and infant daughter, Schaefer moved to another state and started over. He opened a small practice, specializing in treating the elderly. And never again, in all the years of his medical practice, did he leave a dying patient alone. He stayed and saw their souls into safety, each and every one.

A few years later he and his wife had another child, a son. His wife wanted to name the boy William Junior, but Schaefer wouldn't have it. "I've never liked the name William," he said, refusing her offer. They called the boy Steven, after his wife's father.

"Don't you hate working with old people?" his son asked him once. The boy was sixteen that year, bursting with energy and life, and clearly distressed by the nature of his father's work.

"They need my care," said Schaefer.

"But they're dying," said Steven.

"I know." It was all Schaefer could give the boy in reply.

It wasn't enough. It never was. His obsession with the lives and deaths of his patients drew Schaefer away from his family. In time, his wife left him, and his children dismissed him as someone who had little meaning in their lives.

The ages of Schaefer's life were listed like the etched lines on a gravestone. His marker was his work, his patients. The old and the dying, they claimed him. Never again did he fail to answer their calls to stay with them, to watch with them and stand guard against their fears.

Grave Promises

When he thought of that night in the cemetery, Schaefer told himself it couldn't have happened the way he remembered. What had he seen, really? Nothing he could describe. He told himself it had been a reaction to his guilt over Emmons's disappearance.

But in the lonely times before morning, he had asked himself, What really happened to Emmons?

He kept his secret quiet as the grave. It was his memory, no one else's. He brought no one into his fear. Not his ex-wife, or his children. Not his patients. Not the minister of the church where he worshiped God on Sunday mornings. No one.

As he grew older, colleagues said he should take a partner into the practice. They said the workload was too much for him. "Bring in a young doctor," they told him, "someone fresh out of medical school."

He didn't. He would carry this weight alone.

Schaefer practiced medicine until a minor stroke stopped him in his seventieth year. He'd been at work, felt a sudden heat sear through the left side of his brain, and collapsed. The result of the stroke was partial paralysis of his right side. His right hand shook, he walked with a noticeable catch in his stride, but he could take care of himself well enough to manage on his own. He didn't need a nursing home, or long-term care in a hospital. For that he was grateful.

He managed an independent life for three more years, firmly resisting anyone's suggestion that he move to an adult care community or elder village. Schaefer had seen enough of old people. They talked of dying, and worse, of where they wanted to be buried.

Lately, the thought of graveyards had begun to prey on his mind.

Long ago he'd given up the practice of attending funerals. Even when his ex-wife died, and his son and daughter made a point of asking him to be there—a gesture of reaching out to a distant father after so long, he understood—still, he didn't go.

Over time, many of his friends died, relatives, even some of his patients, but Schaefer never went to their funerals. People began to think he didn't believe in religion, that he wouldn't step inside a church. He let them think whatever they wished. He believed in God. It was graveyards he feared.

In the spring of his seventy-fourth year, when the country-side blossomed in beauty, Schaefer began seeing the old man. At first he thought it was a trick of his eyes. He took off his glasses and rubbed the lenses with a corner of his shirt. His hands shook. He feared he'd drop the glasses, but didn't.

When he put them back on, the old man was gone.

Schaefer told himself his vision had been getting worse. Lately, much worse. He tried to convince himself the old man had never been there. It didn't work. That night, he left the light on in his room when he laid down to sleep.

A week passed in uneventful peace. Schaefer had very little sleep, but nothing happened. He almost convinced himself the vision had been a dream, or his imagination. This worked in the daylight, but when it grew dark, he stared at the windows and watched for unbidden shadows.

Often, these vigils became so intense, he forgot to eat his evening meals. His already thin body became gaunt and frail. He forgot to take his medicines too, those needed to help prevent another stroke.

A week before Easter, he saw the old man again.

He'd been invited to his daughter's house for Easter dinner, and this time he intended not to disappoint her. She'd moved back to the town where she'd been born. Her aunts and cousins were there, and other members of her mother's family.

Schaefer decided to fly there. He was getting too old to travel any great distance by car. He'd fly to the city, rent a car at the airport, and drive the rest of the way to her house. He was thinking of the trip, waiting at the airport and wondering if the presents he'd brought his daughter's children would be all right, when he saw the face in the crowd.

The old man was ahead of him, in a group of other people. Emmons turned and stared at Schaefer. The crowd kept moving, passengers hurrying to their planes. Before Schaefer could call out to him, Emmons had disappeared.

Schaefer felt sudden weakness overwhelm his body. A pounding began in his left temple, moving to a place behind his eyes, like a balloon blowing up in his brain.

"They're calling your flight, sir," said the attendant from the desk. "Do you need help boarding the plane?"

"No," Schaefer told her. He started toward the gate. The pounding grew worse, like an ocean hitting the shore of his skull. He wondered if he'd make it to his seat, so many people in the way.

"Excuse us, please," said the flight attendant, clearing a path for Schaefer, then helping him store his carry-on bag in the overhead compartment. "This is your seat," she told him.

He fell into the seat, his breathing labored.

"Are you all right?" she asked, concern showing in her eyes.

He nodded. Couldn't speak.

"Would you like me to get you something? A drink of cold water?"

He shook his head.

She went away, and he was left with only the sound in his head . . . pounding, pounding, pounding.

A kind of peace came to him when the plane took off. He felt safe above the graveyards of the earth, above the spirits of the dead. He could see every passenger on board the plane. Cyrus Emmons was not among them.

It was a five-hour flight, during which the flight crew showed a movie. Schaefer closed his eyes and rested. He was so tired. The weight of his age and ill health pulled at his strength. He wanted to see his daughter and her family. He had never seen his grandchildren, two boys and a girl. If he could only get there . . .

The plane landed safely. Schaefer moved down the length of the airport terminal, barely able to walk. He knew he couldn't drive, but if he could manage to get to the front of the airport, he would hail a cab to take him to his daughter's house. He could rest there until he felt stronger, until he—

Cyrus Emmons stepped out before Schaefer.

"William," Emmons said, "it's time. A promise is a promise."

Schaefer tried to speak, but something heavy slammed into his brain. He fell, his forehead hitting the floor with a sickening crack.

* * *

"Dad."

The voice intruded into a place of unconsciousness.

"Dad, it's Jenny. Open your eyes."

Recognition, like a candle lit in a dark room, brought William Schaefer back to a world of thoughts, sights, and sounds. He didn't know the voice of his daughter, it wasn't familiar, but he knew her name.

"Where am I?" he asked. His vision was double. It was sickening to look around the room. Double windows, double doors, double Jennys.

"You're in the hospital, Dad. You fell."

"Fell?"

"At the airport, remember?"

He remembered the airport, how awful he'd felt, and then he remembered seeing Emmons standing right before him. At the recollection, panic flooded through Schaefer's veins. He tried to sit up.

"Where is he?" He couldn't see clearly. The damn double vision made everything look so strange. Emmons could be right there in the room with him and he might not know it.

"Where's who?" asked his daughter.

Why wasn't she little? She used to be little and cute, blond like her mother. He remembered calling her Lady Jenny, because she was so small and wanted to be grown-up. Now she was grown-up.

Emmons could be anywhere. It made no sense. If the man were dead—had died nearly fifty years ago—how did he keeping showing up? Unless he wasn't really dead, had never died.

"I've got to find him. You help me, Jenny."

"Find who?"

"Emmons!" He hadn't meant to yell at her. She didn't know, of course she didn't. He'd never told her about Emmons, or that night so long ago.

"Your doctor's name is Ryan, Dad—not Emmons. Do you want me to call him for you?"

"Ryan? No, help me find Emmons. You'll do that for me, won't you, Jenny? Help me find him before it's too late."

"Sure, I'll help you. Don't worry. Everything's going to be fine. Lie down and relax. I'll stay here while you rest."

He was exhausted by his efforts. Couldn't get up. Tried,

but couldn't. If he could slip back into the place of unconsciousness, that would be best. He didn't want to see this room with its double images. He didn't want to see anything at all.

"Rest, Dad. I'll stay with you while you sleep."

He closed his eyes. *Rest.* That's what he needed. He'd rest a little, and then he'd . . .

The day turned to night while William Schaefer slept. Into the darkness of the room, a presence entered Schaefer's consciousness.

"William."

He knew the voice, remembered it from forever. It dragged him from his sense of peace. No peace now. No rest. No life.

"Go away," Schaefer said, not opening his eyes.

"A promise is a promise," said Emmons, his voice sounding like a tumble of running water, the hum of electricity, or harnessed energy.

Schaefer wouldn't look.

"You left me alone," said Emmons. "I was afraid, like you are now. I told you what they'd do, and you left me alone."

"I'm sorry. I'm so sorry," said Schaefer. "How could I know—"

"It's time," said Emmons. "Take him."

Schaefer opened his eyes and saw dark shapes surround his bed. Denser than the dark of the room, they moved closer. . . .

"No!" screamed Schaefer. "Don't let them—"

The door opened. "Dr. Schaefer? Are you all right?"

"Turn on the light!" cried Schaefer, his voice high as a child's.

The man switched on the light and stepped into the hospital room. "Is something wrong, Dr. Schaefer? Sometimes it can be frightening to wake up in an unfamiliar room. You probably don't remember too much about arriving at the hospital. I'm Dr. Ryan."

Schaefer looked everywhere but couldn't see them.

"You may not remember much about where you are right now," said Dr. Ryan, "but people certainly remember you at this hospital. You worked here, I've been told."

Now he knew where he was, back in the same hospital where Emmons . . .

"What floor is this?" he asked.

"You're on the fourth floor," said Ryan.

"What's outside that window?"

"The window?"

"Is it a graveyard?" Schaefer had to know.

"Why, yes."

Schaefer felt his muscles bunch and release, bunch and release. Fear hollowed him. Terror seeped like a drug into his veins.

"My daughter, where did she—"

"She left, had to go home to her children. She'll be back tomorrow."

"She promised to stay."

"She couldn't stay all night, could she? You wouldn't expect that? You were asleep."

He knew what would happen. They would come for him, just as they had come for Emmons so long ago. They would take his body before he was dead. The stark fear of what they'd do to him penetrated every fiber of Schaefer's being.

"Don't leave me alone," he asked the fresh-faced young doctor. "I'm dying. I can feel my life going from me," he said. "Stay with me until then."

"You're not dying."

"I am, I know it."

"Calm down, Dr. Schaefer. This kind of upset isn't good for you. You've had another minor stroke. You're going to be fine, but you have to—"

"Don't leave me. Promise?" Schaefer pleaded.

"It's all right. I'll stay with you. Settle down," said Ryan.

"Promise me . . . on your life. You won't leave, even if I fall asleep? Don't let them take me before I die."

"Don't worry," said Ryan. "I'll stay right here, but you have to try to relax."

Schaefer lay back against the pillows, his body drenched in sweat. He smelled fear on his skin. And death.

"Close your eyes," said Ryan. "Take some deep breaths."

Schaefer's eyes closed. Let me die before it happens, he thought.

"A promise is a sacred oath," he whispered to the doctor,

and then his breathing became heavy with exhaustion and sporadic sleep.

Dr. Ryan stayed in the room, monitoring the old man's fading heartbeat and labored breathing. It didn't seem possible, but it was true—Schaefer's vital signs were worsening incredibly fast. If Ryan didn't do something immediately, the man would die right in front of him.

Ryan hit the emergency button in the room. The code should bring running footsteps and the rattle of a crash cart down the hall. He wanted to take an immediate EKG on the patient, and if his suspicions proved founded, he needed to administer an injection of adrenaline. An injection of adrenaline would regulate the old guy's heart. Imagine, having worked in this place as a young doctor, and winding up in the same hospital.

No one came.

Ryan pressed the emergency button again. The hospital was short-staffed. They'd had radical cutbacks since last winter. He waited, alarmed by how fast Schaefer's condition was worsening. He reached for the man's wrist. The pulse was thready; he could barely feel it.

"Damn!" Ryan knocked over his chair in his rush to get out of the room. He was losing him. Adrenaline could still make the difference. Where was the damn crash cart?

It's not too late, he thought, leaving the room and stepping only a few steps into the hall.

"You left me." The old man's voice grated on the air, harsh and menacing.

Dr. Ryan turned back to his patient. Surrounding Schaefer's bed were nightmare visions of death . . . images that burned like hot iron into Ryan's mind.

"He broke his promise," cried William Schaefer. The man's eyes were stark and terrified-looking. "On his life, he swore it! A promise is a promise. Take his life in exchange for mine. Look at him," he pleaded, pointing his feeble finger at Ryan. "He's young, a much longer life for you. Take him."

The grave terrors twisted around and stared their eyeless orbs at Ryan. His mind shouted, *It's real!* But he couldn't run, his muscles paralyzed with desperate fear. Bony hands grabbed him, tearing at his flesh.

They lifted him, the thieves of life. Skeletons and demons. Cold eyes. No eyes. Dead. Lifted him off the floor and raced with the spoils of their victory, down the hall to the fire stairs, out the exit and across the dark stretch of land between the hospital and the graveyard. To the graveyard itself, and the hill.

In the hospital bed a faint smile played at the corners of the patient's mouth.

William Schaefer heard running footsteps coming toward the room from the nurse's station, and the rattle of a crash cart. A team of three, two nurses and a doctor, ran into the room.

He suffered their ministrations without protest, the hurried placing of six adhesive-backed patches from the sterile pack, attaching the monitor lead wires of the EKG machine, the LED monitor readout.

"Normal rhythms," said the doctor, a woman.

Schaefer felt much better. Stronger.

"Where's Dr. Ryan?" the doctor asked him.

Schaefer lifted his shoulders in a weak shrug.

"Ryan called for a crash cart, then left?" asked the doctor, sounding amazed.

Schaefer said nothing. His condition improved steadily.

When the team of doctor and nurses left his room, Schaefer turned his head toward the window and looked out. Clouds covering the moon parted. By the silvered luminance of moonlight he saw the graveyard and the standing tombstones, like sentinels on the hill.

Shadows moved between the stones, chasing something up the hill. Someone. A finger of moonlight touched the dark slope. Schaefer saw a figure turn, as if caught by the overwhelming shadows. Sealed in the band of light, he clearly saw the face of Dr. Ryan.

Schaefer turned away. A scream, the terrified cry of a child, carried from the hillside crest of the graveyard . . . carried on the chill April air . . . and pierced Dr. William Schaefer's soul.

Oh, God, he thought, trembling inside, *I've always hated graveyards.*

THE FEAR OF FEAR ITSELF

Del Stone Jr.

The First Hour

FROM FIVE MILES UP, PAUL WESTERBROOK THOUGHT THE ground resembled an impossible dream of heaven.

Impossible, he thought, his depth of focus shifting to his reflection in the airliner porthole. Impossible that I could be here and the ground could be so far away.

He watched his image. Shafts of sunlight slanted through the row of portholes on the opposite side of the cabin, back-lighting his head so that his face was masked in shadow. Darker pools filled in the spaces around his eyes and mouth.

He might have been staring at a skull.

And he could hear a rushing sound. Not the dull thunder of a flood, but a fine sandpapery hiss, the sound of air whistling over the bright aluminum skin of the 767 as it hurtled through the thin atmosphere, its engines and wings maintaining a hair-trigger equilibrium between thrust and weight and lift, and he could feel the plane sinking and rising as variables of air density and wind velocity and engine compression altered the formula in tiny but notice-able increments that brought mists of perspiration to his forehead as he tried to calculate the forces of turbulence necessary to send the airplane spinning out of control—

He slammed the porthole visor down.

He squeezed his eyes shut.

And he recited a silent prayer: Please, God. I'll do anything you want. Just get this plane on the ground safely.

Somebody was speaking to him. He blinked.

"Did you want something to drink, sir?" A flight attend-ant. She was older than most, with thin, blond hair, pale skin, and high cheekbones. She had the calm look of a kindergarten teacher handing out waxed Dixie cups of warm Kool-Aid. The aniline-blue uniform of South Air smoothed the curves of her body and gave her a confident, almost motherly aspect.

A bump rattled the plane. Paul grabbed the backrest of the seat in front of him and felt his palm slide greasily over the plastic upholstery.

Finally he said, "A drink? Yes," and was instantly ashamed of the tremor in his voice. "Bring me a couple of Valiums and a bottle of Crown Royal. That should do the trick."

The attendant smiled warmly. "White knuckles, eh?" she whispered, and he nodded too quickly. He thought he must look to her like a contrite child.

"Do you fly often?" She was easing into the seat next to him, and he thought he could feel a shuddering vibration passing through the floor of the airplane and up through the frame of his seat. Or was that a change in engine pitch? Was the pilot throttling back as a warning light suddenly blinked red, or was a turbine starting to rattle as hairline cracks widened into chasms of flawed metal and the blades pre-pared to fly off the shaft like knives thrown by a blindfolded magician—

"Not much. But from now on, yes," he said. And he had made the decision himself, hadn't he? In spite of Gail's subtle coercion, he had accepted the position of regional buyer for the McAndliss chain of department stores, a promotion that would give him more opportunities—a final chance, as it were, because twice before he had refused offers like this for whatever reason had seemed important at the time, and if he'd refused again . . . Well. Gail would have said nothing, but her measured ways of doing things when she was angry would have spoken volumes. You are an indecisive and fearful man, she would have thought, adding: I don't know why I married you.

So he'd accepted the offer.

But the job required flying.

"It's nothing to be ashamed of," the attendant said, and laid an utterly cool palm on his hand. Her skin was as dry and smooth as a pool hustler's chalked cue. "Most people experience a little anxiety while flying. Sometimes it's acrophobia, claustrophobia, or even a combination of the two. Are you afraid of heights?"

Paul nodded once. Heights. God, yes.

She patted his hand. "My father used to say, 'We have nothing to fear but fear itself.'" She shook her head sadly.

Paul nodded without enthusiasm. At that moment he didn't care about borrowed aphorisms. He simply wanted to be on the ground.

"My father was an airline pilot." She smiled mysteriously. "He never worried about . . . the unexpected."

A staticky voice scratched from the cabin speakers. It was the captain, announcing that South Air's nonstop service from Los Angeles to Atlanta had reached its cruising altitude, that passengers could remove their seat belts, that their flight time would be about four hours and forty-five minutes—Paul stopped listening. His heart seemed ready to jump out of his throat.

The attendant gave Paul's hand a reassuring pat and stood up. "I'll bring you a cocktail and check to see how you're doing." At that moment the whining throb of the engines shifted to a lower, almost subliminal pitch that seemed to resonate through Paul's bones. His stomach looped into a tense knot.

She looked at him and said, "Try not to worry, Mr. Westerbrook," and her gaze hardened for a moment, as if a layer of ice had formed over her eyes and melted, long enough for her to whisper, "If the plane crashes, all the worrying in the world won't change a thing."

Then she was padding silently toward the rear of the

airplane, and the terror was swarming all over Paul again as he tried to remember when he had told her his name.

The Second Hour

Paul wondered what Gail was doing at this moment.

In his mind's eye he saw her at the dining room table, her leather portfolio beside her with papers spilling between the teeth of the zipper—homework papers or tests to be graded, the things teachers carried with them. She would remove the papers and arrange them into neat stacks and attack them until they were back inside the portfolio.

That is, if she were there. And not next door.

When he landed at Hartsfield International Airport, he would go home in a taxi. After seventeen years, their marriage could no longer support airport reunions.

But he envied her. He envied her discipline and her stubbornness and her immunity to fear.

"Here's your drink, Mr. Westerbrook," the flight attendant announced. Two other attendants were pushing a drink cart up the aisle, tossing ice cubes into plastic glasses like crap shooters and popping the tabs on cans of 7UP and Coca-Cola.

He thanked her nervously and drained half the glass in a single swallow. The liquor seemed to cauterize the lining of his throat. Bourbon and Coke—mostly bourbon. He wasn't a bourbon drinker, but anything with alcohol would have served the moment.

He glanced at her name tag: It said TESS.

She slid into the seat next to him again and in a conspiratorial whisper said, "Do you like the drink? That's the way my father liked them—heavy on the bourbon."

Paul took another sip. Why hadn't she asked him what he wanted to drink? He thought to ask, but said, "You mention your father often. You must love him very much."

Her gaze became unfocused, and a tracing of a smile crossed her lips. "Yes," she said. The smile dimmed to an expression Paul approximated with regret. Then she was back to business. "Now finish that drink because the first officer tells me we're headed for some rough weather."

Paul felt ice crystals forming in his blood. Rough weather? Turbulence? Something cold was sliding along the lifeline in his palm—a drop of moisture, either condensation from the cup or chilled sweat. He managed to stammer, "Will—will it be bad?"

The flight attendant—Tess—shrugged. "You never know, especially with this flight crew."

He raised an eyebrow and took another hit of the drink.

"The first officer has been drinking since we left LAX," she said.

The liquor burned like lye. It caught in his windpipe and he choked, spraying bourbon over the tray. He hacked until his eyes burned and tears smeared everything into watery blots of shadow and light. When he was finally able to breathe, he wheezed, "But isn't that—isn't that against the rules?"

She frowned. "You're darn right it's against the rules. Honest to God. My father would have a heart attack if he could see what goes on in the cockpit these days."

"But why doesn't the captain put a stop to it?" Paul babbled.

She shook her head wearily. "This sort of thing goes on all the time—it's not unusual. All the airlines have problems with alcoholic pilots." She hesitated and cocked an ear. "Did you hear that?" She listened a moment longer. "It sounded like they shut down an engine." Paul felt his eyes goggling. She tittered, and it was a sound without mirth. "I guess not."

She walked away, humming softly. Paul stared blankly at the seat back ahead of him. A pit seemed to have opened in his stomach, claiming everything inside him and giving back nothing but black fear.

He wished he could fold himself into that pit and simply disappear until this ordeal was over. He wished he could return to the heavenly ground.

The Third Hour

Paul sat rigid in his seat. He could hear a metronomic pulsing, the sound a wheel bearing on a car makes when the grease has been reduced to sludge and metal is rubbing against metal and the entire wheel assembly is about to fly apart. He listened closely, his ear filtering out the extraneous noises of people chatting, and he could hear it: a droning throb modulated by regular basso pulses that seemed to beat through the air frame itself, the sound of weary machinery about to fail.

He listened.

It was the sound of his own heart.

God, he thought, if Gail could see me, she'd—she'd—

Tess was suddenly in the seat next to him. "Did you enjoy your drink?" she asked happily.

Paul nodded, and asked distractedly, "And how is the first officer enjoying *his* drinks?"

"Fine, fine," she said dismissively, ignoring the sarcasm.

"What about"—Paul hated to say the word, as if saying it would make it real—"those storms. Are we through them yet?"

Tess's eyes narrowed into a playful squint and she shook her head. She raised the visor and pointed. Paul risked a quick glance and then twitched his eyes away as the vertiginous change in perspective caused him to swoon. On the horizon he had seen . . . clouds. He was no meteorologist. But they resembled volcanoes of turbulence and violence. He slid the visor back down.

"Cumulonimbus, Mr. Westerbrook," she said gravely. "Thunderstorms. Hell breathers." That last part came out in an overdone stage whisper. On the ground he would have laughed at her melodrama, but up here, trapped in this cabin, he could only stare, dumbstruck with terror.

"Those are the same clouds responsible for most airplane crashes," she said. "For instance, the worst disaster in aviation history occurred on the Canary Island of Tenerife when two 747s collided during a thunderstorm. Over five hundred people . . ." She clasped her fingers around an imaginary matchstick and blew silently.

Paul squeezed his eyes shut and turned away. Why was she telling him this? She knew he was afraid. Why was she doing this to him?

"To quote my father," she said, her voice suddenly solemn, as if she were about to recite a catechism, "'God created thunderstorms to keep pilots humble.' But then thunderstorms aren't the only reason airplanes crash." The fingers came up for another accounting. "Mechanical or structural failure is the second-leading cause, followed by pilot error, midair collisions—and did you know, Mr. Westerbrook, that even disturbances by passengers have been blamed for airplane crashes? Did you know that?"

He dared to open his eyes and look at her. She looked back with a knowing smile.

He heard loud voices from the rear of the airplane. Tess's head went up like a wolf sniffing the air for deer scent. She hauled herself out of the seat with surprising litheness.

Paul looked back, fearful of what he might see. An elderly woman was standing by her seat, and the man next to her—Paul could see only the man's bald pate—seemed to be in some kind of distress. Paul settled into his seat and shivered.

A man wearing the South Air uniform appeared in the aisle, striding toward the rear of the plane. He was tall, his hair grayed at the temples and his face framed with lines. Paul thought he must be the captain, and the sight of him came simultaneously as a comfort and a shock. What could be happening that required the captain's intervention?

After a few moments the captain reappeared, moving toward the cockpit. Paul loudly cleared his throat.

The man stopped, and Paul said quickly, "Is everything all right, Captain?" He thought his voice sounded muffled and indistinct, as if a ventriloquist had spoken the words for him.

The man grinned and said, "Everything's fine. An elderly gentleman was having a problem with his ear." He pointed to his own ear. "The pressure. But now he's fine." He hesitated and added, "Oh, and I'm not the captain. I'm the first officer."

A tremor shook Paul. This man didn't look intoxicated. But Paul had heard stories about pilots' abilities to hold their booze. Maybe this first officer would return to the cockpit and knock back a stiff belt of bourbon and snicker about the chickenshit in seat C15 who was about to crap his drawers.

Without thinking, Paul asked: "Sir, are you a drinking man?"

The first officer chuckled. "Excuse me? I'm a member of the LDS church. We don't drink alcohol."

"And what about the storms," Paul blurted, hearing the panic rise in his voice, but not caring. "We're flying into storms, aren't we? Thunderstorms. Hell breathers."

The man looked baffled. "No," he answered tentatively. "We've got a few stratocumulus at about seventy degrees compass heading, but no thunderstorms." He tucked his tie into his shirt. "Just relax and enjoy the flight, sir. We'll be in Atlanta in about two hours." He walked away.

Paul felt a prickly sensation across his body, as if his skin were cooling and shrinking back around his bones.

Lies.

She'd lied to him.

In the jumble of his emotions a thought loomed— something he could never quite forget. A lie Gail had told him. About the man next door, and the afternoons she spent over there, "tutoring" his son. He remembered the vow he'd made to never believe anything anyone told him without confirming it himself.

Lied to. He'd let himself be lied to again.

"My God, I'm not believing this. I'm really not believing this." Tess was in the seat next to him, smelling of spilled bourbon and patchouli and a faint whiff of sweat. "That man in B28—he had a gun! He threatened to shoot up the airplane!"

Paul shook his head. He said, simply, "No more."

"Thank God that Karen—she's the flight attendant responsible for rows twenty through thirty-eight—saw what was happening and stopped him."

Paul closed his eyes. "We're not flying into bad weather."

"She wrestled the gun away from him before he could pull the trigger," Tess continued, a hard edge forming on her words.

"The first officer hasn't been drinking either," Paul went on. "He's a Mormon, for Christ's sake."

"Do you have any idea what a bullet would do to this airplane?" She seemed to be talking to no one but herself. "What *would* happen?" she murmured questioningly. "The cabin would lose pressure, and rapid decompression might damage the flight controls—no, this airplane has electronic flight controls. It's the older jets with mechanical flight controls, like the 727, that might have problems. But the pilots could lose consciousness. The plane *could* crash, I suppose."

"Have you heard anything I've said?" Paul asked, his voice rising. The plane jiggled and his heart raced a moment. "What were you trying to do? Scare the shit out of me?"

She shook her head, her gaze refocusing into a glare. "Mr. Westerbrook, are you familiar with desensitization therapy?"

That caught him off guard.

"It requires that a person who is afraid of something be repeatedly exposed to the source of his fear until he becomes desensitized to it." She paused and sighed. "That's what I was doing. I apologize if I frightened you, but it seemed the best way to handle the situation. Like my father said," she added cheerfully, "'You have nothing to fear but fear itself.'"

Paul clenched the armrests until veins stood out on his hands. "Is that so? Well tell me, what do you think your father would say about a flight attendant who scares the living shit out of her passengers? That's not exactly standard procedure."

Her expression chilled to absolute zero. "He wouldn't say anything, Mr. Westerbrook. My father is dead."

Instantly, Paul's anger swirled away. He mumbled, "Oh."

Her stare was blank. "He was killed in a plane crash. Three years ago. In Houston."

The breath eased from Paul's lungs in a slow, defeated sigh. Some emotion, yellow and bitter like shame, began to gather inside as he tried to imagine the grief she must feel when she came aboard an airplane. He found that it was beyond his comprehension.

She picked at her jacket. "I was only trying to help."

He nodded slowly. Maybe he had been too harsh. Finally, unsatisfactorily, he said, "Okay, let's just . . . forget it. No more fairy tales about storms or drunken copilots or crashes."

Tess said, "Fine," and got up to leave. Paul touched a finger to her sleeve and added, "The first officer told me the man in the back was having problems with his ears. So no more fairy tales about whackos shooting up the airplane. Okay?"

She gave him a puzzled look. "I guess he was trying to reassure you. Truth is, the man really did threaten to shoot up the airplane. Karen took the gun away from him and gave it to me." She whispered urgently, "Look, Mr. Westerbrook. This airplane is like a miniature city—all the things that happen in a city can happen up here too. People fight, get drunk, die—"

"No more fairy tales!" Paul said out loud, fresh panic making the hairs on the back of his neck brush against his damp shirt collar. His voice warbled beyond the narrow perimeter of the seats around him. Another passenger, a young woman who was reading a novel, glanced his way. "We agreed. No more fairy tales!" He started to clamber out of his seat but realized he had no place to go, so he sat back down and stared stonily in the opposite direction.

Tess tapped him on the shoulder. He refused to look at her. So she said in an exasperated tone, "Does this look like a fairy tale?"

He looked. Resting in her palm was a tiny revolver.

The Fourth Hour

Impossible, Paul thought, squeezing a sweat-soaked lump of napkin as if he were pumping a vein to give blood. This is impossible.

The airplane had entered an area of clear-air turbulence. It roller-coastered through the ice-blue sky like some kind of Six Flags ride, sliding down invisible flumes of air to abruptly surge higher. His inner ear told him this was all wrong, and the glands in his jaw began to ache, a prelude to motion sickness. But he promised himself he would not puke. He would not add that to his list of miseries.

He thought of the old man and the dainty gun Tess had showed him, and his heart pancaked into a spin. It made no sense. Why would the man want to kill himself *and* everyone else aboard?

Then a final question occurred to him: How could the man have smuggled a gun past the metal detectors and X-ray machines?

The first officer has been drinking since we left LAX.

Thunderstorms, Mr. Westerbrook. Hell-breathers.

And, finally, *The man really did attempt to shoot up the airplane. Karen took the gun away from him and gave it to me.*

Lies.

He couldn't stand it. He undid his seat belt and marched toward the rear of the airplane. An attendant who was sitting in the last row of seats spotted him, rolled her eyes and moved to get up, but he was already upon the bald man hunched in seat B28.

Paul's first impression was that the man had died a thousand years ago and the airline was returning his body, filched by grave robbers, to its rightful resting place in some Egyptian tomb. The man was *old.* His flesh was wrapped around his skinny bones like yellowed cellophane, and his hand shook with a palsy that seemed to consume all his energy so he could do nothing but squat in the seat and stare straight ahead, his drooping lips permanently bent into an atrophied frown.

Paul thought: This man couldn't have brought a gun aboard.

The elderly woman sitting next to him glanced up. Paul asked, "How is the problem with his ears?" and the woman answered in a brittle rattle, "Oh, he's doing much better—"

Somebody planted a hand on Paul's shoulder and he jerked around, expecting to see Tess's leering smile. But it was the other flight attendant. She said irritably, "Sir, you'll have to return to your seat—"

Paul seized her by the shoulders and her eyes grew round and afraid. "Tess," he hissed. "I don't know what's going on, but I think Tess has lost her marbles. She's got a gun!"

The woman shook off his hands. "I don't know what you're talking about, but you'd better return to your seat—"

"I'm talking about Tess!" he said angrily. "She's got—"

"Keep your voice down!" she snapped. "You'll cause a panic. I'll make sure the captain hears what you've got to say."

The plane dropped suddenly and they both grabbed seat backs to hold on. An overhead bin unlatched and the lid flew up with a plastic clatter that startled the woman with the novel, who glanced up apprehensively and then buried herself in the book with a look of ferocious concentration. Paul turned and scuttled down the aisle.

A newspaper clipping lay in his seat.

Next to it was a bullet.

He held the bullet before him like a jeweler assaying a gemstone, his emotions bouncing between fascination and outright terror. And then he turned to the clipping.

The headline read: FORTY SURVIVE CRASH AT HOUSTON. Paul could not stop himself from reading the story.

A South Air jetliner carrying 62 people crashed at Houston's International Airport on Monday, but only 22 people were killed in what authorities describe as a heroic effort by the flight crew to land the crippled jet.

South Air Flight 6212 was only one and a half hours into its nonstop flight from Atlanta's Hartsfield International Airport to Los Angeles when the crew radioed a distress call and asked for emergency clearance to land at Houston.

Emergency crews stood by as the South Air jet, a Boeing 727, attempted to make a wheels-up landing. The jetliner broke into three pieces before finally coming to rest on a taxiway.

Paul scanned the story, and then his eye came to rest on a string of cold paragraphs midway through.

FAA crash investigators on the scene said the pilot reported a rapid decompression incident at altitude that resulted in damage to the jetliner's control systems.

Officials would not comment on the "incident," but survivors who spoke with reporters said a hysterical passenger apparently opened an emergency hatch to "get off the plane."

Officials would not confirm the report, but one of the survivors, a man identified as Paul D. Westbock of Atlanta, was taken into custody by airport security personnel and later transferred to the federal detention facility in Kingwood.

The date on the clipping was three years ago.

It all came to him, all of it, the pieces falling together, and Paul found that he could not sit down, that he had been overtaken by a kind of numbness as explanations finally meshed with events, and he would not sit down until this airplane was on the ground, his memory serving up a final shocking image of Tess and the dainty little gun—a lady's gun, really. He had to tell the captain what was happening. He had to. Because there was nothing left for Tess to do now but kill him.

He stepped out into the aisle and began hurrying forward.

As he approached the bulkhead that separated coach from first class, he heard her say, "Where are you going, Mr. Westerbrook?"

She was sitting next to the emergency hatch. She motioned for him to sit down. He paused and weighed his chances of making a dash for the cockpit. The gun was cupped in her palm.

She stood and pushed him into the seat next to the hatch.

"You should be in your seat, Mr. Westerbrook," she hissed.

"It wasn't me," he whispered. He heard his voice starting to crack. "The names aren't even the same."

"I was on that flight," she said, ignoring him. "I tried to help the man who was afraid. But as you read, I didn't do my job very well." She swallowed noisily. "My father was the pilot. He died. But I lived. So did the man. He never undid his seat belt." A tremor ran through her. "Somehow that doesn't seem right."

Paul watched her hand. He wondered if he could grab the gun. In his mind he saw Gail laughing at him: Why would you even consider such an absurd thought; you're an indecisive and fearful man. I should've divorced you and married Thornton next door.

"I want you to do something," Tess said, and Paul knew she was no longer speaking to him. "I want you to make it right."

Paul shook his head. "I don't know what you mean," he said, but he thought he knew exactly what she meant.

She turned and skewered him with a stony stare. "I want you to open that door."

His heart clenched around the words. He tried to imagine doing that—grasping the release lever and pulling out, then up, and the hatch popping away like a champagne cork and air blasting out, into a sky-blue void, sucking him with it, with nothing below but miles of tumbling emptiness and gyrating terror—

No, no, his mind rejected it with a convulsive shudder that brought real tears to his eyes and had him fumbling for his seat belt.

"Unfasten your seat belt and open the door," she said evenly.

"No," he whimpered, scrunching his eyes shut. "It wasn't me." He winched the belt tight and grabbed the armrests and sat that way a few trembling moments, daring to peek after nothing happened. He saw that Tess was gazing at him almost tenderly.

"Don't you understand?" she asked softly. "I know it wasn't you. But it doesn't matter. You'll do. You're the best I can do." Then her eyes narrowed into slits and the last inflection of sanity departed her voice and she whispered slyly, "Unfasten your seat belt and open the door."

He shook his head no. No. No.

He could see the rage building in her, a flaming, almost artificial blush of crimson rising in her cheeks. A vein pulsed in her neck. She appeared ready to explode.

She undid her seat belt with a practiced snap and stood and glared down at him. The color of her uniform seemed to go from blue to black.

"All right," she muttered hoarsely. "Then I'll shoot the goddamned pilot and copilot, and we'll all go down. And it'll be your fault, Mr. Westerbrook. Just like before."

Later, he would reflect on this moment either consciously

or in nightmares and realized he had acted without think-ing, in a way that was decidedly untimid, and that his actions came not in response to some admonition or coercion. He simply acted.

He grabbed the emergency hatch handle and pulled out—

—she turned and her face was a smiling rictus of tri-umph—

—and then he pulled up—

—her expression collapsed into dawning horror—

And the cabin exploded as the hatch blew out and was snatched into the screaming slipstream, and then everything was pouring through the socket in a bellowing shock wave of frigid air and papers and pillows and every loose thing inside the cabin that could fill the vacuum. The plane lurched sharply and began to dive. Paul felt himself being sucked into that freezing, screeching storm and grabbed the armrests of the seat next to him, his heart whamming with sledgehammer blows, until the seats themselves began to tear away from the cabin floor and jitterbug toward the opening.

Something larger flew overhead and banged into the hatchway.

Tess.

He peered over his shoulder and saw her clinging to the edge of the hatch, her body flapping against the 767's aluminum skin, and beyond her was empty sky and clouds—a confluence of every terror Paul could imagine brought to horrifying reality only inches from his face. But again he acted without thinking, and this too he would look back on and wonder where the courage had come from.

He reached for her.

They locked eyes for a moment, and what he saw in her was malice refined to its purest essence. She mouthed two words. She gave him an evil smile.

And then, she let go.

All the Hours Afterward

They let Paul go.

He passed every lie-detector test. The gun was registered

to Tess. And another passenger, the woman who had been reading the novel, corroborated parts of Paul's testimony.

So they let him go.

And when he returned to work, he told his superiors he could not do the job. He didn't care what Gail thought.

Because Tess had told him, just before she let go.

She had said, "Next time."

And there would not be a next time.

THE ANOMALY OF MONDAYS

Billie Sue Mosiman

R EVEAL TO ME YOUR SOUL, SINFUL AND NAKED, SHOW ME
from the beginning how it was with you. . . ."

Dr. Cayman Key glanced down to see if the voice-
activated recorder paused recording at the termination of
his voice. It had. Why couldn't he trust machines? It was
another obsession taking hold.

He bit his lower lip, glanced to the closed office door and
then shut his eyes.

"It's Monday," he said softly, his voice but a rustle of
wind moving down his shirtfront. Beyond the echo of his
voice he heard the tiny whir of the recorder capturing every
word. "You don't have patients on Monday. Concentrate
instead on your soul."

Again he paused to recall why Mondays were his chosen
day of rest. He had to say it. Tell it to a machine since he
could not tell it to a human being. If he told anyone, he'd
never work again, and besides, the confession would break
his heart. He had never let them know during his own
psychoanalysis about the secret, and it had festered, spewing
puss and fume and froth into every crevice of his being. It

had been running around in his psyche for forty years and he wanted it out. Out.

"Every Monday, Father left for the weekly inspection of the books at his two jewelry stores in Evergreen, Alabama. Although it was a small town and the customers were mainly farmers and their wives, Father had done well. On the other days of the week he remained at home, having taken an early retirement.

"My father was basically an indolent man who cared nothing at that time for business or enterprise or wife or child or life, even, it seemed, if it required effort. I think that's why he died before he was sixty.

"Every Monday, Mother took me to her bed just as soon as she heard Father's car leave the drive. She took me to her bed and she . . ."

His eyes snapped open and in the shining blue depths a great fear lay exposed.

"Tell me," he said, now harshly, "why your soul is in peril. Don't hold back, don't block, don't subvert it!"

His mother first fondled his back and shoulders, giving him the gentlest of massages. Then she turned him over, cupping his small form with her own body where she lay on her side.

"I could smell her sleep scent, her pores releasing an odor of parched almonds. Later in the day, after she'd showered, she would smell otherwise, not of almonds at all, but of Ivory soap and delicate baby powder."

He could not to this day help the sickness that crept over him when he smelled almonds or accidentally bit into one in a sweet or a cake.

"Once she had me on my back, she made tracks down my rib cage with her fingers, walking them past my belly button and to the elastic of the small briefs I wore."

All the while she sang to him of periwinkle rains and azure skies over shadowed mountains, of indigo spring days and cobalt summer nights.

"Her favorite color was blue, she said, all the blues of the spectrum, but my eyes, she told me, were her favorite blue in all the world, an unusual turquoise that meant I would have luck and charm. No one but me, she promised, possessed the Aegean Sea locked in their eyes the way I did."

The Anomaly of Mondays

The recorder stopped. The room stilled, was a tomb for some moments.

"How she loved me!" he said.

How she used him for her selfish ends.

"And then forgot," he cried, startling himself and biting down again on his lip to keep from weeping inconsolably.

He set aside the recorder on the glass-topped desk. His right hand strayed to the top drawer at the right of his chair.

"If I use the pins," he said, "she will never know. If I am careful, no one will never know. Only I know and I approve."

Because it made him feel so much better, well enough in fact to live through Monday one more time without taking a gun to his head and ending it all forever.

He did not know when he opened the drawer or when he brought out the plastic case of stick pins or when he took the first one and embedded it a quarter inch into his left forearm. Or when he followed the first with a dozen more.

All he knew was that it was Monday and he might live until Tuesday if he hurried. If he was quick and he paid close attention to the blood.

"What would you do if there was someone you just couldn't deal with anymore?" Dr. Key asked.

He and George LaCross loped across a bridge that crossed a freeway in Birmingham, their brightly colored jogging suits catching the attention of passengers in cars. Key wore blue, as always, and George was in orange this morning. On their feet were Nikes, and soaking the sweat from their brows were matching white headbands.

"Huh," George said, overweight, panting, in real agony now for they'd run half a mile farther than the day before. "I'd get rid of him. Is it your new secretary? I can't find reliable help either, Cay. Hell, they all go to work for lawyers these days, the bright ones. I guess they don't think there's any future with doctors. At least with attorneys they can turn into paralegals."

Key did not like his secretary, it was true, she never got his calls right, but she was not the dumbest girl he had ever hired, though she might be one of the skinniest. She looked like a mop handle. No buttocks whatsoever, arms like soda straws. He thought he might have to send her to George to check her out for anorexia or bulimia, but that would mean she'd need therapy, and Key certainly did not want another patient right now. His workload was overwhelming enough.

"She's stupid, right? I heard her answer the phone this week when I called. 'Dr. Key's office, will I help you?' She doesn't even think when she speaks." George was still talking about Key's secretary. Key, on the other hand, was now contemplating his friend's advice and finding it acceptable. He'd get rid of the person.

Hadn't he thought of that a million times?

But the pins had worked until now. And talking into the recorder, getting all that evil and sickness into the open, that had worked. Until now. What if . . . what if getting rid of her cured him of all his obsessions? Couldn't he do it then?

He was beginning to wash his hands more than five times a day. Might that turn into something rather obscene if it continued? And he found that nights frightened him so that he couldn't get to sleep thinking about the dark. So much dark out there and in here, dark everywhere, no sun.

"Cay, did you hear me?"

Key looked around and saw George standing alongside the hedge bounding a huge sloping lawn, catching his breath. He was all red-faced, and combined with his shocking white hair and the orange jogging suit, it made him look like a clown. "What's that?" he said. "I'm sorry, I was thinking of something else."

"I said that girl needs some meat and potatoes. Wish I could give her some of my extra pounds. Do you ever advise your help?"

"Oh. Oh, yes, sometimes I do. You're right, Maggie's too thin. I was thinking either I'd fire her or send her over for a physical."

"Send her over. Though getting her to eat is not going to put brains in her head, Cay. You have a problem with her, fire the girl and hire another."

"Yeah, I might have to do that."

He had no intention of firing Maggie. Or advising her to eat. Or sending her over to George.

The Anomaly of Mondays

His intention, on the recommendation of his best friend, was to murder his mother.

She was sick to have sexually abused him, and that was what led to his interest in abnormal psychology and his lucrative psychiatric practice. She was sick all the years of his growing up, but around the time his father died, she began to forget just how destructive she had been to him. He noticed this one day when he remarked, "We used to have a 1955 red and white Ford just like that one."

He sat with his mother under a canopy in the back garden of her home. From the hillside they could see several city streets below, and the Ford, a beautifully kept antique, moved past just below them.

"We never had a Ford," she said. "Your father favored Dodges."

He turned to her, puzzled. "We never had a Dodge at all, Mother."

"We certainly did. Every new car your father bought, it was a Dodge, just like the one I have parked in the garage."

He thought she was tricking him. Playing some sort of game. So he began a test. "Well, I do remember that Father used to give you a smack when he had had too much whiskey and you two were playing gin rummy." How many times had he witnessed that scene, a hundred, a thousand? His father never hit her any other time that he knew about, but when she won too many times, he reached out and slapped her square in the face. Why she consented to continue playing with him so often really intrigued the young Cayman.

His mother, reclining on the chaise lounge in the shade of a flowering, fragrant mimosa, sat up and gave him her deepest frown. "Your father never hit me in his life, Cayman Roger Key. And I don't like you making up lies like this, it's cruel of you to speak evil of the dead."

He nodded. Cruel she called it. But in her voice he recognized the ring of sincerity. She meant it. She really did not remember the abrupt and brutal smacks in the face. Had she rewritten the past?

He was a college premed student then. He did not know what this meant, psychologically, but it did not make him happy to think she might have forgotten . . . what she'd done. This test would not be complete until he knew for certain.

"Mother, remember all those Mondays?"

"Mondays? What are you talking about? What about Mondays?"

"When I was about three, Father semiretired. He went to town on Mondays when we lived in Evergreen, remember? He checked on the stores."

"I don't remember it was on Monday specifically."

"Well, it was. Every single Monday morning he dressed in a suit and his polished shoes he kept for that day, and he went to inspect the books and to handle any problems the stores had encountered the week before."

"You're mistaken, Cayman. He didn't go on just a certain day."

Key felt a relentlessness seize him. He had never confronted her, blamed her openly, never spread that wound and let it bleed for her to see. He continued in a tight voice. "When he left the house on Mondays, you took me into your bed. You hugged me and crooned to me songs about the different colors of blue, you massaged my shoulders and then you took off my underwear."

Now she was sitting straight up, her back a flat board, her eyes staring straight into his. She was not moving or attempting to interrupt. From the look on her face, he couldn't tell what she might be thinking. Remember this, he thought. You must remember it. I will you, goddamnit, to remember.

He continued reciting the ritual she enacted upon his younger self for six years. Until his father died. And then she quit abruptly, falling into reverie and a miasma of depression from which she had not ever truly exited.

He did not leave out one single detail of the act. He mentioned her smell and his trumpeting heart, the slickness of her saliva, the pull and the tug on his penis until it was erect, the many small deaths she had made him endure until finally there was no one left alive inside to feel a thing, ever again, not pain or humiliation or the torture of perverted love. "You killed me," he said finally. "You murdered your own little boy because you were a sick, twisted, demented, perverted woman."

When he finished, he sat forward in his chair and said, "Now do you remember? Surely you remember what you did to me."

She stood up shakily, holding to a limb from the mimosa and swaying. She brushed tears from her sagging cheeks and said, "I never did those things. I am not an animal. I would never do that to a child of mine. I was always good to you and loved you more than anyone else. I'm not a monster."

It was then he knew for sure she had rewritten history, that the past was a slate wiped clean and existed for her no more.

He was alone with it. It was his world, and she had deserted him in it.

She left for the house. He sat in the chair smoking, watching the traffic below. Within fifteen minutes she returned carrying a tray of glasses holding ice and a pitcher of tea with lemon slices floating on top. "I thought we could do with refreshment," she said, completely recovered.

"Do you remember when I was a kid and our Mondays together, Mother?"

She looked dumbfounded. "Mondays? What did we do so special on Mondays?" she asked.

The slate was clean again.

But he knew he could not let her get away with it with such merciful ease.

It was not long after, when he had earned his degree and had begun his own practice, that he first discovered her claustrophobia. It was when she tried to get into his car to go for lunch. "I can't," she said simply. She turned, walked rapidly up the walk, and entered the house.

He followed and braced her in the formal living room that was cold and austere and as lily-white as her flawless skin. "What's wrong now?"

"I can't stand to be suffocated. There's not enough air in a car."

"I'll turn on the air-conditioning."

She shook her head.

"We'll open the windows, then."

She began to tremble. "You won't make me go in the car today, will you? I'll scream if you do. I can't stand it."

He probed and found that she avoided the smaller rooms of the house and that she could not ride in elevators or attend society functions or parties where there would be a lot of people crowding her. She was terrified of losing her breath and not being able to suck in air.

When George LaCross told him he should get rid of someone who could not be handled, Key knew in what way he had to murder Lydia Broadworth Key. He would use the common method of curing her claustrophobia. But with a slight twist at the end.

It was Monday, and he sat at his desk in the office he had installed next to his large 1840s mansion, talking into the recorder.

"I'll do it Wednesday," he said. "I'll close the office and tell Maggie I have a cold. If I do it, I'll be all right. I won't need the pins. I won't need to talk anymore, scouring my soul this way. It will all be over, once and for all, thank God, oh, thank God. . . ."

"You're sure I'll be able to do this?" she asked, holding tightly to his hand as he led her into his cavernous dusky parlor.

He shook loose from her grasp and turned on a lamp. He patted an easy chair and told her to sit down. "It's most important that you make yourself comfortable," he said. Suddenly he thought he could smell almonds, and he hurried to the mantel over the native stone fireplace and lit a cone of sandalwood incense. He watched the smoke curl into the air and thought if it was just one shade darker, it could be called blue.

With his back to her he explained. "We begin with this room because it is the largest one in the house. I'll sit with you. It shouldn't take but a few minutes, and when you feel you're secure, we'll go to the next smaller room. We'll continue through the house, taking you to smaller and smaller rooms until you're able to overcome your phobia."

"It sounds horrible." She shuddered and her teeth clicked loudly enough that he could hear them from where he stood. He turned around.

The Anomaly of Mondays

"It's called behavior modification. It works, Mother, it's been working for decades."

"You'll stay with me . . . and talk to me?"

"Of course." He smiled winningly, clasped his hands in front of him, and breathed deeply of the incense.

After twenty minutes she seemed ready to move on. "I want to get it over with," she said. "If I get scared, I'm going home."

"Whatever you say. I want you to be comfortable."

He took her next to the living room that was not quite as large and open as had been the parlor of the house. He sat with her. He talked of pleasant things and told her to think of azure skies over a field of nodding daisies.

From there they went into the kitchen, it being approximately the third largest room in his rambling home. They sat at the table and he offered her coffee with real cream from a silver service. That made her smile and relax. She admitted this was not such a bad therapy as perhaps she had thought it might be.

In one of the bedrooms she began to sweat, her brow dotting with droplets silver in the reflected light of the lamp. Her hands shook for some time. He talked to her soothingly. When she calmed, he said, "Now I'm going out, Mother. You need to make yourself comfortable on your own without my help. I've helped enough. If you're to be cured, you'll have to take some responsibility for your own thoughts and actions."

She protested mildly, but twenty minutes later when he returned to the closed room, she was smiling in triumph. "I can do it," she said. "I know I can lick this silly thing."

He led her to a dressing room off the bedroom. It was twelve feet by fourteen. It had no windows. There was but one door that he warned he must close. He had put a chair in the room. She took the seat, but she was jittery again, a tic playing havoc with her left eye. She repeatedly wet her lips, and when she tried to speak, she stuttered. "I—I . . . ca-ca-can't. . . ." She tried again. "You . . . have to . . . sta-sta-stay."

"You're doing fine, Mother. We're almost finished. After this there's just one more room, and you're going to make it, I know you are. Aren't you tired of being a prisoner of that

343

phobia? Don't you want to be free of it? Of course you do.
Now I'll be back in thirty minutes. Think about blue
hydrangea and hollyhocks. Think of the Aegean, Mother,
how lovely it is in the moonlight."

He walked out and shut the door. He stood rooted to the
spot, listening. Smiling. He thought of the pins once and,
furious, sent the thought scampering to the back of his
brain. No pins! No punishment to his flesh! He had done
nothing wrong, damnit. His erections with her did not mean
he was a freak. She made him get the erections. She was
warped beyond redemption, and she was the one who had
not been punished yet.

He checked his wristwatch. Time to proceed.

"Well? Now wasn't that all right? Aren't you feeling just
fine and dandy?"

She sat in the chair rigidly, her face blanched, and
sweating even more profusely. Her linen suit was stained
beneath the arms and her knuckles were white where they
gripped the chair edges. She couldn't speak, but she nodded
agreement.

"Wonderful! You're doing marvelous, Mother, really.
Only one more room and you'll be cured. You'll never again
be afraid of enclosed places. I'm your son, would I lie to
you? I've helped countless victims of claustrophobia this
way. They were all cured. Instantly!"

She walked stiff-legged at his side. He led her by the hand
through a maze of rooms and dim hallways. He opened a
door on the second floor just at the top of a flight of stairs.
"In here," he said. "Step inside."

It was like the cell in an asylum. He had had it specially
made. The walls were padded and covered with thick
creamy vinyl dotted with vinyl-covered buttons. The floor
was white tile, and the space was empty of all save for one
straight-backed ladder chair. A single lightbulb in a wire
cage hung from the high ceiling.

She did not notice that on the inside of the door there was
no doorknob.

"This is it, Mother. The final frontier where the last battle
is fought. If you master this room for a mere thirty minutes
alone, you'll be absolutely cured."

He pushed her before him toward the chair. The room

hardly held the two of them and the chair. It was a square area, six feet by six.

Key looked around proudly. "Isn't this lovely? It's quiet and simple. No distractions. I want you to sit down and keep your mind trained on cheerful thoughts. Meditate on your breathing, breathe in, breathe out, count your breaths."

"Cay?"

"Yes, Mother?"

"I can't do it." She said it in the smallest possible voice, the voice of a damned child.

"Sure you can. You've come this far, you can go the whole way."

"This is like a . . . like a coffin."

He laughed. "Don't be silly. It's like no such thing. It's a padded room so there won't be any noise to bother you. I've used it for a dozen people, and not one of them failed me. You won't fail me, will you, Mother? You're resilient, aren't you?"

She closed her eyes and wrapped her arms around her quivering body. "I need to go home."

"Think of blue-gray mist rising from asphalt in early morning," he said, backing to the door step by step. "Visualize a sapphire lake lancing streaks of gold into your eyes from the overhead sun." He was at the door and closing it.

"Mother?"

She opened her eyes.

"Think of blue Mondays. They're blue, aren't they? Think how you killed me when I was just a small child and could not defend myself. Will you? Will you think of that?"

His turquoise eyes narrowed, and just as she rose to lurch forward, hands outstretched in pleading, he slammed the door and locked it with a final snick of the dead bolt.

"I'm so sorry about your mother." Maggie half rose from her desk in his outer office, but he motioned her down.

"Thank you, Maggie. Did anyone call yet?"

She shook her head and tried to look busy with a sheaf of typed papers.

He strode into his office, took the seat at his own desk.

The intercom buzzed. Maggie's voice intruded, tinny and uncertain. "It's Dr. LaCross on line three."

"Thanks." Key answered the line with a slow, drawling hello. It could be interpreted a variety of ways, either suffused with weariness or simple melancholy.

"Cay, you know how much I liked your mother. Would you like to come over for dinner tonight with me and Caroline? You shouldn't be alone."

"Thank you, George, but I'm not up to going out yet. I'd rather just stay in."

There was a moment's hesitation on the line, then, "Well, you know what's best. Give me a call if you need someone to talk to, okay?"

"Sure, George, thanks again."

For an hour Key sat at his desk with templed fingers, thinking. His lower lip had a permanent canal where he had been biting into it.

His mother died on Thursday around noon, said the coroner, and it must have been a painful passing, considering the look frozen on her face. Too bad she lived alone, with no one around to call for help when her heart gave out.

She was buried on Sunday. On Monday he walked the rooms of his big house and never once went near the tape recorder or the drawer of his desk to get the pin case.

He was sure he was cured. He drank himself into oblivion Monday night and passed out on the parlor sofa. That must be why he did not feel so well this morning. Alcohol always gave him nightmares and hangovers.

He pushed the button on the intercom. "Maggie, call and cancel my appointments today."

"Uh, I already did, Dr. Key. I didn't think you'd be up to much this soon after . . . uh, you know."

"You can take the day off."

She sounded relieved when she thanked him. He heard the front door to his office close not more than two minutes later.

Alone again.

His gaze kept returning to the drawer to the right of his chair.

No. He did not need to stick himself with pins now. She

was dead, gone, buried. She had paid for her sins. Let God take the hindmost.

He glanced up and found minutes must have passed without his noticing for there was blood on his trousers, leaked there from the pinpricks in his forearm. He stared incredulously at the thick field of pins he had stuck from the bend of his elbow all the way up to his arm socket. It was rather lovely, the more he stared at it, all that silver and red glinting like armorplate over a field of poppies.

But still. This was getting out of hand. He was becoming like his mother, forgetting whole blocks of time and the past, recent and far, forgetting also the hazy dark things that lurked in that lost time, yet in some way expecting they would get him.

Dear Jesus hear me, he thought, there is no cure.

He knew it was so when he shifted his blue stare and the desk calendar reminded him this was only Tuesday.

SPOOR

Thomas E. Fuller

The wind is a world, high and warm, a solid substance beneath the arch and boom of the wings, an invisible sea where the proudest predators swarm.

Her name was Laura Slaton and she couldn't remember when she had first become afraid of griffins. Perhaps it had started when she decided to go freelance rather than when she had worked at Microcon.

The environment at Microcon hadn't been very conducive to mythical creatures. It had been all white tile and exposed pipes and soft gray work stations with the occasional fern for contrast. Proud leonine eagles could not exist in that stylishly sterile landscape. They would have collapsed unnoticed next to the soft drink dispenser, unable to rise into the cool germ-free air. If something didn't register on a computer monitor, it didn't exist, no matter how bright its plumage. Or how it smelled.

Laura shook her head against the sudden sharp odor of overheated metal and musk, thick and heavy. Then, just as quickly as she had noticed it, it had gone. She shivered. That's what they smell like, she thought. Like an overheated car engine, like parrots in a cage.

Like the lion house at the zoo.

She had gone over to her work station and turned on the computer. Work made it go away. Once the words and figures started flowing across the monitor, once the steady hum started singing, her foolish fears would be gone and she could get on with her work.

And try to ignore the thought that somewhere eyes like molten gold were watching. And waiting.

The strength flows out from slim shoulders, slicing sharp and graceful through the shimmering air. Wings with feathers like liquid emeralds stab down, rip up, then glide like ice through silk, an aerial hunter's dance.

Laura Slaton's apartment was on the twentieth floor of the Aberdeen House, a rather stylish high rise in the city's center. She had bought it with proceeds from her first big freelance contract. It wasn't very large, just a living area, kitchen, bedroom, and bath. But it had a tiny balcony, and when the sun went down, the retreating sunlight would explode from tower to tower, a tide of brillance ebbing away. Just as the advancing darkness seemed to be triumphant, the windows and neon would blink on to transform the night into a velvet background for thousands of shimmering square-cut gems. She would stop work, shut down her machines, and stand on her little balcony with a glass of wine and watch the kaleidoscopic glory of it all.

Or at least she had.

Until the hot metal smell had come. Until she thought she had seen lithe shadows flicker across the warm window glow. Until she had felt molten eyes upon her and the hot taste of blood in her own mouth.

She very seldom went out onto the balcony anymore. She felt too vulnerable out there, as if she were naked on an empty street corner. Now she just wandered her little apartment with her evening drink—wine abandoned for vodka and orange juice.

Her money had gone for carefully selected furniture that met her eclectic tastes, but more importantly, into the work station, an elegant collection of beige boxes on teak tables.

Everything in order, everything state of the art, everything just for her. With the flick of a switch, words flowed from her mind, through her fingers and into her machines. Then out into the world alone. Once it had just been practical. Now it was her only chosen contact with the outside.

Laura Slaton would never go out again.

The glide is smooth with the wind, one with the wind. It is the seamless melting, silent communion with the jagged empty horizon. It is the peace before pursuing.

She had never been really happy at Microcon. Of course, she had never been really happy anyplace. Laura didn't get along well with other people. They made her nervous. She had never known what to do or say, so she would just stare blankly until the conversations went away. And they always did. It wasn't that she was unattractive—she was rather cute in a small washed-out-blond way, if forced to an admission. Several of her coworkers had even asked her out to lunch, and one determined young man had persevered to a dinner date. But it never went beyond that, and now she had decided that nothing ever would.

Instead she had devoted herself to her work and built up her contacts and taken courses and studied until she was acknowledged as one of the best technical writers in the field. Then she had taken those skills and contacts and left the sterile labyrinths of Microcon behind her for her own business in her own little apartment.

She had rather wanted a cat to break the monotony, but her lease wouldn't allow it. So she created one on a computer program and talked to it occasionally when she'd had a little too much to drink.

The fear had arrived in her sleep. Sleeping well had suddenly turned to dreams that woke her in the middle of the night, tangled in sweat-stained sheets and gasping for breath. At first she couldn't remember the dreams, not completely. There was running, fleeing from something floating in the air above her, which then devolved into impressions of great wings flailing, of sharp things flashing and cutting with talons, beaks, and claws. And the reek of hot metal and musk.

Spoor

The dreams had become more and more intense without becoming any more comprehensible. Hot milk hadn't worked. Alcohol had given her headaches, and drugs left her groggy for most of the morning. She'd actually begun to dread going to bed. But she had to sleep, and the fitful dreams had continued, becoming more and more chaotic and violent.

Until one half-light morning she had awoke to discover herself seated at the keyboard, typing one word over and over and over: griffin griffin griffin griffin griffin griffin griffin griffin griffin griffin griffin griffin griffin griffin . . .

The brass glazed eyes scan, searching soullessly like beacons across the blank bowl of the sky. All is jagged lines and burning angles. And the sharp clear pulses of the Prey.

Why griffins, of all godforsaken things? she asked herself. Why not werewolves? Great masculine brute-things, hulking forward through the fogs and mists, clad in tattered trousers, their cruel fanged mouths gaping wide. She shuddered.

Or vampires. Vampires were even more frightening—and infinitely more romantic. She herself was especially enamored of the Frank Langella *Dracula*. Yes, dreams about vampires, that would make some kind of sense. But griffins . . .

She rubbed her eyes. What did she know about griffins? They were composite creatures from mythology, half lion, half eagle, but when she tried to picture them, her mind was filled with images of wings and talons and sharp feline claws. She forced the image back into her skull with the heels of her hands on her eyes until the darkness exploded into dull flat colors—purples and blacks, dusty greens and flat, faded yellows.

The colors bloomed across the inside of her eyelids like bruised clouds. She stared into them until something flickered in the dullness, a cluster of gems on old velvet. The gems floated closer, vibrating like a clockwork hummingbird. Tears ran from her eyes as she strained to see. Wings, sharp and clear and emerald green, a head more like a raptor parrot than an eagle, and a tawny amber body steel-sculpted behind it. She jerked her face away from her hands and blinked rapidly in the brilliant dawn sunlight. Laura knew that if she had waited just a few seconds longer, the image would have screamed and then plummeted into her, a fur and feather dagger stabbing at her heart. Even now she could still hear that unborn scream echoing inside her head.

Talons fixed like bladed fists slice the toxic air rising from the cars clustered below. And grasp.

Laura Slaton had a very organized mind that lectured on the irrationality of her fears. Buried beneath that thought, another, more pressing one, also worked on the problem, though not quite as rationally. It told her that griffins were real, and justified her caution in not confronting them. This highly formed thought process began to hold more and more of Laura's attention. It would be entirely possible now to banish her fears by simply avoiding places that might be interesting to a griffin.

But what interested griffins? What do they eat? Where do they live? The questions chased each other around and around in her meticulous subconscious, like imaginary rats in a mental maze.

She rose and walked stiffly to the balcony. The air was like a tonic, warm and moist. The city rose up around her, massive towers surging up from the concrete and noise below. Above it all the bloated morning sun rose sullen through the early mists. She stared at the blood-colored orb until it seemed that something dark streaked across it.

Raptor razor beaks snap then open wide in a scream both deep and shrill. It echos soundless, lost in the all consuming roar that rumbles up from beneath it.

Laura had forced herself to spend every Monday at the Football Widows Literary Club, a mostly female circle that met at Price's Bookstore one block down from Aberdeen House. She had never been a widow, and rather liked football, but her world had been shrinking down to her

monitors and her apartment, so she went more as a nod to
mental health than anything else.

The ladies discussed Great Books—there had been a
particular run on F. Scott Fitzgerald for some unknown
reason—but occasionally a mystery or even a romance
would slip in. When it did, Laura would try to join the
discussion, but ended up staring at her tea cup or eating
entirely too many wedding cookies.

One particular evening the group was once again mount-
ing an attack on Mr. Fitzgerald, *The Great Gatsby,* to be
precise. Laura was hiding in the back of the room, trying not
to think about griffins and failing miserably. Griffins didn't
belong in the city. They belonged in the mountains, where
they could launch themselves into the air. Bodies that
aerodynamically unsound needed height to get airborne.

The scent of hot metal and musk rose up around her, and
she gulped another cup of ginger and peach tea.

"She was so terribly upset, my dear, positively irrational!
She started to hyperventilate, and I thought we were going
to have to call 911!"

The voice was brittle and chatty, pitched so it couldn't be
heard up front or ignored in the back. Laura turned to her
left, peering cautiously over her tea cup. Two elderly ladies,
armored in blue hair and mink, sat conspiring together.
Mrs. Bradshaw, the one speaking, babbled brightly. The
other, Mrs. Stanley, kept glancing blankly back and forth
from her friend to the guest speaker, looking for all the
world as if she were watching a tennis match.

"Well, we finally got her calmed down and into bed with a
nice hot toddy, but nothing would do but we all had to go
and look for Ferdinand. We didn't find anything, of course.
Poor dear, she probably took him out for walkies and forgot
to bring him back. She's gotten so forgetful lately." Mrs.
Bradshaw sighed theatrically and waited for her companion
to comment, but Mrs. Stanley's attention had once again
been captured by the speaker. Mrs. Bradshaw sighed again,
and staked out her next victim.

"It's Mrs. Silverberg, my dear. You know her—the older
lady with the *unnaturally* black hair? She's frightfully upset,
she's misplaced her Ferdinand!"

"Ferdinand?" Laura asked, her cup vibrating in her trembling fingers.

"Dreadful little thing! A Pekinese shouldn't weigh that much—she overfeeds him, you know."

"No, no, I didn't. She misplaced him, did you say?"

"Well, she can't find the horrible little thing. And she got so upset! Just ruined our regular bridge club! Said she put him right out on the balcony just like she always does and he was gone! Or so she says." Mrs. Bradshaw leaned forward conspiratorially. "Thinks he jumped right up on the wall and then right over the edge. Can you imagine? Ferdinand couldn't jump over his dinner dish, let alone a wall! She even made us go down to the ground floor and look for him! Didn't find anything, of course. If a thirty-pound Peke had fallen from a fifteenth-story apartment, one would think it would be rather conspicuous." She laughed merrily.

Laura said nothing, but saw in her mind's eye a small fat dog with bulging eyes plummeting like a furry stone, stubby little legs frantically churning in reverse. She managed to put the tea cup down before she dropped it.

"Of course, she'd had Ferdinand for just years and years and years, since before Mr. Silverberg died, and he's been gone for almost ten." Mrs. Bradshaw's chintz-blue eyes sparkled at the thought of such devotion.

Mrs. Stanley blinked back into the conversation. "Mrs. Massey lost her Bitsy."

Mrs. Bradshaw swiveled in the other direction. "Not that precious Siamese of hers! Oh, how dreadful!"

"Yes," nodded Mrs. Stanley. "Been gone for almost a week now. Figures she must have left the door to the apartment opened. She very upset, very upset."

"Oh, I can see how! Bitsy was such a lovely thing! Siamese are such perfect creatures! Don't you agree?"

"Oh, yes . . ."

Freed from the attention of her two neighbors, Laura quietly gathered up her things and slipped out where she almost welcomed the muted roar of the city. She clutched her bag to her chest and hurried down the street toward home. But her mind kept going back to the missing pets.

Pets were allowed in the larger apartments in the Aberdeen House, most of which were rented to the elderly, perhaps the only people in the world more lonely and isolated than she was. All of them had pets, horribly pampered, spoiled, overweight, and arrogant pets. She would pass them on her forays into the world, dragging their hovering owners behind them like heavy balloons on tethers. Now they were disappearing, vanishing off balconies tens of stories above the . . .

What do griffins eat?

She tilted her head back and stared up at the towering apartment buildings. They rose up like geometric mountains, straight and sheer-sided, the balconies miniature ledges clinging to the tiers. Ledges where small plump creatures preened and strutted, totally unaware of what hunted them among their man-made peaks.

They come in low and fast, silent on the air. One fast snatch with razor-sharp talons and the balcony would simply be empty, only an overturned water dish or scattered pillow to leave any hint of what happened.

Her mind tried to logically explain the foolishness of this line of thought. The other now dominant part sent her scurrying through startled pedestrian groups and across rapidly braking traffic as she ran panic-driven toward home.

I know what they eat, she screamed in her mind.

I know what they eat.

The Prey struggles stunned in the Hunting grip and surrenders, ripped open like a bloody flower, spilling the rich wet insides into the air with an aroma like sanguinary perfume.

First the front door—primary lock, dead bolt, two chains. Then the bedroom—both windows locked, heavy nails driven into sills secured. Curtains closed, always closed now. What she cannot see, cannot see her. The lights were dim, to cast no shadows on walls and windows when she moved so that no raptors would see her panicked movement beneath them. She stabbed under the sofa and chair with a broom handle, just to be sure. Her electronic cat stared out at her from the monitor and then went back to playing with its electronic ball. She patted the disk drive as she hurried past. Nothing hid behind the shower curtain, curled and purring on the cool porcelain.

Not quite completely buried, the rational voice still strove for order beneath the griffin fear. Make a gesture, it murmured, before capitulation. Face the fear and see that there is nothing to face. Laura looked around the almost sealed room and took a ragged breath. One last try. She turned to the draped double doors of the balcony.

With an almost steady hand she drew back the curtains. Light streamed in, making the dust motes dance in the stale air. Swiftly she snapped the lock and slid the glass door open. The air was warm but fresh. Laura stepped out onto the balcony, her eyes straining for a flash of emerald and amber darting between the neighboring towers. There was nothing but the gray softness of pigeons. Pigeons are good, if there are pigeons, then there is nothing hunting them. Nothing else stirred, and she felt the tension flow out of her. She ran her fingers through her hair and shuddered. All her life she'd hidden herself away, but at least that was from possible dangers. Griffins were not possible dangers. Griffins were not possible, period.

Laura turned and reached for the sliding door. Then she just stood there, her arm outstretched and frozen, and stared at it. At the soft metal frame and handle.

And at the deep gouging scratches, like sharp silver scars, cut into the frame.

So silent in shadows. So silent in the light. So silent on the rising wind and in the full lust of the Kill. So very silent.

Laura never went out again. Supplies of rice and flour and black beans and canned meat and vegetables, or anything with a long shelf life, were delivered in one large order that depleted her checking account. She had bought powdered milk and fifteen different kinds of tea from the gourmet shop.

Then she sat in front of her computer and set to work. She switched all her bills and accounts payable over to electronic banking and served notice to all her clients that she would only be available through voice or E-mail. No mailboxes. They were all in the lobby of her building, and the lobby just wasn't secured. But you can't seal an imaginary creature out. She closed her eyes and shoved the nagging voice further and further away. Can you?

You can only seal yourself in.

Circling around the artificial heights, antique gold eyes questing, the killer lover soars.

Laura's world contracted and turned in on itself. She ate oatmeal for breakfast now. All the cornflakes had been scattered in front of various windows and doors to serve as an organic early warning system. She didn't know how well the idea worked—she never went near windows and doors to find out.

Instead she sat in front of her computer, ripping through her projects and assignments. She filled her head with minutia, with anything that would keep her from thinking of griffins, thinking of wide-spanning emerald and jade wings and bronze raptor beaks that could so easily mimic her thoughts if they really wanted to. Push them back and she'd be safe. Push them out and she'd be safe. Outside, the wind whispered forlornly over the abandoned balcony rail, making disconcerting flapping noises that she tried to ignore.

Closer, closer, spiral down . . . whisper in her ear, in her mind.

When she could no longer stand the keyboard's static clicks, she would make soup or a sandwich—there was no longer enough for both—and retreat to her big chair. There she would curl up, legs tucked protectively under her, and watch television. But no matter how interesting the program, she would soon find herself changing from channel to channel until her hands would start to shake. So many people, so out in the open, so vulnerable to each other, to anything that might happen along. Eventually she would turn it off and try to read the same words over and over while the off-white walls of her apartment arched over her like an overturned bowl.

Or the inside of an egg.

The faint scent seeks, touching and tantalizing over all other coarser aromas. Involuntarily, talons extend, claws unsheathe. Spiral down, spiral down . . .

Laura disconnected her phones since she no longer recognized the voices. She carefully stepped over the cornflakes and sealed the edges of her windows and doors with duct tape. The few personal messages on the E-mail had dropped off one by one, as did the assignments and contracts. She no longer heard voices in her head. The sound came from outside, of something gliding by beyond the sealed curtains.

The spoor grows stronger, sun-scorched tin and heavy musk. Spiral down. Spiral down . . .

She lost the computer during the sixth week while playing with her electronic cat. Hers had been a tabby, a calico, a Persian, even a manx. Currently, it was Siamese, a lean, shallow-stomached seal point happily batting an electronic mouse with red shorts back and forth. On a whim she decided a domestic short-hair would be more appropriate. That's all she'd meant to do as she'd reached for her own mouse. She certainly hadn't meant for those extra lines to rise up from that playful feline shape. Certainly hadn't expected them to divide and divide again, then arch up into the air and fill themselves in with rippling shades of green. She watched in horror as the ascetic Siamese face flattened and flared and hardened under eyes like burnished coins. The beak had opened—the tongue was round and purple— and the beast had reared up as its lungs had filled with air to scream. Her scream. She smashed the screen into a thousand shimmering shards by ramming the keyboard into it.
Then she cried over the death of an electronic cat.

The air is intoxication, a ripe promise like a skyborne wine. Follow it. Spiral down, spiral down . . .

She had forgotten to buy lightbulbs. The one in the bathroom was the first to go.

Spiral down, spiral down . . .

Spoor

The constant odor of hot metal and musk was everywhere now. It permeated all her clothes. She stopped wearing them.

Spiral down . . .

Nothing rang anymore. The TV was a blank cataract. The computer a pile of fossilized crystals and dead chips. There was no light, no dark. Only a small naked woman curled tight in a chair in the middle of an apartment-sized egg.

Spiral . . .

Laura Slaton woke to pain, nasty petty pain. She was stiff and cramped. She blinked and looked around her sealed apartment. Dust was thick in the air. Nothing moved, nothing stirred. She tottered to her feet and nearly fell as the pain stabbed up and down her legs. She rubbed her fingers into her eyes, gritty from sleep. Something awoke her constantly through the night. Not wings, not soundless cries. Rain, it had rained during the night.

She rubbed her arms, hugging herself as she did so. I'm waking up, she thought, I am actually waking up. The hot metal and musk smell still clung to everything, but it didn't seem as threatening. I'm not frightened anymore, I'm scared, but I'm not frightened. A lethargic calm was seeping over her. She touched her hair. It was slick and matted. Her nails were black-rimmed and cracked. There was no way she could face a mirror. If she saw herself, she wouldn't care anymore.

Laura staggered toward the curtains that covered the balcony's double doors. Dazed, she reached out and touched the faded fabric, tacked shut with row upon row of safety pins. She shook her head in a vain attempt to clear it, grasped the curtains and with one supreme effort ripped them apart.

Sunlight stabbed in around her, an avalanche of light, nearly burying her in its brightness. Almost blind, she felt **for the duct tape plastered over the doors and tore it down.** The tape screamed as it parted, leaving a sticky residue of itself on the shiny aluminium. Then it was only a small flick of the wrist and the doors slid open. As she stepped out, she glanced down at the door handle and wondered how the marks that had seemed so deep and raw now seemed like the scratches of a key stabbed drunkenly at a lock.

It was early morning. Everything was clean after the rains, slick and new as she was drawn out onto the balcony. She stepped naked into the open, anonymously displayed high over the still sleeping city. She swayed in the light.

The griffin smell had followed her from the shattered shell of the apartment. Out here it was a more heady aroma, something that tickled her nose and made her slide her cracked nails lightly down her sides. She was still scared, but it was so different now. Griffins. She started to giggle, hugging her own nakedness in the breeze. Her head tilted back and swiveled from right to left, taking in the panorama of the city from horizon to horizon. There was nothing there, no flash of yellow and green, no griffin swooping down from above. Of course there wasn't.

It came swooping up from below.

Exaltation of the quest exploding through heart and lungs and eyes! Twined shoulders reach out and beat down with emerald perfection. Spiral. Spiral?

It hung in the air, just beyond the balcony railing. Laura stood defenseless before it, a scruffy child trying to keep from screaming.

With studied grace it reached down and perched on the weathered wood. Buried deep in the back of her skull, a voice that had been stilled for months began to calmly analyze the creature that had begun to groom itself with a round purple tongue.

Its wingspan was twelve feet from tip to tip, all green, emerald and jade and lime. The body was smaller than she'd pictured, more like a cheetah than a lion, carved amber, sleek and elegant. The beak was a parrot's, only sharper. It was nonchalantly straightening the great wing feathers, but the eyes that stared over the wings at her were those of a raptor. And something else. She stepped forward.

Spoor

Sun dance, star dance, dance of clouds and wind and
the long hot soaring that lasts forever . . .

She stepped again, nearly falling as her bare feet crunched
the cornflakes the griffin's wings had blown out. It sounded
disturbingly like eggshells.

Blood dance. Fire dance. Dance of raptor heart and
talons, beak and wings . . .

She stepped again, tears cutting down her cheeks. There
was a horrible itching across her shoulders and her feet
clicked as she walked.

The surge and the calling and the high high soaring.
Spiral out, spiral out . . .

Her face felt stiff and immovable and her arms seemed
impossibly long as she reached toward those burnished
golden eyes, those gently fanning wings.

The final mad mating. Spiral out, spiral out . . .

Her heart bursting, her tongue round and large in her
mouth, Laura Slaton reached out to that proud narrow
chest, framed in feathers green as a Han emperor's burial
armor. Reached out and through . . .

Spiral out, spiral out . . .

Off balance, she shrieked like a startled gull and plummeted through her insubstantial stalker out into the breaking dawn. As she did, something seemed to pull free of her in
a burst of feathers and fur. Something bright and powerful
and wonderfully free. She spread her own wings not in fear
but in imitation, and held the air in her own proud grasp.
And as she fell toward the final embrace of the concrete and
asphalt far below her, Laura Slaton twisted in the air. The
last thing she saw was two soaring specks of emerald and
amber climbing into the sun. Then they were gone.

And so, smiling, spiraling, was she.

IMPOSTOR SYNDROME

Lawrence Watt-Evans

GORDON KNEW JANICE LIKED TO PAINT; CHERYL HAD MENtioned it at the party when she first introduced them.

"She paints?" Gordon had asked, while Janice was at the buffet stocking up on scallops in bacon.

"Mm-hmm," Cheryl said, pulling a toothpick from the hors d'oeuvre she'd just put in her mouth.

"Is she any good?"

Cheryl had held up a hand until the hot little tidbit was out of her mouth, then said, "Don't know—I've never seen any of her work. She's shy about it."

Gordon had nodded and not thought any more about it at the time. Oh, he'd been interested—he was interested in everything about Janice just then, and besides, he'd majored in art history, and even if he'd wound up a broker instead of an artist or an art critic or a museum curator, he was still interested in art.

But it didn't seem especially important at the time.

They'd had dinner together two days later, and met for lunch the day after that, and one thing led to another, and six weeks after the party he had moved his belongings into the big old house on Thornton Street that her parents had left her.

She'd made it clear, though, that she didn't want him

362

prying into the closed-off rooms on the second floor—not that there was anything terrible about them, but they were private, full of family relics.

And Gordon hadn't been pushy; he liked Janice very much indeed, liked her shy, crooked little smile and the way she seemed to always be looking sideways at him, liked her childlike, high-pitched laughter. She had a sly wit and a slender, sexy body, and their tastes in any number of things—movies and music and manners—were neatly aligned. He didn't want to antagonize her. If she wanted to keep a few rooms to herself, that was fine with him. He hadn't exactly told her the whole story of his own life either. They had plenty of time to get to know each other better.

So he kept himself to the ground floor and the big master bedroom, and that was plenty of space, far more than he'd had in his old apartment.

Janice liked to paint, Cheryl had said, and it did occur to Gordon that he hadn't seen any sign of it, hadn't seen an easel anywhere, or any of her paintings on the walls anywhere, but maybe she'd lost interest, maybe she'd just taken a few classes and then given it up.

He didn't worry about it.

But then, about three months after they met, he came home one wintry evening and found the downstairs dark and empty, even though her car was in the driveway.

Puzzled, he turned on the hall light, then put down his briefcase and hung up his scarf and overcoat.

"Jan?" he called.

No answer.

He walked down the hall and stuck his head into the kitchen, and that was just as dark and deserted as the front of the house.

"Hello?" he called, in case she was in the pantry or down in the basement, but no one answered.

Taking a nap perhaps?

He walked back to the front and up the big staircase, and turned to head for the master bedroom, then stopped.

The door of one of the other rooms was open, and light was pouring out into the unlit hallway.

Curious, he stepped over and looked in.

She was sitting there on a tall stool, working on a large

painting, a painting done mostly in cream and shades of gray, a painting of a mother in late nineteenth-century dress stroking a young girl's hair.

"Wow," he said.

Janice started and dropped her brush. She turned and stared blankly at him for a moment.

"I'm sorry," he said, "the door was open, and I couldn't help—"

Before he could finish the sentence, she bustled off the stool and slammed the door in his face.

He stood there, blinking, trying to decide what to do next and absorbing what he'd seen.

He'd heard that she liked to paint, of course; what he hadn't heard was that she was *good*.

He hadn't had a proper look at it, of course, but from the glimpse he'd had, the painting was excellent—a bit sentimental and old-fashioned in its choice of subject perhaps, but the composition was original and very, very good, the colors subtle and effective, with the warm creamy hues of the woman's face and clothing in vivid contrast to the cool background.

Mere technical details such as light and shadow and perspective didn't even come into it, so far as he could tell—they were all perfect.

That was why he had said "Wow," instead of clearing his throat or otherwise politely making his presence known.

Smart and sweet and sexy—and *talented* too. He'd really found himself a prize!

Then the door opened again, the light in the room went out, and he was still standing there stupidly as she pushed past him and closed the door behind her.

"Hi," he said.

She looked nervously up at him. "Hi," she said. "I'm sorry about the door. . . ."

"Oh, it's okay—I'm sorry if I intruded."

"I shouldn't have left it open, but it gets chilly in there with it closed—the radiator doesn't work right."

"Maybe I could fix it."

"Maybe," she said, in a tone that clearly meant no.

"So, you paint?"

"Sort of," she said, looking down.

"What I saw looked really good."

She didn't answer, and in the dim light from downstairs, he couldn't really see, but he thought she might actually be blushing.

"Come on downstairs," she said. "I'll make us some dinner."

She didn't want to talk about the painting; she made that obvious as she conveniently didn't hear his comments and questions over the bustle of cooking supper. He let it drop—for the moment.

He knew he should probably let it drop for good, but the image of that woman in the creamy Victorian dress haunted him—something about the expression on her face would not leave him alone. He would stop sometimes on his way along the upstairs hall and stare at the closed door.

He didn't try to open it, though. He wasn't going to sneak around. He valued her too much for that.

It was almost a week later that he brought the subject up again.

"So, did you ever take art classes?" he asked over dinner.

She nodded, not looking up from her plate. "Years of them," she said.

"I thought that painting you were doing was very good," he said. "From what I saw of it, anyway."

She shrugged. "It's nothing special," she said.

"Yes, it is," he told her. "Not everyone can paint like that. I'd like to see it again sometime."

"Maybe sometime," she murmured.

"Are there others?"

She looked up, finally. "What do you mean?"

"I mean, do you have other paintings you've done?"

"Well, of course," she said. "You didn't think that was my first, did you? I thought you said you liked it."

"I *do* like it—I think it's wonderful!"

"Then it couldn't be my first, could it? Painting takes practice."

"No, but . . . oh, I don't know, I thought maybe you'd given the others away, or thrown them out, or something."

She shook her head and looked back at her plate; she fumbled with her fork.

"No," she said. "I still have them all. All the ones that I thought were any good, anyway; I burned the early junk."

"Could I see some of them?"

"No," she said—then softened it. "Maybe someday, when I know you better."

He nodded. "All right," he said. He knew not to push it any further, and changed the subject. "Say, did you see the news today?"

Gordon was patient. It was six months later, six months of carefully avoiding the subject and never looking in, even when she was painting with the door open, weeks after he'd asked her to marry him and she'd put off a decision, that she finally told him one Sunday afternoon, "I want to show you something."

He looked up from his magazine and asked, "What?"

He wasn't thinking about paintings; he'd been involved in an article on Vatican politics. He blinked at her, and realized she was nervous about something. He put the magazine down.

"A painting," she said.

His eyes widened, and he got up quickly. "Please," he said, "I'd love to see it."

She led him upstairs—and he noticed, as they climbed the steps, that she was breathing fast, and her hand on the banister was trembling.

She wasn't just nervous, he realized; she was *scared*.

Of what? Of his reaction to her painting?

That was silly; even if it was trash, didn't she trust him to be tactful?

She led the way into one of the rooms she ordinarily kept locked—a small bedroom at the back of the house, full of dusty sunlight and faded pastel furniture.

The painting was the brightest thing in the room; it stood propped up on the dresser. He stepped over to look at it.

She stepped out of his way, not saying a word.

It was an odd scene—a little girl in a pink party dress standing in a littered alleyway against a nighttime background of pawnshops and strip joints, handing a single red rose to a man in a black leather coat. The dress, the rose, the neon signs, the red bandanna the man wore at his throat, all seemed to shimmer, patches of brilliant color against the washed-out, grayed and decayed background.

The faces looked oddly familiar, but Gordon couldn't place them; he supposed they were just models he'd seen in magazines, or something.

He stared at the painting, taking in every bit of it.

A pawnshop window held a display of watches, and he could read the time on each one; a barroom window reflected a bow in the little girl's hair, and also a woman in a tight black skirt who wasn't in the foreground.

Everything was perfectly realized, no detail missed. The neon lights colored the little girl's shiny black shoes and the man's leather coat; the man needed a shave. The rose was ever so slightly past its peak, the petals just beginning to droop.

"It's wonderful," Gordon said.

"You like it?" Janice said, smiling shyly.

"I *love* it. Did you . . . what did you use for models? All the little touches . . ."

"No models. I made it all up."

"That's amazing!" He turned and glanced at her—she was radiant, basking in his acceptance.

"I'll leave it here, then," she said, "and I won't lock the door."

"Could we put it out on display somewhere?"

Her smile vanished. "Oh, no!" she said. "I couldn't let anyone else see it." She saw the disappointment on his face, and added, "Not yet."

"All right," he said. Then he went back to staring at the painting.

She didn't just have talent, he thought; she was a *genius*. Why did she hide it so completely?

He looked at her with a whole new sense of wonder. Who *was* this woman he was living with? She obviously had depths he hadn't even imagined.

He turned back to the painting.

Why had she painted that particular scene?

Why was that the painting she had chosen to show him, rather than the one of the Victorian woman?

It was a mystery.

When he looked again, she was gone, having slipped silently away.

He took to reading in that little back bedroom, where he could look up at the painting every so often.

It was a month later that the second painting appeared. He went into the room, book in hand, and stopped dead.

The two paintings were side by side on the dresser, the girl in the alley and the new one, of a plump man standing in a forest clearing, smiling beatifically, arms spread wide as he looked up at something that wasn't in the scene, bands of sunlight spilling down between the trees and streaking bright colors across the mysterious dark green forest gloom, the brightest light bleaching the man's face almost white.

Again, it was a stunning work. Gordon stared.

"Do you like it?" Janice asked at dinner that night.

Gordon didn't pretend not to understand.

"I love it," he said.

She beamed at him, and hummed to herself later, when she cleared away the dishes.

Two more paintings appeared a fortnight later—a woman in a white gown trimmed with red, blue, and gold, standing in a ruined church; and a man reading a newspaper on an otherwise-empty subway platform as an express ran by. The newspaper headline was SUBWAY KILLER STRIKES AGAIN, and it was only after he read that that Gordon noticed the bloodstain on the concrete by the man's foot.

Why had Janice painted such a thing? Why had she chosen that as one of the handful he was allowed to see?

And why didn't she let him see the others? Why didn't she let anyone *else* see any? Her younger brother had visited, and had been forbidden entrance to any of the locked rooms, including the back one that had become Gordon's private gallery.

Didn't she know how good they were?

He asked her that flat out at dinner.

"Do you know how good your paintings are?"

She blushed. "No, they aren't," she said. "They're just . . . just playing around."

"They're *art*," he said. "First-rate art. They should be hanging in galleries and museums!"

Impostor Syndrome

"Oh, Gordie, it's sweet of you to say that, but I could never let them be displayed anywhere."

"Why *not*? They're nothing to be embarrassed about—they're fine, fine work!"

"No, they aren't, Gordie. And speaking of work, did you know they promoted that obnoxious Karen Baker?"

Having thus changed the subject, she steadfastly ignored any attempt to change it back, babbling on about her office.

At first Gordon thought she was just trying to distract him, but then he began to listen to what she was saying.

"You should have had that promotion, shouldn't you?" he asked.

"Oh, no, I wouldn't want it—all that responsibility!"

He let it drop, but the next morning he stayed home from work, and around mid-morning he phoned Cheryl, who was a manager in the same office as Janice, and after some chitchat asked, "Isn't Jan about due for promotion?"

"Janice? She didn't tell you?" Cheryl asked, startled.

"Tell me what?"

"We *offered* her a promotion—twice, in fact. She turned it down."

He pressed her for more details. By the time he hung up, he was seriously dismayed, and thinking back over other incidents that had taken place during his relationship with Janice.

There were little things, like thrown-away lottery tickets, and bigger ones, like the secret paintings and the refused promotions, and even the postponed marriage decision.

Janice, he realized, was systematically avoiding success.

A promotion was obviously a success, and she surely must realize how good her art was, so keeping it secret was a way of avoiding success. And marrying him—well, he couldn't help thinking of that as a form of success too.

He'd heard of this sort of thing—sometimes it was called "impostor syndrome," the belief that one didn't deserve success, that any success would lead to disaster because it was undeserved, that sooner or later everyone would realize that one was undeserving, an impostor, and the success would be snatched away, to be replaced with disgrace.

He was angry with himself for not having realized months ago that Janice had it.

He'd read about it. Sufferers would sabotage their own lives, doing it to themselves before anyone else could do it to them, so that their imposture wouldn't be discovered.

He remembered how she had been frightened when she showed him the first painting. She must have been afraid he'd tell her she couldn't paint, he realized—that he'd expose her as an impostor.

He stood in the hall, one hand still on the telephone receiver, thinking it all through.

He had respected Janice's wishes about the paintings, and the marriage, and everything else, up until now; he'd assumed she had sound reasons for her actions. Maybe not logical reasons, but reasons.

But if it was this phobia that was responsible, that was different. She shouldn't let it run her life.

He glanced up the stairs and let go of the phone. Then he changed his mind and picked up the receiver again while he pawed through the phone book.

One of his old college classmates, a fellow art major, owned a gallery now.

Gordon handled the four paintings with the utmost care as he loaded them in his car and drove them to the gallery for Ian to inspect.

He brought them through the back door, one by one, and leaned them up on a framing table.

Ian, at first casual, grew more respectful when he got a look at the first canvas.

"You know the artist?" he asked, looking sideways at Gordon.

"I'm living with her," Gordon explained.

Ian whistled a note through his teeth. "Must be interesting," he said, looking back at the painting of the girl in the alley.

He inspected the four paintings carefully.

"Do they have titles?" he asked.

Gordon admitted, with some embarrassment, "I don't know; I never asked."

"We'd need to frame them before we could hang them."

"You'd be willing to display them?"

Ian glanced at him, startled. "Are you nuts? Of course

we'll hang them! The only question is whether I have the nerve to ask what they ought to be worth."

Gordon blinked.

"They're not for sale," he said.

Ian sighed. "Then what the hell are you doing here? We're not a museum, Gordie; we're a business."

"I was thinking you . . . you know, as a favor, for publicity, I thought you might display a couple, just to see what sort of reaction you get."

Ian stared at him.

"Why?" he asked.

"Well, see, I want to convince Janice how good they are. She's . . . well, she doesn't believe she's talented."

Ian looked back at the paintings.

"She's talented, all right. She's fucking brilliant." He considered, then said, "Look, Gordie, I'd like to help—but I'd also like a chance to sell these. You think there's *any* chance this Janice might be willing to sell something? Maybe not these particular pieces, but you say she's got others?"

"I think so," Gordon said. "These are the only ones I've seen, but I'm pretty sure she has others put away."

"Think she might want to sell any?"

Gordon hesitated.

"I don't know," he said at last.

"Well, find out," Ian said.

"I can't. Look, Ian, suppose I were to loan you more than a dozen paintings, enough for a one-woman show, and I promised you'd be the exclusive agent if she ever *does* agree to sell any? Would you do it?"

"Do what? A show?" Ian considered that. "Yeah," he said slowly. "It'd be good publicity, showing these—get people into the gallery. One day only, on a Saturday. I'd need at least . . . let's see, three on that wall . . . at least twenty paintings, to do it right, but I could maybe get by with one room. A dozen would be the absolute minimum, and they'd all have to be good-sized. How many will she loan me?"

"I don't know," Gordon said. "I'll find out and get back to you."

That night at dinner Gordon sat across the table from

Janice, watching her closely, trying to gauge her mood, how she would react to the suggestion of a gallery show.

She was being unusually quiet, though, and his attempts to guide conversation to the subject of her painting—or for that matter, her fear of success—were unsuccessful. She would only speak of trivia.

Finally he asked straight out, "Jan, are you afraid people would make fun of your paintings?"

She looked up, shocked, from her pecan pie dessert.

"They wouldn't, you know," he said quickly. "The paintings are really *good.*"

"That's not it," she said.

"Then are you afraid they'd *praise* them? And that you don't deserve it?"

"No," she said, looking down at her pie. "That's not it either."

"Then why won't you let anyone else see them?"

She looked up, looked him right in the eye. "You don't know?" she asked.

"No, I don't. I can guess, maybe, but I wish you'd tell me."

"If you don't *know,* Gordon . . . no, I'm not going to tell you."

She pushed away and left the table, left her pie unfinished.

He watched her go, and debated going after her.

She was lying, he was sure. She was afraid people would laugh at her work—or that they wouldn't, that they'd tell her it was wonderful, and she'd never be able to live up to it.

But she wouldn't admit it.

He got up and followed her, and found her standing at the foot of the stairs, looking up into the darkness. He came up behind her and put his arms around her.

"I'm sorry," he said. "I'd never do anything to hurt you, Janice—I just want everyone to see how wonderful you are!"

"I'm not wonderful," she said. She pulled away.

He had to show her, he thought. She *was* wonderful, and he had to convince her of it. She had no self-confidence, that was the problem; she didn't think, "Nothing ventured, nothing gained," she thought, "Nothing ventured, little lost."

But *he* believed in "Nothing ventured, nothing gained"!
And two weeks later, opportunity fell into his lap.

"I need to go up to Chicago," Janice told him. "My uncle
Eugene's moving, giving up his house and taking an apartment, and he's asked me to come help him sort through
stuff, see if there's anything I want."

"Oh?" Gordon asked.

"Yeah, he's got a lot of the old family stuff. My cousin
Charlotte will be there, and maybe Aunt Grace, if her health
holds." She hesitated. "Would you like to come?"

"When would this be?" he asked.

"I'd be leaving Thursday, coming back Tuesday. I've got
vacation days I can use."

He looked at her, then said, "*I* don't; I'm afraid I'll have to
pass."

"Oh, I thought you did," she said.

"Nope."

He was lying; he did have leave time available.

But this was his chance to put on that show at Ian's
gallery.

She seemed disappointed, but he thought about how her
face would light up when she saw the reviews, when she
heard people raving about her work.

"You go ahead and have a good time," he said.

"All right," she said, a bit coolly.

A few minutes later he excused himself and called Ian.

Ian complained about the short notice, but agreed. Gordon provided him with Polaroids of the four he'd already
seen, so that he could advertise the show.

And Thursday, as soon as Janice was gone, Gordon took
the keys from her dresser jewel box and unlocked all the
upstairs rooms, his hands trembling with anticipation.

How many paintings would there be? Would there be
enough good ones?

Then the door of the first room, the room where he had
seen her working on her painting, swung open.

There was the easel, and the stool, and the lamp—and
behind the door a stack of canvases.

A *large* stack of canvases—sixteen in all.

The Victorian woman and child were there; so was a
stunning self-portrait that showed Janice's face subtly dis-

torted, her teeth almost fangs, her expression predatory. There was a painting of a steam train, one of a pair of horses, one of a man chopping vegetables as a little girl watched . . .

"Jackpot," Gordon whispered to himself.

He was wrong, though; the jackpot was in the next room, where the canvases were stacked on all sides—portraits, landscapes, still life, even abstracts.

Altogether, there were over 120 paintings.

Some of them were obviously early work; some were so bizarre Gordon didn't know what to make of them. Even so, when he arrived at Ian's gallery Friday morning, he had sixty-six canvases packed into his car.

That was all he could fit and still have room to drive.

Ian, after a few moments of shock when he saw the number, and several moments of awe and delight when he looked through the available material, weeded them down further, and in the end forty-three were hung.

The show was a wild success.

And Tuesday, when Janice came home, clippings of the rave reviews were set out on the living room coffee table, waiting for her.

The reviews were all just from the local papers, there hadn't been time to get any serious attention, but it was a start. He couldn't wait for her to read them.

He met her at the door, kissed her, and took her bags.

"There's a lot more stuff in the car," she said.

"I'll help you with it," he answered. "Let me drop these in the bedroom."

As he hauled the luggage up the stairs, he glanced back and saw her drifting into the living room, looking at the clippings, and he smiled nervously.

She might be angry at first, he'd taken a really great liberty, but when she saw what everyone *said* about her work . . .

He dropped the suitcases by the bed and hurried back down.

She was sitting on the couch, holding one of the clippings, staring at it, stunned.

"I'm sorry," he said, "I know you were afraid that people

wouldn't like your paintings, but I *knew* they were good, so good I had to share them—and see? Everyone loves them!"

She finished reading the review, then turned and stared up at him.

"You really don't understand, do you, Gordon?"

"Sure I do, Jan," he said, but she was already on her feet, pushing her way past him.

He turned and followed her out to her car—as she had said, it was full of boxes and bundles. She circled around to the driver's side and opened the door.

"What should I get first?" he asked, reaching for the passenger door.

"Lost," she said as she tapped the power lock switch. Then she climbed into the car, slammed the door, and started the engine.

He stood and watched helplessly as she pulled away.

She was angry. He should have known. But she'd have to come back sooner or later, and maybe he could make her see that he hadn't done any harm, he'd been saving her from her own fears.

He turned and went back into the house.

She'd be back. And she'd see that he'd done her a favor. She'd be back.

But she wasn't back when the phone rang about eight, and he snatched it up ready to apologize, ready to beg, but the voice on the other end was Ian's.

"Does she want to sell any?" the art dealer asked. "I think I could get ten thousand for that big one of the old woman and the cobwebs right now."

"I don't think so, Ian," Gordon said. "I'll talk to you later." He hung up.

Janice hadn't come home by midnight, and Gordon finally gave up and went to bed.

He was awakened by the phone; he snatched it up.

"Hello?" he said. "Janice?"

"No," said a man's voice, "this is Lieutenant Arneson, with the police."

"Police?" He blinked and sat up.

"Is this Gordon Webber?"

Nightmare scenarios ran through his mind—Janice in a car wreck, Janice mugged, Janice raped.

"Yes," he said, "I'm Gordon Webber."

"If you could come to the Holiday Inn on Route 35, we'd like to talk to you."

"Is this about Janice?"

"Yes, sir, it's about Ms. Fletcher."

"Is she okay?"

"No, sir, I'm afraid she isn't. If you could come to the hotel, please?"

"I'll be right there."

He hung up the phone and quickly got dressed. Fifteen minutes later he hurried into the hotel lobby.

There were three cops standing by the entrance to a first-floor corridor; he approached them and shakily said, "I'm Gordon Webber—I think Lieutenant Anderson wanted to see me? About Janice Fletcher?"

"Lieutenant Arneson," one of them corrected him. "Room 122; he's waiting for you." He pointed down the corridor.

At the door of the room he was ushered inside, and met by a man in plainclothes who introduced himself as Arneson.

Janice wasn't there; Gordon had half expected to see her lying dead on the floor.

The bed was unmade, he noticed.

"Where's Jan?" he asked.

"The hospital," Arneson said.

"Then why am I *here?*" Gordon demanded, starting to turn.

"The hospital *morgue,*" Arneson told him.

Gordon stopped, and sagged.

"I thought it would be easier here," Arneson said. "We'll be going over there later, so you can confirm our identification of the deceased, but I thought we should have a little talk here first."

"How'd it happen?" Gordon asked, not looking at anyone or anything in particular.

"Pills," Arneson said. "Sleeping pills. Lots of 'em."

Gordon blinked.

"She left this," Arneson said, holding out an envelope.

Gordon looked at it, and saw his name and their shared phone number written on it. He took it and pulled out the sheet of paper inside.

"That her handwriting?" Arneson asked.

"Yes," Gordon said, starting to read.

"Gordon," it began, and at the omission of the customary "Dear," his eyes began to tear.

> I know you don't understand what you've done to me. You thought I was afraid I'd be laughed at, afraid of failure, but that was never it. You thought I was afraid to marry you for the same reasons—but that wasn't it. I couldn't marry you because you didn't understand. You didn't see what my paintings were about. I didn't show my paintings because they were *private,* Gordon—they were my innermost soul put down on canvas. I was never good with words, so I used my pictures. I never cared one way or another about money or success, I had enough of both and didn't need any more, but I cared about my privacy— and you put my soul on display, you invited the public to trample through my most secret feelings, feelings you never understood. In a way, you raped me, Gordon—a psychic gang-bang. I can't live with that. So I've left you these two notes, and I'm saying good-bye. I hope you'll understand at least *one* of them.

It was signed "Janice," and underneath was a P.S.: "Not Jan, you son of a bitch."

Gordon swallowed hard, then looked up from the note to Arneson's hostile face.

"It says *two* notes," Gordon managed to say.

Arneson nodded, and gestured to one of the other cops.

The man picked up a piece of board, about two feet square, that had been leaning against the wall. He handed it to Arneson, who held it up and displayed it to Gordon.

Gordon looked at it, at Janice's final painting, done in cheap hobby-shop pigments on masonite, and finally understood.

It wasn't anywhere near as finished as any of her others, parts of it were little more than hasty sketches, but it was still a fine work of art in its way.

The painting showed a magician and his assistant, standing on a stage before a crowd of reporters. The magician was a man in top hat and cape—and Gordon recognized his own face.

And seeing it there, he also realized that he was the man in the leather coat in the first painting she had shown him, and that Janice had been the little girl.

The assistant was Janice, as well—Janice standing stark naked, teeth clenched as she fought against pain; the magician had sliced open her belly and pulled out a double handful of her intestines, and was displaying them to the applauding crowd with flamboyant gestures.

Blood dripped through the magician's fingers, but he smiled proudly, oblivious to the blood and the woman's agony as he performed for the crowd.

And Gordon knew that that smile, and the entire painting, would haunt him for the rest of his life.

The Contributors

Jerry and **Sharon Ahern** have authored more than eighty novels, numerous short stories, and nearly a thousand magazine columns, articles, features, and interviews. **Samantha Ahern** is being published professionally for the first time in these pages. She has acted in various theatrical productions, done commercial voice-overs, and appeared in several instructional videos.

Robert Bloch writes: "I was born on April 5, 1917, at 9:45 pm., and have a birth certificate to prove it. Since the age of seventeen I've written short stories, novels, a variety of nonfiction, and scripts for radio, television, and films. Sixty years later I'm still a professional writer, and offer *None Are So Blind* as proof. Unfortunately, I don't have anything to prove that I'm still alive, so you'll just have to take my word for it. Or the words of my story." [Editor's Note: Robert Bloch passed away on September 23, 1994. His stories, however, live on. Thanks, Bob.—W.W.]

Alan M. Clark was born in Nashville, Tennessee, in 1957. He graduated in 1979 from the San Francisco Art Institute with a bachelor of fine arts degree. After college he tried several occupations he found bitterly unsatisfying. Howev-

The Contributors

er, in 1984 he decided to devote himself to freelance illustration. In between bouts with the paintbrush, he writes. He lives in Nashville today with his collection of mummified animals and wife, Melody, and is a founding member of the Bovine Smoke Society.

Douglas Clegg lives in southern California with his spouse, a black cat, and a border collie mongrel. He has written six novels, and has seventeen short stories forthcoming in the next two years; his most recent novel is *Dark of the Eye.* In addition to his horror novels, he also writes suspense fiction and contributes time and energy to the AIDS Service Center of Pasadena.

Nancy A. Collins is the author of the contempory horror novels *Wild Blood, Tempter,* and *Sunglasses After Dark.* She has worked extensively in comics, predominantly for DC/Vertigo with *Swamp Thing* (1991–93) and *Wick* (1994). She is a winner of the Bram Stoker and British Fantasy Awards and her short fiction has appeared in such venues as *Year's Best Fantasy and Horror* and *Best New Horror.* Born in rural Arkansas, she now lives in New York City with her husband, underground filmmaker and anti-artiste, Joe Christ.

Ron Dee has been dealing with a number of phobias since he can remember, and chose writing as an outlet to try and understand them. Born and living in Tulsa, Oklahoma, until recently, he has been writing since the early 1970s. He has several stories appearing in other anthologies, including *The Ultimate Dracula, The Ultimate Alien,* and *Hottest Blood,* and two of his novels were published by Dell Abyss during their first year. More recently he has written the novels *Blood, Succumb, Shade,* and *Horrorshow* under his pseudonym, David Darke.

Nicholas A. DiChario has sold approximately two dozen works of short fiction in the past three years to science fiction and fantasy markets, professional magazines, and original anthologies. He was nominated for the 1993 John W. Campbell Award for Best New Writer of the Year, and has also been a Hugo and World Fantasy award nominee.

The Contributors

Born on Halloween in 1960, he has a B.A. in English from St. John Fisher College in Rochester, New York, and is currently working as a technical writer for Blue Cross/Blue Shield of Rochester.

Nathan Eliot is an Atlanta secondary school counselor and retired mental health technician. He has written and published many articles on child sexual abuse, and regularly speaks at both local and regional conferences. Nathan has received numerous recognitions for his community service. This story is his first published work of fiction.

Randy Fox was born in 1963 and grew up in Dunmor, Kentucky. He presently lives in Nashville, Tennessee, with his wife Stephanie and their two cats, Samantha and Kallie. His biggest influences are Richard Matheson, Sir Cecil Creape, and Jerry Lee Lewis, and he is a fan of fifties juvenile delinquent movies, rockabilly, and Warner Bros. cartoons. He is the author of *Not Broken, Not Belonging*, published by Roadkill Press, and a founding member of the Bovine Smoke Society.

Thomas E. Fuller is the author of nineteen stage plays, two outdoor dramas, the books to four musicals, and has been produced by theaters all across America. He is perhaps best known for his more than thirty audio dramas written as head writer for the celebrated Atlanta Radio Theatre Company and as editor of "The Centauri Express" audio magazine. Thomas is married to artist Berta Fuller, has four children, and lives, strangely enough, in Atlanta.

Richard Gilliam's writing career includes more than twenty years of freelance nonfiction, a dozen short stories, and the editing of several well-regarded anthologies. Richard is possibly the only person to claim both *Sports Illustrated* and *Heavy Metal* among his credits. He is the film critic for *Horror* magazine and a contributing editor for *Pulphouse*.

Ed Gorman has been described by Britain's *Million* as "One of the world's great storytellers." Winner of mystery's Shamus, and nominee for both the Edgar and the Anthony, he is the author of a dozen novels and two collections of short stories. His novella "Moonchasers" is being developed for the screen by Hollywood Pictures. (Thanks to Blaine Stevens at O'Keefe Elevators for his help with the technical details; and to Richard Gilliam for several good editorial suggestions.—E.G.)

Martin H. Greenberg is a professor of international relations at the University of Wisconsin at Green Bay and the author of several well-regarded texts, including *The International Relations of the PLO*. He has edited more than six hundred anthologies, and serves as an advisor to the Sci-Fi channel.

Lucretia W. Grindle was born in Boston, Massachusetts in 1960, and grew up part-time in the United States and part-time in England, where her family owned a riding school. In 1981 she quit competitive riding to go to Dartmouth College and Oxford University, where she read Philosophy and Theology. In 1992 she began to ride again, and now competes three Three-Day-Event horses full-time. Her first book, *The Killing of Ellis Martin*, was published in 1993 by Pocket Books. Her second, *So Little to Die For*, is due out in 1994.

Rick Hautala is the author of eleven novels, including *Twilight Time, Ghost Light, Cold Whisper*, and *Winter Wake*. He has had more than thirty stories published in such anthologies as *Stalkers, Shock Rock 2, Narrow Houses, The Ultimate Zombie*, and *Night Visions 9*. He lives in southern Maine with his wife and three children.

Dana Edwin Isaacson is an editor and writer living in New York City. His work has appeared in *Mademoiselle* and *The New York Times*.

Nancy Kilpatrick has published over sixty horror/dark fantasy/mystery short stories. She won the 1992 Arthur Ellis Award for best crime story. Under a pseudonym she edited *Love Bites*, an erotic vampire anthology, and published two novels for Masquerade Books—*The Darker Passions: Dracula* and *The Darker Passions: Dr. Jekyll and Mr. Hyde.* Her limited edition collection *Sex and the Single Vampire* is just out from Tal Publications, as is a horror novel from Pocket Books, *Near Death.*

Edward E. Kramer's credits include over a decade of work as a music critic and photojournalist. Directing his interests to writing and editing fiction, his numerous anthologies have received acclaim. A graduate of Emory University of Medicine, Ed is a clinical and educational consultant in Atlanta with a private practice specializing in addictions. He is deathly afraid of extremely low places and designer luggage.

Jill M. Morgan is the author of seventeen novels, some written under pseudonyms. Her books are in the genres of: suspense, horror, science fiction, historical, young adult, and middle grade. A Texan by birth, she grew up in Southern California and has lived there most of her life. Recent novels are *Cradle of Fear* and *Cage of Shadows* by Meg Griffin. Her short stories have appeared in *Phobias, Freak Show, Excalibur, Stalkers 2,* and many other anthologies. Her phobia is driving on California freeways.

Billie Sue Mosiman is the author of five novels of suspense and more than sixty short stories that were published in various anthologies and magazines. The fifth novel, *Night Cruise,* was nominated for an Edgar Award in 1993 by the Mystery Writers of America. An upcoming novel of dark suspense, *Son and Shadow,* will be a lead title from Berkley Books in April 1995. She lives in a rural area just outside Houston and spends her time gardening or playing computer games.

Kathryn Ptacek is the author of eighteen novels, including *Shadoweyes* and *Ghost Dance,* featuring Chato Del-Klinne, as well as numerous short stories. She edited *Women of Darkness I* and *II,* both landmark anthologies, and works as a compositor for the *New Jersey Herald.* In her copious spare time she publishes *The Gila Queen's Guide to Markets,*

The Contributors

a monthly market guide for writers and artists. She collects unusual teapots and cat whiskers, and is a member of Horror Writers Association and Sisters in Crime.

Carrie Richerson lives on thirty acres of Texas hill country near Austin with her partner and thirteen cats, who supervise all of her housebuilding, bookselling, and writing efforts. Her stories have appeared in the *Magazine of Fantasy & Science Fiction, Amazing Stories, Pulphouse, Noctulpa,* and the *Year's Best Horror Stories XXI.* In 1993 and 1994 she was nominated for the John W. Campbell Award for Best New Writer in the science fiction/fantasy field.

Shawn Ryan lives in Birmingham, Alabama, and is the author of two novels, the recently published *Brethren* and the upcoming *Nocturnas.* Writing fiction at night and on weekends, he writes nonfiction during the day as music writer for the *Birmingham News,* the largest newspaper in Alabama. He has been in Birmingham for ten years, moving there after earning a degree in journalism from Georgia State University in Atlanta. Single and thirty-six, he currently is working on a third novel, *Triad.*

Wayne Allen Sallee was born September 9, 1959, and has been writing professionally since 1985. He's worked as a skip-tracer for a law firm in the Loop, a PR man for an Elvis impersonator, and as unwitting Mafia dupe: the place he washed dishes for was the front for a chop shop. His favorite Catwoman was Julie Newmar. His novels are *The Holy Terror* (Zeising), *Girl With the Concrete Hands* is being marketed, and he has just started *Marnie's Near Morning.* His chapbooks include *For You, The Living* (Roadkill Press), *Pain Grin, Insanitized Streets,* and *Untold Tales of the Scarlet Sponge* (all by TAL). He's been in DAW's Years' Best Horror for the last nine years. This story is for Diana Gallardo.

Pamela Sargent's most recent novel is *Ruler of the Sky* (Crown, 1993), a historical novel about Genghis Khan; two new *Women of Wonder* anthologies edited by her will soon

The Contributors

be published by Harcourt Brace & Company. Her other novels include *The Shore of Women, Venus of Dreams, Venus of Shadows, The Golden Space,* and *Earthseed* (chosen as a 1983 Best Book for Young Adults by the American Library Association). She has won a Nebula Award and a Locus Award and lives in upstate New York.

Harold Schechter is Professor of English at Queens College, the City University of New York. His books include the horror novel, *Dying Breath* (co-written with his wife, Jonna Semeiks) and the true-crime trilogy *Deviant, Deranged,* and *Depraved,* all published by Pocket Books.

Del Stone Jr. is a new writer, having published in *Amazing Stories,* Bantam's *Full Spectrum 4,* Marvel/Epic's *Hellraiser,* Dark Horse's *Underground,* and Karl Edward Wagner's *The Year's Best Horror Stories XXII.* His illustrated novella, "Roadkill," was published in 1993 in collaboration with artist Dave Dorman; a sequel, "Heat," will be published in 1994. His story "I'll Wait for You" appeared in three issues of *Thumbscrew.* He is single, bowls, still smokes, and has the uncanny ability to mangle ANY dirty joke.

Brad Strickland has written or co-written sixty short stories and sixteen novels, including two *Star Trek: Deep Space Nine* books, *The Star Ghost* and *Stowaways,* and a *Star Trek Academy* novel, *Starfall,* which he wrote in collaboration with his wife Barbara. He contributed to *Phobias,* and twice his short stories have been selected for *The Year's Best Horror Stories.* He teaches English at Gainesville College and lives in Oakwood, Georgia, with his wife and their children Amy and Jonathan.

Lawrence Watt-Evans is the author of two dozen novels of fantasy, science fiction, and horror, as well as six dozen short stories and innumerable articles and curiosities. In the horror/suspense field he's probably best known for his 1990 novel, *The Nightmare People,* and for his short story "Stab" in Dennis Etchison's anthology *Metahorror.* He also has stories in *The Ultimate Dracula, The Ultimate Zombie, Dead End: City Limits,* the original *Phobias,* and elsewhere.

The Contributors

Watt-Evans minored in art history at Princeton, but left without a degree.

Wendy Webb is a Registered Nurse and professional educator having taught in such places as the People's Republic of China and Budapest, Hungary. Writing credits include nonfiction and short fiction that has appeared in major anthologies. She has acted on stage, film, television, and in radio, and lives in fear that should she entertain the thought of dancing at this point in her life, she would make Lucille Ball look like a prima ballerina at the *barre*.

George Zebrowski's previous novel, *Stranger Suns*, was a New York Times Notable Book of the Year. His many highly praised, award-nominated stories and novels have been translated into a half-dozen languages. He writes for several magazines, among them *Omni* and *Amazing Stories*. Forthcoming from Avon/Morrow is *The Killing Star*, a major new novel with scientist-author Charles Pellegrino.